TEAR ME
DOWN

THE ENSLAVED SAGA
RUBY MEDJO

Published by Ruby Medjo

Edited by Vickie Vaughn

Cover Design and Interior Formatting by L.J. Anderson of Mayhem Cover Designs

CONTENTS

To my momma. You've taught me the beauty of resilience and unconditional love. I would not be where I am today without you by my side.

PLAYLIST

"The Last of the Real Ones"—Fall Out Boy

"Ruins"—Olivia May

"Radioactive (Ft. Kendrick Lamar)"—Imagine Dragons

"Hold Me While You Wait"—Lewis Capaldi

"Afterglow"—Ed Sheeran

"The Good Ones"—Gaby Barrett

"Only Love"—Mumford and Sons

"Aeon (Ft. Juliet Lyons)"—Nick Murray

PART I

A STICKY SITUATION

"The sun, with all those planets revolving around it and dependent on it, can still ripen a bunch of grapes as if it had nothing else in the universe to do."
—Galileo Galilei

1

Year 3045
The Ruins (Previously the United Kingdom)

Olivia Donne

I watch with wide eyes as the sadistic Erathians march forward through the ancient, crumbling city. I'm hidden by four walls, three stories high; they cannot find me here. I am quiet as a mouse, and probably quieter still. I cannot say the same for the ragtag group of other humans I've been trekking through the Ruins with.

There are six unearthly beings in total, most young males. The one with greying hair is at the front, finger poised over the trigger of his malicious gun. I've seen the damage their weapons inflict. My eyes pinch shut against the memories, edging away from the glassless window, creeping back into the shadows of the decrepit building.

I hold up my fingers to the wary, waiting eyes of the group. Two men, near their forties, a woman in her thirties, and a younger man, closer to my age. I met them a month ago, and being some of the few wild humans remaining, there was no question of our allegiance. It would always be us versus them.

They had come some two hundred years ago. In peace, they promised. Their sun was dying. Humanlike in every aspect—and vastly superior in every aspect as well. It wasn't long before wars were waged and millions of human lives were lost. They came to conquer, and conquer they did. To still be a free human is a miracle, one I never intend to squander. The alternative is slavery, and the very thought of submitting to such a vile race leaves an acrid taste in my mouth.

I will never kneel to them. Death is preferable to a life in chains.

The woman's eyes mist over, fear wrinkling her forehead. I frown. Of course, I am afraid too, but I will never show it.

"Let's pray they are simply passing through," one of the older men whispers. I nod in agreement. The day is bright, but clouds are thick on the horizon. I yearn for the cover of darkness, even if these beings have incredible eyesight. For some reason, night has always made me feel secure.

We pass the hours in silence, no sounds but the wind whistling past the window and the occasional chirp of a flittering bird. I am bored but I try to sit still, leaned back against the wall with my bag on my lap. Everything I own fits in it.

Night finally falls. I've twisted my long, dark hair into a thick braid. The boy close to my age is staring at me. I stare back until he blushes and looks away.

Rain begins to pelt the roof, a chill breeze rising. It makes it difficult to distinguish any other important noises. I fall into a fitful sleep, my mind on edge knowing these aliens are on the prowl.

My body jolts awake at the sound of a keening scream. I am

on my feet, my backpack thrown across my shoulders before I can fully register what is happening. The staring boy is staring still, his face illuminated by many flashlights. I rush at him, colliding with his chest and shoving him across the debris-strewn floor to the stairs on the other side of the spacious room. He stumbles and cries out as gunfire cracks through the night, but I push him still. I cannot let him die, even if I hardly know him. He's human, and that's enough for me.

The heavy metal door is wrenched open; shouts and confusion and screams all mingling into an abhorrent circumstance from which we try to flee. I feel a sharp tug, the straps of my backpack biting into my shoulders. All I can see is how wide the boy's eyes go before I slam onto the dusty, gritty ground.

My eyes stare up at the barrel of a gun, shock and the impact from hitting the floor knocking the breath from my lungs, and I'm blinded by the light emanating from the alien's headlamp. Even though I face certain death, I cannot die like this. Mustering my hatred for their kind, I clench my muscles taut, rolling to my stomach as fast as I can while I kick out and knock the freak to the ground with a rewarding thud.

Grinning, I waste no time springing up to flee through the melee, but I am struck in the jaw with the butt of a rifle. My vision darkens as I tilt. The floor once more rushes to greet my falling body.

My head is throbbing. I am cold, wet, and it smells as though I'm back in the cover of the forest that surrounds the Ruins. My eyes open, greeted by darkness. As they adjust, I see I am correct in my guess. A small fire blazes under the cover of a tarp, giving off an orange glow to the shimmering ferns and trunks of sturdy trees.

My hands try to move up to rub my cheek where it hurts the

most, only to find they are bound tight with rope. I test my legs, gritting my teeth as my chances of escape are dwindled to near nothing at the moment. My only option is to roll and adjust myself to a half-sitting position, kicking with my tied legs against the mud.

The freaks sit around the campfire, enjoying what smells to be a delicious meal. I count five. Their leader is not present. Has he somehow died?

They are all perfect—flawless. Tall, broad-shouldered beasts, bred for destruction. The main distinction between our kind and theirs is their eerie eyes. If the light catches them just right, they shine back, like a wolf in the darkness. None are looking this way.

I peer around, making out two other lumps near me; the woman, and one of the older men. It's easy to assume the others are dead. Carefully, I slouch back down, rolling to the woman. She has a gash near her temple, congealing blood plastered to her pallid skin. I swallow hard at the sight of her, tied up like I am, awaiting our fate.

My forehead nudges her, wishing to wake her, to form an escape plan, when I hear one of their booming voices over the patter of rain on the canopy above.

"Aww, the little one is awake," he says. I roll onto my back, doing a half sit up to see over the brush as the alien approaches, his eyes slit in a predatory way with a cruel smirk on his face. I kick away as he draws nearer, but it's no use. He reaches for my bound wrists and tugs me upright without so much as a grunt of exertion.

His smirk widens, light hair cropped close to his head. His eyes are light brown up close. I shiver in his dominating shadow.

"I bet you're starving," he says. My brows furrow. I don't want to answer him, to give in at this point in my capture. So they don't think me a weak target. Instead, I simply ignore him. His smirk falters.

"Come, eat," he says, dragging my bound feet forward through the mud and bracken before plopping me in front of the fire. Four other pairs of eyes stare at me. I bring my knees up to my chest, feeling the alien's presence behind me as he takes his seat once more on his log. His knees cage my head in.

He reaches around me for his plate, picking up an unidentified piece of meat and holding it before my mouth. I shy away, feeling the heat emanating from between his thighs.

"Eat," he growls, voice taking on a dark edge. I eye the piece of meat, my stomach undeniably growling. In a flash, his other hand grabs my braid, pulling my head back as I let out a pained yelp. He takes his chance, shoving the food in my mouth. It makes me choke at the intrusion and subsequent explosion of flavor, but it's the best food I've had in years, so I chew and swallow automatically.

He pats the side of my face.

"Good human," he mocks. "How does it taste to eat your own kind?"

His words take a moment to sink in, but when they do, I lurch forward, retching up everything in my stomach. Even when I think I'm done, bile rises to finish it off. The group laughs, but an even deeper voice looms above the rest.

"Knock it off, Brutus."

I'm panting, shivering. The alien whose legs I'm sitting between—Brutus—grips my hair again, giving me a shake. My eyes fall across the fire into a pair of dark brown orbs. His squared jaw is flexing, traces of stubble across his cheeks and chin.

"Why, Pax-y?"

The alien's glare deepens, heavy brows pulling low over his eyes. He is menacing, powerful. Brutus grips my cheeks, squeezing them so hard my jaw flares in pain from its previous run-in with the butt of the rifle. I let out a whimper.

"Aww, cute noises humans make, huh? What other ones can I make you do, human?" he jests, turning me around to face him. He stands, pulling me so I'm on my knees. A heavy palm rests on the back of my head, the touch almost gentle. I raise my eyes to his in confusion. He smirks, and this time I recognize the evil. His hips jut forward, the hand on my head smashing my face against the zipper on his pants. The group chuckles as he presses me aggressively into him. I understand there is some demeaning significance, and my blood boils. I'm about to fight back when he releases me.

I waver on my knees, never seeing the hand flying toward my face. The back of his massive hand catches my cheek. I fall to my side with a cry of pain as it explodes over my skin.

"What a little whore, like the rest of them," he seethes, reaching down to pluck me off the ground. I whimper, straining to be free of his grasp, but he is inhumanely strong.

"Enough, Brutus!" the other one says. Brutus snorts.

"That's all they are good for. Cleaning and fucking. May as well break her in now—"

"I said *enough*," he hisses. I crane my neck in an attempt to see this alien, but it's of no use.

"You can't command—"

"By law, you must register to own a human. By law, you must have them screened for diseases and have them inoculated."

Everyone is motionless, tense. I'm shifted around before being tossed to the ground. My eyes find the dark-haired alien. He is staring down his counterpart, face contorted in fury.

"And yes, Brutus, I can command you."

I don't see the angry boot flying toward me, and I can't even cry out when it connects with my stomach. Brutus gets his last bit of torment in before stomping away. My body gasps on the cold forest floor as they watch me.

I'm roused at dawn, tied to the woman, the man tied behind me. We are marched through the Ruins, due north. I haven't seen a map in years, so I have no clue what kingdoms could be this way, but I do know we aren't far from one. We never are.

The sun streams down, and I ache for water. The woman, Sarah, begins to beg for water and food. I keep my mouth shut, not liking how she grovels and pleads, sounding so weak. She is ignored in the presence of their stoic leader. My eyes often wander to Brutus, to my left and ahead of me. He often jests with two younger freaks. On my right is another alien, his hair a strawberry blond. A few feet ahead of him is the dark-haired one.

The Ruins thin until there is no trace of humanity left. Just the forest surrounds us now, which I find somewhat peaceful, save for Sarah's continued bargaining tactics. I'm starting to not like her, human or not.

My feet ache in my worn shoes, legs wobbly by the time we are allowed a reprieve. The aliens begin to set up camp, the leader tying us to a tree a few yards away from the fire. They ignore us, cooking, resting, some coming back fresh from some nearby body of water.

"Water? Please, we will die!" Sarah cries. I pinch my eyes shut, thudding my head against the back of the tree. Does she not see they don't care? I thud my throbbing head a few more times, seeking oblivion. For the first time since my capture, I see this situation for what it is, and a few sorrowful tears escape.

It is dark. There isn't even any light from the fire. My body is jostled awake as unsteady fingers work at the knot tying me to the tree. My wrists are raw, the skin around the rashes red and peeling.

"No—"

A gag is shoved in my mouth, stifling me as Brutus throws me over his shoulder, walking me to what I assume is his tent. My stomach flares in pain from his previous kick. Another freak follows, but all I can see are his boots.

"Me first," the greedy alien insists. Brutus tosses me to the ground. I fall on my tailbone, crying out at the sharpness of pain that radiates up my spine. I'm in their shared tent, on a pile of blankets. He unbuckles his tan pants.

"Fuck off. You can have her after I'm done."

I kick away, but my legs are bound together again, making my motions slow and cumbersome. There are four other sleeping aliens in here, and my eyes land on a mop of dark, spiky hair.

I roll as the two squabble, ramming right into his back. I don't expect his reaction, however, and my throat cries as his thick, strong fingers wrap about it, his dangerous eyes inches from mine. He sneers, and it's then I realize just how quickly he has moved. He's on top of me, pinning me down. His hand lets up his hold on my neck, and I gasp in a breath as best I can.

"You're not allowed in here, human," he hisses, raising his hand. Perplexed, I don't see this strike coming either. His slap resounds around the tent, my face flying to the side. Tears spring into my eyes—ones of pain and frustration. Everything stills.

"What in the fucking hell—" the alien on me growls, standing. I curl in on myself, shivering. Brutus and Kel hold their hands up to declare their innocence as the rest of the monsters begin to awaken. The evidence is damning, though. Brutus' pants are unbuckled, his zipper half down.

The dark-haired alien casts me a glance, connecting the dots. His jaw ticks. "What did I say about the laws, Brutus?" he hisses.

"Listen, Pax, she's nothing. She's going to die before we get home, so we may as well enjoy her—"

"That is not what I asked," he seethes, his bulging arms straining against his olive-toned shirt.

Brutus crosses his arms. "Fine, whatever, I'll *obey*," he mocks. "You may as well just take her since you're already so attached."

Pax sneers before looking down at me once more. He reaches to me, gripping my bicep and yanking me up before dragging me out into the cool night. No one follows. He finds me a separate tree, one closer to their tent. Taking his time, he finds a new length of rope to keep me in place. But I am beyond playing nice.

He reaches for me and I pull my bound hands away. I turn my back to him. He lunges, pinning me by my throat to the tree. Hatred rolls off him.

"You will obey us, human," he spits, cinching the rope tight about my chest. I wrinkle my nose in a sneer, shaking my head. His teeth grind, yanking the gag from my mouth. I'd spit in his face if I had any saliva left. I settle for the next best thing.

"You're all freaks," I say. He's pissed.

"Some tongue for someone in such a position."

"Go back to your own planet, you fucking leech." I hiss. Fury flashes in his eyes. His hands clench and unclench. He's showing restraint. I intend to push him over the edge. If I make it to wherever they are taking me, they will make me a slave. I'd rather die, out here in the wild, where I belong; free.

"Speak to me that way again, and you will regret it, human," he growls. The gag having been gone from my mouth for a minute or so, I finally have enough wetness in my mouth. I gather it discreetly before pursing my lips and spitting directly between his eyes.

He doesn't flinch, doesn't react other than to wipe his face clean, and when his eyes reopen, they are livid.

"I will enjoy breaking you," he swears. He stands, smirking down at me as I squirm and glare. He's wearing loose shorts that reach just above his knees, his legs rippling with muscle. What have I gotten myself into now?

"You will never break me, freak."

His fist connects with my jaw, and his boot with my side, so hard I feel as though a rib may have broken on impact. I choke on air, tears coating my cheeks. "Sleep, human, you will need it come tomorrow."

And with that, he saunters back to his tent.

I awake as a blast of cold hits my face, and for a moment it feels as though I'm drowning. My eyes spring open as I gasp. There is nothing but light filtering through a cloth. A new wave of water hits my nose and mouth. I can't breathe. Whoever is holding the cloth is tightening it across my aching face. The water relents, and I gulp for air, choking as more water hits me. There is laughter.

The cycle continues until the cloth is pulled from my face. My chest is heaving for air, my body shivering from the cold. I'm met with Pax's dark eyes. I glare.

"That is for your words against me, human. Tonight, we can discuss what your actions will cost you."

"Just kill me," I seethe. His eyes waver, always on edge, always angry. He unties me from the tree, untying my legs as well. A thinner rope loops between my bound wrists, anchoring me to him. My wide eyes search our surroundings. No one else is here. It's just us two. Panic begins to creep over me like a shadow. They must have left while I was being tortured.

He thrusts a metal water bottle into my hands. I stare at it in shock. He quirks his brow before I peer inside, inspecting the contents.

"It's water."

I hold it to my lips, so thirsty I can't bring myself to care if it's poisoned or not. I down the whole thing, wiping my mouth on my torn shirt sleeve. He passes me another full bottle. I gulp it down greedily, but his giant hand stops me halfway, pulling the water from my cracked lips.

"You'll be sick."

My head shakes, reaching for it with desperation. He frowns, studying me. My belly is protruding with the onslaught of water, but I am afraid I'll be deprived again, and I need my strength if I'm to keep my wits.

He caps it, placing it in his huge frame backpack. I am disheartened when he stands straight, but hope flutters in my chest. He's holding what looks to be a protein bar. I remember my mom buying them in the store whenever she was trying to diet.

My mouth waters, my stomach grumbling as he peels the wrapper off. And then as if teasing me, he brings it to his mouth, taking a huge bite of the chocolatey bar. I bite my cheek to keep from flinging more insults at him. I won't beg, as Sarah did.

He smirks as he chews and swallows.

"Obey, and you'll be rewarded."

I frown, quirking my brow at him. So that's how it's going to be. His eyes narrow.

"You don't own me."

He stows the other half of the bar.

"I will, human."

My jaw slackens as he hefts his pack onto his broad shoulders with ease. He gives a sharp tug on my rope, starting forward. I've no choice but to follow.

We stop when the sun is at its highest point. I am panting, sweating, and my ribs throb with every breath. He sheds his pack with a thump on the forest floor, reaching for his water. He guzzles it, water droplets snaking their way past his lips, through the scruff on his chin, and down his bobbing throat. I am white-hot with anger, but he turns his dancing eyes to me, holding out the water.

I take it without thought, downing the other half. He seems to have an endless supply. I am gasping by the time I'm done, clutching at my side. When my eyes peel open, a protein bar is there, perched delicately in his huge palm. I move to take it, but he snatches it away faster.

"Manners, human."

I don't want to play his game, but I need my strength if I'm to somehow get away. I choose the path of least resistance.

"Please," I say, attempting to keep the disgust from my voice. His eyes simmer, gaze darkening. He hears it, all the same, but he ignores it, holding out the food to me. I grab it, ripping it open and shoving it to my mouth. The chocolate melts on my tongue, and as I chew, peanut butter is mingled with the flavors. My eyes widen in horror. I spit it out, wiping at my tongue, but fear it may be too late.

Of all the ways to die, my own stupidity would be the way I get killed.

I let out a whimper, bringing my pleading eyes to his. He's staring at me as though I am the foreign invader, as though I've sprouted three heads.

"Human—"

"My...bag..." I rasp, feeling my tongue already begin to swell.

My eyes water as adrenaline courses through me.

"What is wrong—"

"Peanuts..." I gasp, lurching forward to his bag.

His thick hands stop me, both holding my shoulders. "You are bright red, human."

"I know!" I screech, trying to shove past him. "I'm going to die, I need my bag!"

He shoves me down, hard, and I fall back onto my already aching tailbone with a hiss. My bag appears before my feet.

"Untie me!"

For once, the brute listens, his deft fingers working fast. I dive into my bag, the feeling of using my arms without hindrance a welcome feeling. My fingers brush over the cylindrical bottle—the last EpiPen I have. I bring it out, uncap it with my teeth, gasping now as my throat closes. I jam the needle into my thigh without a second thought, pushing the plunger down before withdrawing and rubbing the area to work the medicine into my bloodstream.

I am still gasping, but as the minutes tick by, breathing is less stressful. The alien sits on his knees, his fingers resting on his thighs. His eyes are wide, his brows risen. He has a chiseled face, with a long, perfect nose to match. The way he's looking at me makes me think he somehow cares whether I live or die.

"Are you dying, human?"

I shake my head, the adrenaline fading, leaving me weak.

"What has happened?"

They don't have allergic reactions to food? I'm shocked and intrigued if I'm being honest.

"I'm allergic to peanuts," I say, my voice hoarse. His brows pull together in confusion. "They can kill me. Make my airways swell."

He still seems unsure, but he nods, reaching back into his pack. He hands me an apple and another bar.

"Peanuts?" he asks, brows pulled together and pushing up in the middle. He looks...*concerned*, about me. It makes me feel strange, the thought these freaks have any capacity to care about another race—about a race they have decimated.

I check the label. I'm not one of those unfortunate people who can't even be around air contaminated with peanuts. This bar looks to be mint chocolate chip. I don't feel like eating anymore, but I know I must.

"No, I think it's safe."

I never learned to read, but I can recognize certain words.

"What is your name, human?"

I roll my eyes, chewing the soft bar, the explosion of flavor tickling my already swollen tongue. In a flash, he grips my cheeks, hard, but not so hard as to hurt me. More stern than anything. His eyes are dark—I've upset him.

"Do not make that gesture at me again."

"What are you gonna do about it?" I grumble through my pinched cheeks. His jaw ticks before a sadistic smile etches its way onto his face. I swallow hard, my stomach in knots. He turns away with a confident aura and I stick my tongue out at him.

We make it to camp at dusk. Only a few freaks mingle around, their leader one of them. He nods to Pax before ducking into their tent. Pax sheds his frame backpack, walking me to a nearby tree. I should have expected this. Sarah—her face battered—is tied to a tree across from me, ten yards or so away. I can't see the man.

He sets to work, cinching my torso to the tree so I'm left standing, my arms pulled taut above me. His handiwork is finished by tying the rope about my throat, tight enough to bring discomfort, but loose enough that I can still breathe. I am beginning to understand his punishment before he has to speak.

"You will stand, and you will not be allowed dinner. If you make noise, I will gag you. The more you move, the tighter this gets. Your choice," he growls, running his fingers over the rope on my neck.

"You took all my choices already, dumbass."

Now I can recognize the way his jaw ticks when I've pissed him off. I should probably stop tempting fate, but I can't help it. We stare into one another's eyes, testing each other. His gaze flickers a moment to my face. I haven't seen myself since my capture, but I know I'm swollen and bruised, can feel it in the constant throbbing of my cheek and ribs.

"Pax!" a deep voice calls from inside the tent, sparing me. With a final sneer, he marches off, leaving me alone with my thoughts. I wonder what made him such an insufferable asshole.

It's late. Pax hasn't reemerged from the tent, but their deep voices still make their way to my ears, the sound almost a lullaby now. There is the rush of a nearby river, and crickets and frogs sing to the night. It's cold, but not so cold that I can't handle it. I've endured worse. It's springtime, so the days— though often rainy—should continue to get warmer.

I need to find a weapon, maybe I can distract Pax tomorrow, fake another allergic reaction. His guard was down, then. The thought of killing him churns my stomach, but it's a necessity at this point. I refuse to be a slave.

I'm just nodding off when I hear the brush rustling. My eyes snap open, falling to the darkened tent. If it's an animal, I'm screwed. I tense in apprehension, and my fears are assuaged, only to be heightened when I recognize that close-cropped blond hair.

Brutus is grinning as he saunters near, his intent clearly malevolent. My eyes skip from his form to the tent, wondering how much trouble I'd be in if I screamed.

"Pax must love me. He has you all tied up like a present," he grins, standing so close now my nose is tickled by his shirt. My heart races in fear of the unknown. He reaches out, hands gripping my sides, sliding up underneath my shirt. His skin is clammy and sticky against mine. I feel sick to my stomach. His hands travel down to my hips. My body begins to shake, and if it wasn't for the ropes holding me up, I'd be a puddle on the ground.

His long fingers move to the front of my tattered jeans, deftly unbuttoning them, the sound of my zipper obnoxiously loud in my ears. I swallow hard. "P-please," I whisper. Tears form in my eyes.

"You want me so bad you're going to beg for me? Fuck," he hisses, his voice holding humor. I shake my head, the rope cinching down more and more as I struggle. His fingers dive down. I cry out at the intrusion. He covers my mouth with his, his hot tongue running along my lips as I whimper. Pain blooms between my legs as he thrusts his fingers up into me. I cry harder. I don't understand what is happening, but it is worse than anything I've ever been through before.

"Shit." he hisses, pulling my shirt down and dashing quietly into the forest, leaving me weeping and shaking. I feel disgusting, used. My chest rises and falls as panic courses through me. I can't handle that torment and torture. It's too much.

I don't see him through my tears, but I hear his deep, gravelly voice.

"What did I say about making noise?" Pax hisses, standing right before me. I flinch away, cowering, an involuntary sob creeping past my lips. There is no way to slow my breathing, and the rope is making it way more difficult to gulp in air. His fingers tug at my braid, the rope loosening as he holds my head to the side while untying it. It's not enough. I'm still spiraling.

"No, no, no," I chant, my voice tremulous.

"Human?" he says, his deep voice laced with what sounds like concern.

"Hey," he says, jostling my shoulders. My eyes snap to him. His brow is furrowed, his face pinched. My lips tremble as another small cry escapes.

"Is this allergic thing happening again?" he asks, stepping back to inspect me, still holding my shoulders. His keen eyes dart down. I try to bring my knees up, to curl in on myself. He grips the hem of my shirt, yanking up, then his fist turns white on the fabric. I know what he sees. My jeans unbuttoned, my zipper down. A furious blush rises in my cheeks.

"Look at me."

I shake my head.

"Dammit, I said look at me," he growls, gripping my cheeks and forcing my eyes to his.

"Who?" he seethes. His anger astounds me. I know it's not because of the treatment I've received, but because Brutus broke their laws. I shake my head again. I'm not saying a word.

"Why didn't you yell for me?" he growls, his grip tightening.

I whimper, but he doesn't notice.

"Why—"

"You told me not to make any noise," I choke out, attempting to defend myself any way I can. His jaw slackens, his hand falling away. He stares at me, so long I become uncomfortable. Without another word, he begins to untie me, even my aching wrists. Once loose, I stand before him, free to run but much too weak to do so. He grips my forearm, leading me to the tent. He pushes me against the canvas.

"Stay." He says, letting me go as he disappears inside. Again,

I know I should run, but I am far too weak to get anywhere. He reappears with a bag similar to mine. His hand clamps around my arm again, and he leads me through the forest. The sounds of the river grow louder. Is he going to drown me?

I tug away at the sight of the water, moonlight sparkling and dancing across the top. The river is wide and shallow here. His grip tightens.

"Knock it off," he grumbles, though his voice has lost some of its menacing edge. He tosses the bag aside, turning to me. Without any preamble, he strips me of my purple flannel, tossing it aside before reaching for my dirty tank top. I back away, hugging my stomach as my fear mounts again.

"I'm not telling you again, human."

I shake my head, my lip wobbling. Does he want to finish what his friend started? He sighs, annoyed. He points to the river.

"You have ten minutes to bathe. If you don't, I'll do it for you."

I am stunned. He fishes in his bag, tossing me a white bar of soap that I almost drop. His fingers tap his wrist. I'm rooted, though. I don't want him to see me nude, and I don't want to be this vulnerable around him. I grip the scented soap, wavering, still reeling from my earlier attack. He takes a threatening step forward, his body massive in comparison to mine, his arms again straining against his olive-hued shirt. He's wearing shorts again, but no boots. Just normal athletic shoes.

He takes another step forward, cocking his head to the side. I step back, stumbling over the uneven rocks. He is fast, reaching out to me before I fall. His arms are warm around me. His scent is nice, like cedarwood. Not like Brutus; he smells foul, like sweat and dirt.

"Go on, human," he urges again, his voice lower, more gentle.

"I...I don't..."

He frowns as I peek up at him.

"Don't look at-at me..."

He sighs through his perfectly straight nose. I'm still in his arms, close enough to feel his breath leaving his lungs, close enough to see the dots of stubble along his jaw and chin, dark like the spiky hair atop his head. He wears it casual, short on the sides and back, but longer on the top.

"Ten minutes," he says, releasing me. I take my time, allowing the cool water to calm my nerves as I assess my injuries and scrub my body clean of Brutus' touch. My tailbone screams in protest along with my ribs, and my face thuds with a dull ache. Those pains I can handle. The one between my legs burns, and I am left ashamed, wanting to vomit. I've never felt an injury like it before, and though it worries me, I refuse to ask Pax if I'm in danger.

I scrub my hair, running my fingers through it to smooth the tangles. He waits longer than ten minutes, but his back is to me, his arms crossed over his broad chest. When I'm done, I rise, shivering, thankful for the bit of moonlight. My bare feet shift on the slippery rocks, but I keep my balance, scanning the shoreline for my clothes. They are gone, and my breath hitches in my throat.

"Here," he grunts. My head snaps up. He's still facing the forest, but his thick arm is outstretched, holding a towel out to me. I grip it, drying my face and body and hair as best I can before wrapping it around me.

"My...my clothes..."

"Too dirty," he says, crouching down to dig through his bag. He stands, facing me, holding a matching olive green shirt and a pair of what look to be shorts. My brow furrows when I realize they are men's boxers. I want to say no, but I am too exhausted and hungry and thirsty. He turns away as I hastily dress. His shirt is clean, hanging to just above my knees, his boxers loose and slipping down.

He glances over his shoulder, frowning.

"Take those off. I'll find you something else."

I obey, thankful for such a height difference between us. It's made his shirt into a dress of sorts.

"Come," he nods to the forest, taking his bag and the towel before his hand clamps around my forearm. We emerge in the clearing, and to my surprise, he doesn't take me to my tree, but to the tent. I hesitate at the entrance, but he pulls me through. No one is in here, save for his leader at the very opposite end, sleeping peacefully. He tosses his things side, pointing to a sleeping bag on the far left.

"Sit there."

I obey once more. He follows, unzipping the bag for me as I hesitate. My body slips inside, warm almost immediately. I push my hands beneath the silky material, my eyelids heavy with sleep. He sits on a canvas stool at my feet, digging in his other pack. He hands me a full bottle of water, a pouch of dried fruit, and two of those protein bars. I dive in before he can stop me.

"Manners," he grunts, seeming as tired as I am.

"Fank—ooo," I manage to say around a mouthful of mint chocolate chip. His eyes waver for a moment, hinting at a smile, but it never crosses his face. After sucking down an entire bottle of water and eating my meal, my stomach feels full for the first time in weeks. Even before capture, my situation was rather dire.

He rubs his palms together, leaning on his knees. I lean away, remembering the brutality he is capable of.

"Who touched you tonight?"

Tears prick my eyes. I was trying to shove that away, but he brings the pain and humiliation to the surface again. I bring my knees up, circling my arms around them, shrinking under his gaze.

"Human—" he growls.

"My name is Olivia," I whisper through my tears, answering his question from this afternoon. He straightens, and my diversion works.

"O-liv-ia?" he repeats, checking his pronunciation. I nod, resting my chin on my knee caps, keeping my eyes on his midsection so I will know if he makes a move.

"Hmph," he mutters. "That's kind of a mouthful."

I glance up at him, and his face is contorted as he studies me. There's no need to tell him I was named after my grandmother on my mother's side. My name is special to me, a source of pride, and it feels like he is diminishing that.

"What about Livy?" he presses.

"You want me to change my name?" I whisper, glaring at him through a new wave of tears. He gives a sharp shake of his head.

"No—just shorten it, for my sake. A...what do you humans call it? Nickname?"

I can't help the small smile on my face. But I still want a say in what he calls me. "Livy or Liv."

"Alright," he says with a nod. He stands, and I cower with a whimper, covering my face and curling into a ball. I wait on edge, but nothing happens. When I peek my eyes open, I see he's kicked off his shoes.

"Scoot over," he demands. He doesn't give me a chance to think over what he's saying as he unzips his sleeping bag and slides in beside me. The zipper closes back up, his warm body dwarfing mine. My heart races in fear. I'm not wearing enough clothes to protect me from an attack if he wishes to.

"Face inside the tent and lay down, Liv," he grumbles. I feel my panic rising, and I listen automatically. My head lands on his pillow, and his breath is hot on my neck, our bodies flush. He rests his heavy hand on my hip. I let out a squeak and jump as far away as the bag allows. His grip tightens, pulling me back to him.

"Hush. We have a long trek tomorrow."

My heart takes a few moments to calm. I roll my eyes to the darkness, thankful he can't see. With a full belly and warmth enveloping me, I cannot help but fall into a deep, dreamless sleep.

2

Pax

The little human stiffens in my arms as she awakens, her heartbeat quickening as she comes to her senses. I am cautious as I hold her, for I saw myself the bruises that littered her torso last night. We Erathians are strong beings. I forget how fragile humans can be, never having been around them for any prolonged period of time.

I tighten my hold on her. She is warm, a notion I somehow find comforting. She doesn't resist, but rather relaxes once more, settling into sleep. I let her. She will need it today for this last stretch before we reach the Kingdom of Sardone—the kingdom I am from.

I am rested enough, and so I listen to her breathing become more even, her heartbeats slowing. I wonder at her age. She is a woman, if I've interpreted her features correctly—not a young child. Judging by the way Brutus is attracted to her, I'd say she is close to his own age. Just the thought of what he has put her through is enough to set my teeth on edge. It goes beyond breaking our laws. He's being sadistic for the entertainment of her torture. I cannot let it slide; if there is dissent in our ranks, we will crumble as a unit.

I will address it with the human again today, will force her to answer the question I already know the answer to. She sighs in her sleep and rolls. I release her, allowing her to move. Her body is facing me by the time she settles again, her little features pressed into my chest. Her face is swollen from everything she's endured, and purple bruises smatter and mar her otherwise comely face. For a human, her looks are alluring.

She's dark-haired, deep brown woven through with caramel tints from her apparent time under the sun. Her wide eyes—when open—are as green as the forest we've been traveling. She is small in stature, short and starved. Not an Erathian woman by any means, but it is somehow endearing. The other woman she was traveling with is annoying and grating and her looks do not make up for her groveling ways.

This one is smart—perhaps too feisty for her own good, but a survivor all the same. When we reach the kingdom, I'll be forced to turn her over to the authorities for proper training and testing. I've never owned a slave. I'm still not sure I want to. I suppose I have time to decide if I'll keep her or not.

Her nose crinkles. I realize my grip on her has become too tight, pressing against her injuries. I loosen up my hold. Her round eyes blink open, and for a moment she is confused. They find mine, and she blinks in quick succession. So strange. We do not have to blink so much to keep our eyes moistened.

"Will you be ready for this last stretch today?"

She stiffens, frightened.

"Last stretch?"

"Before we reach my kingdom."

"Uhh...which kingdom would that be?" she questions. Her brows pull together in concern.

"Sardone."

"Oh," she says, gaze falling to my chest. She nibbles on her lip. I decide on a new tactic to get her talking—compromise.

"If you tell me who touched you, I will give you breakfast before we go."

She brings her knees up as best she can, a strange thing she often does. Why would she want to appear smaller in the face of a perceived threat? "Liv?" I growl. Her lip is wobbling, but she shakes her head. I sigh in annoyance. I cannot punish Brutus if I don't hear it from her mouth. I need a new tactic.

"Was it Kel?"

She shakes her head.

"Was it Jeven?"

I know for a fact it isn't; he's my closest friend.

She shakes her head.

"Was it Brutus?"

Her body stills before spasms of shivers rock her.

"Just say yes." I whisper to her. "Nod, *anything*," I press. And she does. Her nod is small, and a frightful, pathetic cry leaves her lips before she sniffles. Humans are such emotional creatures. It is disorienting. It is also making a strange feeling creep into my chest. I do not like it when she cries like this. The feeling her crying gives me is uncomfortable because it is so foreign and new.

"Hush," I say, cupping her head, pressing it to my chest. My parents own slaves. My mother used to calm the children this way when they were inconsolable, and though I never spent much time around them, I learned from afar. Her tears wet my shirt.

"Why do you...even care?" she grits out through her quieting cries. She's angry with me.

"He broke the law—"

"You're sick, all of you," she hisses, pushing against me. I keep my hold, but her head snaps up, shimmering green eyes glaring at me.

"Do not test me, Liv."

"Don't call me by my name, freak."

"Enough, dammit!" I growl.

"Why? Don't you feel like beating me today?"

Her fingers, once pressed to my chest, now curl in, gripping my shirt as fury writhes on her bruised face. I am stunned, remembering with distinction each time I struck her, each one with intent to correct her foul behavior. It wasn't something I enjoyed doing.

"Your actions warranted punishment—"

"I'm not yours to punish!"

Somehow, I wish she *is* mine to punish.

Her voice rises in her agitation. I grip her harder in my anger, our strong wills on display as we eye each other.

"This is your last warning. Watch your tongue."

"I fucking *hate* you," she seethes, wriggling to be free of me. I take a steadying breath before I wrench open my sleeping bag and drag her up by her arm.

"What—"

"I'd keep your tongue behind your teeth for the rest of the day, human," I spit as I drag her back to her tree. I had pity for her last night for what she'd endured, but I was beginning to see that humans were rather pathetic creatures, bent on their own destruction. Slavery is as common to me as walking down the street and seeing my own kind. Her mistreatment had snapped something within me, likely because my parents had always been kind to their slaves.

But she is pushing me to my limits, and I crave her submission.

Again I tie her up, placing the rope around her neck. Her hate-filled eyes tell me she knows the rules.

"Am I allowed to speak when your disgusting leech of a friend attacks me again?" she seethes through clenched teeth. I sneer down at her. There is something in her eyes, something I have overlooked these past few days. *Fire.* She is filled and over-flowing with it. Her spirit is strong, stronger than I imagined a human's spirit could be. Her words sting. Why, I have not a clue.

"No one will come near you."

"You're psychotic."

My anger is mounting at her insults. Perhaps allowing the authorities to train her will be a good thing. I feel as though my mind is decided; I want to keep her. That look in her eyes is as mysterious as it is chilling. My life is rather dull when not on a mission or a raid. She will quell that boredom while also keeping my home clean.

Her eyes widen before they dart to the ground, her cheeks reddening where they aren't bruised. I feel his presence behind me. My shoulders tense in anticipation.

"Nice," Brutus says, clapping me on the shoulder. "I do enjoy seeing more skin. For a human, you've gotta admit she has some delicious legs—"

His sentence is cut short as my temper overflows. I whirl, my fist connecting with his jaw. I am satisfied as I hear it pop and feel it shatter. He howls in pain. It will heal in a week or two. I turn my eyes back to my stunned little human. She gapes up at me, tears glittering on her face. I nod once to her before I break camp.

Olivia

We walk past midday, the land sloping steadily upward the entire time. Pax has given me back my shoes, but with a new pair of socks. They are thick, itchy, and too big, but I refuse to say anything. The dress-shirt is more troublesome, especially with no undergarments. He is patient as we walk, never tugging on the rope that tethers me to him. My wrists still burn, though.

He pauses at the top of a hill, turning to frown down at me as I stumble. Hiking is difficult when your hands are tied together. His pack goes on the ground and he trudges back to me before scooping me up and carrying me the rest of the way. He doesn't even seem to break a sweat.

He pauses near his backpack, and my eyes follow his line of sight. I let out a small gasp. A wide, lush green moor greets us. With the golden sun streaming down on the verdant fields, it looks like heaven. I wander forward in awe, having never traveled to such an untainted place before. The tug of the ropes pulls me back to reality.

"Eat," he says as he sits on a rock. I ache to sit as well, but I don't want to risk flashing him. He hands me a protein bar and a bag of dehydrated cheese.

We eat in silence before he glances up at me.

"Sit," he growls before he resumes his chewing.

"No," I bite back. He gives a sharp tug to the rope, and I nearly lose my bag of cheese. I wish to kick him.

I remember, then, my plan. Like a fool, I forgot to finalize the details. There are no visible weapons that I can reach; even his gun is broken down and packed away. He doesn't fear anything, not even me.

"Liv—"

"Ok, bossy asshole," I grumble, sitting. He whirls, catching the back of my neck. His hold is tight, forcing my gaze to his.

"Enough with the foul language. You're a lady, not a mongrel."

"Do you torture all ladies you come into contact with, or am I just special?"

His eyes dance with malice and contempt.

"I have not tortured you."

"You tied me to a tree and told me if I spoke—"

His grip on me tightens as his mouth twists down, effectively cutting off my retort.

"I apologize."

His words stun me into silence as I blink at him. I never knew these creatures were capable of saying a simple sorry. Then again, he did break Brutus' jaw right in front of me today.

"I know how you can make it up to me," I press, coming back to my senses. He lets go of me, biting off a chunk of apple as he turns his gaze back to the scenery.

"Hmm?" He muses.

"Let me go."

He chokes, eyes bulging as they fly to me.

"Not a chance."

"Why? No one is here, no one will know—"

"No."

"Why? What good am I? I can't cook, and I sure as hell can't clean, and if I'm sold to some asshole who just beats me...I can't live like that!"

"Who says I am selling you?"

Again, I am stunned into sheer shock. My mouth hangs open, my half-eaten protein bar abandoned.

"You...can't...no, please," I beg, tears welling in my eyes.

"Livy, calm down."

I shake my head.

He pinches the bridge of his nose in clear exasperation.

"I just need someone to clean and cook. I can teach you those things. And if you follow the rules, you'll be fine."

I may not be turning into a slave that is used solely for horrific manual labor, but this is still demeaning and belittling and *taking away my freedom*.

"Where—"

"You'll live with me, in the city. We can figure out rules when we get home."

"Home?" I echo, breathless. I feel like I've been kicked in the chest. His brows dance, inching closer.

"In time, you may see it as home."

I turn my gaze to the horizon, drinking in the overwhelming beauty of the wild. This is where I belong. *This* is my home.

"No," I whisper. "I will never see it as my home."

The walls of the Kingdom of Sardone loom into view. Though they look like ancient stones, I know they are not. These aliens seem to like how humans of the past decorated their landscape, and in turn they copied it. Storm clouds roil above, a foreboding welcome into this hellish place. I've never been inside a kingdom full of Erathians. I've never been inside a kingdom, period.

We pass through the gates. Pax hands over his backpack to the authorities. They wear grey uniforms and strange head coverings. I watch as they pull apart everything in his bag and lay it out on a wide, steel table.

"Identification?"

"Paxton Harper, First Platoon, Ranger 002." I stare up at him, wondering what his title means. The man going over his belongings pauses, eyeing him through his dark face shield.

"An honor, sir."

Pax nods, unfazed.

"And this one?"

"A recently captured human. She's on her way to the Facility."

"Everything is in order, sir. A pleasure to meet you," the guard says. Pax simply nods again, pulling me after him after shouldering his pack once more. We pass through a stone tunnel before we are funneled out into the grandest city I have ever seen. It looks like photos I saw as a child of the Royal Mile or Victoria Street.

The sun is setting, casting an orange and pink glow over the grey stones. There are green plants sprouting from pots or boxes in window sills. The windows and doors seep gentle light onto the cobblestone street. Erathians walk to and fro, smiling, nodding, ducking into pastry shops or pubs. It is overwhelming.

"Welcome to Sardone."

His voice coaxes me back to the reason why I am here, and a stone drops into my stomach.

"What was this city called before your kind took over?" I try to keep the malice from my voice. He scratches his head, frowning.

"I'll have to find out. Why?"

I look back out over the sprawling, bustling city with sorrow filling my heart.

"Because. That is what I wish to call it."

"You'll be at the Facility for three days or so. Just simple training and vaccinations to keep you healthy," he prattles, clearly excited as we walk through the winding streets. I'm exhausted, overwhelmed, and filled with deep sadness. My life is over.

My face bumps into his backpack, rubbing my nose from the impact. I look around him, following his gaze. Dread pools in my gut.

"Come on, Liv," he says, giving my rope a tug. I plant my feet. There is a courtyard, surrounded by a stone wall and an iron gate. It's nothing more than another form of prison for me. And I'd rather take my chances with Pax than some unknown freak. He gives an angered growl.

"Liv," he warns. I shake my head, pulling my burning wrists. He relents, coming toward me, resting a heavy hand on my shoulder.

"Three days. That's all, alright?"

I shake my head, unable to speak around the lump that has formed in my throat.

"Can't I just stay with you?" I whisper, my voice hoarse. I hate how pathetic I sound, like a child begging to stay in their parents' room for the night. His normally stoic face flitters with a mix of unreadable emotions.

"It's the law, Livy. We both carry diseases that can kill one another. You need this check-up."

"And the training?"

I try to keep my voice from sounding fearful; I need to be strong. But my words come out as a whimper. His thumb brushes up and down on my shoulder.

"Basic etiquette. Stuff you won't even need to know unless you're in public."

"I'm going to be your slave," I breathe. The words—now out—feel more real. His lips dip down in a frown. His hand slides from my shoulder down my arm before he reaches up. I flinch and cower away. He pauses his pursuit as he eyes me, then slowly cups my chin, more gentle than I ever thought him capable.

"Don't look at it that way, Liv. You'll have a home, food—clothes that fit. What's wrong with that?"

My tears threaten.

"I'd rather have freedom than all of that."

He sighs, releasing me and tilting his head back to stare at the stormy sky.

"Come, it's getting late." He forces me over the threshold. My own personal hell awaits.

~

Pax

I sit across from the nurse, her desk cluttered. She clacks away on her ancient computer. This place is old, as is the technology. They must not receive adequate funding. I begin to worry that Liv will suffer some sickness from being in here.

She stands behind me. I can feel her shifting; it is cold, and she isn't dressed properly. I'll have to find out what humans need to survive. My heart lurches in remembrance.

"She has an *allergic* to peanuts," I say. The nurse nods, giving me a simpering smile before glancing back at Liv. Her blond hair is pulled into a tight bun, showcasing her strong cheekbones and sharp jawline. After staring at Liv for so many days, this Erathian woman's features are harsh, masculine.

"It's very common for humans. I'll keep her segregated and attach a note to her file, and we can send you home with some medication."

"That being what?"

"Humans called them 'EpiPens.' We haven't changed what's in them or how they are administered because they do work well in emergencies."

I nod, relaxing.

"What is her name?"

"Olivia."

"Surname?"

I blank, turning to ask. She glares down at me, pressing her lips thin. She's being an insolent brat. I'd rather be the one training her, so she knows what I expect, but I know I must follow the law. I quirk my brow. She turns her face to the ceiling.

"Just put Harper," I grunt, waving my hand.

"Alright, and age?"

Again, I turn to glance at her. Her hair is wavy after her

wash in the river, hanging down in thick curtains past her ribs. The sight is pleasing to me.

Her eyes are wide.

"Answer," I demand.

She opens and closes her mouth, frightened, confused. "What...day is it?" she whispers to me, leaning in. She doesn't want the nurse to hear. I clench my teeth, feeling mild pity for the human.

"May 2nd."

"I'm eighteen," she whispers back, casting her eyes down. The nurse hears, typing it into her notes. I wonder how long she's been eighteen.

"Alright, Mr. Harper, I just need your handprint. We will call you when she's ready for pick-up."

She shuffles papers around on her cramped desk, clearing the scanner. I press my palm to it, feeling the slight tingle as it memorizes me. "How long?" I ask. She pulls her drawers out, filing Liv's paperwork.

"Typically, three to five days. We administer her first vaccines this evening. Some humans have adverse reactions, so we must monitor them. Once she's medically cleared, her training starts. Never takes long," she says, leaning in with a smile. My gut writhes. She could be here for five days? And she could have adverse reactions? I glance back at her. Tears are pooling in her eyes again.

"Do not cut her hair, or alter her appearance."

"Of course, sir." She stands. "I can take her from here."

"I would like a moment alone, please. Tell me where I need to meet you," I demand, allowing my authoritative voice to wind into my words. The woman is stunned but recovers quickly.

"Yes, just meet us down the hall. You'll see the double doors at the end."

I nod as she clacks out in her heels. She's almost as tall as me, another trait of Erathian women. Liv is short, the top of her head reaching under my chest. She is so small, so frail, I find that I am now worrying constantly about her health here. I have no choice though, so I stand. She backs away until she hits the wall, keeping her eyes on the ground.

"Come," I say. She shakes her head. Still defiant. Fire courses through me at her refusal, but it's not anger. It's another foreign emotion. I like this one more than the others she gives me.

"Now, Liv."

She shuffles forward at the tone of my voice. I reach down, unknotting her bound wrists, chucking the dirty rope into the garbage can. She rubs at her bleeding, cracked skin. I grit my teeth.

"You...you said three days."

"I wasn't aware it could be more."

She feels betrayed, I can see it in the hunch of her shoulders.

"Please, I'll go with you, I will clean—"

"I can't, Livy. You're from the wild. Even being around me for this long puts us both at risk for disease, understand?"

After some sniffling, she nods.

"Can you get me before training?"

I wish that I could. I don't want her to learn bad habits. My cheeks puff out in a long sigh. I am feeling the weight of this decision—of accepting responsibility for a human life.

"I will do my best."

Her eyes snap up at the words, hope and fire mingling in her striking green orbs. I've never seen such a color. Most Erathians have dark eyes.

"Be good. You can eat any meal you want when I come to get you."

Her eyes dance, a sly grin creeping onto her face.

"Ice cream?"

"Not a meal."

She huffs in annoyance.

"Chocolate?"

She's stalling.

"After a well-rounded meal, yes. Whatever sweet you want is yours."

She seems to glow through her shadowy bruises at my words, radiating an aura that is hard to ignore. Seeing her happy over the simplest thing is endearing as much as it is intriguing. I make a note to grab some reading on humans before I leave. If I'm going to do this, I will do it to the best of my ability.

"And then, of course, after that you're going to let me go, right?"

Her words, though clearly a joke, still hold some hope. I frown at her. Are all humans like this?

"You're better off here, trust me."

I don't bother telling her the horrors we encountered before finding her small band of misfits, horrors that were mere feet from her that would have—I bite my tongue to stave the thoughts, hard enough that I taste the coppery tang of blood. I feel she won't believe me. She crosses her arms, darting her eyes around the room.

"Let's go, it's getting late," I say, nudging her to the door. She plants her feet again, her shoes squeaking against the polished linoleum. With my forward momentum, my sternum collides with her shoulders. She turns, panic clear in her eyes.

"Do you promise to come back?" she whispers through her tears. I feel my frown deepen. Why would I go through all this trouble if I didn't intend to come back? She is being silly.

"Yes, Liv."

"Say it."

"Say what?" I grumble.

"That you promise."

I wonder if this is a normal human custom that I am not aware of, and so I do it to placate her.

"I promise."

She gives me a final, wavering stare, before turning around and opening the door of her own accord. I repress a chuckle as she marches forward down the hall of her own volition. I remember my words to her, about wishing to break her.

If I could take those back, I would.

3

Olivia

M y first night isn't so bad. I'm poked with a needle, which is nothing new to me, and shoved into a cage on the floor. It's demeaning, but my sights are set on getting out of here. Once I'm back with Pax, I will find a weapon, and I will be on my merry way. I'm freezing here, scrunched up on the floor, so I tuck my knees up into his shirt. I'm exhausted from the hike, so sleep overtakes me easily.

I awake before dawn feeling hot, which is a surprise. My stomach, though empty, is roiling. I know I'm going to vomit, and there's nowhere to do so in a cage this small. I bang on the bars, but I know I am alone. I was told I'd be segregated. I vomit yellow bile until I gag, a splitting headache rearing up. It isn't long before I pass out.

I'm awoken sometime later. Harried voices are muttering about a reaction. So, their medicines are going to kill me. *Super.*

I'm taken out, poked and prodded and stripped before I'm strapped to a bed. Many machines are hooked to me, but I am too feverish to remember much. I waver in and out of consciousness. For how long, I do not know.

I finally awake, feeling more normal, though hungry. The blonde nurse is there, dabbing my face with a cool washcloth. I don't mind her. It's the men that worry me.

"Training starts today," she quips, eyes dancing with excitement.

"You'll make your master incredibly pleased when we are done. He's captured such a pretty slave!"

I want to vomit again, but keep my mouth shut. I need to get out of here if I want to escape, and if that means playing the game, then so be it. My eyes just watch her in silence, wondering how she can be excited doing this—how she can find joy in aiding her kind in dominating ours.

I'm cleaned, dressed in a white gown with flowers dotting the otherwise blank canvas, and cuffed. I walk down the hall to a classroom full of girls—all human, all of varying ages. Their eyes stay down on their desks, hands folded neatly atop the grainy surfaces. I'm pushed into the front row.

A man stands at the front, a baton in his belt, a ruler in his hand. His eyes are shifty, dark, and snakelike. I feel my anger returning at the injustice that has been done upon me, my family, my species as a whole. I don't know how I will make it through this. I eye the room. No one looks back at me.

"Eyes down, human," the man spits. Another walks through the rows of desks, the women trembling in his shadow. Where is the kind nurse? I wish for her.

The women recite the words written on the board, words I myself cannot read: *I will obey my Master or suffer the consequences* their hollow voices say. I feel like vomiting again. A little girl around the age of ten is struggling. I keep my mouth shut, glaring at the man in charge. He sees me, and without any preamble, he stomps to me and batters his baton across my knuckles. I cry out in pain.

The little girl is struck across the backs of her hands with the ruler.

"Leave her the fuck alone!" I yell, lunging for him without a second thought. I'm clubbed by the leader in the back of the head. Blackness follows.

I remember this punishment. Pax did it to me in the forest. I know I will not die, but as the water rushes over my face through the scratchy cloth, it feels as though I will. I try to keep calm, but I am strapped down and helpless. My wrists tug at the cool, biting cuffs. The water relents, and as I gasp, more hits my face. It's not being poured as Pax did. It's being sprayed, and the pressure is relentless.

I'm on the verge of passing out from lack of oxygen by the time they stop. I'm left, shivering in the darkness. They will not break me.

Another day in the classroom. I know it's been over three days, but I'm unsure if I've reached the five day mark yet. The crushing thought that Pax has decided he doesn't want me swirls in my hazy mind. Why I yearn for him is beyond me. He's just as monstrous, just as evil. I begin to hate him.

It's the only thing keeping me alive.

I'm pressed down onto my knees, and then further so my butt touches my calves.

"Palms up," the leader growls. I obey. "Eyes down," he hisses, smacking the back of my head. I grit my teeth. He grips my chin, squeezing so hard I know I'll have his fingerprints bruised into my face.

"You'll be nothing more than a whore to your master," he

seethes. He hates me, just as I hate him. I don't understand what a whore is, but I know the word is meant to be degrading.

"I hope he fucks you senseless every night." I don't really get what that means, but it sounds more vile than anything else, this action he speaks of. I can't imagine Pax being that hateful toward me, but doubt begins to creep in.

"You'd like that, wouldn't you?"

I don't answer, trying to keep my cool. He backhands me so hard I fall to the side. When he bends down, I spit blood in his face and kick out his legs. He falls with a satisfying thud. My temper will cost me greatly. Two guards rush forward, one beating me with a blunt baton, the other with a thin stick that stings and smarts. I grit my teeth, but eventually the pain is too much. I cry out.

Beaten to the point of almost blacking out, I'm dragged back to the water room. I recognize it, and I begin to panic. It's no use. I'm strapped in, and the torture begins again. Little by little, they chip away at my mind.

I'd thought my days were getting worse, but the next one tops them. I spent the night in the water room, dripping and shivering, and as I fell into a fitful sleep, I was awakened by more of the same torture.

When I am taken out, I am strapped to an X. The room is white and steel and the leader stands before me with a sadistic smile on his face.

"I will break you, human."

His words, of all things, are my undoing. Pax said them to me in the forest, that he would enjoy breaking me. He hasn't done it personally, but his kind has. My hatred flares again. I am electrocuted, burned, and stabbed. The hours don't matter anymore. The bottoms of my feet are blistering from the flame of a lighter one of them holds. Another jabs a needle into my thigh, that pain familiar, but after having it done to me relentlessly, I know I would rather die of my allergy than ever stab myself with an EpiPen again.

Three words resound in my head throughout my tortures, my mind focusing with precision on his face. *I hate you, I hate you, I hate you.* If I survive, I promise I will kill him myself.

Pax

My fists are clenched on the front desk of the Facility, the receptionist on the phone with the man in charge. It's been nine fucking days. First, it was a bad reaction to her inoculations. Then, it was the delay in her training. And every day thereafter, it was some other bullshit excuse.

The woman gives me a nervous smile, the receiver of her phone pressed to her ear. She's faking the call; I can hear the dial tone on the other end. With a sneer, I storm past her desk against her protests and down the hall. The double doors are within my sight, and it just so happens that the blonde nurse is in my path.

"Where the fuck is she?" I rumble like the storm that is raging outside. Her eyes widen, her lips falling open. She takes a trembling step back, pushing her palms out toward me in stark fear.

"She—"

I grip her throat, slamming her against the wall. Erathian men are still the dominant gender in our society, even more so than human men were to their women. With my high rank in the government, she has no choice but to obey me.

"Take me to her now, or I will ensure you are all imprisoned for treason."

I release her. She gasps and coughs before nodding and rushing to the doors. I follow close behind. A few shocked men stare at me with anger in their eyes. The batons on their hips infuriate me. One steps in my path.

"Move," I growl.

"You're not allowed back here, sir," he sneers.

"I'm sure my father, Penn Harper, would love a tour of your Facility. Shall I give him a call?" I threaten. His eyes widen. He steps aside, trembling like a coward in fear. The blonde skirts around them, keys jangling in her shaking hands.

"I had no part in this," she whispers, her wide eyes frightened, seeking my forgiveness for what I'm about to witness. I steel myself, those strange emotions swirling in my chest. She pushes open the door, and my knees nearly buckle at the sight.

"*Liv.*"

Her name escapes my lips in a breathless plea. She hangs on an X, one that I know is typically used to torture insubordinate Erathians because our bodies can withstand more pain, more brutality. I was strapped to an X once for initiation. It was some of the worst hours of my life. I've no idea how long she's suffered in here.

I rush forward, loosening the binds that keep her sagging form attached to her prison. She slumps into my arms. I can feel her heartbeat. It is slow, weak. I pull her light body away from the X, tucking an arm under her butt while my other hand cradles her head to my shoulder. I feel like a father holding their child. She is small enough to be a child.

I turn my livid gaze to the quaking nurse.

"You best find a new job," I hiss in warning. I will personally ensure this place is shut down, that those responsible will suffer. Slaves are meant to aid us in our daily lives, but it seems some have lost sight of that notion.

I hold her tight to my chest, feeling her shallow breath on my neck as I storm out and into my vehicle. I lay her down across the front seat. There is no middle console like the vehicles humans made, for there isn't a need. I close the door, making my way around as thunder rumbles, threatening rain. I wrench my door open and climb in, starting my vehicle and blasting warm air onto her cold body.

I read a lot about humans over my nine days without her. I know all of her basic needs now. My hands grip her shoulders, pulling her languid form until her head rests on my lap, face up. She's more bruised than before. I attempt to keep my eyes on the road, but they keep falling to her.

My apartment is in the nicest part of town, therefore marking it as rather expensive, even if it is only a one-bedroom, one bathroom. I am thankful for the cover of darkness as I pull Liv from my vehicle, holding her the same way as before. I wait as a man and his slave woman pass by on a walk. Her eyes are cast to the ground. She is being led by silvery chains attached to her wrists. The sight is so typical, it would normally not give me a reason to pause.

But now, I wonder at her treatment behind closed doors.

I brush it off, entering my building with my thumbprint and walking us to the elevator. I am on the fifth floor, overlooking the city. I unlock my door with my thumb again, nudging it open with my knee. My elbow taps the screen on the wall and the warm light turns on, illuminating my long kitchen, living room, and makeshift office in one corner near the big window. The door locks automatically.

I bring her to the couch, careful as I set her down. Even in her state, she immediately curls her knees up, whimpering at the pain this inadvertently causes her. I crouch down, pulling her thick hair from her face to inspect her. I need Jeven. He's our medic, and the only one I'd trust with her.

I inspect her bruised face, then her arms, wrists, even her ankles and feet. The blisters are not from our hike. They are too fresh. I unbutton the side of her gown, pulling it away enough to see the bruises that litter her torso. My teeth grit. There are hundreds of tiny holes that my keen eyes home in on. Needles. I remember the pain, having endured it myself.

Then there are the long, screaming welts. Her skin hasn't broken, but I know the pain. I shake my head, sinking onto my knees. I know the pain as an Erathian male, not as a human woman.

Her heartbeat quickens. I button her gown, smoothing it flat once more. I do not know what reaction to expect. She pries open roving eyes. They are confused until they fall to my face. There is no more fire, no more spark. If anything, I was expecting her to attack me.

With a pitiful cry, she pushes herself back as far as she can into the couch, clutching her hands close to her chest as a shield from whatever horrors she thinks I may do to her.

"Livy—" I begin.

Her weak voice cuts me off and cuts into my soul as well.

"I am yours, master."

I leave her be, pacing in the kitchen as I rub my forehead. My tea is long abandoned. I crave something more potent. I feel disgusted. I do not want her like this. She's not the same. Despite how infuriating she was, she at least had life within her.

Jeven instructs me to clean her from head to toe, to coax some food into her, and force her to rest. I agree with his remedies but am at a loss as to how to proceed. I make my way back to the couch. She is drifting in and out of consciousness.

Gentle, I pull her into my arms, carrying her to the bathroom. I lean her against the wall, turning on the tap to run her a bath. The noise jostles her awake.

"I need to clean you up—"

She whimpers, eyes locked on the water.

"No, no, I've been good!" she wails, attempting to stand. My hands clamp around her shoulders, holding her in place. She refuses to meet my eyes.

"Yes, you have, Liv. You get a bath, and anything you want to eat, and I'll even let you choose where you sleep. How does that sound?"

She's trembling and crying and sniffling. Those strange feelings enter my core again. I wait until she nods. I help her stand.

"Please, master, don't l-look," she stutters, wringing her hands together.

My temper flares.

"Do not call me that."

Her eyes would normally find mine, would normally question me and push my buttons. She doesn't this time. It's pissing me off, how different she is—how she's not the same young woman that went into the Facility.

"What would you like to be called?" she mutters, her voice hollow.

"Just bathe, Liv. I'll leave you some clothes."

She bobs her head as I release her. I close the door, rubbing my temples. I fetch her one of my shirts. I have been so enraptured with work and studying humans that I forgot to buy her clothes and other necessities.

I go to my kitchen, pulling a head of lettuce from the cooler and other supplies to make her a decent salad. My book instructed me that humans need protein, vegetables, carbs, and fruits in moderation. I go back to my cooler in the wall, searching for the dressing I made myself. My eyes land on a brown and tan tub. Her pint of chocolate ice cream.

I slice up chicken, other vegetables, and warm a piece of bread for her. Overanalyzing every ingredient label, I check for peanuts for the fiftieth time. I hear the bathroom door creak open. I offer her battered face the most convincing and gentle smile I can muster, but her eyes are trained on her feet.

"Sit on the couch."

She obeys without hesitation now. I grumble to myself, bringing her food to her with a glass of water and her pain meds. My white shirt is stained with water droplets from her damp hair. I slide her salad onto the coffee table, seating myself next to her.

"You may eat," I say when she doesn't move. I know she is starving. Her eyes are stuck wide on the salad. I glance at it, wondering if it looks appetizing to her. Maybe she needs help? I pick up her fork, stabbing a piece of chicken, holding it out to her. She jerks away, pressing the back of her hand to her mouth. I drop the fork with a clatter, rushing to the bathroom to retrieve my small metal garbage pail. I can hear the bile rising up her throat.

The pail moves under her chin just in time for her body to expel nothing more than a yellow substance. I am worried. I've never seen anything like this before. She vomited at camp that first night, but I wasn't as concerned then.

She's shaking, clutching at the pail as her body writhes again. It looks so painful. I reach out, placing my hand between her prominent shoulder blades. She spits, calming, but she's whimpering.

"What can I do, Livy?" I am at a loss. She shakes her head, sniffling. She's crying again. I stand, going to retrieve a damp washcloth. I read it helped calm humans in physical distress. Holding it to her forehead, I sink down onto the leather couch again. She lurches away with a frightened whimper, wide eyes on the damp rag. I pull away, holding my hands up to declare I mean her no harm. I watch as her bottom lip trembles as she quivers in fright, and then it sinks in. The wet rag. Her torture.

My stomach is in knots. I know she endured waterboarding at the Facility, but what's worse is knowing it was something I personally did to her. I didn't know, didn't understand how badly a human would react to that, and now that knowledge feels like a white-hot knife plunging into my stomach and twisting my guts. When she speaks, it only makes that relentless guilt worse.

"Why...why didn't you come back?" she asks, her voice hoarse.

I nudge the pail to the side, tossing the rag away.

"I did."

She shakes her head.

"I counted. I was there for thirty days."

I feel like I've been punched in the chest.

"You were only there for nine, Liv."

Her green orbs flash to mine, rimmed in red, surrounded by purple and yellow and blue. I wish to see her face as I had on the day I captured her, the day she swept my legs from under me and knocked me to my ass. Her brows wage a war of confusion.

"Nine?" she whispers. I nod. The fact that she felt like she was there for more is a testament to her torture.

"I'll be a good girl," she says finally. I want to shake her, to demand she fight back like she used to. Now is not the time.

"You be whatever you feel you need to be, Olivia."

The use of her full name has her face scrunching in pain and sorrow. I place my hand on her back again. Her bones stick out far too much.

"Please eat."

She shakes her head.

"Do you not like salad?"

She points to the chicken.

"You don't like chicken?" I press. Her shocked eyes find mine. I'm thankful she still looks me in the eye from time to time.

"Ch-chicken?"

I can hear her stomach growl, which makes me confused.

"What else does it look like?"

"I thought you ate humans," she whispers, casting her eyes down. Fucking Brutus and his cruel prank. I sigh through my nose in deep frustration.

"We do not eat humans, Liv. You ate pork that night."

"Oh," she mutters.

"Eat, you need something in your stomach before you take these," I say, holding out two white pills. To my shock, she digs in. "Manners," I remind her automatically.

"Fanks," she says. I feel a small smile crack my face. She's still in there, somewhere. I will find her.

"Where would you like to sleep?" I ask after ensuring her food has settled well. She twists her hands together but doesn't answer. I am annoyed. "I will choose for you if you don't make up your mind."

"On the floor, by your feet."

Her words are quiet, robotic. Rehearsed. I grit my teeth. I point to the ajar door at the end of the short hallway, my room.

"Go in there. I want you on the bed, on the left side, under the blankets."

She nods, but I can feel her apprehension. What else have they crammed into her mind? I retrieve her promised tub of ice cream and a spoon. I wouldn't normally allow even myself to eat in my bed, but she needs it.

I am satisfied to find she has listened, but her eyes stay stuck on my white duvet. I tap the lights on with my elbow before I move forward, sitting down by her feet, holding the dessert beneath her gaze. Her eyes jump to mine in shock.

"Go on. Just don't make yourself sick."

She gingerly takes the spoon.

"Don't you want some, mas—"

My glare cuts her off, and she shrinks at my wordless reprimand.

"My name is Pax to you."

She nods.

"I'm going to change. When you're done, I need to go over some basic rules, and then I want you to sleep."

She fiddles with the lid, but she nods.

"Yes, Pax."

I stand, moving to my closet and grabbing a change of clothes before I head to the bathroom. I don't take too long, worried about leaving her alone in any capacity right now. I return to my room, tossing my dirty clothes in the hamper. She's nowhere to be seen. There's no way she can escape; only my fingerprints or handprints allow for an exit. The half-eaten tub is abandoned on my nightstand, and my eyes home in on a minuscule chocolate stain on the white cover.

I pause, listening for her rushing heartbeats. I crouch down to her horrible hiding spot beneath my bed. Her hands are clasping her mouth, her tears numerous.

"Come here," I say in exasperation. She shakes her head, sending a thrill through me. "Now, Liv," I demand.

"It was an accident," she squeaks, fearing my retribution.

"I know, come here."

It takes her a moment, but she comes out and stands before me. I yank the blankets back before gripping her hips and hoisting her onto the bed. She's so light it feels as though I am picking up a rag doll.

"Lay down. Are you done?" I ask, nodding to her ice cream. Her chest is heaving in fear, but she nods. I take the spoon to the sink, stowing the ice cream for another day. When I return, she hasn't moved a muscle. I seat myself at the end of the bed again.

"Relax, please."

She nods in acknowledgment but doesn't actually do it. I run my hand through my hair. Best to just get on with it.

"I work from home the rest of this week. Today is Monday. You are free to acclimate for this week. All windows are alarmed and only open with my fingerprints, same with doors, including the bathroom. You will eat and rest. Each night at ten, you will come in here and go to bed, with or without me. Understand so far?"

She gives a small nod.

"If you try to escape or to hurt me, there will be consequences." My eyes bore into hers. There, deep down, is a flicker of a spark. I bite back my smile.

"I will not beat you, starve you, lock you away, alright? You will simply have privileges taken away if you break the rules, and we can figure out other punishments as I see fit."

She pipes up.

"Privileges?"

I nod.

"Tv, books, games, unhealthy food. Whatever else you want, it is yours. But if you break rules, those will be taken for a time I determine."

I am shocked as she crosses her arms and glares at me. It takes a moment for her to realize her actions, but as she does, she quickly changes her stance. Again, I bite back a chuckle.

"I'll implement more rules as need be. Alright?"

She is gritting her teeth. It is curious, how quickly she is wanting to resist my authority after just being freed from hell itself. I do not understand how she is capable of that, but I have to remind myself she's a survivor. This is all she has probably ever known. I quirk my brow, waiting for any response. She nods.

I turn off the light, crawling into my side of the bed. It is unheard of to allow your slave to sleep next to you, even ones used for sexual purposes. I just can't imagine making her sleep on the floor or the couch after what I've inadvertently and explicitly put her through. She shifts beneath the covers. I remember how warm she was in my sleeping bag next to me, how quickly I fell asleep once I was sure she couldn't escape.

I reach out through the darkness, scooting closer to her. I hear her heart rate spike, her breath gasp. I pull her body flush with mine, calmed immediately. I do not want to hurt her, so I keep my hand on her hip instead of my arms around her as I wish to do.

I wonder if I've gone too far. I know humans have boundaries as far as physical touch. She *is* my property, though.

"Do you mind this, Livy?"

She hesitates, but shakes her head. I hope she isn't lying to me out of fear of retribution. I press my nose to her hair, feeling how soft it is against my face. Erathian women's hair is coarse and wiry.

I am surprised by how quickly she falls asleep in my arms. She rolls, as she did in the tent that morning, pressing her face tight to my chest. I run my fingers up her spine, feeling her bones. She is calm, her sleep peaceful. I rest my chin on her head as nightmarish thoughts plague me. They always do when night falls.

I didn't realize how badly I needed a companion before this moment.

4

Olivia

I stare out the window. The day is sunny, and I presume it is warm. Pax has insisted I take a nap on the couch, but I cannot get my eyes to close. I fear I will wake up back in that water room, or the X room. A shiver runs through me. I pull the thick blanket up to my chin.

Pax sighs, the sound aggravated. I am curious, poking my head up over the back of the couch. He sits in the corner at a small desk, a tablet-computer thing perched in front of him. His cheek is in his fist as he stares at the words on the glowing screen. Behind his desk is a tall bookshelf. I cannot remember the last time I saw so many books.

He picks up his navy blue mug, holding it to his lips. He pulls it away, the muscles in his back tensing through his grey shirt. The mug is empty. He's already had four cups of coffee today.

A loud knock sounds at the door, and panic races through my veins. I squeak in fright, diving down and pulling the blanket over my head. He stands up, his chair scraping against the dark wood floors. I roll onto my stomach, chancing a peek over the arm of the couch with the blanket still covering me. The door is open, and through it, I can see a hallway and other similar doors. Pax signs something, that frown always on his face, and the man standing opposite him hands him a brown box.

They exchange pleasantries, and Pax shuts the door, tossing the box to the kitchen table. He meanders to the empty coffee pot, grumbling to himself before he checks the watch on his wrist. He curses again.

"Sorry, Livy. I didn't realize it was so late." His eyes somehow find mine. He smirks. "Aren't you hungry?"

I nod. He made me something called oatmeal for breakfast and even topped it with strawberries. My stomach growls, hoping that it's for lunch as well. He wouldn't let me have coffee, though. He said he wanted to make sure it was safe for humans first. We never had coffee or anything besides water on the run. If we were lucky, we'd find old cans or bottles of soda sometimes.

"Come here," he calls as he turns to the sink. I obey, shivering as the blanket falls from my body. I stand beside him, staring at the beautiful concrete countertops, the color of faded brown rust.

"This is the cooler," he says, pointing to a glass box framed by metal. It's in the wall. I've never seen anything like it.

"Tap once, and it lights up," he says. I peek at him. He nods to the cooler.

"Go on."

I reach a shaky hand up, fingers brushing the smooth glass. I jump as bluish light illuminates the contents. When we had a home we had a fridge, a box that was outside of the wall. I barely remember that.

"Now tap twice to open it."

I do as he says, smiling as it opens.

"What do you want for lunch?"

The tub of velvety ice cream jumps out at me, but so do the strawberries and the salad, and there's a whole roast chicken in there, and some sort of steak marinating. All I can do is stare, overwhelmed. Even when I was little, we never had this much fresh food.

"I...I..." I stutter. He reaches around me, his warmth soothing as the cold continues to blast my face. He grabs supplies for another salad.

"We can have steak and potatoes tonight, and you can help me if you wish."

The cooler closes as he sets the food on the island counter. I chance another peek at him. He's shaved his face, but under his eyes there are rings. He was up before me—well before me. I slept until ten. I watch as a vein in his neck pulses, bringing precious, vital blood to his brain and back to his heart. I learned about the body when I was in the Settlement, a drab place where I spent a few years of my life before it was wiped off the map by Erathians. I learned because I wanted to know how people could die.

Could I kill him? I wanted to when I was being tortured. Yet here I am, one day free of that hell, and I am grinning at the sight of food and a cooler. I bite my cheek, hating myself.

"Liv?" he asks, chopping up the lettuce. I don't realize I am staring off at nothing, that he has asked me a question.

"Yes?" I say, shaking my head.

He nods to the table.

"Bring me that box, please."

Still distracted, I do as he asks, bringing it back around to him. The knife in his hand is abandoned as he searches for something else. I can swipe it, but it's much too big to conceal easily. He produces another knife from the pocket of his jeans, the blade flying open. I jump back at the noise. He ignores me, cutting through the tape and stowing his knife once more. He pushes the box to me, resuming his salad making.

Confused, I peer inside. My chest tightens. There are at least ten EpiPens. My face warms. Sarah was the last person to have an EpiPen, one she found at an abandoned pharmacy. She nicked it for trading purposes. I carried all her supplies for eleven days straight just to own that last EpiPen. And now Pax has given me ten, without asking anything in return. I may be his slave, but something tells me he would do this small kindness for me no matter what.

"Are those the right kind?"

He stands with both hands on the counter, leaned over, the tendons in his muscled arms jumping out at me. I pick one up for closer inspection, looking for the right symbols. I squint at the label. *Epinephrine.* It's one of the few words I recognize. My mother used to make me stare at the bottles to memorize it, same with the word *peanut.* We didn't have much time to worry about other words, but she used to say some and make me remember their meanings.

I nod.

He straightens, brushing his hands together.

"You can put them in your nightstand after you eat. I'll keep a few, too, just in case."

"Thank you," I say, my voice quiet.

He shakes his head, waving his hand. "Of course." It almost feels like I am his equal.

I sit down to eat, raising my fork to my lips just as he's settling back in to work, another pot of coffee brewing.

"Manners, Livy."

I grit my teeth, deciding to play nice, but on my terms.

"Thank you, *sir.*"

His eyes snap to me, simmering, but I just shovel the food into my mouth, always afraid it will somehow run out.

"Slow down," he comments. I give an annoyed huff. After I

eat and tuck my EpiPens away, the sun is streaming in and landing right on the couch. I decide to watch the clouds scuttle by, but as my tired, beaten body is warmed, I drift off into a dreamless sleep.

I awake as someone jostles my legs. My eyes spring open in fear. I sit up, so fast my head swirls. The sun has dipped low on the horizon, but it isn't very close to sunset yet. My eyes fall to Pax. He's seated himself on the far end of the couch, my legs in his lap.

"Just me," he says in reassurance. I take a steadying breath, rolling to my side and pulling my legs away from him. For some reason, his touch bothers me right now. He doesn't seem to notice as he stares at his phone, sifting through what looks to be photos.

"Shit," he mutters, letting his head fall back. I pull myself up into a sitting position, wrapping my arms around my legs, keeping the blanket on me. It's another barrier between me and him. His deep chocolate eyes find mine. He frowns.

"I need to get you clothes and other things. I forgot."

I chew my lip, giving him a small nod.

"Here," he reaches to the side table, grabbing a pen and paper.

"Write down your sizes and things you need."

He holds the pen and paper out to me, and my mouth runs dry. He nudges it, indicating I should take it. I reach out a shaky hand, staring at the white blank page. He waits as I stare.

"I'm gonna go change."

He stands, leaving me alone for a few minutes. I uncap the pen, poising it over the paper. I haven't used one in forever. Still shaking, I attempt to write my name from memory. My handwriting is horrid, and I'm not sure if I have spelled it correctly. The sight of my scratchy scrawl makes tears well in my eyes.

I sniff, wiping them away. I don't hear his approach. His hand snatches the pad of paper, making me jump.

"Seriously, Liv? Are you trying to piss me off?" he growls. I shrink into the cushions, unable to meet his eye. It feels so stupid. I can't even remember how to spell the name my parents gave me.

I heave a shuddering breath, hiding my face in my knees. It feels like he is gone after a few minutes, but when I chance a peek, he is sitting across from me on the coffee table, leaning forward on his knees, eyes trained on my messy writing, an intense look on his striking face.

I bite my cheek.

"This is your name," he says, voice low, eyes still on the paper. I shrink further in on myself, shifting my eyes away from him. "When were you uprooted, Liv?" he asks, his voice gentle, quiet. I can't meet his eyes, but I feel them staring me down, nonetheless.

"Six."

I hear him shift, then sigh.

"Look at me, please."

It's not his usual demand. He has used the manners he forces on me. My gaze drifts to his. He tears the top sheet off the stack of papers, setting my name aside. He writes something down, then shows it to me.

"What does it say?"

His writing is blocky, square—and for some reason, it reminds me of him as a person. I squint, the letters familiar. It is my name.

"Olivia," I whisper, finding his eyes. Something swims in those depths, something I can't understand. He nods, then jots something else down before showing me.

I stare for longer. Only three letters, but I cannot remember what sound the 'x' is supposed to make, or if the 'a' is long or short. I shake my head, not wanting to embarrass myself.

"Pax," he urges.

I should have guessed that.

"What is your last name?"

For some reason, I want to tell him. He will be the first person I've told it to in five or so years.

"Donne." I say. He sets to work on a new sheet, writing down a few different things. He turns the paper to me.

"Which spelling looks more familiar?"

I frown, leaning closer. There's Done, Donne, Dunn, Dun. I wring my hands together, nervous, as though this is a test. Eventually, I am almost certain I know which one and point to the second option. He glances at it before offering me a small smile.

"Good," he nods. I feel as though I've passed some test. He's still staring at me, though, and that feeling of unease creeps over me again. I want to be away from him. I don't like how he touched me while I was asleep, and I don't like how he is staring at me now.

"May I go to bed, please?" I tack on manners so he can find no reason to deny me.

His brows furrow.

"It's just after four, Liv. You need dinner."

"I'm too tired."

"What's wrong?" he presses.

I shake my head.

"Talk to me—"

"Nothing!" I snap, my voice biting, my heart thundering. I feel like a wounded animal, caged in while some stronger being pokes at me with a stick. His face clouds over. I've made him mad again, but I don't care. His feelings aren't the only ones that matter.

"I demand you tell me," he seethes.

"Just beat me. Hold me down and pour water over my face until I can't breathe anymore. I don't fucking care," I hiss, shaking as my emotions mount.

"Watch your language," he growls.

I feel my eyes are so wide they may bulge out of my skull. "I can't do this," I say, my voice quiet. He throws his hands up.

"Do what, Olivia?" he raises his voice in his anger. I shake my head as tears well, training my eyes down to the fuzzy, velvety grey and white blanket. I feel as though my words flow through me with the utter truth of how I feel in this exact moment. My eyes find his.

"Kill me, please. I can't do this," I beg.

"What?" he breathes shocked, his face slack. I nod, wiping at my cheeks, mustering my bravery. I sit a little straighter, unable to quell my words.

"I don't want to live this way. I want to be free, or I want to die. And you've taken my freedom."

He grits his teeth, finally tearing his eyes from me. His jaw is clenching and unclenching, his arm muscles twitching. After an eternity, he stands. I still cower in his presence. His eyes seem to be unable to meet mine.

"Go to bed."

I don't make a move. He's quaking with rage. He flexes his fingers. I know he wishes to hit me. I smirk up at him. I've won, in some small way.

"If you don't get into bed—"

He's raising his voice again.

"What? You'll what, you coward? You can punish me, but you can never hurt me so bad I will die? What kind of life is that to live? You're a fucking *monster!*" I yell, standing before him. He can barely contain his fury. I poke my finger at his chest.

"Everything they did to me was *your* fault. The only reason I wanted to live was so I could kill you!"

He catches my wrist, his hold bruising. Good. My smirk deepens. If I can push him over the edge, he will kill me, on purpose or accident, I don't care anymore. He walks me forward, forcing me to walk back until my shoulders hit the wall. He is slow, his gaze and his hold unwavering. I glare up at him the entire time, attempting to not betray my fear. I feel it fluttering in my chest.

He releases me, taking one step back. He raises his arms, but I am too enraptured by his movements to flinch this time. He pulls his long sleeve shirt over his head, exposing the expanse of his muscles. There is not one part of him that isn't perfectly sculpted.

He tosses his shirt aside, and it is only then that my eyes focus on his lightly bronzed skin.

Scars.

They are *everywhere*, littering every free space. Some are small nicks, some are long, ragged, grisly. My mouth clamps shut, eyes bouncing to meet his livid ones.

"Freedom has a price, Livy. Choosing death over the unknown is the most cowardly thing I've ever heard."

I want to be enraged, I want to make him hurt as badly as I am right now, but I am left empty at his words.

"Go to bed. On the *floor*."

"I'm—"

"Now, before I do something I will regret."

I snap my mouth shut, leaving his sight but I slam his door as my final word. I slump to the floor, allowing my emotions to flow forth as sobs wrack my sore, exhausted body.

Pax

It's midnight. Her cries quieted some time ago. I've yet to check on her, my mind swirling around her words. She is being irrational, more than what I feel should be normal. I lean back on my couch, bringing the whisky to my lips. The remnants sear through me. I set my glass aside, standing and stretching. My eyes fall to the wrinkled slip of paper she wrote her name on. Without a thought, my fingers gently pluck it from the wooden top.

I make my way to my room, cracking the door and peeking in. A small lump is curled on the floor at the foot of my bed. She's tucked her legs into my shirt to keep warm, her body in a tight ball. I move past her, setting the paper on my nightstand and changing in my closet before rolling into bed.

I twist and turn, half sleeping, still angry, still frustrated. No one has ever gotten this deep under my skin before. I am angered that I want to cave and pull her into bed with me, angered that my resolve is so thin already. What is this human doing to me? Maybe I should sell her...

The thought makes my chest ache. With a mouth like hers, she'd be beaten daily, or worse. I can't bring myself to do that to her. I am a monster, as she has said. I left her to be tortured, and I suppose this is my punishment. *I deserve it.*

I sigh, pulling off my down comforter, leaning over the end of my bed. It's not needed to stay warm, it's simply a comfort. Humans, however, need warmth to stay alive. I gently drape it over her little form, tucking it up to her chin. She rustles and sighs but doesn't wake. Her face is peaceful. I continue to stare, laying on my stomach, watching her shoulders rise and fall, watching her eyes twitch. Erathians rarely dream. I believe she is dreaming right now.

Laying back the normal way on my bed, I glare at my nightstand. There, perched innocently on the polished wood still, is her handwriting. I reach for it, holding it up to the pale moonlight. *Olivia.* Her 'o' is wobbly, her 'a' much too ornate. It's as if a child has written it. I smile. I press my fingers to my nightstand drawer, unlocking my hidden safe and tucking the piece of paper away next to my weapons. Sleep evades me.

Olivia is on the couch, staring out the window as she did yesterday. She's been quiet, only muttering small pleases and thank you's when necessary. She ate her breakfast, but mostly pushed it around her plate. Her depression is obvious. I take a break from work, shooting Jeven a message. He has a slave. He may know what to do.

I stand and stretch, peering over the back of the couch. She is fast asleep. I know she needs it. Her bruises are beginning to fade. I decide to take the rest of the day off, to focus on her. I need to go shopping for her, and though I feel she may not be ready for her public debut, it may help bring her out of this funk.

I shift her legs aside, settling onto the couch next to her. She wakes immediately with a small gasp, pulling her legs out of my lap with a sharp tug, her wide, green eyes swirling with fear and angst. "I didn't mean to wake you," I say.

She pulls her gaze away, scooting to the farthest end of the couch, wrapping the blanket tighter around herself. She tucks her knees up, looking away from me as she rests her cheek on them. I frown. I see a pattern in her behavior.

I woke her the same way last night, and she reacted the same way—pulling away from me, giving me that look as though I'd somehow betrayed her. I find it puzzling; she's let me hold her while we sleep before. Why would this gesture seem any different to her?

"Liv?"

She moves her face to me but doesn't meet my eyes. She's trying to obey enough to not get into trouble. I study her hunched demeanor.

"Have I done something to upset you?"

She shakes her head. I can see her thinking, can see her confusion. Maybe she doesn't understand her emotions. I can only imagine what a tangled web they must be. Humans are terrible at processing anything.

"I...won't touch you, while you sleep. I had no ill intent with the gesture," I say. Her eyes snap to mine, her brows pinching together. There's a small divot between them. Eventually, she nods.

"Why does that bother you?"

She shrugs, staring at the floor. I decide not to push it. I need to find her a doctor, someone who specializes in all this human stuff.

"Will you go to the stores with me today?"

She tries to hide her interest, but she nods.

"I..." she begins, her voice hoarse. I wait. She glares at the floor. "They took my shoes."

"That will be our first stop, then."

Her face brightens, but she still won't fully look at me.

"I'm going to shower. Do you want to watch TV?" I know leaving her alone, unsupervised, is a risk, but I have to begin trusting her at some point, especially if I expect her to trust me. She straightens, nodding.

I find the remote on the coffee table, flicking on the box above my fireplace. I surf through channels until I find some children's show. For some reason, I know this will be the best choice for her. She's already engrossed, smiling the slightest bit. I leave her be, giving her a chance to feel like a child again—to give her back a part of herself that has been robbed from her.

Her eyes are round as saucers as we enter the shoe store. It is only a few minutes' walk from my complex, so I give her a pair of my hiking socks to wear. No Erathian gives her a second glance. Liv, however, stares at *everything*.

"What brings you in today, sir?" A teen Erathian boy asks. His eyes drift to Livy, lingering for longer than I like. With her fading bruises, her beauty is more evident. It is rare for our kind to find humans appealing.

"Shoes for this one," I say nodding down to her. She stands at my side, shoulders hunched, fiddling. I don't cuff her or chain her to me. I doubt she has any inkling to run away, and I don't want her feeling worse than she already is about her circumstances.

"Oh...the slave store is just around the corner, sir." The kid says, pimpled face reddening. I grit my teeth. Out of my peripherals, Olivia shrinks even more, hugging herself. My same shirt still hangs from her bony frame.

"And?" I bite back, the kid jumping at the sharp edge in my voice.

"Women's shoes are this way," he says, motioning us to follow. I reach for her, my fingers around her elbow as I lead us to the right side of the store. It is empty in here, and I am thankful.

"Sit," I command, nudging her to the bench. She does, pulling down my shirt to her knees. I can feel her palpable discomfort.

"May I check her size, sir?"

I step back with a nod, crossing my arms.

He pulls out a foot measuring device. "Just place your foot right here—thanks," he says as she listens. She is curious as the scanner sizes her with precision. "US size 6. She may be able to go smaller for some brands. What kind of shoe does she need?" He asks me directly. I scratch at my jaw.

"Umm...athletic ones. And slippers, for the house...and something for when it's raining...and she can choose whatever other pair she wants," I say with a wave of my hand.

Shopping is a bleak affair to me. The boy's eyes widen as he stands.

"Right away, sir."

He jets off.

"Socks, too!" I call. I lean against the wall across from Liv. She's swinging her little feet, my socks abandoned on the bench next to her.

"I'm not supposed to be here," she says. I know she wants to sound tough and biting, but it sounds more hollow and sad than anything. I am beginning to feel empathetic toward her.

"You can be anywhere I say you can be, Livy."

She peeks up at me. There is still pain in her eyes, but it seems my words have helped. The boy brings back a plethora of shoes. He takes his time talking about the pros and cons of each, and before long, he is talking directly to her, as though she is his equal. I watch their interactions, watch as she gives him a small smile, tucking her hair behind her ear as she eyes a pair of light pink and white tennis shoes.

Her eyes dart to mine for permission. I try to hide my smirk, but it is impossible. I give her my nod of approval. She ends up with those, a pair of shiny black rain boots, a pair of fuzzy grey slippers, and a pair of soft boots with sheepskin lining that she wears out of the store despite the warmer weather. I don't tell her how ridiculous she looks.

I carry her bags, reaching for her wrist. It is a busy time of evening, and though this is a safe part of the city, there are still those who would take one look at her and do anything they could to have her. She doesn't mind my touch. Her free arm swings, eyes jumping from shop front to shop front. We pause at a crossroads, and she is fixated on a boutique with lots of lights and crystal chandeliers.

"There?" I ask. She shakes her head, wide eyes on mine.

"No, no, that's too fancy."

"Have you ever even been in a place like that?"

She presses her lips together before she shakes her head. I pull her toward the shop and we enter. It is fancy, but the clothes are quality, and she seems happy. A tall, lanky redhead saunters over, her eyes on me alone. Her intentions are clear, and lust rolls off her in waves.

"We don't get many men like you in here," she purrs. I feel Liv's eyes dart up to me, but I plaster a fake smile to my face to remain pleasant. This woman thinks she's hotter than she is.

"Just need some clothes—"

"For your girlfriend?"

I want to snort. She's fishing for information about me. I pull Liv a little closer until her side is pressed to me.

"Nope, for this little one here."

The woman's eyes fall to Liv, who is smiling up at her. Her grin is genuine. Her interaction with the boy at the shoe store has boosted her confidence, but not all of my kind are so lenient when it comes to humans.

"Oh," she says, barely hiding her disdain. "We sell clothes for Erathian women, not slaves."

I feel Liv flinch. I glance down at her in mock confusion, then back to the spiteful woman.

"I didn't realize masters were only allowed to shop in a specific store," I growl. She simmers, but that disdain is still there on her flawless, blunt face. Her eyes betray her disgust.

"There are lingerie shops and adult fantasy shops in Hillsyard," she hisses, crossing her arms. I know the part of town that she speaks of. It is where there are brothels, drugs, and slaves for sale for...other purposes.

Liv picks that moment to pipe up, her confused eyes searching my face.

"What's a *lingerie*?" she whispers. I can't hide my snort. I release her arm, instead folding her into my side, chafing her hip.

"Something I will thankfully never see this woman wearing. Let's find somewhere else to do business."

The woman's mouth drops in shock, and Livy is still confused, but we turn and leave. I am glad she doesn't grasp how segregated our society truly is. We eventually find a store that is run by a kind woman. She is older, near my mother's age, and she employs slaves. I allow Liv a chance to wander and find what she likes. I notice she often is drawn to comfort over the latest fashion, dark hues, and oversized tops.

The owner is folding her growing pile at the counter, making small talk with Liv.

"You've got yourself quite a nice master, little lady," she says, leaning across the wooden top. Liv averts her eyes, giving a bashful nod. The kind woman chuckles, leaning closer.

"I think you're missing some necessities."

Red creeps up Liv's neck and seeps into her face. Again, she nods. The woman looks at me.

"Do you mind if I borrow her, sir?"

"Not at all."

She comes around the counter, reaching for Liv's hand, before leading her back to the undergarments section of the store. I am thankful for that gesture. Liv would have let us leave without saying anything.

We finish up, my arms straining from the amount of bags I'm carrying. Night is falling, music drifting to us from decadent restaurants. I'm starved, and I bet Liv is, too. She keeps close as we meander towards home, but she stops when we near a cafe. A slave woman is on her knees before her master, a thin chain around her neck. I know the slave is about to be punished for some unknown crime. I nudge Liv forward, but she plants her feet.

"Move," I growl.

"But he's—"

The slap echoes, but the world doesn't stop. No one else

bats an eye. I need to get her to move before she does something irrational. For the first time today, I regret my decision not to tether her to me in some way.

As I am trying to maneuver all her bags to one side so I can grab her, a loud bang echoes through the square. My trained ears recognize it as nothing more than a firework; Erathians are quite fond of that human invention. In that short moment, Liv sprints away. I realize I've forgotten to share with her the most vital law of our kind; a slave on the loose without a master can be shot on sight.

5

Olivia

I run without a thought. The gunshot reverberates in my mind over and over and over. I clutch at my ears, whimper as I shove past warm bodies and hard elbows and soft sides. I do not know where I am. It is familiar, this feeling, this moment. I was much smaller the first time I fled their gunfire. I was much smaller when I pressed my hands to my mother's stomach as blood seeped between my fingers and stained my soul.

I ram straight into a solid, cool force, but before I can fall, something behind me is pinning my arms to my sides in a death grip.

I writhe and wriggle and let out a scream. They are wearing that armor—white and grey. Seamless. Lethal and impenetrable. A gloved hand squeezes my throat, crushing my windpipe as he pulls me off my feet. I claw at the hand and arm, their cackles like crows.

"Pretty, for a slave."

"Very. Should enjoy her before we kill her."

My heartbeat hammers in my ears, but I can still hear it. Still hear *him*.

"Liv! Olivia, get back here, dammit!"

I lurch, reaching for his voice as black spots fill my vision. He can save me. He *did* save me. Even if he did this to me, he has still saved me. The hold on my throat loosens, and I sob for air as I'm tossed to the ground.

"What the fuck—"

His voice is livid. I remember I am wearing a shirt-dress. I pull my knees up, pebbles and cobblestone biting into my flesh. I kick away from the monsters, toward the familiar voice. His heavy hands wrap around my biceps as he lifts me onto my feet.

"A slave on the loose is ours to do with as we please, citizen."

I am panting, leaning heavily against Pax's warm, strong body. One of his arms wraps around me, tucking me into his side to shield me.

"She wasn't escaping," Pax hisses. I wonder at his words. It should seem to him I was running away, so he's either lying to them and I am in deep trouble, or he thinks I was simply scared. I hope it is the latter, hope I do not have to defend myself against him. That is a battle I will lose.

"She was running toward us—"

"She heard a firework and panicked. She has PTSD."

I don't know what those letters mean. All I heard was a firework? I have only seen one firework in my life before, and it simply fizzled on the ground. The guards snort derisively.

"Humans do not suffer that type of mental affliction."

"The hell they don't," Pax growls, standing his ground. The guards are agitated.

"Hand her over, citizen. You are not fit to properly control your slave."

"You will have to go through me first, officers," he spits.

They glance at one another before sizing him up. Pax is near half a head taller than them both, and twice as wide. Even two against one, they do not stand a chance.

"We will just call our commander—"

"Go for it. Tell him I say hello. His family photo is on my desk."

They shift nervously. I don't realize I am shaking. After a moment, the two glance at each other and seem to back down.

"Keep that thing under better control, or we will be forced to act as the law demands."

Pax's grip on me tightens, whether in anger at their words or anger at me, I do not know.

"I will keep that in mind."

The guards leave and the street is empty and quiet. I am still shaking, now fearing his retribution.

"Pax..."

"Not now, Livy. Grab some bags so we can get home."

I obey, unsure of what is to come.

I am sitting on the couch as he's instructed. I can hear him lugging my things to the bedroom, hear him starting what I assume is the washing machine. He marches to the bathroom with my bag of toiletries. I could do it myself, but I keep quiet. His silence is unnerving.

I keep my eyes down, staring at my tan, sheepskin boots. My feet are warm and wrapped in luxury. I've never owned shoes so comfortable before. My eyes begin to water.

He approaches, settling next to me on the couch. I shy away, but he grips my wrists, turning me to face him. I stare at his broad chest.

"I'm not mad, Liv."

I am shocked, my eyes bouncing to meet his. They are

warm, gentle, but he is frowning as usual, and his brows are low over his eyes. I shift under his gaze, feeling scrutinized.

"Part of that was my fault. I didn't explain the repercussions your actions would have."

"They wanted to hurt me," I say, my voice quiet. He quirks his head to the side.

"Guards are instructed to shoot loose slaves on sight. You were seconds away from death."

Though I am shocked, I shake my head.

"They said I was pretty. They wanted to enjoy me..."

His face storms over.

"And you understand what that means?"

His voice goes up at the end in question. I chew my cheek. I have an idea, but I don't want to voice the wrong thing and embarrass myself. He sighs when I don't respond.

"You're not in trouble. Do not ever leave my side in public like that again. Next time, you won't be so lucky."

I nod, staring at his knees.

"Go shower and get cleaned up. I will make dinner and dry your new clothes. Dirty clothes go in the hamper. I will leave your clean clothes on the bed."

I nod, but he doesn't release me. I feel as though he wants something.

"Thank you." I whisper. I'm too tired to want to cause trouble right now, too mentally drained from everything to fight him on his demands. The warmth surrounding my feet also seems to make my chest burn, too, and I don't know why.

"You're welcome. Bed after dinner, understand?"

I glance at him, unsure.

"The...the floor?"

He cracks a smirk.

"Not tonight."

～

I am stuffed after dinner. I sit on the edge of the bed in my new pajamas—long, red flannel bottoms and a loose t-shirt. My braid is loose, my hair still damp, but it is fragrant, like roses. At least, that is what the picture on the bottle says. I picked it out because I thought it was pretty. Having my own things makes me feel different—special. I even have my own hairbrush. I spent an hour smoothing my hair out before I went to dinner.

Pax was quiet when we ate, drinking something out of a short glass. It smelled fiery, and he winced when he drank it. I was curious but let it be. He made us steak and potatoes. I ate everything on my plate.

He enters the room, going to his closet to grab his change of clothes before going to the bathroom. I watch the way he walks. Head up, shoulders back, chest forward. He is dominant—a king, and this is his kingdom. I wonder where that leaves me, but I know, with a sinking feeling, that I am still lower than a peasant. I am a slave. No amount of shoes or new clothes will change that fact. I need to work on my escape plan.

He reenters, wearing shorts and a tank top. His arms are massive, his skin lightly bronzed. He doesn't even have to flex for me to see the strain of his muscles.

"Lay down, Liv."

I obey, tucking my legs up under the cool blankets, resting my head on the soft pillow. It is so comfortable, I want to sleep right away. The lights flick off, and we lay in silence for a while. I stare at the ceiling, replaying the day's events.

I am startled as he shifts, bringing himself closer to me. I am not used to sleeping so near someone. My heart is thumping hard.

"Come here."

I want to resist, but I don't. I scoot closer to the middle. He sighs, reaching out and wrapping his arms around my waist.

"Face the other wall."

I don't want my back to him. I roll, facing his chest. He stills but doesn't say anything about my insubordination. Instead, he pulls me closer, until our bodies meet. He is warm, his hard-muscled chest surprisingly soft against my face.

"You always face me," he notes. I glance up. All I can see is the underside of his chin and his neck, his Adam's apple bobbing when he speaks.

"Why?" he asks.

"I don't know," I answer, honest. We fall into silence again. The skin of my legs and bum still burns from being shoved to the cobblestone earlier.

"Pax?"

"Hmm?"

He sounds tired.

"Never mind."

He squeezes me.

"Speak."

"What is PTSD?"

I am unsure if I remember the letters correctly. He stiffens, pulling me away, staring down at me. In the moonlight, his jaw is even sharper, his wide almond eyes bright as they catch some unknown source of light.

"Post-traumatic stress disorder."

"I...I have that?" I ask, confused. How does he know if I have that? Was he a doctor or something?

"You have all the trademark symptoms."

"Oh...am I...am I going to die?"

He cracks a half-smile.

"No, Livy. It's a mental thing."

He must see my confusion.

"You've endured traumatic instances. You heard fireworks. They sounded like gunfire, am I correct?"

I am shocked, nodding.

"And you felt like you were back in a bad moment, didn't you?"

How does he know this? Again, I nod.

"I...wasn't trying to run away. I'm sorry," I whisper, feeling guilty after everything he did for me today.

"You are forgiven. Next time, try not to run. I will be there."

I nod, biting my lip. His strong presence is reassuring. I've never felt that security before, even with my mom.

"How do you know what I was feeling?" I whisper, hoping I am not prying. I want him to keep talking to me. His face darkens. He pulls me closer, tucking me under his chin again. His next words rumble in his chest.

"I have it, too, Livy."

Pax

I allow her to sleep in, knowing her healing body still needs all the help it can get. I am stuck answering emails that were missed yesterday afternoon. The idiocy of some coworkers is enough to bring on a splitting headache. My fingers massage my temples. I need to attend a conference call later today, another thing I am dreading.

I hear the shuffle of her slippers across the wood floors, and I turn. She stands in the hall, rubbing her tired eyes, her hair a mess. It is hard to keep the smile from my face.

"Breakfast?" I ask.

She brightens, nodding. I hope she takes it easy on me today. I stand, motioning her to follow.

She stands next to me expectantly at the island. I nod to the cooler.

"Grab what you want and I will show you how to make it. Today, you will do dishes."

She frowns at the last part, jutting her hip out. Her fire is on display. Though I feel I don't have the energy to battle with her today, a thrill rolls through me. I don't know how to place the emotion. Part of me wants her to act out, part of me enjoys the power struggle. I don't understand why.

She retrieves strawberries, then goes into the pantry for oatmeal. She loves this for some reason. Her round eyes look up at me, green orbs wide and bright, her face open and expectant. Her bruises are just yellow now—still ghastly, but I can see the shape of her face better.

"Bowls are in that cupboard," I say, pointing up near the sink. She opens it but cannot reach the dishes. Her feet are on her tiptoes, stretched out, fingers wiggling. I chuckle, reaching around her and handing her a bowl. Erathians being tall, everything is built to accommodate us. I will need to buy her a stool.

She huffs, annoyed, bringing it back to the island. I tell her how much to pour, instructing how much water, how long to heat it for. By the end, she hasn't said much. I feel her frustration at not knowing how to do this. If I handed her a skinned squirrel, she could likely cook it with ease. She is a wild being, now forced to domesticate. I feel guilty.

She rinses the strawberries, holding them up by their stems, giving me a pleading look. I press my fingers to the knife drawer, unlocking it. Her keen eyes watch my every movement.

"I know exactly how many knives I have," I mention, so she knows I am watching. She grits her teeth. I hand her a knife.

"Slice here near the green part."

She fumbles a few times, the berry rolling away from her. I worry she will injure herself.

"Here," I say, moving behind her. My hand goes over hers, tightening her grip on the handle. I show her how to slice slow, gently, so the berries stay in place. Her bony shoulders brush against my stomach. I lean in, enjoying the way she feels. Her hair is wavy, fragrant, shiny. I want to touch it, to feel it for myself. I've only ever felt an Erathian woman's hair.

"How old are you?" she quips. I've released her hand, letting her chop the strawberries on her own. Her voice is light, simply curious. I pray her good mood lasts long enough for me to get through my workday.

"Twenty-eight human years."

Her head bobs. She's cut up almost half the box of fruit, but I let her keep practicing. She tilts her head back, looking at me upside down, smiling. My hand wavers near her hip, my other hand on the counter, caging her in. She waggles the knife.

"Can I keep this for practice?"

I snort.

"Very funny."

She shrugs against me.

"Can't blame me for trying."

"No, I can't."

"So," she says, turning back to her work, jutting her hip out again. She is being sassy today.

"When I escape, what's the best way out of town? I really liked that moor we were on."

I can't help my chuckle now.

"If you escape and live, I will set you free there myself."

"Challenge accepted."

She isn't watching her motions and nearly slices her finger.

"Careful," I growl. She looks back again, rolling her eyes. I grit my teeth, my hand clamping down on her hip.

"No, Livy."

She narrows her eyes, then rolls them again and adds a huff just to piss me off further.

"Can you wait to be a brat until later, please?"

"Since you asked nicely...no."

I bite my cheek as my anger begins to simmer. As a child, the only thing that worked on me was corporal punishment. My father never beat me out of anger, though. He'd only reprimand me when he'd had time to cool off. And it worked.

Having my hide tanned on occasion taught me more than words ever would.

I smirk, pinching the back of her arm.

"Ow!" she hisses, jumping and glaring at me. The knife clatters to the countertop.

"Knock off that attitude, Liv."

She is stewing, her jaw clenching.

"I don't want to."

"Then there will be consequences. Your choice."

"What? Are you going to beat me?" she grumbles. She isn't going to forgive me easily for that. I still hear the pain and fear in her voice.

"No. I will never do that again."

"But you want to hurt me."

"In some capacity, yes. Because I think it is the only thing you will respond to."

Her chest heaves for a minute. I grip her hips, turning her to face me. She refuses to meet my eye, but I can see tears glimmering, ready to fall.

"I do not wish to make you cry, Liv. Weren't you ever paddled as a child?"

She sniffs and shocks me by letting out a little laugh. She looks up at me.

"Yeah. My dad had to do it all the time."

"And did it work as a deterrent?"

She shrugs. I doubt she remembers her past in great detail.

"Did he ever harm you to the point you hated him?"

She seems to think about it, then shakes her head.

"It is no different, then. I do not wish to scare you, hurt you so bad you need time to recover. I just think sometimes that will need to be my way to get through to you."

She crosses her arms, thinking my words through with careful consideration.

"It needs to be fair."

"How so?"

"You can't make up rules as you go."

She is willing to compromise. My chest flutters. It is working.

"I will finalize rules by this evening, and we can put them into practice starting tomorrow. Do we have a deal?"

She twists her mouth in thought.

"Sooo, I can do what I want today?"

"Don't push it."

"Fine. Deal. But I want a say in the rules."

I consider this. If it makes her have a sense of control—and therefore a sense of freedom—then I am willing to do it.

"Alright."

"And I have a say in how you punish me."

I sigh, drumming my fingers on the cool counter, eyeing her.

"Yes, that is fair."

I do not wish to cross certain boundaries, to undo the work we've been doing to get her past her torture in the Facility. The thought reminds me of the important conference call. I check my watch.

"You will need to eat in the bedroom. I have a call soon. I will get you when I am done, okay?"

She nods, her big eyes wide and earnest. She is trusting me because I am trusting her. The notion is interesting to me.

"Good girl," I say, straightening. "Clear this and take your food."

She nods, her face reddening out of the blue. I frown. God, she already wants to get into trouble?

"Take the knife out of your waistband, Liv."

She glares at me. I reach around, plucking it from her back, wagging it in her face.

"You're not off the hook for this."

There is a devious glint in her eye as she smirks. That thrill runs through me again. Am I excited to administer my control? Part of me is, I think.

"Room," I say pointing. She grabs her bowl, that look still in her eyes. I have to hide my smile.

"Yes, *sir*."

"I want this looked into with very careful consideration," I say into the phone.

"Of course, sir. Let me jot down some notes so I can ask them—"

"No, it needs to be undercover."

"Why, son?" my father asks. His friend—the man in charge of all slave facilities—is quiet on the other end. What I am requesting is unheard of.

"I want it discreet. Their practices have gotten out of hand, as I saw for myself recently. They implement the use of torture."

It is quiet on the other end for a moment.

"Unfortunately, I have been hearing rumors of such instances from masters upon retrieving their slaves. I thought it was a fluke, but now there is substance to it. I will launch a full-scale investigation across five major Facilities in Sardone."

I nod to my empty desk, Liv's limp body flashing in my mind the night I took her from there.

"I want the men and women held accountable to the fullest extent for their actions. They have been given too much leniency, and this is what happens."

My voice is a growl. My father remains quiet, allowing me to take control. This is, after all, my issue to remedy. I hear papers shuffling.

"I will send some of my men in tonight, unannounced. I will

forward you a full report once I have rectified this issue. Again, I apologize, Mr. Harper."

I am not pacified, but at least it's something.

"Thank you. I look forward to hearing your results," I say. We exchange parting words, and he is off the line. My father sighs. I can picture him rubbing his forehead.

"So, anything you wish to tell me, Pax?"

I chuckle, leaning back, relaxed. My fingers scratch at my jaw, glancing out the window. The day has turned from sunshine to possible rain, but I don't mind.

"I found a wild human on our last raid. I decided it was time for some help around my place," I shrug to no one.

"Your one-bedroom apartment?" he says, his voice chiding. He knows there is more.

"She would have died on her own out there, and she would have been killed here for the way she talks and acts."

"Sounds like you've done her a justice, then."

"I...I left her there, dad. Nine days, they had all sorts of excuses as to why I couldn't come to get her, so I finally just went in myself."

He chuckles. My headstrong ways come from him.

"Sounds about right, son."

I shake my head.

"She was on the X. She could barely move..."

He sighs, taking his time before speaking.

"No one—human or not—deserves torture. You did the right thing, Pax. How is she now?"

I lean back, crossing my arms.

"Better. Still wild. I didn't realize humans were so..." I fumble for the right word.

"Confusing? Intelligent? Irritating?" he says with a laugh. I join him, nodding.

"Exactly. She loves to push my buttons and try to reason with me."

"Sounds like a handful. Your mother just took in an eleven-year-old girl. Smart little thing. They seem more like companions than anything."

Companions. Is that was Liv is to me? My parents have always been kind, understanding, and patient people. Living on a farm in the country, they've cycled through their share of slaves. Growing up, I don't remember many interactions with them. No slave was ever chained, and none ever tried to escape.

"Well, any tips would be greatly appreciated."

Again, he laughs.

"They are more like us than we think. Be a leader worth following, and she will follow you anywhere."

I know his words are deep, and they cut through me to some degree.

"Thanks, dad."

"Anytime. Come visit when you're able."

I snort. With work, that is near impossible.

"I will try. Tell mom hello."

We say our goodbyes, and I am left staring at my bookshelf, musing. *Be a leader worth following.* I like to think of myself as a decent enough person, even with all the damage I have caused in my line of work. I squint at the books, a million different plans of action forming in my mind. I can make this relationship work. I know there will be battles, but I know if I can earn her trust, things will smooth out. She wants freedom, and I can give her that in the confines of my home. I just need to make her see it that way.

I clear my throat, standing to go retrieve her. I peek my head into my room. She's sitting in the window seat, her face pressed to the glass as she watches people mill about below. She doesn't even know I am here.

"Liv?"

She jumps with a yelp and whirls, clutching at her heart. I chuckle.

"Sorry. You can come out now."

There's that devious glint again. She stands and makes her way near me.

"But first, there's a matter we need to settle."

She quirks her head to the side, crossing her arms. She isn't being insolent, just curious. It is easy for me to tell the difference now.

"Bowl to the sink, then wait for me on the couch."

"Yes, *sir*."

My teeth grit and I walk out to my desk. I hear her follow, listen as she places the bowl in the sink. She's soon back and seated on the couch. I would write down the rules, but she cannot read them. I seat myself before her on the coffee table, and she leans away, avoiding my gaze. She is nervous.

"Let's talk day to day, what I expect."

Her eyes that remind me of the lush grasses on that moor flash to me. She sits on her hands and nods.

"You'll clean up after yourself, whether that be dishes, laundry, any messes you make. You will make the bed every morning, do your laundry when need be, and make all your meals. With me so far?"

"I don't...know how..." she flushes, embarrassed. I nod.

"I understand that. I will take my time and teach you, and once you have the hang of something, you will be expected to do it."

She chews her cheek.

"This isn't fair."

I am stunned, and a little pissed. I straighten. I haven't even gone through everything yet.

"What isn't fair?"

"You're making me work for you. Isn't work done supposed to be paid? I had to lug around a twenty-pound bag for two weeks just to buy a freaking EpiPen!" she growls, throwing her hands up. I calm down, understanding what she sees as an injustice—what she sees as slavery.

"I buy the food, your clothes, your necessities, pay for the electricity and rent and water. This is your exchange."

Her face changes: she sees my point of view, and she isn't upset. I feel relief.

"Fine," she mumbles.

"Good. Now, privileges. I will show you how to work the TV, will buy you games or other things to entertain you while I am at work. I expect you will be rushing through your chores each day," I say. She gives her little smile. I rub my palms together.

"In exchange for that, each evening we will work on education."

She perks up but soon becomes closed off. Always prideful and stubborn. She doesn't want me to think her stupid. If only she knew I don't think that at all.

"I want to teach you to read and write. There may come a time where I need you to know those skills, to pay bills for me and whatnot. You'll also have access to lectures on any topic of your choosing. You must watch those before any fun things."

"Ok," she mutters, thinking. I can see her excitement building.

"Now, rules. No foul language—"

"Bloody hell," she says, rolling her eyes. I glare at her. She smirks, smug. I continue with the knowledge I will reprimand her soon.

"No rolling eyes, crossing arms, or any disrespectful displays. No stealing cutlery—"

"What's cutlery?" she interrupts. I pinch the bridge of my nose.

"No interrupting me when I speak, Liv."

"Sorry," she mumbles.

"Cutlery is knives, or any utensil used to cut."

"Oh."

"No escape attempts. If you somehow get past me, and the guards find you, it will be out of my hands, Liv. Understand?"

She is upset, and the wheels in her mind are turning.

"I've ordered a tether, it attaches from your wrist to me. You only have to wear it in public."

Her eyes flash to mine in fury. My muscles tense.

"No."

"Yes."

"That is demeaning. I am not your slave," she hisses.

"It's for your safety. We live in a decent part of town, but having human women stolen is not uncommon, alright?"

Her brows inch together.

"Someone would steal me from you?"

I nod.

"It can happen, Livy, and I can promise you that wherever they take you it will not be good."

She shrinks.

"Fine."

I sigh.

"Last, punishments. If you break any of the rules, I will administer one of three punishments of varying degrees. Foul language and the like will warrant pinching, in the moment. Sound fair?"

She is gritting her teeth.

"Sure."

"If you don't finish chores before doing other activities, I will take away privileges, such as TV, games, you get the picture."

She nods.

"Fair."

"If you attempt to steal knives, escape, become physically aggressive, or any number of worse things, I will paddle you."

Her eyes widen, jaw slackening.

"Fair?" I quirk my brow.

"We are forgetting this morning, right?" she asks.

"I told you I wouldn't."

She thumps back into the couch.

"I intend to correct, not to hurt, right?"

Sour, she nods, not meeting my eyes.

"What about if you do something bad?"

Her words pull me up short.

"Like what?"

"Like...lie. Or..." she trails off. Her eyes are watering. She stares at her knees. I understand her train of thought. I need to give her some sense of control.

"What are your rules for me, Livy?"

She is surprised, bringing her face to mine. She hardens her look, but there is still a visible part of her that is a frightened child, lost and alone.

"No lying."

I nod, wondering why this is her number one rule.

"Alright. I will always be honest with you."

"No touching me while I am asleep."

I should have seen that one coming. I nod. For some reason, it bothers her, and that is the last thing I want to do.

"You can't punish me after just making up a new rule."

"Fair enough."

She sits, thinking for a few moments.

"That all?"

She nods.

"For now."

I chuckle.

"Alright, let's get on with it. Five paddles sound fair for stealing the knife?"

Her face blanches.

6

Olivia

"I won't do it again," I say, trying to reason with him. His face is normally so stoic. Here, and now, it is open, earnest, his eyes bright.

"I know. Come here."

I stay rooted.

"Liv," he growls in warning.

"You won't hurt me?" my lips whisper. I am scared. I know the strength he is capable of. He shakes his head, serious.

"Not like that, Liv."

I nod. Best to just get it over with so I can go back to my window and look outside at the people walking down the street. I stand on shaking legs. He is still perched on the coffee table. He brings his knees further apart, looking up at me. We are almost the same height, even if he is sitting. My heart is thundering in my ears.

He grabs my hips, turning me to the side, before one hand snakes up to my lower back, bending me over. I understand what he wants. I lay myself across his knees.

I try to control my shaking, but it is impossible. One of his big hands is on my shoulder blades, the other gripping my hip. I stare at the ornate rug, my mouth dry with nerves.

He seems to want to get it over with as quickly as I do. His hand yanks the band of my pajama pants down. I am thankful I have underwear now, but I am still uncomfortable, knowing he is seeing so much of me. I wonder what these aliens think about us humans, physically speaking.

He rests that hand back on my hip before he slides it down to my butt. I tense as he pulls away, feeling the rush of air. The smack makes me jump, and though it stings, it is nothing more than that. Relief floods me, sending my heart beating into a wild frenzy. I jump again, letting out an involuntary whimper. It still does not hurt. I am simply scared, being this vulnerable.

The hand he rests between my shoulder blades moves up under my hair until he is cupping the back of my neck. *Smack.* He says nothing. I cannot see his face, nor do I want to. I am mortified. His calloused thumb rubs up and down the side of my neck. Is he soothing me?

Smack.

That one makes me whimper. My backside is stinging and sore. Only one more. I tense for it, my toes curling. *Smack.*

It is over. I am breathing hard, my heart still pounding. He is gentle, pulling the band of my pants back up. Without a word, he sits me up, standing and grabbing my hips. He replants himself on the couch, pulling me onto his lap. I am straddling his hips. He doesn't allow me to see his eyes, using his palm to press my face into the crook of his neck. I don't realize how badly I am shaking.

His other hand snakes down, his palm rubbing circles and soothing the area he paddled me. It is all strangely comforting. As though he feels guilty for doing it. Either way, I am questioning ever stealing a damn knife again.

He is warm, holding me tight to him. I am comfortable, but

the fading adrenaline coursing through my body has left me weak and trembling. His hand continues to soothe me, the same palm that smacked me, so tender as he does so.

"Calm down, Livy," his voice rumbles in chest broad chest. I can't move. I don't want to move. This entire situation is so strange to me—so new. There are feelings, emotions I have never felt before. I want his comfort, want his gentleness, but I want to provoke him as well. How can I want both?

It is too much swirling in my chest. I let out a whimper against his neck.

"I've got you," he hushes, pulling the blanket over us. He rubs his palm up and down my back, grips my butt to adjust me on his lap, pulling me even closer to him. How is it possible that after all that, I want to be near him in such a way? I feel safe here, in his arms.

His cheek is pressed to my forehead.

"I do not enjoy that."

His voice is low. I know he isn't lying. I can tell by how he is holding me now.

"I don't, either," I mumble against his neck. He surprises me by chuckling, the sound bouncing us both.

"No more stealing knives."

I have stopped shaking. I am exhausted.

"We will see about that," I mutter.

My body tenses before my mind can comprehend what is happening. My eyes shoot open. Another reverberating bang echoes through the space before rumbling in the distance. I whimper, pinching my eyes shut, shaking my head.

Strong arms hold me. I am warm, cocooned in a nest of blankets and a hard-muscled body that is three times my size. I curl into him, his scent of cedar wood pulling me back from the brink of drowning in horrid memories.

"Just thunder, Liv. There's a pretty nasty storm rolling through."

His voice is now familiar to me. I like the way it rumbles through his chest against me. For some reason, it is soothing. I want to hate him. My instinct is to want to get away. I just know it will be more difficult now. He's thought of everything, from the locks on the doors and windows and drawers to his rules. Escape will not be easy anymore. My best chance to be free was during our trek here, and I squandered it.

I pull away to look at him, feeling different after the punishment I received. It's impossible to place the emotions. He loosens his arms, allowing me to sit up on his lap. I like the way he holds me facing him, like he knows my preferences and never once questions them.

"I think we both took a nap today," he comments. There's a small smile on his lips, but his eyes are still tight. He checks his watch, then glances out the window. Rain batters the panes and floods down the glass. It is beautiful.

"I need to go to the store once this storm lets up, and Jeven wanted me to go to the gym with him after dinner. Will you be comfortable by yourself for some time tonight?"

I fiddle with my hands. They rest on his stomach. Being this close to him simply feels normal now. I've never been this close to anyone besides my mother. I don't realize how it makes my chest feel full. I have missed such comforts.

"What's a gym?"

He chuckles, his hands on my hips, holding me steady. Lightning flashes, illuminating his dark eyes.

"A place where you work out. Lift weights, run, play sports."

I am utterly confused, but also intrigued.

"May I..." I cut myself off from asking, my shoulders slumping. For a moment, I felt his equal. I am not, though.

"Would you like to come run those errands with me, Liv?"

I can't hide my excitement.

"Yes, please."

He fully smiles now, reaching up, tucking my wild hair behind my ear.

"You're so much sweeter after you wake up."

His words and the way he is looking at me makes me want to always be sweet to him. He is actually happy right now. I feel utter guilt for enjoying this new turn in my life. I should want freedom, I should hate him and his kind and what they have done to me and my family. But right now, I can't. I push the bitterness away. I need to take this one day at a time.

He checks his watch before he says *weather*. He narrows his eyes at the face.

"Rain should let up in an hour. Go get ready. I'll finish my work and we can go to the store. I'm craving a cappuccino."

"What's that?" I don't even attempt repeating the strange word. Again, he chuckles.

"It's a coffee drink."

I cross my arms, ready to argue now. He sees it, quirking his brow in warning. I am not being defiant, though. At least, not yet.

"Humans can have coffee."

"And?"

I uncross my arms. I want to ask him to try this new thing, but I am too nervous to do so. I don't want him to say no. I can already feel how that will crush me. He waits, patient, but eventually his hands fall back to my hips and he gives a squeeze.

"If you shower and get ready and can rinse your dishes from earlier, you can order a coffee."

I beam, jumping to be free of him so I can complete my tasks. He doesn't release me so easily.

"Remember the rules for public, Livy."

I nod vigorously. Even being tied to him is no big deal at the moment. I don't care, as long as I get to map out this part of town and memorize it for when I one day escape.

I stand by the door, bouncing in my new rain boots, zipping up my thick rain jacket. I wanted the black one at the store, but the kind lady told me I needed some color. It is a bright, luscious red. She told me it complimented my hair.

My hair is still damp, but it is French braided down my back. Pax is on the couch, pulling on his boots. He is on the phone with his friend.

"Yeah, I'll be there around six-thirty. Yeah...bring Deidre. Might be good for her. Okay, see you then."

He hangs up, tucking his square phone into his back pocket as he stands. He pats his other pockets, coming near, distracted as he shrugs on his sturdy jacket. He's just adjusting it when his eyes find mine. They widen for a moment. Something flashes in his gaze, something intense. I do not know the look, so I shrink, taking a step back. Have I done something wrong?

"Come here."

I take a step forward, keeping my eyes averted. What did I do wrong now?

"Look at me."

I obey. I really don't want to screw up my chance at getting a moment to see new things. His eyes are on my face, and they linger until it becomes uncomfortable. I feel myself heat up under his gaze.

"Did I mess up something?" I ask, voice small. I put on my jeans first, like my mother used to do. They are snug, hugging my body, but this way they slide easily into my boots. My jacket reaches my upper thighs, keeping me warm and hopefully dry, and I tied the knot as best I could. I do not see how I could have screwed this up.

"No...no, you did very well, Liv."

His voice sounds strange.

"Here," he holds out his palm. I see the flash of something silvery. I place my left hand in his, palm up. The chain is thin, so thin it seems fragile. He attaches it from my wrist to one of his belt loops. The line is longer than I assumed it would be.

"Don't get any ideas. The only way to get this off is with my fingerprints or to melt it at thousands of degrees."

I see a button near his belt loop. It must be where his fingerprint goes to release me. I just nod before peeking back up at him. I am itching to go.

He frowns at me, zipping up his jacket.

"Stay to my side or in front of me, please."

"Okaaayyy," I whine.

"Liv," he warns, his tone low. I flash him a cheeky smile, bouncing in my boots.

"Can we go, please?"

He shakes his head with a snort, pressing his palm to the scanner near his door. Into the city we go. I am buzzing with excitement.

Pax

It is just drizzling now as we round the corner to my favorite local coffee shop. The smell of fresh rain tickles my nose. I chose this part of town to live in because everything is within walking distance from my apartment, and there are many young, single Erathians nearby. The shop is on the upcoming corner, and through the dreary day, the lights inside are like a beacon.

Liv's eyes are wide, looking at everything and everyone. There are a few slaves with their masters, but she doesn't stop as she did last time. I open the door for her, allowing her in before me. She pulls her hood down, giving me a clear view of her face once more. With her hair done and pulled back, I can see her more clearly. She has pale skin, still yellowing in its healing process. Her face is an oval shape, but she has a widow's peak on her forehead.

I watch the way her eyes widen. She is overwhelmed. Seeing her discover new things is perhaps my favorite thing about her; she is so genuine and interested. She is biting her lip, staring at the pastries behind the bulbous glass. An Erathian woman with dark hair smiles at me from behind the counter, smoothing down her apron. She is attractive, holding herself well.

I realize I have forgotten to feed Livy. My fingers brush her lower back, nudging her forward.

"Pick out some food, too."

Her bright green eyes flash to mine in surprise.

"Really?" she breathes. I smirk, nodding down to her. She is at the glass, ogling over everything while I wait at the register.

"My name is Tarex, how may I help you today?" the young woman says, beaming at me with a row of perfect teeth.

"A cappuccino, wet, please, and whatever she wants," I say, nodding down to Liv as I fish for my wallet. Tarex's eyes fall to Liv, and she beams. Liv is still looking over each pastry with such careful consideration, I can't seem to look away from her. The woman's voice pulls me back.

"Oh, how sweet! What a cute little slave. I love how you've dressed her!"

Liv's eyes bounce up at the words. I tense, waiting for her to mouth off, but I can see her chew her cheek instead. Something like pain flits in her forest green eyes.

"What looks good, Livy?" I ask to distract her. She ducks her head, ashamed now. Slow, she points to a chocolate croissant.

"One of those, please," I tell the lady. She is still smiling at me, not seeing anything amiss.

"What to drink?" I ask quietly to Liv. I can see the rise and fall of her chest, can see she is battling tears. I grit my teeth. She doesn't want to speak. Doesn't want to cry in public.

"Same thing as me?" I press. She just nods, staring at her feet.

I relay the message to the woman, ensuring there are no peanuts in sight, and pay, moving to the side with her pastry in hand while we await drinks. The receipt has her phone number scribbled on it. I moved here specifically to find peace, to find someone to share my life with, but all I have managed are one night stands and a few flings. I save the phone number in my wallet, but at the moment my stomach feels sour.

Our drinks are done. I hand Liv hers, walking her to the corner of the cafe. We sit at a metal table, and I pass her the croissant. Her tears are gone, but she is still withdrawn. My cup warms my hands.

"Careful when you drink. It's really hot."

She bobs her head, eyeing the crinkly bag.

"Eat," I say, nodding to it. It seems even the words from the woman haven't deterred her appetite. She rips off a flaky hunk of the croissant as chocolate oozes over the buttery dough. Her eyes are wide, her face brightening. She shoves the pastry in her mouth, bouncing in her seat.

"Manners, Livy."

She grins.

"Fanks Pax."

I shake my head at her habit of speaking with her mouth full to annoy me, sipping at my coffee. My eyes wander as she eats, her little boots swinging. She is happy once more. Her dainty outstretched hand surprises me. In her fingers is a piece of the croissant.

"For me?"

She nods, cheeks turning a slight shade of pink. Her gesture warms me. She is being kind—caring about my needs in some small way. I feel hope that this will all work out, that I will be a good leader and she will be a good follower.

I take the morsel, ensuring to thank her as I eat it. She tries her drink. She seems stumped, unsure of whether or not she likes the flavor. I wonder how badly caffeine will affect her. This may be a decision I come to regret.

We leave, carrying our drinks out into the misty afternoon. The grocery market is a few blocks north, and we will pass by many shops. I already know I will have to go slow to allow Liv a chance to see everything.

"What's that?" she asks, pointing to our left.

"Pet store," I grunt. She stops, and I feel the tug of her chain. She has pressed her face to the glass in wonderment.

"Animals?" she breathes, fogging the window. Has she never seen a pet store?

"Like fish and dogs and cats," I explain, coming to stand beside her. She points a thin finger to a glass cage.

"What is that? It's so tiny!" she says, grinning from ear to ear.

"I think it's a hamster. Like a small, fuzzy rodent."

Her round eyes bounce up to me. She is beyond excited.

"I've never seen one before!"

Perhaps caffeine was a bad idea.

I nudge her arm, gentle.

"We can come look another day as a reward for good behavior. Sound like a deal?"

She twists her mouth down but nods. It seems every time she is subtly reminded of her situation, she clams up. I will have to speak with her about that, but not anytime soon. Our trust needs more building.

We enter the store, and I show her which basket to grab. She complains, wanting to push the cart instead.

"We don't need a cart, though," I explain for the fifth time. Her argumentative ways are creeping back to the surface.

"Olivia," I growl as she glares at me, crossing her arms. I reach over, pinching where her shoulder meets her neck, the only bit of exposed skin she has.

"Ouch," she hisses. Her glare deepens.

"Do we need to revisit some other punishments when we get home?"

Her arms fall to her sides, her face paling. Good. It is working. She is quiet the rest of the trip, and I feel guilty. I know she is excited when she begins to pull toward something, but she stops herself and drops her head.

Paddling her had the desired outcome in most ways. It was strange for me, though. I hadn't thought I would feel awkward when doing it. Seeing her surrender herself only proved to me one thing; she is scared of me, knows I will always win a physical battle. And afterwards, the way she shook—I couldn't bear to look her in the eye. I was shocked when she let me hold her. I hadn't intended to do that, but I simply couldn't let her go. She already thinks me and my race are monsters. I don't want to make it worse.

The thrill it sent through me is perhaps the most troubling part, though. The power I held was different; she is weak, a female. I enjoy my line of work because I am able to exercise my power daily, but against my own kind, against the same gender. With her...it made something snap within me.

I stare at her as her fingers brush over cans of beans and corn. Her eyes are still so wide, her face so open and curious. I am stunned to find her attractive; most Erathian men think human women are disgusting. I used to count myself as one of them.

I know there are men of my race that buy slaves for sexual pleasure alone. I never understood that either and found it rather taboo, even if my society deems it very acceptable.

Finding beauty in Liv is surprising to me, but it is not something I will act on. We are two substances that cannot mix in such a way, like oil and water.

She presses her fingers to a can, underlining a word.

"Bean!" she quips, turning her dazzling smile to me. My heart gives an irregular thump. Her smile falters. She looks embarrassed. My eyes dart to the can, surprised to find she is correct.

"God job, Livy. You remember that?"

Her smile returns, smaller this time as she nods. I want to reward her, even if we had some struggles. I walk her to the candy aisle. Sweets seem to be her favorite, but chocolate tops them.

"Pick out one candy."

"Really?" she breathes, overwhelmed. I nod. It takes her five full minutes and lots of questions about labels. She lets me know she recognizes the word *peanut*, but there are other words that mean the same, and she needs my help with those. I inspect the chocolate bar she has chosen, satisfied that it is free of this thing that can kill her.

I have an Epipen in my jacket just in case.

We check out, and she is fascinated by the coins I use. I promise to teach her to count change during some of our lessons. I have ordered her children's books and art supplies, in the hopes I can keep her interest during our studies.

Finally home, I unlock her. She does what I have instructed by hanging up her jacket and placing her boots on the mat. She jets off, though, her candy bar in tow. I can hear the bathroom door slam.

"Livy!" I yell, tossing the grocery bags to the island counter. Her job was to put them away. I stomp to the bathroom, not feeling kind enough to knock. She's snuck off to eat her damn chocolate.

I wrench open the door in quiet fury, but it soon turns to

utter embarrassment. She squeaks, perched on the toilet, jeans around her ankles as she fumbles to cover herself. Fuck.

I back out, shutting the door and leaning against it. Poor thing just had to pee.

"I'm sorry, Liv."

I hear the toilet flush and the water run, but she doesn't emerge. I wait, then knock. Again, nothing. I open the door to peer inside. She is sitting on the floor against the tub, arms around her legs, her face in her knees. I walk in, sitting across from her. It is difficult considering my size, but I manage.

"I didn't mean to scare you," I say. She ignores me. My hand reaches out, touching her knee. She jerks away, her livid eyes flashing to mine. I hold my palms up in surrender. She tears her eyes from mine, but I can see her tears. I think quickly to reign her in.

"What's my punishment?"

She peeks at me, brows furrowing.

"I made a list for you, you can make a list for me," I say with a shrug. She sits up straighter. Soon, a coy smile is playing at her lips.

"You have to sleep on the floor."

I chuckle.

"Don't push it, Liv."

She taps her chin. This is fun for her, and I am relieved.

"I get coffee with breakfast tomorrow."

"That is not a punishment, silly."

She turns a light shade of red.

"I don't want to paddle you."

I let out a laugh.

"No, I doubt I would take that very well, huh?"

She nods, smiling. After a moment, she speaks, her voice soft.

"I...I can't punish you..."

Her brows are furrowed. Something about her words strike

me, hard. How can I so easily do the very thing she cannot bring herself to do? And why did it make such potent feelings enter my veins? This is wrong. She is the human, the submissive, the slave. I am her master. I should not feel strange or guilty about this at all. Yet I do.

"I will make sure to knock next time, okay? And yes, you can have one cup of coffee with breakfast."

She smiles.

"Come help me with dinner. You will accompany me to the gym this evening, sound good?"

She nods, excited. I stand, but she darts around me and out the door. I pop my head out, peering down the hall and into my room. She is stowing her candy bar in her nightstand, next to her Epipens. For some reason, this makes me smile.

She is innocence, and I am sin.

7

Olivia

Dinner is chicken noodle soup and biscuits. Pax doesn't teach me how to cook, per se, but he insists I watch to learn. He's easy to watch while I am perched on the barstool at the island counter. I haven't watched anyone cook a meal this fancy since I was in the Settlement. Even then, it was only what the scavengers and hunters could get their hands on. Since I had no family, I was always last to eat. I grew used to scraps.

My mouth is watering as he shreds the rotisserie chicken. He is wearing his usual jeans and plain t-shirt, this one grey, the sleeves short and showing off his muscles as he moves about the kitchen with precision. I want to ask him about his race, why they are so similar to humans, but I feel a traitor to my own race.

His eyes are on the cutting board as he moves to dicing carrots.

"What is it, Livy?" he asks, not even glancing at me. I jump, straightening, fiddling with my hands under the counter. He peeks at me from under his brow.

"N-nothing," I say, too innocent as I shake my head. He snorts, returning to his work.

"Just ask."

"No," I mutter.

"Why? Are you embarrassed?" he says as he eyes me again. I shrug.

"You don't need to be embarrassed in front of me," his voice is gruff.

"Why do you look so human?" I ask, my voice low and wavering. His dark eyes flash to mine. He sets down the knife. I feel nervous, but he eventually smirks.

"Our planet was very much similar to Earth. It is why we chose it to come to."

"And you were born there?" I whisper. It is a notion I cannot even begin to fathom. He shakes his head, wiping his hands on a dish towel before throwing it over his shoulder. He scoops the carrots and celery into his big hands, dumping them in the pot to sauté with the onions and garlic. He has been teaching me cooking words as he goes.

"Yes. We...slept, the entire way here, our bodies frozen in time."

His eyes meet mine, but his back is half turned to me. I blink, stunned. He seems ashamed, somehow, to share this.

"And your planet—"

"Sargas. It died. Well, our sun did."

"Did everyone make it?"

I am leaning forward, not realizing how intense this story is. He frowns before he shakes his head.

"No. My grandparents on my mother's side gave their tickets to us, so we would live. It was...horrific, or so I have heard. I was too young to remember."

There is a sadness about him, in the corners of his eyes, in the way he speaks of his family. I am beginning to think we may not be so different, at least, not us two as individuals. He turns back to the pot, stirring the vegetables. The aroma is making my stomach grumble.

"You...you all lived in peace, for a while..." I trail off. He nods, but doesn't turn to me.

"What changed?"

I ask, because I was too young to notice, to remember, same as him. I have only heard other people's stories. I want to hear his side, how he defends mass genocide and slavery. He sighs, the sound heavy.

"On Sargas, slavery was very normal. We came to Earth, saw for ourselves the same mistakes we made that aided in destroying our planet before our sun died, and decided to help remedy it. That caused many problems. Wars erupted...and you know the rest," he mumbles the last part, pouring chicken stock into the pot.

I hug my stomach. Of course, I do not agree with how his race has acted, but I will not voice that right now. He glances at me, frowning.

"What do you remember?"

I bite my lip, thinking back. I barely remember my father. He was in the military, always gone fighting the wars these aliens started. I remember my mother and grandmother. Remember fleeing our home when it was attacked. I was lucky, being uprooted at such a young age. I do not miss what I cannot fathom. My mother's death, though, will always haunt me.

"Liv?"

I realize tears have welled in my eyes. He has paused, big spoon in hand, his brows together in concern. Why does he always seem to care about my feelings when he is the one who enslaved me? I feel my temper rise and lock my jaw. I still want a chance to go with him to the gym after dinner, so I keep my words behind my teeth.

I shake my head.

"I don't want to talk about it."

He stares, long.

"I hope you will, someday. I would like to know who you are."

I don't feel like sharing my family with him, for they are mine—the last thing I own are my memories. No one can steal those from me. Not even Pax.

We stay silent as he cooks, the tension suddenly thick. He turns on the news for background noise, but I drown it out. He slides a bowl in front of me, a warm biscuit on a small plate next to it. The meal looks heavenly, especially after such a cold, dreary day.

"Eat up, then go change. We will leave at six-fifteen."

I grip my spoon, glancing at him. He's not eating?

"Aren't you hungry?"

"I'll eat after I workout."

I nod, diving into the luscious meal with abandon. Flavors explode across my tongue, from the onion to the roasted chicken, to the salty broth, to the soft, floury noodles. I am in heaven.

"Manners," he grunts, taking dishes to the sink.

"Thank you, *master*."

He drops his head, clenching the counter. All I can see are the strain of his back and neck muscles. I smile to myself. It's fun to pester him.

"Olivia," he growls.

"Hmm?" I quip innocently. He turns, leaning his hip against the counter and crossing his arms.

"You can stay home."

"No!" I jump, berating myself for that jab. He glares.

"Be nice. That is your last warning." His eyes are serious. I nod, watching him work while I eat.

I am changed, wearing pants that are called *leggings*, with an oversized sweater. He tells me to be warm and comfortable, and so this is the best option. My new tennis shoes fit perfectly, feet bouncing by the door as I wait for him.

He emerges from the bedroom, keys and phone in hand. He is wearing light grey athletic shorts and a black tank top, show-casing the muscles that could end my life in a matter of seconds if he so wished. I grit my teeth against the phantom of pain that tingles through my jaw and ribs. He has hurt me, and though he is more restrained now, can I trust he will keep his word?

Tucking his things into his pockets, he pulls on a hoodie. It looks warm and cozy.

"Come," he says, adjusting his clothing so it sits just right. I obey, holding out my wrist. He clasps the thin metal but has nowhere to attach it to himself. This could turn in my favor. His eyes flash to mine.

"Stay by my side at all times. Do not speak to anyone, slave or Erathian, unless it is Jeven or his slave, Deidre."

I chew my lip, but nod. My hair is loose, and it tumbles all around me in soft waves. I haven't had hair this clean in years. I enjoy the way it feels, brushing against my face.

"If anyone approaches you, touches you, you get my atten-tion, and I will take care of it. Understand?" His eyes are dark, the look in them new, but not unfamiliar. I remember seeing it when he hauled off and broke Brutus' jaw. I swallow hard. Is he possessive? Protective? I cannot decipher. I have never been around someone who values my safety other than my own family.

He flicks off the light, pressing his palm to the door scanner, and we make our way out into the evening. I am stunned, paused before a bulky, forest green vehicle. I don't really remember cars—at least, not ones that could function. And this is an Erathian car, meaning the technology is far superior.

I hear his chuckle as he leans around me and opens the door.

"Get in."

I have to pull myself up, but I slide across the black leather and into the middle. There are so many lights and screens that I am overwhelmed. He slides in beside me, our legs touching.

"Sit in the middle, Liv."

I scoot further, still distracted. He slams the door, pressing his hand to what I assume would be the ignition, and everything fully lights up as the vehicle turns on with a rumble. I feel taller than ever as he shifts into drive and we glide smoothly out of the parking lot. I can feel his eyes on me as I scoot to the opposite window, pressing my face to the glass as the changing scenery whisks by me.

"When was the last time you were in a city?"

I shrug, not glancing at him.

"I don't remember."

We are quiet for the rest of the ride. He pulls up to a large concrete building. The lot isn't very full, and the Erathians that emerge from the doors are all massive. I shrink back in my seat, feeling nervous. He helps me out, and I keep my eyes down on the wet pavement as I walk beside him. We are blasted with warm air as we enter, and there is heavy thumping music playing, along with all sorts of other sounds. Grunts, yells, the slamming of metal, balls bouncing on a wood floor, sneakers squeaking.

There is a huge man behind a counter, talking to an Erathian woman who appears to have been working out. Pax approaches, pressing his hand to a scanner. The man looks his way.

"Need a spot for your slave?"

"No, thank you."

Pax tugs me around the counter. There, in the corner and sitting on the floor, are a few humans of varying ages, all female. They keep their eyes down, their wrists bound with thick chains or biting ropes. I feel guilty, only having this one thin chain on my wrist.

Pax pulls me closer, so close our bodies meet. I tense. Have I done something wrong?

"We have to go into the men's locker room. Only look at the floor or at me, alright?"

I glance up at him to see he is frowning again, and his eyes are even darker. I nod, unsure of what to expect. We round the corner, entering a smelly room. I grimace, pressing the back of my wrist to my nose to stifle the humid, sweaty scent. The tiled floor is wet in some patches, and I can see the bare feet of different men. Pax leads me to a corner, pointing to a bench. I sit, pulling my hands into my lap.

He opens one of hundreds of small doors, pulling off his sweatshirt and stowing his things. He sits next to me, typing into his phone, when another pair of bare feet stomp into view. Pax doesn't seem to notice, lost in his typing. The bench dips as the man seats himself next to me, unlocking his door right underneath Pax's. I glance, simply out of curiosity, and then tear my eyes away just as quickly. He is naked as can be, just a few feet from me. It sends my heart racing in embarrassment and dread.

I turn, angling my body toward the one thing I know, but he moves at the same moment. My face is pressed into his arm as I pinch my eyes shut, shielding them from the sight right next to me. Pax stills, allowing me to hide in his shadow. I feel his heavy hand cup my knee, feel him lean in near my ear.

"Some people have no concept of personal space, huh?"

His words are light, teasing, and they make me feel better. I smile, nodding into his smooth, warm arm. His hand pats my knee, standing.

"Eyes down," he reminds me. He doesn't have to tell me twice. We leave the locker room, the air freshening as we go.

"Hey! If it isn't Paxton Harper and his wild conquest!"

My eyes jump up, finding the familiar strawberry blond man from our trek in the forest. I freeze as he grins down at me. It isn't a kind grin. Behind him stands a tall, thin woman—a human—with a chain around her neck. She has short black hair, pale skin and freckles, and amber hued eyes. She is beautiful, but in her eyes dances something dark, something catlike.

"Very funny, Jev. This is Olivia. Liv for short. Meet Deidre," Pax says, nodding to the woman. She gives a coy smile that I cannot return.

"My well-trained vixen of a pet," Jeven chuckles, tugging once on her collar. I feel sick as she lurches forward.

"Leg day?" Pax asks. Jeven sighs.

"Seriously, dude?"

"Quit pussin' out," Pax says with a chuckle. I eye the hawk-like face of Jeven, deciding I do not like him. The human, Deidre, may be alright. The two men jest each other, finding a corner with the equipment they need. I am instructed to sit, Deidre next to me. I pull my knees up to my chest as Pax crouches in front of me. His eyes are relaxed, playful. He hands me the other end of my chain.

"Earn my trust, Liv," he says, keeping his voice low. I am stunned, but nod. He gives a smirk.

"Here's my water if you get thirsty."

He hands me a large metal bottle before standing and preparing his workout with Jev. Deidre has been chained to the wall next to me. There are loops around the entire perimeter of this space, and I realize it is for slaves. My stomach sinks.

The woman and I do not talk, and I am too nervous to begin a conversation on my own. I fiddle with his water bottle, taking a few sips when I need to. I watch in fascination as Pax hefts heavy metal plates and slides them onto a bar before centering himself under it and lifting. His faces reddens as he squats, but he does this repeatedly, adding more and more weight each time. Jeven, I notice, cannot do even half the weight Pax does.

They go through different exercises, chatting about work and cracking jokes. Almost two hours have passed when they stand us up and walk us to a large open space. I recognize it as a basketball court. I've seen only a handful in my lifetime.

Pax has me sit, and he crouches before me again, grinning as sweat beads along his forehead. His dark hair still stands perfect atop his head. I hand him his water, shifting so my tailbone doesn't ache as bad. Jeven's face is beat read, his hair a sloppy, sweaty mess. He looks gross.

Pax takes a long drink before handing it to me, lid open.

"Go on," he says. I do, rather thirsty, even if I have only been sitting while he works out. He is in a good mood, and in turn, it makes me feel more relaxed. He stands and stretches, jogging off as the two begin to throw jabs at one another, an orange basketball in Jeven's hands.

"So." Deidre's voice makes me jump, and I glance at her with a nervous smile. She is staring at me, and though she is smiling, I can tell it's fake.

"Sooo..." I reply. I haven't spoken to another human in weeks.

"You're just a little princess, aren't you? What's your secret?" she says. I blink a few times, confused.

"What—"

"Oh, don't play dumb, girl," she says, rolling her eyes. "That freak would do anything for you," she whispers. I look to Pax, who is dominating Jeven in basketball as well. I do not understand what this woman is talking about.

"Best thing Jeven ever does is pass out early on occasion."

I bring my eyes back to hers, still so lost.

"I'm...confused..." I admit. She narrows her eyes at me before she snorts, incredulous.

"No way!" she hisses.

"What?" I breathe, clutching the water bottle to my chest.

"He hasn't fucked you yet, has he? God, you're so lucky."

My mind is whirling. I know the basics, but my mother died before she could give me the sex talk. After that, I simply stayed far away from men when possible.

"I don't really understand," I mumble, feeling my face redden as I eye my new shoes. She chuckles, the sound sympathetic.

"Oh honey, you're in for a shock when that day comes."

I feel the impulsive need to know, so I can better arm myself against whatever *fucking* entails.

"What...umm...happens?"

She lets her head thud against the concrete wall, smirking. She nods her head to the men, and I bring my eyes to Pax. He is panting, ball tucked under his arm, as he stands at the top of a curved line. His tank top is gone, revealing all his perfect muscles, beads of sweat rolling down his torso.

"There's a lovely long...*thing*...between those legs of his, and when it gets nice and hard he will shove it into you over and over and over. They *love* it," she says with disdain. I feel myself blanche. I want to ask *where* they put it, but after Brutus' attack, I have a feeling. That burning sensation returns between my legs. Would Pax ever hurt me that way?

"He won't do that," I say, but my voice is shaky. She laughs.

"Just be lucky your master is so sexy. I get a ginger haired weasel. At least his cock isn't so big. You, on the other hand..." she says, glancing between me and Pax. She laughs again.

"That thing will rip you in two."

I feel a steady tremble beginning to take root in me. More emotions flood my chest, ones of fear and angst and hopelessness. I know, even without experiencing what Deidre is talking about, that it is somehow sacred, to share such a bond with someone. I want a choice in who I share it with, right?

"Jeven is insatiable. Every night. Chains me up, shoves that pathetic worm into me, and goes to sleep. Sometimes, it actually feels good, so maybe your master will allow you to get off before he does."

"Get...off?" Does she mean roll off one another? She snorts, about to speak, when I see Pax's shoes approaching. She shrinks and averts her eyes. I cannot meet his eye either now, too embarrassed. He crouches down, and I jerk my eyes away from between his spread open legs. Where does he hide such a thing? Is this human lying to me?

He plucks the bottle from my arms, taking a long drink as his chest contracts and expands. He hands it back, reaching up, swiping his thumb across my cheek. The gesture is kind, gentle. I bring my eyes to him. He is beaming, his teeth perfect, white, his stubble beginning to poke through the skin of his jaw and chin.

"Thank you for behaving," he says. I nod, unable to mimic his smile. His face clouds. I shift and squirm under his gaze.

He leans in closer.

"Are you alright, Livy? We will leave soon. You can watch a movie when we get home, how does that sound?"

I try my best to smile and nod, but my voice fails me. His brows are close together in concern, his chocolatey eyes flicking between mine. He sighs, standing, playing half-heartedly against Jeven now. I dread the moment we return home, wondering if this woman's words are true. The need to escape is more pressing than ever before.

Pax

The ride home is silent. I at least thought Liv would have some excitement, would want to share whether or not she'd made a new friend. Perhaps humans don't think that way? Or had the locker room frightened her? I find my mind worrying on a loop. It is frustrating, not knowing her thoughts.

"I am going to shower," I tell her as we enter my apartment. "Get pajamas on and wait on the couch for me. I'll let you choose the movie."

She fumbles, standing between the living room and kitchen, looking lost. Her hands are trembling, which only deepens my confusion.

"I...may I go to bed?"

I check my watch. It is late, but not so late that I feel she should be this tired. I decide not to press her until we are in bed together. She cannot escape me so easily there, and I can hear her heartbeats better when we are so close.

"Sure."

She ducks around me and disappears into my room. Annoyed at her demeanor, I shower quick and change. My room is dark as I enter, and she is curled on the floor at the foot of the bed in her new pajamas. Why is she punishing herself?

"Liv?" I ask. Her head pops up, but she doesn't meet my eye.

"What are you doing?"

"It's comfy down here," she mumbles. She is clearly lying, clearly avoiding something—or someone. I begin to piece it together. Maybe Deidre said something to her, about my race as a whole. I sigh, sitting down next to her, the only light being one from my nightstand. She is still curled on the ground.

"Come here."

She doesn't move.

"Now, Olivia."

The tone of my voice results in a quick response. She sits up and scoots closer. I grab her wrists, wrestling her as I pull her onto my lap, facing me. She usually isn't so frightened. Finally, she is straddling me, shaking and huffing and refusing to meet my eye.

"Look at me."

She turns her face in my direction but keeps her eyes on my chest. I am clothed, a t-shirt and shorts. I can rule out the naked man mishap as to what is bugging her. I put both her wrists into one of my hands, my other splaying across her lower back, bringing her closer to me. She lets out a whimper, leaning away.

"Have I done something to make you afraid of me, Livy?" I ask, my voice gentle. She shakes her head. She is sniffling—crying. Shit.

"What is it, then?"

"Why did you take me?" she says through tears. "What kind of slave am I to you?"

Her voice is full of fear and pain. It hurts me, to hear her this distraught—a feeling that comes unexpectedly and force-fully. Deidre must've said something to her, something to scare her.

"What did Jeven's slave say?" I growl. She jumps, shaking her head.

"Olivia, if you don't tell me—"

"She said you're going to fuck me..."

I am taken aback at her blunt honesty. It shouldn't surprise me; Jeven is all too fond of his slave and their...*hobbies*. It is not uncommon in my world, but it is not the reason I took Liv. I release her wrists, placing my hand gently on her hip.

"No, Liv, that isn't the case."

Her watery, emerald green eyes flash to mine. She wipes her nose on her sleeve. Her eyes waver between wanting to trust me and wanting to flee this situation. I keep my hold on her hip firm.

"Do you understand what that is?" I ask, cocking my head to the side. She flushes, averting her eyes. I gather she has no real clue. But in all her perfect innocence, she voices it. I bite my cheek to prevent a smile at her childish explanation.

"She said you umm...put something..." she points down between my legs. "Here," then she points between her legs.

"That is the very minimal explanation of sex, yes," I say, chuckling. She hugs herself.

"You're not going to...to chain me up and..."

"Never."

She peeks at me from under her thick lashes. Her cheeks are rosy in the dim light. I reach up, brushing my thumb along her smooth, warm cheek. It is just as soft as it was at the gym. I enjoy the way her skin feels beneath my fingertips, so delicate.

"I don't like Deidre," she says, her face pinched in a pout. She crosses her arms, glaring at me, but I can see she isn't being a brat. I chuckle.

"I don't think I like her, either."

I smooth my hand up and down the bumps of her spine. The trust—the spark is back, there in her cunning gaze. It has been a long day, and I do not have the strength to contend with her at the moment.

"Would you still like to watch a movie?"

She bobs her head. I am glad I am able to distract her.

"Go pick out a snack while I heat up some dinner, ok?"

She rushes to jump up, but my fingers tighten on her bony hips, keeping her planted to me. She frowns.

"You exceeded my expectations today, Livy. I am proud of you."

Something changes within her in the span of a few seconds, something shifts and clicks. Her jaw slackens the smallest bit, her heartbeat quickens, and her eyes brighten. It is a curious reaction, and I wonder what to make of it. Is she pleased that I am pleased, or is there something deeper at work here? Her eyes are swishing between mine. This is the longest she has held my gaze.

"Thank you," she finally says. Her voice is soft, gentle and sweet and innocent, and it is then I understand; she craves such praises, yearns for them. She probably heard them on a rare occasion when not running for her life. My opinion of her and her behavior matters—to *her*. I feel awash with many emotions, one side of my lips tilting up.

Her eyes soon harden, and she soon crosses her arms again. She quirks a brow at me.

"I'm still going to get out of here and be free, *sir*," she says, haughty and confident. I cannot help my chuckle.

"By all means, Livy, keep trying."

8

Pax

The rest of the week flies by in a blur. Each day is filled with moments of peace, interrupted by insubordination, retracted privileges, pinching, and lots of scowling. I continue to aim to be a leader she can follow, and though it is tumultuous, I believe it is working. She is doing her share of chores—from laundry to dishes to cooking small meals. She has even dusted and cleaned the bathroom. Not without a fight, first, of course, but I will take all the small victories I can get.

I have her lessons mapped out each evening for the next few months. I've yet to reveal them to her, wanting her to see education as a reward so she wants to do it. I have learned she craves sweets, becomes whiny when she is tired (which is often, considering her body is still healing) and has developed a game where she will curse and run away from my reprimands. It's easy to catch her, but pinching doesn't seem to deter her foul language very much.

It is on Sunday afternoon, with the sun streaming in through the large windows, that I feel it. I sit on the couch, successful after prepping a casserole for dinner with some help from the grump.

"Shit," I hiss, my ass getting stabbed by something sharp. I reach beneath me and between the couch cushions, producing a pair of scissors we had used earlier when cutting chives. I had instructed her to wash them and put them in the sanitizer, trusting she would do so. My eyes glare at the representation of her disobedience, but I would be lying if I said a thrill didn't chase through my veins.

I haven't had to paddle her since that one morning, and twice in one week seems gracious of her. She appears from my room, hair flowing to her ribs in a shiny curtain. She is wearing thick wool socks that dwarf her little feet, jeans, and a black, long sleeve top. She tried to wear pajamas all day, and though I am pleased she finally listened and changed (after an argument, of course) I am once more in a sour mood. Not angry; I promised myself to never reprimand out of anger. I am simply frustrated.

Her feet halt in the hall, eyes wide as a deer's as they fall upon her hidden scissors. I wag them, frowning.

"I forgot to—"

"I am not allowed to lie to you, Olivia, and you are not going to lie to me."

She gulps, twisting her hands together.

"We've been through the rules ten times today alone. Why are you acting out so much?" I growl. She crosses her arms in defiance, jutting out her hip. She is ready to spew.

"Because I am tired of being your slave. I did my part and tried it out and I hate it," she spits. I rub my forehead in exhaustion.

"Need I remind you how much worse you could have it?"

Her eyes are burning coals of hatred.

"Need I remind you that you kidnapped me, beat me, starved me, and let me be tortured?"

Her voice is quiet, and though she is trying to be tough, I can see her pain. She will not let go of this easily. Humans, I am learning, are stubborn creatures. I take a steadying breath.

"You are in this situation, Liv, and there is no changing it. So you either accept it graciously and move on, thankful to have food and clothes and protection, or—"

"Protection?" she hisses. Her eyes are watering. I feel my chest tighten as my rage jolts my veins. I clench my hands.

"You let your friend shove his fingers into me while I was tied to a bloody tree and at his mercy!" she spews. It is the first time I am hearing this admittance of what Brutus actually did to her. I am stunned, shocked into silence as she fumes. There was no way of knowing the extent of his molestation upon her. I am livid, now, but for a vastly different reason. No wonder she cannot stand to be touched when she is asleep, no wonder she wears so many layers of clothing—no wonder she doesn't fully trust me.

"And you let those people beat me and stab me and burn my feet and pour water over my face until I couldn't breathe! *You* even did some of those things to me! You're all monsters, and you can't protect me!"

Her body is trembling with her own quiet fury, but she refuses to let her tears fall. I wait, allowing her words to sink in. I cannot let this deed go unpunished, but I can take her words into consideration as far as how I act toward her. I smooth my palms together.

"You never told me what Brutus did to you. That is...horrifying, inherently evil."

Her tears finally slip, but she turns her face away. I never cared much what happened to humans—until Olivia. But the thought of someone harming her in such a way—taking away what precious innocence she has—is enough to make me see red. No one, human or not, should be forced to endure such a humiliating and degrading form of torture. I consider my words carefully before speaking again.

"As for everything else, I will never expect your forgiveness, or for you to make this situation any easier on me. I just ask that you try to find some positives, Livy."

She says nothing. I think about what other evils were lurking just a mile from her before I captured her. I think about my decision to keep her, knowing I would be giving her a chance at a decent life, even without her true freedom.

"I can and I do protect you, Olivia. Whether you want to see that or not. I will never let anyone hurt you ever again."

She squeezes her eyes shut, hugging herself as she battles her tears and emotions. I set the scissors aside as they glint the rays of sun off them. Her punishment will have to come later, once we've both had a chance to cool down.

"Go. We can discuss everything later."

She wipes at her face, ducking into the bathroom. I lean back, staring blankly at the TV, my arm stretched across the back of the couch. She stays hidden for a while, but I let her be. When she does emerge, she keeps her head low. I watch her from my peripheral as she pulls her sleeves down over her hands. I am shocked as she comes near, plopping herself on the ground between the couch and coffee table. She is ignoring me, but she wants to watch sports.

I bend at my waist, reaching down and gripping her hips. She yelps and jumps, but I just pull her up onto the couch, tucking her into my side. Her warmth has grown into such a comfort for me. No wonder humans loved dogs as pets.

She grumbles, playing with the ends of her hair.

"Can you just punish me and get it over with?" she mutters. I am shocked, but have to agree with her—I'd rather get it over with as well.

"Ten sound fair, since you actually hid them?"

"No, I think one should do," she says as she crosses her arms and peeks at me in defiance. I frown down at her.

"I sat on them and speared my ass, so ten. Take it, or it can be more. Your choice."

She is snickering. She can have one small victory over me. I have to hide my grin, hard as it is. After a moment, she sobers, knowing there is no way out of this.

"Fine."

She is nervous, same as the last time we had to do this. My chest is on fire, igniting my entire body. I do not like this, but I do like the sense of control it gives me, especially over her. I push her up by her hips until she is standing before me. I scoot to the edge of the couch, spreading my knees to give her a place to lay. She sighs, avoiding my gaze as I bend her at the waist. Her jeans are troublesome, a hindrance, and I cannot easily pull them down.

"Unbutton them, Liv."

She slides off me, kneeling as she obeys, her hands shaking. She doesn't pull them down, but I assume it is simply out of embarrassment. She lays back across my thighs while I give a sharp tug to her belt loops. My mouth runs dry.

Last time, she wore simple, basic underwear that covered the expanse of her ass. This time, she is wearing some form of stringy lingerie, black and lacy. Her entire backside is bared to me, pale and smooth and flawless with just the right amount of curve.

My body reacts before my mind does, sending jolts of pleasure down into my stomach before flooding into my cock. I shake my head, training my eyes on the ceiling. I have never looked upon a human in lust before, and I refuse to start now.

Her heartbeats thudding into my thigh, I feel her little body tense and tremble in anticipation. With a deep breath, I bring my eyes back to her bared cheeks, smoothing my palm over one

side. I will be kind, switching between sides so she isn't very
sore.

My hand raises, and my palm connects with her flesh. The
sound is sharp, but I ensure my smack is on the gentle side. She
jolts forward on impact. My free hand presses between her
shoulder blades, keeping her pinned to me.

I am mesmerized, watching her pale skin turn pink to red,
seeing for myself how large I am in comparison to her. Between
each paddle, I smooth my palm over her heated flesh, doing my
best to keep any pain to a minimum.

Toward the end, she is whimpering.

"Almost done, Livy," I soothe as she jumps. It is over, and I
stand her up. Her jeans slip to her ankles, but I keep my eyes on
her red face, unable to look her in the eye. I pull her too me,
needing her to be close, needing her to forgive me as I have
forgiven her. I wrap her trembling form in my arms, holding
her the same way as last time, running my hands over her pert
little butt. Everything about her is little in comparison to me
and my race.

I feel her tears wet my neck, listen as she sniffles. My hands
pull the blanket around us, squeezing her tight to me.

"You're alright, sweetheart," I say, smoothing her hair down.
It is so soft against my fingertips. I wish to run my hands
through her strands forever. She stills, and it is then I realize I
have called her a pet name. I brush it off. She is always sweet to
me in these moments of high emotions.

After a while, she is calmed, resting. I am left drained. I pull
her down on top of me as we lay on the couch. She snuggles in,
one hand on my chest, her head tucked under my chin. I run
my fingers up and down her exposed flesh, from her thighs all
the way to her lower back. Before long, she is sound asleep. The
steady rhythm of her heart lulls me into peace.

∾

Olivia

"Mmm," I groan as the bed dips. My eyes flutter open, seeing darkness. It must be early. A heavy, warm hand settles on my hip. In the dim light of dawn, I can make out Pax.

"Be a good girl today. I will check on you at some point, alright?"

After getting caught with the scissors yesterday, I do not want to piss him off again. But my plan worked; he hasn't found the knife I hid in the top of the toilet. Ten paddles was worth that. I am one step closer to freedom, assuming he never finds it.

I yawn and nod. He is wearing a light grey beret with a crest on the front. As he stands, I make out the rest of what appears to be a uniform; it is all varying patches and shades of grey, his pants loose but tapering down to fit into his shiny, sturdy, black boots. He wears a plain black short sleeve shirt, but there is a patterned grey jacket at the end of the bed. The way he looks is rather austere—powerful.

I wonder what his job actually is.

"Do your chores, shower, no pajamas—"

"Bloody hell, Pax, let me sleep," I groan. He pinches the back of my arm and I yelp.

"Watch it, Liv."

I shift so I can escape, fully awake now. Taking my chances, I stick my tongue out at him before darting away. I roll to his side of the bed and spring forth to jump off, feeling him scrambling to catch me. My legs become tangled in the sheets, and I am left free falling. I brace for impact with a cry, but nothing ever happens.

Strong arms catch me and pull me up until I'm sitting in his lap, my arms pinned to my sides as I scowl.

"Maybe today you can work on your attitude," he grunts.

"Maybe today you can work on wearing something a little more fashionable."

He squeezes me tighter.

"For fuck's sake, Olivia."

I twist in his arms, surprised when he lets me. Our faces are inches apart, and he is glaring at me. I give him the best dazzling grin I can muster.

"So, that moor—"

His glare cuts me off.

"I left you a mug of coffee to have with breakfast. All cupboards and drawers are locked, but I've set out any dishes and utensils you may need. I know exactly how many there are, so no funny business."

No, you don't know how many, dumbass, I think, feeling giddy that I am getting away with this.

"There will be no breaking or destroying any of my things. You will complete two lectures and all chores, shower and be presentable. If you accomplish all of that without getting into trouble, we can order pizza for dinner."

My mouth immediately waters. I haven't had pizza since I was a girl, but the memory of how amazing it tastes is still potent on my tongue. I nod vigorously. Sure, I'll do my best figure out how to escape, but if I can do so sneakily, I can still get pizza. One thing living in the Ruins taught me was how to be sneaky, sly.

He stands us up before releasing me.

"Remember, I will be checking in on you unannounced today. Be good."

I grit my teeth. I really want to roll my eyes at him. But I will save that for after pizza. He frowns, grabbing his uniform jacket and heading to the front door. I follow in his wake and feel the heaviness of his absence as soon as the door closes. The silence is unnerving. I haven't been truly alone like this in my entire life.

I need to make good use of my time, but all I can seem to do is wander around the living room and kitchen. The bookshelf is useless as far as entertainment since I can't read. He has put controls on the TV, only allowing children's channels, the news, sports, and educational documentaries.

I find myself in the kitchen, sipping my lukewarm coffee. All the cupboards are locked, but the pantry isn't. Maybe there will be something useful he forgot in there. At the very least, I can make requests for food that will not easily perish, things I can stow away for when I run.

I drag a chair from the kitchen table into the pantry to aid in my search. Starting low, I shuffle around tubs meant to keep food, random cans, and a bag of rice. Everything is organized and neat, and everything is boring. I huff, hands on my hips, standing straight. Nothing at eye level is worth my trouble for stealing. I look up. There are different cooking pots, a slow cooker, some metal pans for what I assume would be used for cooking huge meals, and there, in the back behind everything, is something I do not recognize.

I stand on the chair, reaching up, my fingers brushing the cool glass of the bottle. I pull it to me, staring at the fancy label. I cannot read it, nor do I recognize any of the words. It is half empty, though. Curious, I pull the cap off, sniffing it. My eyes burn and water. It smells like rye and fire.

It isn't a cooking oil like the ones shelved below me, and it is hidden high up where it is difficult for me to find it. Therefore, it is forbidden to me. I feel like getting into some trouble. He won't even know.

"This is our secret, mysterious bottle," I say, lifting it high before putting the rim to my lips. I tip it back, guzzling it down. It burns—sears through me—and my empty stomach churns immediately. I pull the bottle away, having no choice but to swallow the poison. I cough and sputter and choke, turning the bottle around to search the label in utter fear.

What if it is poison, or cleaning chemicals? What if I have just signed my life away on a whim? My chest burns, and my head swims. There, on the bottle, is a skull and bones. It *is* poison. I whimper, dropping the bottle. It crashes and explodes in the pantry. I totter on the chair, jumping down. Glass shards shred my right foot, but I stumble and limp crying to the bathroom.

I need to throw up, right? Isn't that what the healers always said? I slip on the tiled floor of the bathroom in my own blood, and the world tilts. My forehead connects with the tub, and blackness consumes me.

Pax

It is just past eleven, and I have a break in my duties. I march to my vehicle, taking the fifteen minute drive home. I am nervous, but I have hope Liv will be doing her chores, or watching her lectures. I ensured I locked up anything dangerous, anything she could use as a weapon.

I unlock my door, shutting it behind me.

"Liv?" I call out. It is silent, and in that silence is something foreboding. My body tenses, ready to spring into action if there is a threat. My eyes scan the living room and kitchen. The pantry is open, the light on, and from it leads a trail of blood. My heart thunders. I follow the trail without thought, straight into the bathroom. Liv is sprawled on the floor, her foot bleeding from various cuts, her forehead bleeding from a gash near her hairline.

I am on my hands and knees in a flash, feeling for her pulse. It is there. I roll her onto her back before pulling her into my arms. The sight of the gash on her forehead is ghastly. She will need stitches. I pull her limp leg up, inspecting her foot. No stitches, hopefully, but I will have to fish the glass out.

What the hell did she break?

And then, I smell it. *Whisky.*

I grit my teeth against my anger. That will have to come later. How the hell did she find it? Will I never be able to leave her unattended? Will I have to lock her up while I work?

She moans, stirs. Her wide green eyes blink open, and she raises a hand to her head. I grip her wrist, keeping her away from the gash. Her confused gaze falls to me, and it takes her a moment to comprehend what is going on. I cannot help but glare at her.

"I can't even leave you alone for four fucking hours, Olivia," I growl. She winces, pinching her eyes closed and curling in on herself as she whimpers and brings her arms up to shield her face. My heart sinks. She thought I would strike her.

"Liv, I'm not going to hurt you."

She is crying now, but the sound is weak. I do not know much about humans and head injuries, only that they are serious if left untreated. I have no choice but to take her to a physician that specializes in humans. I stand, keeping her in my arms. I fetch a towel, pressing it to her forehead. She whimpers and blubbers.

"I'm...sawwy..." she slurs.

"Save it for later, Olivia. I am beyond pissed at you right now."

I manage to get her into my car and make the short drive to the clinic. I carry her inside, stares of slaves and owners alike following me. I do my best to pull off my hat since I am indoors —a respectful gesture that was pounded into me from the time I was a child. Her blood is on my hands, my uniform. It isn't the first time a human's blood has been all over me. And not because I am rushing them to the hospital.

"I need to see a physician," I say to the young woman behind the counter. Her mouth is agape, her dark eyes wide.

"Now," I growl. She jumps, picking up a phone and pressing a few buttons.

"T-through that door, sir. The emergency team will meet you in the hall."

I don't bother thanking her as I storm through the doors. Liv moans.

"Was it...poison?" she hiccups. I roll my eyes before realizing what I have done. Her damn quirks are rubbing off on me.

"No, idiot. It was whisky—alcohol. And rather expensive alcohol, at that," I grumble. She blinks her eyes open as I walk to the end of the hall. Her eyes go wide, her pupils dilating in terror. A team of three physicians gather at the end by another set of doors, donning gowns and gloves. She jumps up, wrapping her arms around my neck as she lets out a wail. The sound stabs at me, making me stop in my tracks.

"Please, no, I'll-I'll be g-good, Pax, p-please!"

She is wailing and sobbing. The team rushes forward. I attempt to pry her away from my neck to look at her, but her hold on me is surprisingly strong.

"Liv, Liv," I chant, pulling at her as she writhes and screams.

"Please, no, I'm s-sorry, I'm sorry, p-please!"

Her sobs are uncontrollable. A harried nurse appears, syringe in hand.

"Humans can be...so...unruly..." she breathes, trying to pry Liv's arm away so she can sedate her. But once Liv sees the needle, all hell breaks loose. She screams, claws at me, throws her pitiful amount of weight back. I thud against the wall, barely able to contain her anymore. She slips from me, but the other physicians are waiting. I realize—too late—my mistake.

"Back off, everyone!"

My voice booms through the hall, and everyone snaps to attention. Except Liv. She is curled on the ground in a shallow doorway behind me, her bloodied face pressed to the jamb. I crouch down to her panting form, sliding my hand across her upper back. She is shivering, muttering her 'sorry' over and over.

"Look at me right now, Olivia."

My tone holds no room for argument. She obeys, her lip trembling, her eyes so full of fear. This is the worst I have seen her.

"You're hurt, okay? You need to be looked over and stitched up. You're not in trouble."

I know she believes this is the Facility. Guilt courses through me. I am the reason she is having these issues in the first place. I have no one to blame but myself.

"I will not leave you here. I will not leave you ever again. Do you trust me?"

She sniffs, eyes darting around the empty hall. Her face crumbles again.

"Look at me only, Liv, okay?"

She listens, trembling from head to toe.

"Will you let them help you? I don't like seeing you hurt."

I unfold my arms, opening them to her. She hesitates, but shifts closer to me. I know this is as far as she will want to move, so I bridge the gap and wrap her in my arms, cradling her head. She lets me hold her, a few small sobs wracking her frame.

"I'm...so-sorry," she cries.

"Shh, shh. Don't apologize. I just want you to be alright."

Her little heart is hammering hard in her chest, thumping against mine. We sit there, hugging in the hall, covered in her blood and tears. I let my eyes slip closed as I hold her. It is the first time I have ever seen such a reaction to trauma. I know, though, that I have done far worse when faced with my past.

9

Olivia

I am sitting on the couch, staring at the blank screen of the television. Pax is in the shower, his bloody clothes soaking in the washroom tub. He's yet to clear the disaster of a mess I made. I want to do it myself, but I am rooted to my spot in fear. What will this mistake warrant me? How bad will this punishment be? Will he sell me, be fed up enough to kill me?

He was silent the entire way home while I ogled at my healed face. He demanded the physicians give me medicines meant for Erathians only. It was searingly painful, but now there is no sign of the gash on my forehead or the tears in my foot. It only exists in my mind's eye. As the minutes tick by, I am more and more afraid of what is to come.

He emerges from the bathroom, towel wrapped around his hips, his dark hair damp and tousled. The scars that mar his otherwise silky skin jump out at me. I wonder what he endured to get them. My back shrinks into the plush leathery cushions, but he pays me no mind, stomping to the bedroom. His muscles look even more menacing now.

By the time he reappears, clothed in shorts and a t-shirt, his eyes are on me. I am breathing hard, feeling faint. Nothing I say can get me out of this hole I've dug myself into. I feel utterly stupid, risking my plans for escape on a petty whim to get back at him.

He seats himself across from me on the coffee table, and this whole situation rings with familiarity. Will this be the last time I endure it, though? I feel tears on my cheeks, but I am too nervous to move even an inch to wipe them away. I can't even bring myself to care if I appear weak in his eyes at this moment. I *am* weak compared to him.

I always have been.

"Liv—"

"P-please," I plead, my voice tremulous, frightened. "I'll...I'll clean it up, I'll never bug you again, I'll do my chores and...just don't k-kill me..."

He straightens as shock crosses his face, his eyes brooding.

"Livy, I don't want to kill you. Not now, not ever."

I shake my head. That can't be true.

"You-you're lying. You promised never to lie," I whisper, my voice thick with more tears. He sighs, rubbing at his clean-shaven face.

"Olivia, why would I have them heal you if I wanted to kill you?"

I blink a few times in confusion. I shake my head, about to speak, but he beats me to it.

"Just tell me why you pulled that stunt."

At this point, I'd give him anything he asked just to save myself from his wrath.

"I...I don't know..."

"Not good enough, Liv. Why did you do it?"

"I...I was bored, so I went looking through your stuff, and I saw it and thought it would make you mad if I drank it...and then I did and I thought it was poison and I dropped it and it broke and I cut my foot and slipped in the bathroom and hit my head—"

My rushed explanation is interrupted by his deep laughter. I am stunned as I watch his shoulders bounce, as he tries to cover his smile with his big hand. He has a dimple on his right cheek when he smiles that way.

"Why...why is this funny?" I say, perplexed and flustered. His laughter only grows until he is wiping at his eyes. I cross my arms as my fear dissipates and my anger replaces it. Finally, he shakes his head, simmering down to his more usual, serious self.

"Though I am pissed at you, I think the best punishment is you thinking you drank poison. *Never* pull a stunt like that again, understand me?"

I nod, sour.

"I missed half a day back at work. It looks bad on my part, so I need to be able to trust that you won't make stupid decisions like that in the future, got it? If I have to, I will lock you up while I am at work."

His gaze is stoic and dark.

"You said you wouldn't do that," I mumble, picking at the blanket wrapped around me. He sighs.

"You've forced my hand. I don't want to do that. It wouldn't bring me any sense of joy, but if you can't be mature, then that's what will have to happen."

Whatever. I'll be gone before that can happen.

"Fine," I grit out.

"I want you to clean up your mess, and I am adding new rules: no consumption of alcohol, unless I specify it's ok, and no consumption of any *burnouts*."

"What's a burnouts?" I question, confused. His smile returns, lighting his features.

"Erathian drugs. Slaves are offered them all the time on the streets. They are dangerous, and they can kill you."

I chew my cheek as I nod.

"Next time I catch you with alcohol," he says, his tone serious, "I will make sure you learn to hate it."

"How?" I challenge, wanting to try it just to spite him. He gives a devilish smirk.

"I'll do what my father did to me. Make me finish the bottle. May be fun for a while, but the next day you'll wish you hadn't been that stupid."

I grit my teeth, quirking my head to the side.

"*You* disobeyed someone?" I say, half-mocking, half-serious.

"Go clean up your mess, Olivia, before you piss me off even more."

Pax doesn't order pizza, instead telling me I have to make my own dinner, and my bedtime is moved up a whole two hours. I stare at the ceiling before I roll, attempting to make myself tired, but it's of no use. I can see light filtering beneath the doorway, and can hear the TV quietly mumbling something. Maybe if I fake having to use the bathroom, he will let me stay up with him for a little bit longer.

I throw back the covers, my heart racing as I take my chance, peeking out into the living room. He's sitting on the couch, eating a salad with one hand while his other holds his phone. His face is serious as he chews, and then a small smile appears. He sets aside his fork, his fingers flying over the screen for a few seconds.

I step out while he's distracted. A creak in the floorboards alerts him to my presence, and his eyes flash to mine.

"Liv—"

I hold up my hands in surrender.

"I just have to go to the bathroom."

He frowns, but his phone makes a noise, sparing me from further trouble as he glances at it and smiles again. I duck into the bathroom, checking the toilet tank. My knife is still there, wrapped in clear plastic and a few pieces of tape to hopefully prevent rust. I grin to myself at my genius. I go through the motions, flushing the toilet and pretending to wash my hands before coming back out.

He hasn't moved, but he is still holding his phone and smiling. What a weirdo.

"Go to bed," he grumbles, not looking at me. I want to press my luck, but he seems to be in a bad mood with me and a good mood with his phone. I stomp off. At least I have a chocolate bar hiding in my drawer.

I jolt awake, feeling frigid arms encircle me. I scream, thrashing about the bed. I don't remember Pax coming to bed before I fell to sleep. It has to be him, right?

"Shit, sorry Liv, I forgot," he says, releasing me immediately. I whimper, scooting away from him to the very edge of the bed as my heart hammers through my chest. The clock on his wall dimly shows it is two in the morning. I sit up, curling into a ball and hiding my face, pushing the memories as far away as I can.

"Livy?" he says after a few minutes of tense silence. I shake my head.

"I'm so—"

I jump up before he can say anything else, dashing out to the living room, praying he doesn't follow me. I just want to be alone. I nestle into the couch, surprised to find it is cold. Where was he for all these hours if not on the couch?

I decide I don't care as I wrap myself in the blanket, laying my head on the stiff armrest. I stare out into the moonlight and stars. I recognize a few constellations. My mother used to point them out to me when we were jumping from city to city, trying to escape the Erathians. She never had enough time or energy to teach me to read or write other than the most basic things, but she would tell me stories, or sing me songs. We had to survive. There was no time for anything else.

I hear his footsteps before I see him. I roll, facing the back of the couch, annoyed at his intrusion. Why can't he ever leave me alone?

I hadn't realized I was crying, either, until I feel the wetness on my arm. His footsteps draw closer across the wood floor, until the sound is muffled by the rug. I stiffen, wishing for him to just leave.

"Go to bed. I'll sleep out here as my punishment."

His words are low, dark and gravelly. My heart jumps; at least he's recognized his misstep. But I am wallowing in my misery, and I just want to keep it that way. He can get to me in the bedroom. He cannot get to me in the bathroom. After him barging in on me, he programed the lock to obey my hand-prints as well. It is the one safe spot I have from him.

I rise from the couch, not giving him the courtesy of even a glance. I pull the blanket with me, skirting around him. He must see where I am intending to go.

"God, Liv, seriously? Stop being so difficult!" he says, raising his voice. I pause at the door, turning to give him one last look. I can't help but hate him in this moment. I feel the weight of my enslavement, of the turn my life has taken. Maybe it would be better to end it, to kill myself. I don't want to live this way, under his thumb.

His eyes shine for a moment in the darkness, but I can still see the helpless look on his face. Good. I want to hurt him. I don't understand why or how my actions have any capacity to hurt a being such as him, but I want it, nonetheless.

"I don't want to see you," I say. My voice is quiet, and even to me it sounds dead and hollow. He takes a step back, his brow furrowing. I push open the door, entering my solace, locking it behind me. I've slept in far worse places and conditions.

Pax

I know I've screwed up, and each night she locks herself in the bathroom to sleep is another flash of searing pain deep in my chest. I have never felt anything like it before, and it is not pleasant. Being an Erathian—and an owner of a human—I should not feel this way, right? She is fortunate to have food and clothes and shelter.

But as the rings under her eyes grow more prominent, as she cooks and cleans without complaint, I cannot help but hate myself for doing this to her. All because I touched her while she was sleeping? It can't only be that, right? It's been four nights, sleepless nights. I am lonely when I get home. There was always loneliness in some capacity before I took Liv, but I hadn't realized how much she filled that void in my life in such a short amount of time.

I rub my forehead, leaning against the bar as I bring the whisky to my lips. A hand slides across my shoulders as a dark haired beauty seats herself next to me, a wide smile on her round face. The night I made my mistake with Olivia, I had been out drinking with Tarex, the woman from the coffee shop. We'd hit it off, and this will mark our fourth night in a row hanging out. At least she distracts me from my problems at home.

"Hey, handsome," she beams, shedding her rain jacket.

"Who, me?" I tease. She laughs, swatting at my arm playfully. The bartender knows her order and slides it over to her.

"How was work?" she calls over the music, catching the tiny

straws between her lips. I give a shrug and a grunt, sipping my whisky. I come here to forget about work and home, not talk about it.

She is bubbly, though, and can chatter for hours, which I don't mind too much. I don't usually have anything to say. I was branded as a geek in my adolescent years for my interest in science and history, so I learned to keep to myself and let others talk.

The more I drink, the more fun Tarex becomes. She even manages to drag me to the dance floor for a few songs. By the time we collapse back into our barstools, the buzz is thudding through my veins. She gazes up at me, eyes glossed, biting her lip in desire. It's been four decent dates. I should see if I enjoy her physically before we pursue anything else. From the way she is looking at me, I have a feeling she will enjoy whatever I do to her.

"My place or yours?" I say with a wink, praying she chooses hers so I don't have to deal with my sulking human. She giggles.

"I live right around the corner."

Perfect.

We walk side by side through the cool evening and to her quaint studio apartment. She wastes no time. As soon as she locks the door, she jumps into my arms, pressing her sticky lips to mine. I hate lipstick or lip gloss or whatever the hell make up these women wear, but I don't tell her that. I kiss her back, lost in a whisky stupor as my hands roam up and down her slim, toned sides.

She is perfection. The only trace of fat are her small breasts. She is tall and thin, with long legs, beautiful dark hair, and eyes that nearly match mine. She is the epitome of an Erathian woman. A woman my parents would love to meet.

I deepen our kiss, walking us back to her bed. I lay her down, her silky, shiny hair a halo about her face as I struggle to undo my belt buckle. She giggles, tugging at her shirt and shimmying out of her jeans. I lean down, kissing her again to heighten both our arousal, and she moans into me. I pull off the rest of my clothing, fisting my length. She lays before me in nothing but a lacy black thong.

The sight sends a jolt through me, and I pause. Pleasure tingles down into the pit of my stomach at the sight, but I don't question it.

"Roll over," I demand, my voice husky. She giggles again, obeying, jutting her ass up into the air for my eyes to feast upon. I smooth my palm over her soft skin. I am mesmerized. She wiggles her butt.

"Like what you see?"

I grunt in answer, unable to think rationally. I give her ass cheek a tame slap. She rewards me by moaning.

"Ohh, Pax...I like that..."

I do it again, a little harder, and her moan becomes louder.

"Yes," she whimpers. She is playing with herself now. I can't wait anymore. I need a release, and she does, too. I tear off her underwear, using my fingers to find my target. She is soaked and eager. I ease in, but I know she is built to handle me, to complement my body as I complement hers.

We as a race rarely have to worry about pregnancy or diseases transmitted through intercourse. Our scientists cured them long ago, and Erathian women only reach a fertile age well into their thirties, and even then are only fertile maybe once a year, at best.

I grip her hips as I drive myself into her, quickening my pace.

"Spank...me..." she moans, her words muffled by her mattress and sheets as her headboard clashes with the wall. A thrill races through me. I do, this smack the hardest yet. My handprint forms on her ass in a bright red, and she reaches her climax at the same moment. I follow soon after, collapsing across her back as I twitch and come down from my high.

All that is left is emptiness.

We lay in bed with the window open, the breeze delicious across our warm skin. She rests her head on my chest, sighing in contentment. My mind is elsewhere, though. It is late, and I should be more concerned about my human and what troubles she has gotten herself into.

I know, with a sinking feeling, she's not done anything worth warranting a punishment. She is hollow and empty, just as I am.

"What is it like, owning a slave? She seems so obedient."

I snort, trailing my fingers up her side.

"She is the furthest thing from obedient."

Tarex giggles.

"She seemed to be when I met her. I heard that is the best combination: a male Erathian and a female human. They somehow respond better to authority if the gender is opposite."

I give a shrug, considering her words.

"Either way, she is cute as a button. You dress her so well!"

"She picked out her own clothes at the store," I say, my voice rather monotonous. Tarex doesn't notice. She never notices when I just want peace and quiet.

"I used to have a slave. She was thirteen, I think."

I stiffen, glancing down at her. Was someone here watching us the whole time?

"Used to?"

She nods.

"I was warned that human females can be wild at that age. They call it *puberty* or *hormones*. Wicked little thing never obeyed and cried about her mother constantly. I was patient enough, but after month three, she got really bad."

I feel my heartbeat thud harder in my chest.

"What happened?"

She sighs, rolling onto her back in a display of how inconvenient her situation was.

"I had her punished, and when she was returned, she bit me! Little devil. I had no choice but to put her down after that."

I pull away from Tarex, staring down at her in bewilderment.

"You...what?"

She nods, and her dark eyes hold annoyance at her past situation.

"I took her to the nearest Facility and had them euthanize her. It was the humane thing to do. I could have been sued if she bit someone in public like that! Can you imagine the embarrassment? God, I would feel so guilty," she prattles. I am grinding my teeth as my body heaves in...what? Anger? Horror?

A *child*.

This Erathian had been an owner to a human child, and she'd ended her life for something that asinine? If I was that crazy, Liv would have been dead the night she spit in my face. I roll off the bed, gathering my clothes as quickly as I can.

"Pax? Do you have work in the morning?"

I take a deep breath, readying myself to break this off. I cannot stand being near her another minute.

"No, Tarex...you're a lovely woman, but I can't do this. I...I need to go," I say, watching as her face crumples. I steel myself, dressing, not even bothering to put on my shoes. I am met with her livid protests, and I do deserve some of her angry words, but only one thing is on my mind right now, and that is the young woman whose life I stole.

Olivia

I am just making myself comfortable on the bathroom floor when he arrives home. I hope he leaves me alone, but I wonder if he will need to shower. His handprint will override mine, of course, so being locked in here isn't as safe as I would like it to be.

To my surprise, all I hear are his footsteps heading into his room. I relax, closing my eyes, ready to drift off. His footsteps stomp past the bathroom and to what I assume is the kitchen. I frown, settling back down. He stomps by again. And again. And *again*.

I am exasperated and confused. Is he trying to be annoying so I come out? I sit up, leaning against the wall as I cross my arms. It was late—after midnight—when I shut myself in. I assumed he would be gone until much later, as he has been every night this week.

I jump as a soft knock sounds at the door. I glare at it, knowing who is behind that thick, dark wood, knowing who seeks to interrupt my wallowing. It's unfair of me to not allow him to use the bathroom if that is what he wants, but part of me is enjoying making his life inconvenient. He sure as hell didn't seem to care about my feelings when he took me.

The knock sounds again, accompanied by his voice.

"Liv? Are you awake?"

I thud my head against the wall.

"No," I grumble, loud enough so he can hear. There is silence for a few moments.

"May I show you something?"

I grit my teeth as my heart leaps in curiosity. What could he want to show me at this hour? He doesn't sound upset or malicious. I have a feeling I can trust him at the moment...But I do *not* want to give in so easily.

"What is it?" I ask.

I hear his chuckle.

"You have to come out. It's hard to explain."

Of course I do. Nice try, trickster.

"I'll see it in the morning."

"Suit yourself. I hope it doesn't melt by then."

That bastard.

My stomach gives an audible growl at the thought of ice cream. Why that dessert is my weakness, I will never know, but he has figured it out and is using it against me. I haven't had anything sweet since I started sleeping in the bathroom, and the temptation is overwhelming.

"I don't want to sleep in the bedroom," I say in my last act of defiance.

"I never said you had to."

His voice is deep, muffled by the door. But I can hear the hope in it. Why does he care? I am nothing to him but a conquest and a slave. His kind treat mine like animals. Even though he's been decent for the most part, that doesn't detract from the overall situation.

I have no self control, and I am resigned to hate myself for this betrayal as I stand and press my hand to the box on the door. I shiver as it tingles against my palm and unlocks. Pax stands at his full height, more disheveled than I am used to seeing him. I cross my arms and jut my hip out, looking around for this ice cream I was promised.

"Well?" I growl.

"First, I want to apologize for breaking your rule. Please reconsider your sleeping spot. Not only is it inconvenient, it is not healthy."

I grit my teeth against the urge to roll my eyes.

"I've slept in worse places," I say, defensive. His eyes waver with different emotions, ones I cannot decipher. I have never been very good at reading people. Erathians are even more difficult.

"I don't doubt that. But don't punish yourself for my actions, Liv. That's not how this relationship works."

"And how does it work, then?" I say, glowering. His jaw clenches. He has stubble, dark, across his cheeks and jaw and chin. It makes his eyes seem even darker.

"It should be symbiotic."

I am lost, having never heard that term before. He must see my confusion, but I refuse to voice it out of embarrassment. He is intelligent, educated. I am not.

"Meaning two different species living in close contact and benefitting from one another."

I tap my foot, mulling this over.

"Yeah, well, you get a maid that has to be chained up and punished, and I get—"

"Look, I don't want to argue. I just wanted to apologize. Take it or leave it."

He's frustrated. He reaches up, gripping at his tousled hair. I glance around him, out the big bay window. It is dark, the sky littered with stars, and across is another stone building used for housing these creatures. No light seeps from other windows into the night, though. We are alone in this moment. I don't see any benefits to how I have been acting. Even if I want to take a stance against him, he will always win. He will win and rule until I escape.

I need to stop being petty if I want a chance at that.

"Fine," I grit out.

"Thanks," he grunts back, clearly annoyed. I peer around him, looking for my ice cream.

"Sooo..."

He juts his thumb in the direction of the kitchen.

"It's on the counter."

I avoid his gaze, skirting around him as I pad to the kitchen with cold toes. I have missed sleeping in a soft, warm bed, and he works well as a heater. My eyes widen as they fall on the dessert. It's in a big, clear plastic bowl, with bananas, and

chocolate, and *strawberries*. My stomach gurgles again in anticipation.

I feel his presence behind me. I turn, giving him a half
smile, feeling sheepish now.

"It's called a banana split," he explains.

I am confused, though, that there's only one.

"Where's yours?"

He snorts and shakes his head, crossing his arms and
leaning back against the island counter.

"It's all for you. I don't need one."

I turn back to the melting ice cream, pulling open the
drawer that houses spoons and the like. I hold one out to him.
His face slackens as he uncrosses his arms.

"I can't eat it all," I say with a shrug. That's not totally true,
but I don't feel like puking up cream and sugar later when I've
overindulged. He gives a gentle smile, taking the spoon and
picking up the bowl. I follow him to the living room where he
turns on the TV to some random show. I retrieve my blanket
from the bathroom, nestling into the plush couch. He sits,
close, holding the bowl for both of us.

"Go on," he encourages, nodding to it. I dig in, my mind
reaching a high of euphoria. It has been so long since I have
been able to get steady meals, and they never tasted this delicious. He chuckles, taking heaping scoops that rival mine, but I
let him.

After a while my stomach is hard, but I just need that last
bite. I let the frigid ice cream melt on my tongue, the chocolate flavors bursting and biting in contrast to the vanilla. But
there, in the midst of such an explosion of flavors, is an
innocuous little morsel. Confused, I chomp down and swallow, but it is only then I realize the flavor. My eyes widen, my
body stiffens.

Pax doesn't notice, still chowing down on his portion of the
banana split. I wait a few minutes, just to be sure, but then I

begin to feel all the telltale signs. How did one damn peanut sneak past? Or was this his plan all along?

"Liv?" he asks, bumping shoulders with me to pull me from my shock. I turn my gaze to his, and he immediately turns dark, serious and menacing.

"What's wrong?" he hisses.

"Pea-peanut," I rasp. I know, in my rational mind, I have enough epipens nearby to save me, but that feeling is new to me. I'm used to a situation such as this truly being life or death. Pax jumps up, striding to his room and returning with the familiar cylindrical tube. I reach for it, but he pulls away.

"I know how," he says, and by the authoritative note to his voice, I am surrendered at his will. I whimper as I feel the effects of my reaction. He stands me up, yanking down the band of my pajama pants. I am stunned, cheeks flaming to life in utter embarrassment.

"Pax—" I gasp, pushing his hands away. I can't be this vulnerable around him. All it does is bring back floods of abhorrent memories. He ignores me, seating himself on the couch and pulling me to his lap as we both face the fireplace. I watch, shaking, as he unsheathes my lifeline. And then, my eyes hone in on the needle.

A scream claws its way up my throat. I throw my shoulders back against his chest, but he catches me with strong, unrelenting arms.

"No, no, no, not anymore, p-please!" I scream through the hoarseness in my tightening throat. His arms clamp around mine like a vise, his legs also trapping my thrashing ones. He doesn't hesitate as he plunges the needle into my thigh and injects. My skull thuds against his shoulder as I strain to get away. He tosses the empty syringe aside, using his knuckles to rub at the spot on my thigh.

I am crying, blubbering, wavering in and out of reality and fiction—reality and my past. My torture. His hold on me is unyielding as exhaustion sweeps through my veins. It is then, as I finally begin to calm, that I realize why he took control of this situation.

He knew.

He knew I would see the needle, that I wouldn't be able to do it myself as I have done so many times before. I crumple in his arms as a new wave of tears constricts my throat and wets my cheeks. I have always been able to fend for myself, and now I am some broken thing that must rely on a stronger being to care for me. I am withering away, fading into their world seamlessly. And I can't even fight back anymore, not when I am crippled at the mere sound of thunder or a firework, or frozen at the sight of a needle.

He lifts my hips, turning me to face him. I can't look at him, and I don't want to, so I bury my face under his chin and sob. It is easier to realize you're weak when you don't have to face the thing that makes you weak.

He smooths his palm up and down my back, saying nothing, his other arm tight around my hips. I am hiccuping, my tears having run out after quite some time, but he is still holding me.

"You need sleep," he finally croaks. I am too wiped out to argue him on that. I wonder if he has work, and I feel bad for keeping him awake for so long. I just nod, my cheek rubbing against his soft t-shirt. He stands, pulling me up into his arms as though I weigh nothing. Once he's settled me into bed, he ducks out to change. I am almost asleep by the time he returns.

I feel him climb in beside me, feel the cool draft of air against my bare legs. I stiffen, remembering my pajama bottoms are abandoned in the living room.

"Come here," his deep voice demands through the darkness. I don't move right away, but he doesn't seem to notice or care, shifting until he is close, until he circles his arms around me and tucks me into his embrace. I am thankful our legs do not touch, and I am reminded of his many promises to me. He will not assault me in such a degrading way. He never has.

"You put the peanut in there on purpose, didn't you?" I say after a moment. He becomes rigid, but a chuckle soon tumbles from his lips. He understands my way of joking.

"Oh, Livy. I've invested far too much into you now to kill you."

I roll my eyes at his chest before I yawn. He chafes my hip with his wide palm.

"Go to sleep, strange little human."

10

Olivia

I awake feeling refreshed. The bathroom floor did me no favors and taking a stupid stance like that got me no closer to my freedom. I will have to remain on Pax's good side, if I want to get any good chance at running away. Part of me is thrilled at the idea, while another part is terrified.

What if I fail and get shot by the guards? What if I fail and get sent to another torture chamber? What if I get caught by Pax and he decides to kill me?

My heart is racing at all the thoughts, so I shove them away. The day is bright and sunny. I wonder if he has gone to work. I throw back the blankets, staring at my bare legs. My pajamas are in the living room. I frown, jumping down and padding to the door and down the short hall, hoping he is gone to work.

No such luck. He sits on the couch in a pair of grey sweats and a t-shirt, sipping coffee from his navy blue mug and reading a thin, crinkly newspaper. We used to get those delivered to our home when I was a child, but as the wars began, the news stopped mattering. All that mattered was surviving our impending genocide and enslavement. My stomach turns into knots. My eyes dart to the floor, but my pajamas are nowhere in sight.

I feel sheepish, going out in just my underwear, but all my other clothes aren't really meant for lounging. Pax sets down his coffee, fluffing out the paper and grunting something.

"I can hear you, you know."

I jump at his deep voice, my hands darting down to cover the bareness of my legs, even though he can't really see me from this angle. He peeks over the corner of the newspaper, frowning at me.

"Come."

"No," I mutter. He sighs, shaking his head.

"If this is about embarrassment, there's no need. If this is about something else, then I would hope you would voice it to me."

I just want my damn pants.

"Where's my pajamas?"

Yes, it is about something else, but the thought of talking to him about Brutus anymore makes me feel sick with dread.

"Hamper," he says, a coy smirk playing at his clean shaven face. He looks better today than he did last night. Last night, when he held me as we fell asleep. When he saved my life because I was too frozen to do so. He's already seen my bare legs. He's never hurt me the way Brutus did.

I take a timid step out, feeling warm sunshine on my legs. He shifts, patting the couch seat. I raise my chin, remembering the way he walks, so austere and confident. I feel confident as I march forward, until I stub my toe on the coffee table and fall onto the couch with a hiss.

He's laughing and shaking his head, that dimple on his cheek visible. I grumble, pulling the blanket around me to stay warm. We fall into an easy silence, my eyes scanning the print of the newspaper. I catch him glancing at me out of the corner of my eye every few minutes. I am frustrated, because I want to read, I want to know what he is seeing, but I am too ashamed of my shortcoming to ask.

"Do you work today?" I ask instead. He leans forward and grabs his coffee.

"Nope. It's the weekend."

"Oh," I mumble. We slip back into silence. After a few more minutes, he sighs, the sound annoyed.

"What?" I ask, defensive. Is he annoyed with me? He glances at me, his brows pulling together. Eventually, he points to big, blocky letters.

"Political shit."

"*Language*," I mock. His nostrils flare as he glares. I pull my knees up to my chest and give him my most winning smile. He lets it slide with a cock of his head, and I am thankful.

"What is political?" I ask, truly curious. His frown deepens as he folds up the newspaper and tosses it to the coffee table. He stretches an arm out behind me across the back of the couch and sinks down a little further. He smells good, the scent strong in my nose, familiar now. I like it, finding that I associate it with a sense of comfort. I feel myself relaxing.

"I doubt you remember, but humans used to elect leaders into power. Those leaders put laws into effect, and policies and so on. Humans knew who they were voting for, which is very strange for us Erathians."

"Why?" I say, confused. He shakes his head, scratching at his jaw.

"Because, we elect leaders based on policy only. We do not know their names, or see their faces, or hear them give speeches. We are tasked with the duty to go through everything they wish to change and implement that could alter our lives, and we make the best decision based on what we see on paper."

I nod. It makes sense, but I know nothing of past politics, so I cannot compare anything.

"So why is it shit?"

His eyes dance at my use of foul language, but they are warm today, like melted chocolate woven through with honey. He doesn't pinch me, and it feels as though we are conversing as equals. I find I enjoy it—I find him intelligent, and I want to know more. Maybe it will help me when I escape.

He lets out a big sigh.

"Because, this is an election year for Sardone. It's the most expansive kingdom, so there is a lot at stake. Most wish to re-elect the current person in charge, since their policies have been rather outstanding. But there's a large group who is vying for control by putting the opponent in charge, and I do not agree with that person's changes they wish to enact."

"Like what?"

His gaze turns dark. I fold my hands together under the blanket, feeling chilled.

"For one, this person seeks to double raid missions without increasing the number of rangers. Meaning my job will become a thousand times more difficult."

I feel the confusion on my face. I knew Pax was a ranger, but is his job only to keep humans in line by enslaving them or killing them? It is a question I am unwilling to ask, for I am afraid of the answer.

"What else?"

"They seek to exploit slaves. We have laws, dictating what is acceptable as far as treatment of humans. We cannot force children to work in factories or...*other* places."

The way he says *other* makes my skin crawl.

"Slaves owned must be registered. They wish to do away with that, meaning the black market that already exists will flourish under this person's rule."

I chew my cheek as I stare up at him. He is stoic and serious as he usually is, but I never thought I'd see him heated over the terrible treatment of humans.

"You care...?" I ask, puzzled.

"Of course I do, Livy. Why do you think I took you?"

I am stunned, blinking away the shock.

"So you could have someone clean for you...?" I mutter in question. He chuckles, but the sound is dark.

"Liv, if any other Erathian owned you, you would be beaten daily or dead by now."

For some reason, his words sting. Have I not been at least somewhat obedient? Have I not attempted to learn his stupid rules and how to cook and clean? I feel tears threaten. He must see them.

"Hey," he says, his voice low, gentle. He drops his arm around me, pulling me into his side.

"I didn't mean that to be rude. I'm just trying to get you to see that I *do* care how humans are treated, ok?"

I hide my face in his warm side, breathing in the scent of cedar wood. I want to be angry with him, but I know he wasn't being cruel.

"You still enslaved me," I mumble. He surprises me by chuckling.

"Oh, Livy. Someday, you'll understand why I did what I did."

Pax

We spend the day relaxing. I feel as though we both could use it. Liv showers and dresses while I prepare to show her a lesson plan. Today feels like a good day to introduce education to her. She seems more open and willing to listen.

"What's that?"

I turn in my seat, stacking together her writing books. I wave her over. She is dressed in her usual jeans and t-shirt, this one white and flowing, and her hair hangs damp and wavy across her shoulders. Though she is slender and still slightly starved in appearance, I can see she is filling out, becoming healthier, and her face is bright and flawless. She comes closer, brows puckering in curiosity. I reach for her waist, pulling her onto my lap. She sets her pale fingers on my oak desk. I can hear her nervous heartbeats.

"Every weeknight, I'd like to take time to teach you things."

She doesn't respond other than to shift her hips and settle more comfortably in my lap.

"Like what?" she says finally.

"Like writing, and reading," I say, reaching around her with one arm to grab a thick writing book. It is meant for Erathian children, but I don't feel as though I should share that with her. We as a race adopted and assimilated with humans in nearly every aspect, for it was easier that way. I've known no other way of writing or speaking, so this comes naturally to me.

Her fingers skim over the glossy, vibrant cover of the book. I hold her to me as I lean around and flip it open. She points to a letter.

"A," she says. I chuckle.

"See? You won't need much help. You're too smart for your own good as is."

Her heartbeat changes for a moment, speeding up before settling back down. She flips through the pages, and I watch the side of her face. She is smiling as she tucks her thick hair behind her ear, but her gaze drifts up to my bookshelf. She points.

"What's in all of those?"

I lean up, gripping her so she doesn't slide off my lap, and grab one of my favorites.

"Mostly boring stuff for work, but there's some stuff for fun."

I place the book in front of her, the cover a gentle, faded

green with embossed gold lettering and borders. She hesitates to touch it until I hand it to her. She holds it delicately, turning to glance sideways at me.

"*The Fellowship of the Ring*. Fantastic work. The author was human."

She gives a small grin, but it fades, and something intense enters her gaze.

"I want to read it."

"You're more than welcome to."

Her shoulders slump in defeat as she reaches to put it back. I stop her hand before I hold her wrist.

"I can read it to you, and once you get better, you can read it to me. It will be good practice," I say with a shrug. She bites her lip and nods with a small smile. Strange emotions begin to swirl within me again. She's been so open today. I am enjoying her presence, but on a different level. In this moment, she feels like an equal—like a friend.

The buzzing of my phone breaks our gaze, and I reach for it, reading through the text quickly. I sigh, tossing it aside. I hadn't wanted to leave the house today.

"What's the matter?" she questions. I rub my forehead.

"There's a new possible recruit that wants me to give him some pointers for the physical aptitude test. How do you feel about going to the gym with me later?"

She frowns.

"I don't want to see Deidre."

I chuckle, hugging her closer to me, feeling her warmth, my hand splayed across her thin waist.

"No worries, she won't be there. I think we should do that, then order some pizza."

She stiffens and attempts to jump from my arms, but I hold her down in confusion.

"What—"

"Let's just go *now*!"

I am laughing at her eagerness.

"Ok, ok, let me go get ready."

We are soon on our way to the gym, and her excitement seems to fill the car. It is nice to be back in her good graces, something I have missed for the past little while. She stares out the window as usual, face pressed close to the glass. It is sunny, the day warm as summer draws nearer. With a devious smirk, I unroll her window. She yelps, falling forward before turning to glare at me. Her chocolate and caramel hair whips about her face in the wind as her bright green eyes glint.

I chuckle, turning my attention back to the road. Her chain makes a tinkling noise as she moves to sit on her knees, raising her butt in the air to get a better view out the open window. Her shirt flutters up in the breeze along with her silky tendrils, and I am given a glimpse at her naked, slim waist that curves out to her hips, where her blue jeans paint her skin and follow the subtle curve of her ass to the backs of her thighs.

I grit my teeth, feeling hot and flushed—feeling something akin to arousal as I stare at what is rightfully my property. If I was an Erathian with loose morals, could I force Liv to fornicate with me?

The thought sends a searing pain into my chest. No. I could never find forced intimacy arousing. Just the thought of how fragile she is, of how broken she would be mentally, is enough to make my head pound in pain.

Something else occurs to me, then. Brutus, the fucking bastard, obviously found her attractive, had no problem hurting her in such a disgusting way. Jeven has made his jokes about how *hot* she is for a human. I've caught a few Erathian males checking her out when we run errands. But until now, I've never thought anything of it. Humans are below us for many reasons. Because of our superior strength and healing, and our brilliance, we are the dominant species. Why, then, do the men of my race continue to be drawn to these delicate, weak women?

It is a conundrum that will have to wait. I pull into a spot, helping Livy out as we make our way inside.

"Remember, eyes on me or the floor, and do not talk to anyone, ok?"

She frowns.

"Do I have to go in that stinky room?" she asks as we walk side by side. I chuckle.

"Stinky, huh? But yes, you do. I'll be quick."

She sighs, puffing out her cheeks. I can see she wants to argue, but I knew I had her when I said we'd order pizza. She is too tempted by food to disobey very much. I have found her weakness. We round the corner as a few men are coming out, and she ducks her head, skirting closer to me—close enough that her shoulder bumps my arm.

She is usually more leery of being so close to me. Perhaps this is a good sign, a sign she trusts me. I test this, turning my palm over, giving her the opportunity to come even closer. We enter the locker room, and I feel her small, cool hands on my forearm, holding me. I glance down at her in surprise, walking us to a bench in the corner. Her head is down, her shoulders are hunched, and she is gripping my arm close to her chest.

It is difficult to hear her heartbeats in such a cavernous space, but I feel it jump by means of her pulse. I stand before a locker, gently nudging her to the bench. She obeys, sitting, folding her hands into her lap as I stow my things and lock up. No naked men barge in like last time, so she seems more at ease.

"The guy I'm training is named Theo. I've only met him a few times, but he's Jeven's friend. He wanted me to prepare him to test to become a ranger," I explain. She peeks up at me, wary, but it is empty in here today. Her brows crunch together.

"What is your job?" she asks, quirking her head to the side. I sigh. I should have known this was coming at some point.

"I will explain that when we get home."

"Because I won't like it?"

She is astute, but that is not the full reason.

"Partially. But there are things I am not allowed to speak of for security reasons."

Her eyes brighten, and she straightens. She is curious.

"But you'll tell me?" she whispers. I feel a small smile on my face.

"If you can keep a secret, then yes."

Her face warms, and she nods quickly. I jerk my head to the exit.

"Let's get going. I doubt this kid can last through one of my workouts."

She stands, giving me a sly grin.

"I bet *I* can."

I chuckle.

"You know, Liv, I bet you can, too."

Olivia

"Hey," Pax says to a stocky, medium height man. He is young, with sandy hair and light brown eyes.

"Hey, Paxton, thanks for coming to help me out," the man replies, sounding eager and sincere. So far, I like him better than Jeven. They shake hands.

"Call me Pax. This is Liv," he says, jutting his thumb at me. Theo nods in my direction, but otherwise doesn't pay me much attention. I am relieved. I'm not here to make friends. Only here to scope out escape routes before I go home to pizza.

Pax takes us to the middle of the gym. There's some huge contraption, with bars and ropes and hoops. It looks familiar, like something I used to play on as a child at the park, but on a much grander scale. Pax leads me to a mat, handing me the end of my chain and his water bottle. I know what he expects, so I sit as he crouches down to give me his damn *rule* talk.

"I know, I know," I say, bobbing my head before he can say anything. He cocks his head to the side.

"I haven't even spoken yet, Liv. Are you giving me attitude?"

"*Me*? Give attitude?" I scoff. He frowns, but there is mischief in his warm eyes. "The nerve," I say, smiling. He finally snorts, shaking his head and grinning, his dimple visible.

"God, I can't even be mad at you right now. You're getting too witty, you know that?"

I smile, shrugging.

"Just be good, and call me if you need me."

I nod, settling in to watch this spectacle unfold. It is interesting, watching Pax work with someone seemingly below him in status and knowledge. You would think he would be arrogant, rude, but he is patient every time Theo messes up an exercise or forgets a sequence to his obstacle course. It becomes apparent after a while that Pax is a born leader—calm, authoritative, smart, and insanely strong.

I remember being stuck in different groups of humans on the run after the Settlement was destroyed. Some young men would inevitably try to become the ones in charge, but they were all horrible, and nothing but fights ever came from their messy leadership. It was annoying to have some cocky kid think they knew everything, when in reality, I probably knew more.

I watch as Pax jumps easily and grips a bar, his body swinging for a moment, before he pulls his chin up past his hands. It's easy to be mesmerized as I watch his thick arm muscles strain, veins bulging with effort to continue supplying blood to his working body. I lose count of how many times he does this in quick succession, not even seeming tired. He drops down, and Theo is shaking his head as he chuckles, hands on his hips. His face has been blotchy with a sheen of sweat since they began.

I enjoy watching their interactions, observing from afar and learning more about this man that technically owns me. In my heart I know my fate could have been far worse. Nothing will ever replace my freedom, and nothing will ever stop me from trying to escape, but at least I am stuck with someone who...*cares.*

His eyes catch mine and he saunters over, crouching down and plucking his water bottle from my hands. So unassumingly confident. He could control this entire kingdom with ease if he wished to.

"Just a little longer," he says before he takes a long drink. I bob my head, circling my arms around my legs. The urge to urinate overcomes me in a flash, and I rock in an attempt to alleviate the pressure. He gives me a curious look.

"What's wrong?"

I frown, feeling slightly embarrassed, but I know I shouldn't feel that way with him.

"I have to go to the bathroom," I whisper, chewing my lip. He chuckles, looking toward the hallway that leads to the locker room. The gym is empty today, only a few men over in the heavy weights section and a group playing basketball on the court.

"There's a bathroom right across from the locker room that you can use. Come right back, ok?"

He stands and I follow, nodding. It is strange, going somewhere without him nearby, with the end of my chain in my own hands. I scurry off, feeling exposed without his protective shadow. I find the bathroom and do my business, smoothing down my loose top and adjusting my jeans as I open the door.

My head is down, and I see more than one pair of shoes blocking my path. My heart stutters in trepidation as I stop in my tracks. I cannot see Pax or any other part of the gym. I need to round the corner before I do. I take a chance, peeking up.

Four sets of dark eyes watch me. It is a group of young men, looking closer to my age. One has a basketball under his arm and a malicious smirk on his face. He is the tallest of the four, but he is thin. It doesn't matter. Fear still ripples through me. I need to get back out to Pax.

I take a step forward, and he mimics my movement. I stop, casting my eyes down once more.

"Ex-excuse me," I say, my voice wavering, my confidence gone. In the face of a bunch of Erathians, I have none. My time at the Facility taught me that.

He snorts, and the others move in closer, too. I take a step back, trembling.

"Where's your owner, human?"

My eyes snap to his in a glare.

"I don't have one," I sneer. He takes another step closer, but I hold my ground, emboldened with fire.

"Lucky me, then."

I have no time to react as he lunges forward, dropping his basketball and pulling me to his sweaty body, covering my mouth with his hand. I twist and scream and struggle, but the others join, holding my legs and torso.

"Fuck, you ever seen a human so fine before?"

"Can't wait to get in that ass."

"I wonder which dumbass owns her."

"He won't want her when we're through."

Their voices mingle and huff as they struggle to subdue me, pulling me into the men's locker room. I feel angry tears, and I am already exhausted from fighting. Even though they aren't as built as Pax, they are much stronger than me.

I am tossed to the ground as pain shoots up my wrists and spine, and before I can scream, water blasts my face. I can't even open my eyes or make a single sound. My body freezes. No, no, no. It is happening again. I feel the panic rising in me, feel my chest heaving and my world tilting as cold water soaks me. Hands grab at my clothes, but I slap them away, still blinded by fear and the torrents of water spewing down on me.

I am whimpering, crying, confused as I waver in and out of the past. I hate this. I hate that this is who I am, now, after all I have been through. I fall to my side, curling into a ball on the slick tiled floor of the showers. Or is this the water room?

Someone forces me onto my back, straddling me. Another pries my wrists from my chest and holds them above my head. I make the mistake of blinking, of opening my eyes to witness my fate. Two stand off to the side, guarding the entrance. One holds my arms. The one on top of me has his pants down. I pinch my eyes shut as he fondles himself, feeling bile rise in my throat. Deidre wasn't lying.

I kick and thrash, and then I feel it. His fingers on the button of my jeans, then my zipper. I feel cool wind, hear the sounds of the rushing river, smell the scent of dirt and trees. I am back, tied to that tree, surrendered to my fate. And I scream.

Pax

It is blood curdling, the scream that echoes from the locker room. And I know who it belongs to. Ice and fire fight a war in my veins as I storm in the direction of Livy. My vision pulses with fury, and I shake out my arms, preparing to battle.

I made my promises to her.

And I intend to keep them.

They stand, laughing and mocking her, never seeing me coming. I reel back, cocking my fist and connecting to a young man's temple. He thuds to the ground before the others can even figure out what is happening. I grip another pair of shoulders, twisting them to face me as I pull back my head and brace myself for my own impact. My forehead connects with his as a sickening thud reverberates through the space. I throw his limp body to the side like a piece of trash.

The one holding Liv's wrists releases her, wagging his hands and pleading, but I am on him faster than he can cry out like the fucking coward he is. I envelope his throat with my hand and slam him into the wall with enough force to shatter the tiles. He slides down to the ground as consciousness leaves him.

The one on Liv stands, foolish enough to take a stance as though he wants to fight. We are both soaked. I know why they drenched her. They believe humans are unclean, and in Erathian culture, a metaphorically wet woman is a whore, even lower than an animal.

I wait until the scum throws his first punch, all the while listening to Liv's choking sobs. The sound cuts through me more deeply than anything I have ever felt before. She is mine. Mine to care for. Mine to hold. Mine to protect.

I have failed her yet again.

I grab his wrist, twisting his arm back and up before throwing him to the slick ground. I drive my knee in between his shoulder blades, keeping his arm at a very precise angle. He is crying like a blubbering, sniveling child, pleading and begging for me to stop.

"Didn't seem like her tears meant shit to you, motherfucker," I hiss, using all my strength to wrench his arm back further. The sound of his dislocating joint sends a thrill through me, and his screams and howls of pain make me grin.

I am heaving, wishing to spill more blood, but all my mind centers on now is Olivia. I stand, turning off the taps to stem the flow of water. I know Theo is in here, I know the gym attendants are as well, but I ignore them all.

She is shivering in the corner of the shower, sobbing. Her white shirt is soaked through, giving everyone a clear view of her simple white bra, her hair dark and plastered to her face in thick tendrils. I need to get her home. I need to be alone with her. I do not need witnesses for what I wish to do to her right now. I step forward, closing our distance, crouching in front of her.

"Olivia, come here."

I keep my voice as gentle yet commanding as possible. She whimpers in response, teeth chattering as she peeks one eye at me.

"We need to go home."

She is afraid of me, afraid she is in trouble. I can see her, balancing on a dangerous cliff as she thinks this through. Her face crumbles when she realizes my anger is not directed at her.

"Pax," she croaks, voice hoarse as a new wave of tears comes over her. The way she says my name tells me how broken she is. She is too afraid to move. I reach out, pulling her up into my arms, feeling for myself how cold she is.

I ignore everyone who stands gawking, gathering my things and leaving without a backwards glance.

Olivia

I am curled in a ball on the bathroom floor as Pax runs a bath. Steam swirls up and chokes the air. I can't even think straight. I have never felt more helpless in my entire life before. I am unharmed physically, but my mind is another matter altogether.

I have also never seen Pax become so enraged before. It is truly a frightening thing to witness. He is skilled, controlled—lethal. There was no emotion on his face as he easily fought those men off me. No emotion other than a kind of fury I have never seen on anyone's face before. I watch his back as he leans over the tub, testing the water. He is trembling, his whole frame quaking. I shrink, nervous. I thought he wasn't mad at me.

He turns to me after shutting off the tap. His jaw is clenched, his eyes dark. He reaches for me, and I am too numb to shy away. He attempts to pull my shirt off, but I finally snap to reality, kicking away until my shoulders hit the wall. He stops, his eyes locked on me as his nostrils flare.

"You need to bathe, warm up."

His voice is monotonous.

"I can do it by myself," I mumble, hugging my stomach. His eyes blaze.

"I am not leaving you."

His words are curious. I do not understand why he won't let me do this by myself. It has never been an issue before. He is still trembling as he watches me.

"I'll be fine," I whisper, avoiding his gaze. I am embarrassed he had to see me that way earlier, and I feel guilty that he had to rescue me.

"Dammit, Olivia, I'm not leaving you!" he says, his voice rising in pitch and desperation. I jump at the sound, eyes stuck wide on his face. He's never yelled at me before. I feel a new wave of tears coming.

He lets out a hiss of a breath, turning his face to the door before wiping at his jaw. He falls back onto his butt, eyes still locked on nothing. The air is heavy, charged and intense. His body is still shaking, but now so am I.

"I'm sorry," he grunts. He refuses to look at me. His reaction to this whole thing is throwing me off. If he's not mad at me, then who else could he be mad at? Those other men?

And then, it hits me.

He's furious with himself. I blink a few times as I see him anew. He's upset for not being more careful with me. He...*cares*, truly. He didn't want to see me hurt. He never has, but I am just now realizing it.

I scoot forward, my drying jeans beginning to stiffen, my toes and fingers clammy and cold. He's right, I need to warm up, but I don't want to right now. He always makes sure my needs are taken care of first. He always lets me eat first, lets me use the bathroom first, lets me choose stupid shows or recipes I want to try.

He is selfless when it comes to me. Perhaps I can return that selflessness for once. I scoot forward some more, watching my shaky hand reach out for his arm as my heart hammers. His keen eyes snap to it, then to my face, his brows furrowing. I rise up until I'm sitting on my knees. He is confused, but he shifts, dropping his legs, spreading his arms.

I close the distance, carefully climbing onto his lap, wrapping my arms as far around his torso as I can as I hug his hips with my knees. His shaking ceases. I tuck my head under his chin, closing my eyes. He smells like his usual self, more masculine now that he has worked out *and* saved my life, but it isn't bad. It is comforting, being close to him, knowing he is capable of protecting me.

He doesn't hold me back at first, but as the tenseness in his body begins to ooze away, his arms encircle me, holding me so tight it becomes difficult to breathe. How I ever hated him is now a mystery to me. I want my freedom, but having someone who has been unconditionally there for me is filling a void in my life that I've had since my mother's death. It isn't something I ever knew I was missing until now.

"I can't live with myself, Olivia, knowing what I've put you through."

His words rumble through him, thick with emotion. They sear through me, and I pinch my eyes shut as a shiver runs up my spine. I doubt I can make him feel any better right now, but I want to try. I swallow the lump in my throat.

"You've never done to me what those other people have," I whisper. He scoffs.

"I knocked you out with the butt of my rifle. I backhanded you, punched you, kicked you—tied you to that fucking tree," he breathes, his hold on me tightening even more. I shake my head against his chest, against the memories. I blame him for the things he did to me himself, but I can't blame him anymore for the way his society treats me. I know that if he could change it, he would.

That thought hits me, *hard.*

I squeeze him tighter. There is only one thing I can say that I think will work at this moment. I don't know if I am truly ready, but he needs to hear them.

"I forgive you, Pax."

Everything stills, suspending in time as I wait for any sort of response. He says nothing as the minutes tick slowly by. But eventually, he hugs me tighter, resting his cheek on my damp head.

"I will never let anyone hurt you, Olivia. Never again."

My chest feels full and tight at the same time. He is being sincere. It is easier for me to read him now.

"I know," I mumble against him. He is warm, but the longer I sit here, the colder I get. He seems to feel it.

"Do you need help?" he asks. I pull away, shaking my head. He is frowning at me. He still doesn't want to leave me.

"I don't think the shampoo bottle is going to attack me, Pax," I say. He cracks a smile, smoothing his palm over my back.

"No, but I'd blow it up if it did."

I suppress a giggle, hugging my stomach as I shiver. He sighs, falling serious once more.

"I'll order dinner. Take your time. I don't want you to get sick, alright?"

I nod. He leaves me be to soak, and I do eventually warm up. My thoughts, though, are all over the place. There is nothing I can do at the moment to change my situation, and so I know I need to be content for now. A chance to run will eventually arise.

Will I be able to take it when it happens, though?

PART II

THE DARKNESS OF STARS

"I was just an only child of the universe, and then I found you."
—Fall Out Boy

11

Pax

I t has been a few days since the gym incident. I am still on edge, and Liv hasn't left the house. She's been compliant, though. Every morning, she wakes up with me and insists on making coffee while I shower before work. I think she does this so she can have more than one mug, but I let it slide.

Each evening, I return home to find her sitting on the floor, using the coffee table as her desk while she works on tracing her letters and sight words. She's almost through her first workbook. I shut the front door, shedding my jacket and beret, rounding the corner to see her perched on the couch, watching a lecture on astronomy.

She turns, giving me a bright smile. Warm afternoon sun makes the caramel tints in her hair shine. I walk to her, gripping the back of the couch, listening to her lecture. There is free reign of which topic she wants to study, but this is the third time she's chosen this type of course. I wonder what it is that fascinates her, but I am also happy. Astronomy is my favorite.

"Learn lots today?" I ask to the top of her head. She leans

back, smiling at me upside down. Her body is wrapped in her favorite blanket, a mug of tea on the side table.

"Mmm hmm."

I quirk my brow at her. She's up to something. It is easy to see by the way her eyes shine. She either wants something, or she's done something questionable. I straighten, crossing my arms.

"What sorts of trouble did you get into today, Liv?"

"Nothing!" she quips, too innocent.

"Don't lie," I chide. She blushes, cheeks a light shade of pink. Her heartbeat quickens. She knows I will get the truth, one way or another.

"Ok, ok. I tried to bake a cake, but I couldn't figure out what meant what...so...I kinda used all the flour and eggs..."

I sigh, shaking my head with a chuckle. It could always be worse with her, I suppose.

"Did you at least finish your chores and work?"

She nods quickly.

"This is actually my fourth lecture today, thank you very much."

I hate to admit I am impressed.

"Good girl."

I check my watch. Now that I am out of eggs, I need to go to the store. I was planning on making a breakfast hash for dinner.

"Get everything put away and cleaned up so we can make dinner. I've gotta run to the store—"

She jumps up, turning around to face me as she sits on her knees, her eyes pleading.

"Can I come with?"

I frown. After the hell of seeing those men attacking her, the last thing I want to do is parade her around town. For a human, her beauty is obvious. She is a target.

"I don't know, Liv..."

"Please?" she begs, drawing out the word, her brows risen in the middle. I can't deny her. She's been on her best behavior, only giving me attitude in the morning or at night when she's tired.

"Let me change. Clean up your things and put them away," I say. She beams, jumping up and pattering all around the living room like a tornado that cleans instead of destroys. Part of me wishes I could have witnessed her cake baking disaster today.

She is waiting for me by the door, wearing her black leggings and a gray, long sleeve shirt. The clothing is tight, showcasing her growing curves. I frown, feeling a hint of rage enter my veins. If I catch a single man staring at her, I will lose my shit. On the flip side, I do not wish to tell her what to wear, especially because a selfish part of me likes the view.

I grit my teeth, berating myself. She is my slave. She isn't *that* kind of slave, though. I hold out my hand, and she rolls her eyes as she gives me her wrist. My fingers curl around her slender bones, so fragile.

"Attitude, Livy," I remind her, giving her fair warning before I pinch her. She simmers down as I tighten her chain, fastening it to my belt loop. She tugs on it, frowning.

"It's shorter," she whines, gem-like eyes sweeping to my face as she pouts.

"Not because of anything you did, alright?"

Something flashes across her face, and I can see she understands before she averts her eyes, chewing on her lip. We make our way out into town. It is bustling at this time of day, Erathians rushing from one place to the next. Liv sticks close to me, but stops in the middle of the sidewalk, causing me to bump into her.

"Liv?" I ask. She points to the coffee shop I took her to, the one Tarex works at. Shit.

"Can we...?" she asks, her voice sweet as sugar. I want to do something to make her happy, but there is no way I am going to come face to face with my one night stand.

"Uhh...hey, after the grocery store, why don't we stop at the pet store? You've done really well with your studies lately," I say, praying she takes the bait. Her cheeks lift in a winning smile as she nods. I am relieved.

We start forward once more, the sunshine warm, with a touch of a cool breeze. The grocery store trip is quick, Liv being more helpful than a nuisance for once, even reminding me we are out of coffee and bread. Her excitement grows more with each step.

A bell chimes on the door as we walk into the stuffy, humid pet store, a kind elderly man behind the counter. He pats the glass top, and I thank him, setting my bags aside. Liv is already tugging me toward yapping puppies.

"What brings you in?"

"Just browsing," I say, nonchalant, tugging her back to my side. I hear her annoyed huff. The man nods with a kind smile, and we turn to wander through each aisle at a painstakingly slow pace.

"Look, Pax!" Liv says, her voice breathy with excitement. I am staring at a tarantula, grimacing, when I feel her little hand slip into mine. I glance down at where we are joined, her hand so small in mine. It doesn't bother her, reaching out to me, touching me. I feel warm at the thought as she tugs me forward.

"It's the...what was it called again?" she asks, peeking up at me. Her hand is still in mine as we stand before a wide glass cage. I hunch down, inspecting the contents, finding the little furry rodent on its wheel.

"Hamster," I say.

"Oh! He's so cute!" she gushes. I watch her as she watches the tiny critter, her eyes alight, her face glowing. I feel myself begin to smile, and I squeeze her hand.

The little gray and black hamster is fast, cruising on his wheel before he jumps off and runs to the glass where Livy is peering in. He stands up on his hind legs, exposing his fluffy white belly, pressing his tiny pink paws to where her nose is. I am resigned to my fate before I even have a chance to consider another option. I stare down at an enraptured Liv.

"What would you even name a thing like that?" I ask. She shoots me a glare.

"It's a *hamster*, not a thing, Pax. And…I don't know…he looks like a Henry, I think," she says, carefully considering her choice. I snort.

"Henry?"

The hamster is still pawing at Liv.

"Yup," she quips, turning her attention and smile back to him. I brush my thumb over the back of her hand.

"If it gets loose in the house, that's on you," I say. She rolls her eyes, but then goes rigid, straightening up to stare at me in confusion.

"Wait…what?" she asks, voice quiet. I can't help but smile

"You can have Henry, but you're getting punished for your eye rolling and other instances of attitude when we get home," I say, keeping my voice stern. Her face goes slack, her eyes wide in shock.

"Really?" she asks, hopeful and beaming. I chuckle, nodding.

"Yes. Let's get this over with," I say, wondering how much I am going to regret this.

∽

Olivia

"Bed time, Liv," Pax says as he marches into the bedroom. My stomach is still full to bursting from the dinner he made, but I am laying on it anyways, staring into the glass box that houses my new pet. Pax said he could sleep in our room on the floor until he made too much noise, to which I rolled my eyes. Henry pokes his nose out of his tiny log cabin, whiskers twitching. I grin, still in shock and awe that Pax bought him for me.

"Liv, come on. Hamsters are nocturnal anyways."

I hear him crawl into bed, so with a sigh I comply, standing and pulling back the covers before I roll in. With the days getting warmer, I find that sleeping wrapped up by Pax's body with all my layers is quite stifling, but it feels weird to go to bed without pants. I am resigned to suffer through the summer, it seems.

"What's nocturnal?" I ask, falling back onto my pillow. He is still sitting up, setting his alarms for work tomorrow, the muscles in his arms flexing. It is then I realize he is shirtless. My mouth runs dry at the sight of his scars. I continue to wonder how he got them, knowing that it can't be good. He was pretty pissed at me when he showed them to me the first time.

"It means he will sleep all day and run around all night," he explains, putting his phone on his nightstand. He glances down at me.

"You full from dinner?"

I nod, eyes wide. I haven't overeaten like that in a long time.

"You're still in trouble for your attitude," he says. I grit my teeth, wondering how he wants to punish me now.

"Just pinch me and we can go to sleep," I say, faking a yawn and rolling over. His deft arms catch me, pulling me to him and across his lap with my butt in the air.

Dammit.

My heart thuds hard in my chest as I attempt to peek at him.

"Three paddles. Fair?"

"Ugh," I groan. Why does he have to ruin a good day?

"Liv—"

"Ok fine," I relent. He still hasn't found my knife. I'm kind of worried for the day he does. He gives me no warning as he rids me of my pajama bottoms, but I don't mind this time; I was already beginning to roast. I tense as his palm rubs across my butt, reminding myself he's always been easy on me, even when I probably didn't deserve it.

I jump as the first smack sounds, but the sting is nothing to me. The second feels a tad harder, and the third harder still, but it's over. He picks me up, putting me on his lap. I avoid his eyes, instead studying the vast array of scars over his chest and abdomen. The sight makes my stomach churn. How painful were some of these? How did he get them?

"....Liv?"

I shake my head, missing the beginning of his question.

"What?" I say, looking at him. He is frowning.

"I asked if I hurt you. You're crying," he says, his voice deep, dark. I am? I wipe at my cheeks in haste, feeling the betrayal of my emotions on my face. I shake my head.

"No...no you didn't."

"Then did I scare you?" he asks, so earnest, looking so lost. I bite my cheek, considering. No, he didn't scare me, either. What the hell is wrong with me? I feel like there is a bubble in my chest, growing quickly, ready to explode.

"What's wrong, sweetheart?" he asks, his voice so gentle. He sounds hurt. My ears perk, though. This is the second time he has called me that. My family used to call me that, amongst other nicknames. It makes me feel warm, as though they are still here somehow. And then, out of nowhere, more tears constrict my throat.

"Livy?" he breathes, pulling me into him, tucking my head under his chin as a sob shakes me. Why do I feel so sad all of a sudden? We were having a good day, until he decided he still needed to punish me. Maybe that's why? I don't know. I feel confused, a mess, and all I want is ice cream. Chocolate ice cream, to be exact.

"Shh, shh," he says, rocking me. "You're safe, Liv, you're home with me. I've got you."

His words plummet into my soul, and a wail escapes me. I am tired, and I hate him, but at the same time I want him to hold me tighter, but I also want him to let me go, to give me my freedom. I feel overwhelmed. I finally control my crying, sniffling and hiccuping.

"Be honest with me, Olivia. Did I hurt you or scare you?"

"No," I say. "I just...I don't like it when you're mad at me... when we're having a good day..." I say, trying my best to vocalize my rampant emotions. I feel him nod, feel his rough, warm palms slide under my shirt to grip my hips. I shiver at his touch, ticklish.

"I'm not mad, Liv. Not at all. From now on, I'll address it in the moment instead of saving it for later, ok?"

"Ok," I sniffle against him. He shifts, reaching for something on his nightstand. A faded blue leather-bound book is in his hands with silvery writing on the cover. It looks like the green one that he showed me from his bookshelf. I sit up, wiping my cheeks before I shiver, finally cooled down but now feeling cold.

"Want to start this series?" he asks, a small, hopeful smile on his face. I bob my head.

"Here, turn around," he instructs, picking me up before settling me back down so I am between his legs and we are both facing the door. I tense, not liking this position, not liking that I cannot see his eyes. I am more defenseless this way, and even if I trust him, there will always be that part of me that is weary.

He pulls the blanket up to my lap, circling his arms around me, the book resting on his leg. He is warm as he surrounds me, his thigh muscles thick as they cage me in. I pinch my eyes shut, thudding back into his chest. Brutus forced me to sit this way before he shoved my face into his crotch.

I feel his hands on my arms, rough and warm, bringing me back from the brink. He's always been warm. I begin to relax.

"Remember, you're safe, Livy. I'm not going to hurt you."

His voice is a low rumble as he releases my arms and instead hugs me from behind, resting his cheek on the side of my head. I heave a shuddering breath, trying to push those awful memories away. I feel the soft bed beneath me, feel his body around mine, smell the cedar wood scented soap he uses.

He waits as I relax, and when I do he picks up the book, thumbing past the first few pages. I understand now why he is holding me this way; he wants me to see the words, to learn. I feel silly for being afraid at first, especially of him. I nestle further into his embrace, feeling tired, comfortable.

"This isn't the same book," I point out. He chuckles, reaching up his fingers and pulling my hair aside so it rests on my shoulder, giving him a clear view of the side of my face.

"No, *The Hobbit* is the first, so I figured we needed to start there. Actually...*The Silmarillion* should be read first, but...yeah, this will do."

I feel myself smile at the sound of his voice. He is genuinely excited.

"I'm ready, then," I say, turning to peek up at him. He is already looking down at me, small smile on his lips. I stare into his deep brown eyes, feeling secure. I like the way he is looking at me right now. I feel something, in my chest, a fluttering feeling. His bare chest rubs against me as he shifts, and I can't shake the urge of wanting to press my cheek to him, to feel his smooth skin.

I swallow hard, still lost in his gaze. He is handsome. It is the first time I am seeing him as such, but it has been obvious all along. Erathian women watch him constantly, and even slaves chance a glance at him when their masters aren't looking. I feel sort of prideful that I am owned by someone who is coveted by others. I feel as though I may be his, but that also means he is mine, right?

He clears his throat, and I feel myself blush, having stared too long. I turn back to the book. He holds it with one hand, and his other sneaks down my side until he is gripping my bare waist where my shirt has ridden up. He's touched me before and does so often, but here and now, it feels...*different*. More meaningful, somehow. I like it.

He begins to read, his low, husky voice enchanting me as an entire new world jumps from the pages.

~

Pax

I know it is late when my eyes flutter open. It is dark, humid—a storm must be ramping up, but that is not what woke me. My heart jolts as my hands pat the empty bed. It is cool. Liv has been gone for some time.I am about to panic when I hear it.

Soft sniffles and quiet cries. I sit up, peering over her side of the bed and down onto the floor. She is sitting there in her t-shirt and pink underwear, tears coating her cheeks as she holds something. Fuck. Did Henry die already? I am afraid to face that issue, if that is the case.

I am slow and cautious as I stand. Her heartbeat quickens—she knows I am awake, that I am walking toward her, but her face is down, avoiding me as she continues to sniffle. I crouch across from her, concerned and nervous, but the little hamster is sitting quietly in her palm, cleaning his whiskers. I fall back onto my ass, confused at her emotions.

"What's wrong, Livy?" I say. I still feel nothing but guilt for punishing her, for ruining her perceived *good day* with me. I don't want her to be nervous around me, but I feel I have crossed a boundary that will be difficult to remedy.

She brings her sorrowful eyes to me. They are so wide, round and innocent. I grit my teeth. I want to pull her to me, to crush her into my embrace and soothe her, to protect her from her own thoughts.

Liv holds up Henry for me to see. He is so calm in her hands, sniffing at her, turning around to lick at her nose. I witness a ghost of a smile as he does this, but she is still distraught.

"He's living in a cage, Pax," she whispers, voice hoarse. I feel stricken at her words and what they imply. She sees herself reflected in this tiny, helpless animal. He is at her mercy, and though I know Liv has likely the kindest soul I have ever come into contact with, she still sees herself as the monster for wanting him.

I know, because it is a battle I have been facing since she was attacked at the gym. I wipe at my jaw, wondering how to bring her down from the emotional roller coaster she's been on today. She's more sullen than usual, and I can't figure out why.

"Liv...he's meant to be a pet. You've given him a home, isn't that a good thing?"

She shrugs, sniffling still. I sigh, running my hand through my hair.

"He's a prisoner..." she whispers. I feel my chest tighten. Does she see herself as my prisoner?

"Livy, you have a kind heart. But if he wasn't adopted by you, he'd probably be some kids' who wouldn't care for him the way you will. You've already given him a ton of treats, he loves being held by you, and he's in a nice, quiet home. What's so wrong with that?"

Again, she shrugs, running her finger across his head and down his back. I've never seen a hamster sit so still before. The damn thing is attached to her already.

"But...what if he has a family out there?" she says, a new wave of tears coming. I sigh, scooting closer until our knees touch. She still doesn't look at me. I quirk my head to the side, studying her.

"Why do you think he has a family out in the wild, Liv?"

"I don't know," she mumbles. That is a dead end for the moment, but I take note of it. I realize I have never asked if she has any surviving family members. I assumed that they were dead, since I found her seemingly alone. I know, from my debriefings, that only the woman survived our capture. I can only assume she has been sold or sent to work in the factories. Liv never seemed too fond of her, so I doubt they are related.

"Well, let's say you let him go. What do you think would happen?"

Her eyes flash to mine, her brows furrowing in thought.

"He'd go find others to live with?" She phrases it as a question. I shake my head, frowning.

"He'd get eaten, Livy, by a cat, or a hawk, or he'd be run over by a car. Say you let him go in the wild, how would he find food?"

"He's smart, he would," she shoots back, defensive. I hold up my hands in surrender.

"So he finds food. Then he has to build a shelter, stay warm through the winter and dry from all the rain. What if he never finds his own kind? What kind of lonely, hard life would that be?"

Her shoulders hunch. She holds the little grey ball of fluff up to her cheek. Henry sniffs her before licking her tears. Her smile is deeply sorrowful.

"I just don't want him to hate me," she whispers finally. I shake my head.

"Liv, no one could ever hate you, especially Henry. He loves you so much already. Look at how calm he is in your hands. He *bit* me," I say with a chuckle. She cracks a smile, giggling, peeking at me from under her lashes. Her face is washed pale by the moonlight, but in it her eyes sparkle and shine.

"You've given him a home, and unconditional love, and a purpose. He will live the best life because of *you*," I say. Her round eyes widen, her pupils dilating the smallest bit as she stares back at me.

"Because of you, too," she says, verging on defensive. I falter at her words. She is giving me credit, seeing me as *good*. It makes me feel hopeful. I offer her a gentle smile.

"Let's let Henry get some running done so we can get some sleep, ok?"

She nods, pressing a kiss to his head before gently placing him into his cage. The little critter zooms to his wheel and hops on, seeming to show off as he pauses and looks around for Liv. I chuckle, watching her smile. She's on her hands and knees, her round butt right in my line of sight. I lock my jaw as my eyes feast on such a view.

She is beautiful, from her heart to her body. I never thought I would see her as such, but I do. I sit up until I am on my knees, leaning across her back and wrapping my arm around her waist. She stiffens as our bodies touch in such a primal position. I hadn't intended it to be sexual, but in reality, it very much is. My mind jumps to fantasy before I can stop myself as I imagine what it would be like to have sex with her in this position.

I pinch my eyes closed, gritting my teeth as I breathe through my nose, but the thought is still playing in my mind. Would she like it? I doubt it. She's still scared of me in some ways. I could never do that to her, property or not.

I cough, clearing my throat as I hoist her up by her waist. I turn her until I am carrying her, cradling her to my chest. Her hands dart up, wrapping around my neck in fear I will drop her. She still doesn't understand the strength we Erathians are capable of.

We lay back onto my bed while I pull her on top of me. She rests her head on my chest, her body slack and relaxed. I trail my fingers up the backs of her thighs, enjoying the silky feel of her skin. I do not want to stop touching her, and I am at war with myself. She would give in to me and my desires, this I know, but she would do so out of fear. She knows I can overpower her, and so she wouldn't struggle.

That is not what I want. I want her to...what? *Want* me? I am her master, her owner. She will never want me as long as I hold that power over her.

"Pax?" her tremulous voice whispers. I am pulled from my dark thoughts, and I realize my hands are gripping her hips, holding her tight to me, as though she will disappear.

"Hmm?" I say.

Her shaky finger reaches out to my pec, and she traces a particularly jagged scar. I still beneath her touch, feeling fire where her cold finger trails. My heart thumps erratically. I am a mess tonight, from wanting to fuck her, to now having her touch me in such an unsolicited way.

"How did you get these?" she finally whispers. The question and subsequent memories are enough to pull me back from fantasyland. I feel my mind growing dark, and I feel her tense on top of me in fear. I release her hips, wrapping my arms around her, pulling the blanket up around us. I do not want to share this with her, or anyone.

I never have.

But how can I expect her to reciprocate when I don't share myself in some capacity, slave or not?

I suck in a deep breath before I sigh.

"I...survived, Liv. From darkness that I pray you will never know," I whisper into her hair. She says nothing. We fall into sleep, her fingers still tracing my scars.

12

Pax

I am exhausted as I sit through the morning's debriefings. It is taking much longer than normal, but that is to be expected in the current climate. There is civil unrest in certain parts of the city of Sardone, the capital of the kingdom, where we live. A few other cities to the east are displaying the same symptoms of rebellion.

My commander, Tark, rubs at his forehead as he explains what we should look for while surveilling the CCTV's. He is becoming more grey by the day, now. He is ranger 001. When he retires, I will ascend to his position. I can't help but feel resentful toward that notion, for I don't want that much responsibility.

He coughs, reaching for his mug and taking a long sip before he clicks to the next slide. Jeven visibly tenses next to me. Kel, Brutus, Dax, and a newly promoted man named Kip all groan. The photo is of a map with elevations marked out, a dotted red line leading to a target. Tark chuckles at our misery.

"Enjoy your warm showers, boys, we ship out in three weeks."

My stomach sinks. I know my duty as a ranger—knew exactly what I was doing when I signed up for this job, but the excitement that once came with raiding is now replaced by dread. Dread, because I do not want to find more humans. Dread, because I do not want to leave Olivia behind. Raids can take anywhere from a week to a month.

I pull out my notebook and pen, shoving aside all my other woes as I jot down notes and listen carefully. Tark makes a good point, letting us know that if Opponent Two is elected into office, this will become our lives. I know which way I will vote, and it is insane to me that the other men of my unit are still so unsure. They are tempted by the looser restrictions on slave ownership, though.

Tark releases us, and I pack up my things, pulling on my beret as I fish my keys out of my pocket. Liv had a hard night with all her crying, so I feel I should check up on her while I have some free time in my duties. The slap of boots on concrete makes me turn. Jeven is jogging up to me, wide grin on his face.

"What now?" I grunt. He claps me on the shoulder as we continue forward. He is out of breath. He wouldn't be so out of shape if he worked out with me more.

"New guy needs some hazing, don't you think?"

"No," I say, shrugging off his hand as I reach my vehicle.

"Aww, c'mon, we haven't had a get together with the group in a while. Should be a good time bonding before our next big trip."

I grit my teeth. Jeven is always positive, but sometimes his optimism is too much. He has not seen the world as I have. He has not seen the true darkness that is just outside our kingdom walls. It is one thing to decimate a threat from the safety of a rooftop, but it is another thing entirely to come face to face with it.

"My place, Friday night. Bring what's-her-name," he says. I unlock my car and pull the door open.

"Who?" I growl.

"Please, keep acting so high and mighty. Your slave, idiot," he says, leaning on my hood so I can't leave. God, I want to run him over.

"I'll think about it."

"Good, because I want to hear all about that pussy—"

I glare at Jev, starting my vehicle and revving the engine to drown out his words. He chuckles, backing away and saluting me. Fucker. I stop at the store with the idea to get something sweet for Liv. That usually brightens her up, and she did try to bake a cake yesterday. I choose a few chocolate cupcakes, excited to see her excited.

"Livy?" I call out as I enter our home, pulling off my hat. I hear no response, but the space is clean—untouched. It is past noon, but it seems as though she hasn't even been awake. I am annoyed. I let her sleep in based on our late, tumultuous night, but this is too far. I stomp into the bedroom, pausing when I see her.

She is curled on the floor with a pillow and blanket, fast asleep with her fingers pressed to the glass of Henry's cage. I sigh, frowning. I cannot be mad at her when she does such innocent things as this. I leave her be, setting her cupcakes on the counter before I sift through some mail that was in the box. My eyes bounce up as I hear a small whimper. I toss the mail aside, striding back toward our room.

"Liv?" I call out so I don't frighten her. I pause at the door, staring down at her. She rolls, her face pinched and pale. My brow knots as I come closer, crouching down to her and pressing my hand to her forehead. She is warmer than usual, but it is not a fever.

"What's wrong, Livy?"

Her face is devastating, and she sucks in a trembling breath, about to cry. I note the way she is curled, clutching at her stomach.

"I...I don't feel good," she says finally. I am immediately worried. Has she somehow contracted an Erathian virus or disease? Did *I* give it to her? Or is this a human sickness?

I reach for her, pulling her and the blanket up into my arms before I walk us out to the couch to better assess her. She seems zapped of energy as I sit down, her cheek resting on my shoulder. I coax her up until she is straddling me, capturing her cheeks with my palms. There are rings under her eyes, which are puffy and swollen from crying, and there is a hint of yellow at the tops of her cheeks. Her body is weak, sick.

"What do you feel?" I ask, more worried now. She hasn't even dressed. She seems to hate being around me in just her underwear, but at the moment she doesn't even seem to notice.

"Just...like I'm gonna throw up...and my...my stomach hurts so bad..." she says, still hugging herself. Though Jeven is our medic, I still know enough from training to be able to rule out certain things. Gentle, I grip her wrists and pry them away from shielding her stomach before I press my fingers to her lower right side.

"Here?" I ask. Humans have an appendix, which can rupture. I learned that in one of my human books. She shakes her head, lips puffed in a pout.

"Here?" I press beneath her sternum. She shakes her head. She reaches up, grabbing my wrist in her delicate hand, guiding my fingers down, down, down. I feel my face grow flushed, but she stops just above the band of her underwear.

"Here," she says. She reaches behind to my hand that is holding her back, lowering that one as well.

"And my back, down here, too," she explains. By the tone of her voice, I can tell she is in severe pain. I wrack my brain.

"Have you ever felt this before, hun?"

Her cheeks turn a light pink, and she bites her lip.

"I...maybe...but it was a long time ago..."

I shift, pulling her off me so I can call Jev.

"I'll be right back," I say. Her wide, emerald eyes follow me. I tap into my phone, and Jev answers, his mouth clearly full.

"Decided to tell me about—"

"Shut up. She's sick, I need your help."

I hear his exasperated sigh on the other end.

"So worried about a little human. Never thought I'd see the day you cared about anything other than yourself."

"And who was it that saved your ass from the quicksand two raids ago?" I growl. He sputters and coughs. I know I have his attention now.

"Ok, ok, what are her symptoms?"

"She's kind of warm, not feverish. Umm...her lower stomach hurts, and her lower back...I don't know how long this has been going on, but she's been crying way more than usual—"

I am interrupted by his laughter.

"What is so funny, asshole?" I growl.

"Shit, was wondering when you'd call me freaking out about this."

"What?"

He's pissing me off.

"You need to take her to a physician that specializes in human women. I'd take the day off and do it now, *before* she starts bleeding everywhere."

"Wait...what the fuck are you talking about?"

I am met with more laughter. I am beyond worried now, but he doesn't seem to be.

"Trust me, I found this out the hard way with Deidre. Imagine enjoying a nice fuck and then looking down at your dick thinking it was somehow massacred."

"You're not helping," I growl through clenched teeth.

"She's going through...what do they call it? Menstruation? I don't remember. Deidre takes care of herself now when that happens, but the first time was a shit show."

Fuck.

"Fine, where do I take her?"

He lists off a few places. I jot them down, sending a message to my commander. I never take time off, so all my accrued hours for leave are just piling up. At least I can use them on Liv, now.

I go back to the couch where she is curled into a ball. She peeks up at me, misery written on her face. I do not understand what human thing is happening to her, but I cannot stand seeing her hurting.

"Can you get dressed? I'm taking you to a doctor to make sure you're alright," I say. Her eyes go wide with panic as she sits up.

"No, no, no please!"

I come around the couch, seating myself next to her, pulling her to me. I don't want to be stern with her right now, flex my authority, but I will if necessary.

"I will not leave your sight. When we get home, you can have all the cupcakes I bought you, ok?"

Her tear filled eyes waver.

"What kind?" she sniffles. I chuckle, pulling her into my embrace.

"Chocolate, of course."

13

Olivia

"Dr. Andrews will see you now," the male nurse says from a doorway. Pax stands, holding my hips as I slide off his lap. He's changed into jeans and a t-shirt, the grey color clashing nicely with his dark hair. I do not want to leave his side, and he has promised me he won't, but I am still frightened he will somehow be lying to me.

We are led back into a room with a few chairs and a long table covered by paper. The memories of such a place are faded, yet somehow familiar to me. Pax sits, and I follow, attempting to sit back on his lap. The nurse leaves, the door clicking closed.

"You need to sit on the table," he says. I stand between the two, holding myself. I shake my head, and he sighs, unfurling his arms. I take my chance, not caring if I appear desperate or weak. He is the one thing I know, the one thing I sort of trust, so I fold myself onto his lap, hiding my face in his soft shirt.

We stay silent as the minutes tick by, until a knock sounds on the door. I jump, but his hold on me remains firm. A tall, older woman pokes her head in, a beaming smile on her perfect face. I shrink into Pax. Even these Erathian women are intimidating with their height and dark eyes.

"Hello, Mr. Harper, I am Dr. Andrews," she says, shaking his hand and ignoring me. She moves to the sink, washing up and drying before putting on some gloves. Her eyes never stray to me as she sits on a rolling stool in her perfectly crisp lab coat.

"Thank you for getting us in so quickly," he says, his voice deep, different. He talks this way in front of other people, like he is so official and stern. He doesn't talk this way at home.

"Of course. What seems to be the problem?"

"She's saying her stomach hurts, and her back...her temperature spiked a little today as well."

The doctor gives a sympathetic nod, her blond and grey ponytail bobbing as she does so.

"Alright, I will run through a list of questions, and then we can examine her and figure out what is going on. How old is your pet?"

I bristle at the word she calls me, and Pax's arms tighten. He knows I am upset.

"Eighteen."

"And has she ever experienced these symptoms before?"

I feel Pax look at me. I give a small nod, not meeting anyone's eyes.

"How long ago?" she asks to him. I shrug. Hell if I remember. I was more concerned about food and shelter and not getting captured.

"Not sure."

The doctor sighs, sounding annoyed.

"Has she been more emotional lately?"

"Very much so."

Screw you, asshole. You would be too if you felt like this.

"She was captured from the wild near on two months ago, correct?" she asks. I feel him nod.

"Alright, and history of sexual activity?"

Both Pax and I stiffen. I feel a deep blush rise in my cheeks. He coughs, clearing his throat.

"Umm, none."

"Ok, well Mr. Harper, based on symptoms, age, and her overall appearance, I'd say your pet is close to menstruating."

"Umm...ok?" he says, phrasing it as a question. She quirks her brow before she gives a breathy laugh.

"Ahh, another man new to this process. I'll give you some pamphlets before you go, but I can explain briefly right now."

"I'd appreciate it," he says. She clasps her gloved hands, holding her knee.

"Female humans reach sexual maturation much sooner than Erathians, sometimes as young as eleven."

I can hear Pax gulp, feel his heart thud harder in his chest.

"Seriously?" he asks, sounding shocked. She chuckles and nods.

"Yes, and unlike Erathian women, they are fertile once a month versus once every eighteen months or so. It is a strange evolutionary byproduct, but it ensured chances for quick impregnation. When a human does not become pregnant, their body floods with hormones, and they will bleed for typically a week before this process starts all over again."

"So...once a month she will go through this?" he says, still shocked. I feel stupid for not realizing it was my damn period. I got it once when I was twelve, and then my mom died and it stopped for a few years, and then I just hadn't seen it since. I didn't know it was supposed to be once a month, either.

"Precisely. My guess is she was so malnourished and stressed being in the wild that her body shut down such processes. Human pregnancy is fragile, and their bodies will fight to give their species the best chance of survival."

I feel him nod.

"Going forward, there are many options Erathians use to

remedy this issue, especially males concerned with interruptions in their sexual activity."

His hold on me tightens again.

"Remedy?" he asks, his voice dark. She gives him a sympathetic look.

"She is going to be highly fertile, and tracking that can become tedious. Pregnancies can arise easily."

Pregnancy? Wait what?

"What do you suggest?" he grits out.

"We can remove her sexual reproductive organs. Her healing time will be a tad lengthy, and she will be placed on replacement hormones to keep her moods balanced."

I feel myself drain of color, feel clammy with dread.

"Absolutely not."

"Alright. Another route most take is tying the tubes that release mature eggs. Less recovery time, and you do not have to worry as much about hormonal balance."

"No," he grits out, beginning to tremble. Thank God he seems as pissed as I am at this shitty doctor. I don't understand this whole process of how exactly a baby forms, and I have never thought about having kids, but I don't want this freak messing with my body, especially a part of me that feels so...*sacred*. A part of me that makes me *me*.

"The least invasive route is birth control. There are pills, implants, shots...all prevent ovulation, therefore preventing pregnancy, but those are not as effective as surgeries."

"Can we skip to the non-invasive routes?" he grits out. I peek up at the underside of his chin. His jaw is clenched, his veins throbbing. He looks red, angry. Is he angry for my sake? The thought makes me feel warm, protected.

"Of course. You can simply track her cycle, looking out for symptoms such as mood swings, cravings, cramps, blemishes and fatigue. She will need to wear feminine hygiene products—"

"Let's just get some of that," he interjects. She is becoming flustered by his surly attitude. Good. I've been on the receiving end of his bad moods for a while now. It's time I watch him take it out on someone else.

"Well, Mr. Harper, it depends on which kind you want her to use."

"Whatever kind she wants," he grunts. For the first time, the woman's eyes flash to me, and there is nothing but hatred in her cold gaze.

"I will send you home with instructions and different options. You will also need to be aware of any changes in her breasts going forward. Humans have a disease called *cancer*. It is curable now, but only if caught early. I will demonstrate how to check, and you must do this once a month."

Check? Check how?

The lady pats the crinkly paper table.

"Have your pet undress completely so I may examine her."

No, no, no. *Hell* no. I am not getting naked in front of these two. I begin to shake my head, but Pax gently pinches the back of my arm.

"I am a trained medic for a ranger unit. Tell me what to look for and I will do so myself."

He's lying. Why? Because he knows I will freak out if she touches me? The woman sighs, really annoyed now.

"Mr. Harper, with all due respect, this is my profession, and I must keep track of all females in case a disease breaks out, or—"

"I don't think you heard me correctly," he interjects, his voice dark, deep and menacing. It makes my toes curl in my shoes in fear, and I retreat further into his embrace. The doctor is stunned.

"She is mine, and I dictate who touches her. Thank you for the information, it has been insightful and helpful," he says, standing and pulling me up with him. I am nervous, clinging to the back of his shirt with one hand and the front of his shirt with the other, cowering into his side. I feel myself begin to breathe rapidly. *He's not going to leave me*, I remind myself. He's here, he's taking me home.

The doctor stands, jaw locked tight, her face red.

"You can settle with the front desk. They will give you everything you need," she says, cold as she opens the door and clacks out. I breathe a sigh of relief. I feel Pax chafe my side, and I glance up at him. He's frowning down at me.

"Do you know how to use those things?"

I flush, shaking my head. I only ever was given something to put in my underwear, and I remember hating the feeling of it. He turns a few shades of red.

"Looks like we're both in for a lesson today, Livy."

∽

Pax

"They've been in there for a half an hour," I grunt, pacing in front of the bathroom door. It is late afternoon now, and after reading through everything the doctor gave us, we both decided it would be better if someone else helped her out. Someone who actually knew what she was going through. There was no way I could sit in there and attempt to show her how to use this thing called a tampon. I shiver at the thought of where it resides in her body for the duration of this hellish week.

"Calm down," Jeven says as he watches the rugby game on TV. His feet are on my coffee table as he reaches for a beer and shoves chips into his mouth. His nonchalant attitude is pissing me off. He cheers at a rough hit, and I slump beside him on the couch.

"I don't understand how you handle this human shit," I

mutter, feeling drained. I saw a side of society today that was darker than I could have ever imagined, and the reading material was even worse. Jeven shrugs, but I can tell he's listening.

"They wanted to take out her...what's it called? Uterus? The spot they grow babies?" I say, glancing at him. He sighs, setting aside his beer to level me with a serious look. I am surprised. Jev is usually the more joking type. He scratches at his jaw.

"Yeah, they wanted to do that to Deidre, too."

He seems bothered by that notion. I cross my arms, speculating.

"And what did you say?"

"I said fuck no. That would be like getting our balls chopped off, right?"

He has a point. Erathian women have essentially the same parts as a human woman, but they have different scientific names for them. Either way, those parts are what make them who they are. It is utterly cruel to imagine ripping that away from Liv and forcing her to be on hormones for the rest of her life.

"Yeah, true. How did you handle this, then?"

He chuckles and reaches for his beer again.

"I asked the professional."

"And who would that be?"

He nods to the bathroom.

"Deidre. We went home and I asked her what she wanted, and we came to an agreement."

"That being what?"

"The first two years I had her, I had no clue they had implanted a contraceptive device in her. It was old, so we had that taken out. She's on a pill now so there's little to no chance of pregnancy. The week of her period, I buy her whatever she wants to eat and don't touch her in any sort of sexual way. It's worked out well for us, I suppose," he says with a shrug. I am surprised. Deidre makes it seem like Jeven is evil, but this kind gesture from him doesn't seem that way at all. I nod as I absorb his information.

"So, how is she in bed?" he says with a wink as he jostles my arm. I grit my teeth as I glare at him.

"She's not that kind of slave."

Jev shakes his head, chuckling.

"So defensive. I bet you are curious. How can you not be? She's pretty damn sexy, with that whole wide-eyed innocent vibe."

I grip my jaw, feeling the stubble beneath my fingertips.

"I couldn't do that to her," I say finally, staring at the coffee table. Jev sighs, setting aside his empty beer bottle. I feel his eyes on me, but I can't look at him right now.

"You know, when I bought Deidre three years ago, she was Liv's age."

I am surprised. He's never talked about how he came to own her. I glance at him, at his deep frown. He nods, turning back to the TV as he muses about the past. He breathes in a big breath, scratching at his neck.

"She was living in a cage at this store, covered in dirt and blood. She was filthy. Couldn't even look me in the eye. I just needed someone to cook and clean, because I am shit at it, so I figured even if she was shit, we could make it work, right?"

I chuckle at his reasoning.

"I got her home, was trying to clean her up...and she freaked...it took two years, but she finally came around, told me everything she had been through prior to me owning her. That was the first night we fucked," he says with a laugh. I wipe at my face, laughing with him.

"I...told her not to tell anyone. I was embarrassed. She's a human, she's below me, but...it was so different, so much better. I don't think I could ever sleep with an Erathian woman again."

I feel my brows rise in shock.

"She...well, she's kind of a brat, so we had to figure out how to give one another what we wanted and needed. She's not too crazy about sleeping with me, but in return she gets whatever she needs or wants. Sometimes she even initiates sex."

I nod. I am still surprised Jeven seems to have such a soft spot for his slave.

"So, better how?" I ask, curious. He snorts.

"I think I need another beer for that."

I grab him one, kicking his feet off my coffee table in the process. I pop the top off one for myself. After today, I deserve some booze.

"Humans are...so much softer, in every way. They are kind of fragile, delicate. And fuck...them being so much smaller, they are so tight," he says, shaking his head. My mind floods with racy thoughts about Liv. She is tiny, fragile. I enjoy holding her while we sleep, knowing she cannot escape, but also knowing I can protect her.

He nudges me conspiratorially.

"I bet Liv is going to be *way* tighter," he says with a laugh. I flare, feeling possessive. I do not want to fuck her, and I do not want anyone else getting ideas. But part of me is highly intrigued, and quite aroused, if I am being honest with myself.

"Why do you say that?" I ask, bringing the cool rim to my lips. Hops and wheat mingle on my tongue.

"She's a virgin, right?"

"A what?"

"It's what humans call those who haven't had sex."

"Oh...I...I mean, I would assume so. *We* haven't done anything," I say. He snorts.

"Well, unless she had some boyfriend before you or she was forced, she's probably a virgin."

"Should...should I ask her?"

He shrugs, looking back at the TV. My mind wanders back to when we captured her. She was shoving a boy around her age toward a stairwell. Brutus shot him. Was that her boyfriend? Someone she had shared herself with? No, there's no way. She didn't even know what fucking meant until Deidre told her.

I shake my head.

"No, she is one."

"Lucky you. But also, good luck when you try. Make sure she's good and ready."

I punch his arm, and he hisses.

"What the fuck was that for?"

"Don't talk about her like that," I grumble.

"So touchy. Are you on your period, too?"

"Fuck off," I growl. We fall into silence for a while, and I keep checking my watch. I can hear their hushed voices, and the toilet has flushed probably a thousand times, but they've yet to emerge.

"How do I make her feel better? None of the books I read had any pain relief instructions, but they all said that women could suffer through days of pain reaching levels of eighty PTs," I say. In Erathian terms, PT means Pain Threshold. It is a scale of one to one hundred. The thought that a woman could have pain that high for that many days is insane to me. Jeven frowns.

"Yeah, it can get pretty bad. I read that during labor, they can cross that threshold, get up to one-twenty or higher."

I feel nauseous at the thought. I have endured horrific amounts of pain before, so part of me feels as though I can sympathize with her, but another part of me knows I cannot.

"She's small, so you can give her two painkillers every four to six hours. Try a heating pad on her back or stomach. D likes warm baths and tea. She also becomes way more clingy. She likes to cuddle and cry," he says with a laugh. At least I did one thing right by getting her some chocolate. I make a mental note to run to the store and get her more pain killers and a heating pad.

"What are you going to do with her during our next raid?" he asks. I frown. I hadn't given it any thought.

"Probably take her to my parents' farm. They could always use the help."

He nods, absentminded.

"I take Dee to my sister's. I put her in a boarding facility once, and she came back way too shook up. It's not good for them, being locked up like that."

Don't I know it. I am about to go check on them when the door slides open. Liv is white as a sheet, keeping her eyes down as she emerges. I stand, my eyes locked on her. Deidre comes around, standing in front of her in a protective stance as she glares. I am stunned at her boldness.

"All good?" Jeven calls from the couch.

"As long as he keeps his hands off her—"

"Dee," Jev says, his voice low in warning. She grits her teeth, still glaring at me with her strange amber eyes. Livy shifts behind her, reaching up to pat her arm before she whispers.

"He won't, he promised me."

"Good," Deidre says, giving me one last look before she skirts around me. I stare down at Liv in surprise at their newfound camaraderie, and I quirk my brow at her. She peeks at me, sheepish, as she twists her hands together.

"You ok?" I ask. She bites her lip and gives me a small nod. I can hear Jev preparing to leave.

"I've got to run to the store. Take a bath and I'll be back," I say. She is confused, but she is too tired to fight me.

"Ok," comes her little voice. I reach out, tucking my fingers under her chin, raising her eyes to meet mine. She gives me a small smile. I can tell we are alone, Jev and his slave by the front door. She shocks me as she reaches out, wrapping her thin arms around my waist in a hug. I fold her into me, hugging her back as I smooth my palm over her hair.

"Be a good girl," I say. She nods against me. Unable to stop myself, I lean down and press my lips to the top of her head.

Olivia

I am sitting on the couch, wrapped up tight in my favorite blanket, waiting for Pax to get home. Today has been awful in some ways, but good in others. I hadn't thought he would care this much about me, about my pain, but he seems to be in a sort of pain himself. I am thankful, yet again, that Pax is my owner, that I don't have someone who would have forced me to have surgery. To get *fixed*, as Deidre called it.

A cramp surges through me, and I groan. I finally started as soon as Deidre got here. It was embarrassing, but she made me feel better about all of it. We tried a few different options before she talked me into tampons, saying they were way less messy and you didn't even feel them. It took me a while to learn how to do it, and all the while I could only think about what Brutus did to me.

She seemed to know where my mind was, and she shocked me by sharing her own horrific stories. Before Jeven bought her, she was a slave in something called a brothel. They got rid of her when she was eighteen because she looked too old. I shiver, thinking about that, thinking about how lucky I am. Was I a fool to ever want my freedom? Was I a fool to hate Pax?

It is strange, these emotions I am feeling. Deidre warned me about the highs and lows of hormones. She was right on one thing, though; all I want to do is curl up next to Pax. He is capable of fending off four attackers by himself. He is certainly capable of making me feel better, right?

The door slides open, and I can hear the rustle of grocery bags. I peek over the back of the couch, surprised to see so many. I stand, intending to help him, but his warm eyes catch mine, a ray of light from the sunset washing his face golden.

"Go sit, Liv, I'll bring this over to you."

I bite my lip and nod, returning to the couch, listening as he bumps around the kitchen. He approaches, holding a few things as he seats himself next to me on the couch. I sit straighter.

"First, take these," he says, holding out two white pills and a bottle of water. I obey, knowing what they are. He then holds out a square piece of thick looking fabric, pressing a button on one side before holding it between his big palms, his face pinched in concentration.

Finally, his lips turn up in a smirk, and he holds it out to me.

"Lay down on your back," he says. I frown, but obey, my hands resting below my breasts. Gentle, he presses the square to my lower stomach. Warmth spreads through me immediately, and I relax with a contented sigh as my pain begins to ebb. He is smiling down at me, and the pressure of his palm across my stomach is actually helping stem some of the pain. I feel like I can fall asleep and stay that way for days.

He lets me relax as he tidies up and makes me tomato soup and grilled cheese for dinner. It is amazing, and after dinner he lets me eat as many chocolate cupcakes as I can. I feel sick, bloated, but sated. He's watching sports, the heating pad back on my stomach, my feet in his lap and his hand still pressed to where the cramps emanate.

He even bought me a pair of shorts for pajamas in the summer, and a loose tank top. I changed into them after dinner, feeling special that he has chosen to dote on me so much today. He brings a glass to his lips, and this time I know it is whisky. I want to ask to try, but the thought of what it tasted like last time churns my stomach.

I eventually fall asleep, only to be jostled awake as Pax

carries me to the bedroom. I feel him slide in behind me, pulling me into his body. I tense, my back pressed to him, but his lips are at my ear, his voice husky as he whispers.

"You're safe, Livy. I've got you."

I relax, allowing him to pull me even closer. It seems as though every part of his body is pressed tight to every part of mine. I don't mind. He's allowed to touch me, but no one else. I wrinkle my nose at the scent of whisky on his breath as he sighs into me, burying his face in the back of my neck. He reaches up, pulling my hair away, exposing my skin to him. I shiver at the draft, at the feel of his breath on my neck.

And then, he presses his lips to the top of my spine. I freeze, my heart thudding hard in my chest and throughout my veins. He kissed the top of my head today before he left, which was strange behavior for him, but I brushed it off. Here and now, though, why is he doing this? I move to roll, move so I can face him. I am not necessarily afraid of him, but I am wary. After finishing so much whisky, he is acting not quite his reserved self.

His hold on me tightens, preventing me from rolling. He trails his nose along the side of my neck before stopping below my ear. I shiver, ticklish. Different feelings erupt within me at this gesture. I know it means something, but I am not quite sure what. It feels intimate, and therefore like something I shouldn't allow to happen, right?

I clutch at his hands that hold me in my anxiety. His breath is warm against me, but he says nothing. His lips again find a spot on my neck, this time just below my ear. My heart is in my throat, my mind buzzing. It...feels good, in a strange way, but it's too new, and I feel guilty for some reason. My parents were religious, as most humans I knew were. They believed in maintaining purity until marriage. Now that I know more of the world, I understand what that means.

"Relax, Livy, I will never hurt you," he says, his voice deep and raspy. I am shaky, but I nod, my mind jumping all over the place. One of his hands moves, until he is gripping my hip beneath my tank top, his skin rough and warm against my own. He kisses me again in that same spot, and I feel his tongue this time. A noise between a sigh and a whimper escapes my throat. His hands slides up further, resting on my side before he grips me, hard. *Possessively.*

"Fuck," he growls, rolling his hips. I feel it, then, something hard pressing against my butt and back. My mouth runs dry with nerves. Again, Deidre wasn't lying. I've never seen a male appendage before, so I have nothing to compare it to, but I can tell it's huge.

He groans, releasing me. I lay in stunned silence, my hammering heart shaking my entire frame. What the hell was that? Why did he do it?

And more importantly, why did I sort of like it?

14

Pax

I stare down at Liv in the cool hues of dawn. She is still fast asleep, her cheeks puffed out, her lips open as her eyelids flutter. She is dreaming again. I wish I knew what she dreamt of. I am dressed and ready for work, but I can't seem to make myself leave.

I shouldn't have done that to her last night. I shouldn't have kissed her, shouldn't have given in to my selfish desires. She was scared of me, I could hear it in the hammering of her little heart. She doesn't know what to expect, other than pain and humiliation. Even if I was able to show her it was enjoyable, I would still feel guilty. I would still be taking her choices about her body away from her.

I can't stoop that low. I also shouldn't drink around her anymore, because then I only want her even more. I rub at my face, glancing down at Henry's cage on the floor. He runs up to the glass, whiskers twitching as he presses his paws to it.

She makes a small noise in her sleep, akin to a gasp, and I turn back to her. She is rigid, her face pinched as her heart rate picks up speed. I draw nearer as her eyes flutter open, awash with tears.

"Liv?" I ask, concerned. Her eyes blink before falling to me, and she sags in what appears to be relief. She wipes at her face, but more tears come. I sit down by her feet, leaning over her.

"Hey," I say, keeping my voice gentle. Jeven warned me to watch how I speak with her during this time. She peeks at me before she sniffles.

"I'm...I'm sorry. It was just a nightmare," she whispers, voice hoarse. I feel my forehead scrunch in confusion. She must see the look on my face.

"A bad dream?" she asks. I didn't realize dreams could be bad. I have never given them much thought, seeing as I can't remember ever dreaming.

"About what?" I ask, nervous for her answer. She goes quiet, staring at my chest. She seems as though she wants something but doesn't want to ask it. I want to comfort her, but I know that holding her close will only make me want her more. She heaves a shuddering breath, wiping again at her cheeks. Fuck the consequences.

I lean over, wrapping my arms around her, pulling her up, cradling her in my lap. She relaxes immediately, pressing her nose to the hollow on my neck. I smooth my palm over her back, resting my chin on her head.

"I was remembering my mom," she finally whispers. I choose to say nothing. I need to let her feel she can speak freely to me about these things. I hear her small laugh, feel her breath on my neck.

"She used to bake the best sugar cookies."

I feel myself smile, but I am also feeling her sorrow, feeling it as my own.

"She died...when they came for the Settlement. They shot her in the stomach. I tried to save her...I've...I can never escape that," she finally whispers. I can tell by the change in her voice that she is far away from here and now, deep into the horrid past. I give her a gentle squeeze. If only she knew I could relate, if only I had the strength she had.

"I'm so sorry, Livy."

"But you're not. You still kill us. Hunt us. Enslave us."

Her words aren't angry, but defeated. I feel my own anger flare toward her for lumping me in with the rest, but I simmer down. I deserve it. I have done my share of destruction. But I have also helped, right? I saved her life, doesn't that count for something?

It is as I hold her that my world begins to shift. I suppose it was shifting well before this moment in thanks to her, but I finally feel it clicking into place, now. Our society needs to change. We as a species are more alike than different. Why does mine feel dominant? Why does any one thing feel superior to another, when in the end, we all face the same fate?

It is impossible to change things overnight, but I vow to take a stand, here and now, to ensure the rest of her life with me is one worth living, one where she feels free—truly free. It is the least I can do after everything she has been through, things she never deserved.

I pull her away to look at her. She stares back, sullen, tired, but there is still that glimmer in her eyes, that spark of hope and fire. I do not know what to say, but I know I must say something.

"Olivia Donne."

I hold her cheeks between my palms. She gives me a curious look.

"I vow, from here on out, to do whatever I am able to do on my end to ensure your kind are not slaughtered or mistreated."

Her face blanches as she blinks up at me a few times.

"This will not be easy, and it will take years, but if I can begin to implement changes, then I will do so."

Her heart races beneath my fingertips. I watch as her eyes

glisten, the sunrise streaming in and painting her face orange and gold. It is wild, the way she looks—the way she should always look. *Free.*

"Are you...are you being serious, Pax?" she whispers.

"I would never lie to you, Liv, you know that."

It takes a few more moments, but a beaming smile crosses her face. She is so beautiful that it stuns me. My desire for her is now akin to a rampant wildfire, and it is torture to not be able to act upon it. I do not want to ruin anything, though, not with her—not with something that is so important to me.

She wraps her arms about me, hugging me tight. I press my cheek to her head, unable to stop my smile.

"You're my best friend, Pax. Besides Henry," she corrects quickly. I chuckle, her innocence so confounding and endearing. I feel full of happiness for the first time in many years. I feel we are on the precipice of a monumental change, and it is the most excited I have been for such a change in a long, long time.

It is my lunch hour, but I have too much to do in preparation for our departure in the coming weeks to go home and spend time with Liv. I stride to my office, but a deep voice stops me in my tracks. Tark calls me over, a few other commanding rangers next to him. I change course, saluting them as I approach. Tark nods, a grim look on his face.

"Paxton. You know Xerxes and Rom."

I nod to them in acknowledgment, but their faces remain stoic, hands folded behind their backs. They are near the same age as Tark, greying and weathered from years spent raiding. My stomach feels sour at the thought. If I had made my decisions concerning humans earlier, I would have done everything I could to opt out of this mission.

"It's no secret I am retiring soon, Pax, and with all this civil unrest bullshit, I hope I can push it up a few months."

I feel my brow furrow as the men stare me down, seeming to measure me—my worth, as a man, as a ranger. I feel ice seep into my veins, mingled with dread. Tark's eyes darken. I have been under his command since the beginning, since I was eighteen. Ten years I have been by his side, through more than just raids. He is a good man, an excellent leader. He does not kill for the sake of killing, he does not take joy in torturing or harming humans. Perhaps he is partially responsible for why I have always had such a soft spot for Liv.

"What is it you wish to ask of me, sir?"

"Before anything formal comes of this, we would like to offer you the position of head ranger. Should you choose to accept, you will have access to all tiers of the government, including classified information," Xerxes says, his eyes dark and brooding.

"Not to mention, you will choose new recruits, train rangers, and assemble your own units for raiding," Rom says. I glance toward Tark. His eyes are dancing with some sort of glint that I cannot place, but it isn't good. It is not jealousy, or animosity. I can see he wants me to say yes. I just wonder what he knows that I do not.

"If you do this, son, you will hold as much power as our elected official, current or otherwise," Tark says. His words are cloaked, meant to sound like a bonus to accepting this job, when in reality, he is giving me a glimpse into my future. By holding as much power as our elected official, I would be able to make good on my promise to Liv. My heart thuds hard in my chest.

I knew this was coming, but I knew this before my life's course had been altered. I am treading dangerous waters, that much is clear in Tark's warning gaze. But if I do not take this chance, another one will not present itself. It is all or nothing.

"It would be a great honor to follow in your footsteps, sir," I say. Everyone's answering smiles are tight. Tark gives me a subtle nod, and in his eyes is the confirmation I needed. I chose the right path.

I have just been gifted enough power to change the course of our future.

I am just leaving, striding to my vehicle, my mind buzzing with this massive shift in my life. I do not hear Jeven calling me until he is right behind me.

"Fuck, you deaf?" he asks. I shake my head to scatter my thoughts.

"Uh, no. What were you saying?"

He snorts.

"Party, my place, Friday. Bring Liv."

"No," I say, curt as I open my door. It feels as though he often traps me while I am trying to leave. His hand on my door stops me from an easy escape.

"Dude, you never go out anymore. It will be low key and fun."

I frown.

"If Brutus is going—"

"Fuck no, you think I'd let him around Deidre?" he says, face pinched in what appears to be a protective look. I smirk at him. I wonder how deeply he loves her, and I wonder how long he has known he loves her.

"I'll ask Livy," I say, climbing up into my vehicle. He backs off with a sly grin. I drive home, ready to enjoy my time with her, especially after all the craziness lately.

"Liv?" I call out, hanging up my uniform jacket. I come around the corner to see her on the couch watching her lecture. I grin as she beams at me, but she doesn't move. I come closer, and it is then that I see Henry perched in her lap, gnawing on a carrot. I chuckle.

"How was your day?" she asks, smiling up at me upside down like she always does. I grip the back of the couch, stifling the urge to press my lips to hers.

"It was...a big day. How was yours?"

Her brows crinkle.

"How was it a big day?"

I chuckle.

"We can discuss that over dinner."

She frowns, but she soon moves on, telling me everything she learned today. I smile as I listen. The change in her is monumental, night and day. It makes me feel as though I have done something right in life.

"Why don't we go out to dinner tonight?" I suggest after she finishes telling me she has taught Henry to come when she calls. I don't tell her that holding out treats does not constitute obedience.

"Really?" she breathes, eyes wide.

"Sure. Then I can share my big news."

I check my watch.

"Let me get ready and we can go."

"Ok," she smiles, gathering Henry into her hands to nuzzle his nose. I go into our room, peeling off my boots and socks before I move to the closet and strip down. Naked and not thinking anything of it, I exit the closet to search my drawers for fresh socks and underwear.

I hear her squeak of surprise before I see her. Liv is just standing up from putting Henry back, her eyes wide and stuck between my hips, her cheeks flaming to fiery red in a split second. I jump, doing my best to cover myself, but it is too late.

She closes her eyes, slapping her hands to cover them, before she turns and tries to run out.

"Liv—"

My warning is short lived as she collides with the door jamb. Knowing she is unhurt, I stifle my laugh and reach for an old pair of shorts from my hamper. I tug them on, following her out to the living room. She is sitting on the couch, her face tucked into her knees. Even her neck is red with embarrassment.

I sit next to her, placing my hand on her knee and giving it a slight shake.

"Hey, peeping Tom, I'm not mad at you."

She shakes her head, clearly mortified.

"How's your head?"

"Broken," she mumbles. I laugh at her humor.

"Can I take a look?"

She sighs, unfurling herself but refusing to meet my eye. I pull her onto my lap facing me, brushing her hair away from her warm face. There is a mark on her forehead, but it is only superficial.

"Good news is you'll live," I say with a simpering smile. She bites her lip, finally eyeing me as she tries to hide her own smile. Her eyes fall to my bare chest again. I hold her hips lightly, brushing my thumbs up and down.

"There's no need to be embarrassed, Livy. It's just you and me here, and it was bound to happen at some point," I say, trying to make her feel better. She gives a half-hearted shrug.

"Never seen a naked man before?" I ask with a quirk of my brow. Though I know that answer, I enjoy seeing her squirm. She huffs, deflated.

"No," she grits out. I can't help but laugh.

"All you thought it would be and more?" I tease.

She claps her hands to her face, shaking her head.

"Definitely more," she mumbles. A bark of laughter escapes me, and I wrap her in my arms, holding her close.

"Thank you for boosting my ego, sweetheart."

I can feel her roll her eyes against me.

"Do you still feel like going out to eat?" I ask, rubbing my hand up and down her back. She nods.

"Let me go change, then. You're more than welcome to come spectate, but you don't need to slam your head into the wall anymore."

Her mouth twists down. She looks like she wants to pinch me. But then, a devious glint enters her eyes, and she rolls them. Before I can reprimand her, she jumps off me and flees with laughter. I give chase, her speed surprising, but still no match for me.

Her screaming laughter bounces off the walls, turning to fits of giggles each time I miss her. I go easy, allowing her to escape each time I get close. She loves this game.

Her fatal mistake is when she runs to the bedroom, knowing she is cornered as she backs away from my slow approach. Her chest is heaving with laughter and exertion. I pick my timing carefully, aiming for her waist as I spring forward, catching her off her feet and landing on the bed with her beneath me. She laughs, wriggling as I pin her wrists above her head.

"You almost had me," I say, breathless. She gives me a fake glare, still struggling against my superior strength.

"How to punish you," I muse with a dark smile. She squirms harder, frustrated. I release her wrists, moving too quickly for her to stop me. I haven't shaved in more than a few days, so I press my scruffy face to her neck while tickling her sides. She writhes and laughs and screams as she tries to fight me off, but I continue to twist my face against her neck.

I am laughing, harder than I feel I have ever really laughed. I pull away, staring down at her. She tries to glare, but she is still giggling, tears leaking from her eyes. It is so strange to me how often human eyes water, even when they are happy.

She stares up at me, calming, holding my gaze as I stare down at her. In a flash of desire, I remember what it felt like to kiss her skin, to feel her beneath my fingertips. I want her so badly, even more so now.

"Pax?" she asks, quirking her head to the side.

"Hmm?" I say, pulled from my fantasies all centering on her. Her little brows furrow.

"Why...why did you kiss me last night?"

Shit.

I stare down at Liv, still fumbling for what to say that will remain truthful yet tactful. I can't tell her how badly I want to fuck her. That would freak her out.

I can't tell her it is because I find her simply beautiful. I feel that would freak her out as well. Our relationship has remained one way up until this point—owner, slave. Dominant, grouchy submissive. Erathian, human. How do I blur those lines in a way that will ensure she remains obedient, loyal? I don't want her to hate me, and I don't want her to attempt to run away in fear that I will act upon my desires as so many Erathian males do to their slaves.

I frown down at her, and she continues to stare up at me, cheeks tinged pinked, with her wide forest green eyes. I know she will accept whatever answer is given to her because she is so new to this. I don't want to manipulate her, though. What sort of hole have I dug myself into now?

"I apologize for being so forward with you, Livy. I'd blame the whisky, but that would be the cowardly thing to do," I begin. Her mouth closes, and she gives a small nod.

"I...I have a soft spot for you. I never thought I would enjoy a human's company so much. You've blown my expectations out of the water," I say, scratching at the back of my neck, feeling nervous.

"I just...I feel very protective of you," I say slowly, still searching for the right words. She is quick to pipe up.

"Because I am yours?"

I give a soft snort, smiling at her.

"Yes, Livy, you are mine, but I also hope you can see that I am yours, in a way."

Her blush deepens, turning her cheeks a cherry red. She swallows, her little throat bobbing. She is gracious as she waits for me to continue.

"I...I want to be the only one who touches you, who holds you, who makes you feel good, happy," I say, shaking my head as I breathe out the words. There is a ghost of a smile on her plush lips. But then, it turns into a glare.

"I don't want anyone else touching me, either," she pouts, quite vehement. I can't help but chuckle.

"Well, I am glad you feel that way towards me. Glad you've grown to trust me, at least a little. Right?"

She gives a sure nod, smiling.

"Good. If you do not want me to do those things, I hope you know you can tell me, and I will listen immediately. You don't have to be afraid of me being upset over something like that. You choose who you want to touch you in such a way, alright?"

She is still frowning at me, but she eventually shakes her head.

"I don't want anyone else. It would be...gross," she says, wrinkling her nose in distaste. I laugh, my chest feeling light, happy. The fact that she is voicing this, that she only trusts me, only wants *me*, is astounding.

"You're a beautiful, smart, kind young woman, Livy. I hope you see that, that you know your worth, what it means to me."

Her eyes waver before they glisten. I know she craves such words of praise and affirmation. I make a note to be more vocal about her accomplishments, about her evident beauty. I want her to flourish, to see that despite how my culture views her, *I* see her as such, and my opinion is the one that should matter to her most of all.

"Thank you, Pax," she whispers. I know I have skirted around the truth a little, but I needed to feel out whether or not she was ready to hear it. I still doubt she is, so in order to preserve our peace and our budding relationship, I choose to keep it to myself. I will continue to grow our trust, will allow her to come to me. I feel that is the only way I can do this and not feel utter guilt.

I care much too deeply about her to ruin this.

"So, I'm thinking Hibachi for dinner," I say with a slight smirk. She is confused, as I knew she would be, but I can't wait to see her excitement at such a place.

"What's...Hiba...what?" she asks, screwing up her face in confusion. I laugh, running my hands up her slim sides, proud of the weight she has gained. She still has a ways to go, but I am pleased she is healthier, all the same.

"Get ready and you'll find out."

~

Olivia

Pax drives us to the restaurant, and I am more excited than I care to admit. I haven't been to a public dining place since I was uprooted. People are filtering in and out, all smiling, happy—but all Erathians. I glance to Pax as he maneuvers his large vehicle into a parking space, his arm muscles straining against his black shirt.

"Umm...Pax?" I ask, fiddling with the chain around my wrist.

"Yeah?" he says, checking his mirrors.

"Am I allowed here?"

My voice is small, timid. I can't help but feel shame, for being a human, for allowing this man to enslave me so easily, for assimilating into their culture with such little resistance. But at the same time, I can't help but wonder where I would be without Pax.

Still starving in the wild, fighting over a few morsels of rabbits, hiding from stronger humans, hiding from Erathians. It wasn't the best life, but at the same time I had my freedom to do as I pleased. The consequences were much more dire, though.

"Of course you are, Livy," he says with a grunt.

"I just don't see any slaves."

He turns off the vehicle, glancing at me. He is frowning, his eyes darting to the entrance and back to me. He reaches up, pointing.

I follow his line of sight. There is a man and his slave woman. She is dressed well, and her chain is thin, like mine. It is around her neck, however.

"I know we don't venture out much, so there's some cultural things I should warn you of," he says. His eyes are brooding in the low light of the sunset. It is late, much later than we normally eat. Pax likes to get to bed early so he can wake up early for work.

I nod, wishing for him to explain what it is I do not know.

"It is normal to see slaves and owners sharing a meal, but you need to be sitting beside me, not across. Erathians that are...wealthier, tend to flaunt what they have. Sometimes you will see two or more slaves to one owner, and they will be dressed very well. Try not to stare. It pisses off the slaves and the owners."

I am confused, but I nod. His gaze turns even darker, sending a chill up my spine. He wipes at his clean shaven jaw, looking lost for a moment.

"Umm...you'll probably see overtly sexual incidents at some point. Erathians are very publicly open about such things, especially in the city, where it is less conservative. Again, just don't stare, alright?"

I feel myself redden, but I nod.

"And above all, do *not* leave my side, talk to anyone, or let anyone give you anything. They are sneaky. You will think they are being kind. Erathians in the black market slave trade will use humans to lure other humans."

"O-ok," I say, feeling nervous. I do not want another incident like the one at the gym to happen.

"Come here," he says, opening his arm to me. I slide over, allowing him to pull me close as I breathe in his comforting scent. I like the way his muscles feel beneath the soft fabric. He's always been so strong, so steady.

"I'll keep you safe, Livy. Always. You'll never have to worry about anyone hurting you as long as you're with me."

15

Olivia

My senses are overwhelmed as we enter the restaurant. I find myself hovering closer and closer to Pax. He turns his palm over, like he did in the gym before I got attacked. I take my chance, wrapping both my arms around his and holding it tight to me. He is so steady and warm.

There are so many people, so many noises, and in the midst of all the chaos, there are these huge flat stoves right in the middle of tables where chefs are cooking. It smells delectable, from the sizzling meats, to the searing vegetables. My mouth begins to water.

Pax leads me forward until we are in front of a podium.

"Just one?" the man asks, not glancing at me. I narrow my eyes at him. How can he not see me?

"Two seats," Pax says. I understand as I look around again. Some slaves are on the floor, some on their master's laps, and in the corner a few are tied up. My stomach churns.

"Right this way," the man says, grabbing utensils and a menu. Pax follows, and though I was instructed to keep my eyes down, I cannot help but look around in wonderment. There are those dressed similar to us, but then others who are dressed impeccably well. The clash of classes is interesting to me. I am thankful I see nothing overtly sexual happening.

Pax grips me back. I am puzzled, wondering if he is upset by my wandering eyes, but it is then I understand; we are to be seated next to two Erathian males, and their eyes are stuck wide on me. I feel myself blush as my gaze averts to the ground. Pax sits next to them, leaving the chair on the end for me. I am thankful.

"Go ahead and tell the chef your order when you're ready," the man says, handing Pax the utensils and menu. Despite the noise and overwhelming air, Pax sits straight and seems to command my attention. He pats my knee, smiling kindly as he extracts his arm from my tight hold.

He unfolds the menu, allowing me to see. There are more words than pictures, and I feel ashamed to have to rely on him to tell me what everything says.

"I think you'll like shrimp," he says, pointing to one of the only photos. I wrinkle my nose at the pink curly thing.

"What is it?" I whisper. I do not want to be loud, do not want to draw any attention to myself. He chuckles.

"It's from the ocean. How about I order it and you can try it?"

I am still unconvinced, but I trust Pax, so I nod. He is still smiling softly down at me as I squirm in my seat, sitting on my hands. He stretches an arm out, placing it across the back of my chair.

"Kind of a lot going on?"

I peek up at him and nod as I bite my lip, but I am thankful for his steady presence. He drops his arm, rubbing my shoulder. After a few more minutes of him telling me what's on the menu, I have decided what I want. He orders us drinks and lets the chef in the middle of our table know our order.

My eyes are mesmerized as he begins to cook it right in front of us, even making onions into a steaming, fiery mountain at one point. I can't wipe the grin off my face. We are soon served, both of us digging in.

The food is delicious, and even though the shrimps still scare me, I try one. Pax watches my face, a smile wavering as I consider the flavors. They are new to me, so I am still on the fence about it. As dinner is winding down, we begin to discuss *The Hobbit*.

"How can you not like Bilbo?" I protest, shocked. He chuckles, rubbing at his chin.

"Ehh, just wait until *The Fellowship of the Ring*. There are other characters I like more."

"Who?" I pry, sipping at my soda. I love the bubbles and how they feel dancing across my tongue.

"I can't tell you yet, silly."

I give him a frown. He chuckles, rubbing my shoulder again.

"Ok, fine. His name is Strider at the beginning, that's all I'm going to say."

"And he's your favorite out of *everyone*?"

"Definitely."

"Hmmph," I say, mulling this over. I just want to go home and read now, but then I remember why we came here.

"What was your big news?" I ask. His face falls, becoming serious once more, and I am suddenly nervous. Is he going to get rid of me? Can he no longer have a slave? I feel myself begin to panic.

"I...got promoted, at work. It's not official yet, but it was offered to me today and I accepted."

His dark eyes are brooding as they search my face. I feel relief, but part of me is confused.

"Promoted to what?"

He heaves a big sigh.

"Ranger 001. I will control...well, the military, essentially."

I feel dread seep into my veins. He will be in charge of...what? Killing more humans? Enslaving more of us? I feel myself begin to shake in fury, ready to explode here and now in this restaurant. What about his promises he just made to me? He must see my face, because he grips my knee under the table, leaning into my ear.

"Relax, Livy, breathe. This will help me make good on my word, alright? I will have as much power as the most powerful official."

Relief floods me once more, and I give a shaky nod. He pulls away, but his hand sneaks up from my knee to settle on my thigh, warm and heavy.

"I keep my promises, alright?"

I offer him a smile.

"I know. Congrats, I think?"

He chuckles.

"Thank you. We can talk more at home. I have a mission coming up in a few weeks, and I would like to discuss some plans for while I am gone."

Again, I feel panic. Today is just too much for my emotions. He squeezes my thigh, laughing.

"Livy, sweetheart, you need to relax. I will never put you in danger," he says, his brows furrowing in his concern. I feel tears begin to choke me.

"You...you said you wouldn't leave me..."

He is frowning.

"I was thinking you could stay with my parents in the country. They have a farm. You can even bring Henry."

I heave a sigh, chewing my lip. His eyes are soft, kind, reassuring. If Pax cares this much about me, surely his parents would, too, right? He had to have learned this from somewhere, and the prospect of being in the country is luring. How much easier would it be to escape when I am not surrounded by so many Erathians?

"We'll talk tonight, deal?"

"Okay," I say, giving him a small smile. His hand remains on my thigh as he holds my gaze. I do not mind his touch, not anymore, even after him kissing me in bed last night. He was able to explain why he did it, and I feel reassured he has no ill intent. It is simply nice to have someone to be close to— someone I feel I can trust.

He shifts, reaching into his back pocket for his wallet to pay, and we are soon up and leaving. Night has fully fallen, but it is warm, humid. He opens the door to his vehicle for me, and even grips my hips to help me in. I slide to the middle, but my body freezes and tenses as we both hear a masculine voice. I whirl, glancing past Pax's shoulder. From the dark materializes a man, slender, yet tall, with even darker eyes and a gaunt face.

We are alone, this far out in the parking lot, and on the other side of the vehicle is dense shrubbery. Pax stands between myself and the man, squaring his shoulders, his whole body tight as a spring ready to unleash. I glance back to the other door, praying there isn't more than one man, praying this isn't an ambush.

But then, the man speaks.

"How would you like to become a very, *very* rich person?"

Pax

I unhook Liv's chain from my belt loop, closing the door and locking it as I square my shoulders to the man. Whatever he has to say, I know her delicate ears do not need to hear it. I can give her a less explicit run down later, should she want it.

"I don't need money. Get lost," I growl. The man chuckles, shaking his head and holding up his hands in surrender. I am concerned there may be more lurking in the bushes on the other side of the car, but I am prepared for such attacks, thanks to all my ranger training. If he or anyone else makes a move, they will lose.

"Just hear me out, bro."

I grit my teeth. I hate it when anyone calls me *bro*.

"Your slave, she's hot as fuck—"

I cut him off by taking a threatening step forward. He takes a step back, still holding up his hands.

"Listen, listen! There's some...some new shit goin' around, can make you wealthier than even the traders."

I know he is speaking of slave traders. They do make a shit ton of money. Even though I want to strangle him, I figure if I let him speak, I can get the dirt on the scumbags and report it to Tark first thing tomorrow.

"I'm listening," I hiss. He visibly relaxes, nodding.

"Humans are getting harder to find in the wild, especially ones that look good enough for us to want, right?"

I cross my arms, remaining stoic. He continues.

"There's some guys, started breeding them, but they only want the best. Got a good human male we can cross her with. Their offspring would sell for millions, bro. And you can keep breeding her for much longer and much faster than any Erathian woman. You set the price, they take care of the rest."

His eyes are bright, fervent and earnest, and all I want to do is kill him. I try to control my rage-induced shaking. I can't even fathom allowing some human male fucking her, getting her pregnant—stripping her of her humanity and reducing her to nothing more than an animal. I am enraged that they are forcing male humans to do this as well, but Liv will always be my first priority.

"You got a way to get a hold of you after I think on it?"

"Yeah, yeah bro, of course! Here," he fumbles in his pocket, handing me a black business card. I glare at it in the dark, seeing nothing on it.

"Ultraviolet brings out the name and place."

I nod, gritting my teeth. He still stands there, peering around me and into my vehicle. I can't control myself anymore.

"Get the fuck out of here," I growl. He nods, turning on his heels to scamper away like the fucking rat he is. I will personally ensure hellfire rains down on the operation he's a part of. I ache for the day I take the reins from Tark. Their little business will be in for a shock.

The ride home is quiet, tense. I tell Liv to get ready for bed, promising to read her at least a few pages before we go to sleep. I emerge from the shower to see her perched in her new pajamas, patiently awaiting me. She keeps avoiding my eyes, though, a frightened look on her face.

I climb into bed, reaching for her waist and pulling her between my legs like how we usually read. I just want to get this over so I can think and plot while she sleeps. I reach for the book, but her little hand stops me.

"What happened, Pax?" she asks, voice timid. I sigh, thumping my head on the headboard. I tighten my hold on her. She is so small in my embrace. She leans back into me before shimmying her hips and nestling down. I grit my teeth against what this does to me, against how my body now naturally reacts to her. I do not want anyone else to touch her in such a way, but I cannot stop myself from wanting her—all of her. I know that I, of all people, would care for her, and wouldn't hurt her.

I would cherish something as precious as her innocence.

I press my cheek to the side of her head, enjoying the silkiness of her hair. How do I phrase this to her?

"There's some illegal activity going on with slaves. He offered me a substantial amount of money to...borrow you, for a while."

"Borrow?" she says in a panic, twisting in my arms. I let her, searching her depthless green eyes as I frown.

"Livy...that's not gonna happen. Ever. You are mine, right?" I say, cupping her smooth cheek. She bites her lip, relaxing as she nods. Her brows scrunch, though, and I know she seeks a better explanation.

"What would he want to...borrow me for?" she whispers. I grit my teeth, sighing through my nose as my hand falls to her waist.

"To...allow another human to get you pregnant..."

Her confusion deepens, and I feel myself blush.

"Why?"

I shake my head, sighing.

"Liv...there's some disgusting people in this world. Can we leave it at that?"

"You're mad at me," she says, eyes watering. I give her a smile, pulling her into a hug.

"No, Livy. I'm mad at *him*, ok?"

I feel her nod, but she isn't relaxing. Maybe it would be better to arm her with the truth, to give her the knowledge of what monsters crawl through this kingdom. I doubt she has much inkling to escape anymore, but I think this truth will further cement that notion. I pull her away, studying her.

"There's...less wild humans available. They want to breed humans they find appealing, so they can sell their offspring," I say, my voice dark. Her eyes widen, her jaw clenching. I see her fear, feel her disgust.

"H-how...umm..."

Oh *fuck* no.

I hate that I promised to always be truthful with her.

"Remember Deidre's lovely explanation of fucking?"

Her cheeks burn like a ripe tomato. She gives a bashful nod.

"*That* is how children are made. It's...quite the process, sometimes it can take months or years to get the timing right..." I am fumbling for the right words as she goes from blushing to pale.

"They are...making humans do that?" she says, her voice sorrowful. I sigh, capturing her cheeks to hold her gaze.

"Not for much longer, alright? I'll take care of it."

She holds my gaze for a beat before she nods. Her face screws up into confusion, and I am dreading her line of questioning.

"But...I don't get it..."

"Do you really want to know, Livy?"

She is chewing her lip as she considers. Eventually, she bobs her head shyly. I sigh, pulling her onto my lap so she is facing me. I have no problem giving her a scientific explanation, but I am not sure of a human's biological processes, how much they differ from our species.

"I do not know if it is exactly the same for a human male, so I may not be entirely correct," I begin. Her little hands are folded together, resting on my bare stomach. They twist together, making me shiver as she moves against me.

"When that *thing* of a male's is...in you...it releases a substance. If the timing is correct with the female, meaning she is fertile, then she will become pregnant..."

She is blushing, but she quirks her head to the side.

"Is that...what happens with humans, or with you?"

I shrug.

"I suppose it is very similar. Erathian's have a tendency to become...umm...locked in place, so to speak, seeing as Erathian women are so rarely fertile. It is the best way to ensure a pregnancy every time."

I can see how confused she is.

"Does that...hurt?" she whispers, wrinkling her nose. I chuckle, smoothing my palms over her hips.

"For me or for you?"

"Both...I guess..."

I laugh.

"I can assure you it doesn't hurt me. It shouldn't hurt you, if done correctly," I say. Her eyes waver, and in that small span of time, I can see she has ventured off into her past in her mind. I grit my teeth. Killing Brutus would do nothing for either of us. I need to exact my revenge on him in a much more political manner, or I could end up imprisoned and Liv could be auctioned off.

"What happened to you was...reprehensible, Livy, but I will never let anyone hurt you like that again. And...you don't need to be afraid of when that day does come...because..."

Because what? Who is she going to be allowed to sleep with? I own her, and I would never let her out of my sight long enough to find someone else to do the deed with.

She peeks up at me from under her thick lashes.

"Because you won't hurt me when we do that?"

I stare at Liv, dumbfounded. She said those words with such conviction, with such innocence, like this was supposed to happen someday. I have told her many times that is not why I have her, but does she still not believe me?

"Liv...I..." I croak, shaking my head as I search for the right words. She is sheepish, hiding her eyes now.

"That's...forever your choice..."

She glances at me, and I can tell by the look on her face that she has been keeping something from me. My hold on her tightens. I know exactly who to blame.

"What did Deidre say now?" I sigh. She bites her lip and widens her eyes, but it doesn't fool me; I have caught her red handed.

"N-nothing!" she squeaks. I let out an exasperated sigh before leveling her with a frown.

"I've been honest with you, even if it was awkward."

She looks ashamed, twisting her hands until they turn white. I reach over and clasp them, giving a gentle squeeze. She huffs a bothered sigh.

"She just said that...umm...well for one she said I was lucky because you're *sexy*, but I don't know really what that means, but then she also said your...thing...will *rip me apart*, or something...but I also don't get that...umm...err...she said..." she taps her chin in mock thought as I try to hide my building laughter.

"She said she thinks you really, really, *really* like me, and that when someone really likes someone, they do those things to them," she rushes out after her thoughtful consideration. I finally expel a laugh, and she crosses her arms as her mouth twists into a pout.

"One, *sexy* means attractive, very handsome," I explain. Her crossed arms loosen, her face open and expectant.

"Two, my *thing*, as you've seen, would be considered...large, especially in comparison to you," I say, feeling flushed. The tops of her cheeks are burning.

"But no, size does not necessarily equate to painful intercourse."

She is absorbing everything, her face probably mirroring mine in our shared embarrassment.

"And three, yes, when people really, really like each other, they...do that..."

She chews her lip as she eyes me thoughtfully.

"He...he...he didn't l-like..." she stutters. I sigh, placing my hand on her lower back and rubbing her reassuringly. She is getting worked up. This is too much for her, as I expected it would be.

"Livy, there are evil people in this world, alright? And they can turn even something that is meant to be pure and...beautiful, into something horrible and scary and painful. But it is not meant to be that way, I promise you."

She nods, relaxing.

"But...do you like me, Pax?"

I snort, giving her a gentle smile.

"Oh, Olivia. I like you the most out of anyone on this planet."

16

Olivia

I am eagerly awaiting Pax, excited to show him I have completed my first workbook. He also mentioned something about going to Jeven's tonight to see his friends. Part of me wants to just so I can get out of the house, but part of me is nervous to be around more of his people. And then there's the problem of him leaving soon. We still haven't really discussed it, and to be honest I am kind of mad at him.

I don't really have a say, though.

I am still wearing my pajama shorts and a loose t-shirt when he arrives home. It is too hot to wear anything else, now. I jump up from the couch, clutching the book to my chest. He hangs up his jacket, holding a silvery paper bag. His eyes jump to my face, and he warms with a smile.

"Hey, Livy."

I can't help but smile as I hold the book out to him. He quirks his brow, taking it from me as I bite my lip.

"Wait...did you finish this?" he asks, seeming stunned.

"Yup," I say, twisting my hands together.

"Damn, good job, hun!" he says with a grin. I feel flush with pride. He hands me the bag he is holding.

"I picked out some summer clothes for you, and some things for the farm."

I take the bag, peeking inside.

"Thanks," I say, giving him a smile as we stand awkwardly in the doorway. I want to...well, *hug* him. Or at least have him hug me. I like it when he holds me. He seems to notice, and he steps forward, wrapping his arms around me. His uniform is stiff and starched against me, but I like the way it looks on him. He is so austere, powerful. He always is, but when he dons it each morning, he seems to stand a little straighter.

He reaches up, cupping my cheek as I rest my other cheek on his warm abs.

"I'm proud of you, Liv," he says, his voice lower, gravelly. I smile into him, tightening my hold. He bends down, pressing his lips to the side of my head before he releases me. His actions leave me dizzy, feeling...different, special? I can't tell. It's new, and I like it.

"Why don't you try on your new clothes and we can get ready to go to this damn party," he grumbles, seating himself to untie his boots. I go to the bedroom, trying on the new shirts and shorts he bought me. I finally decide on a black tank top and olive green shorts. They are still a little big around my hips, but I don't mind.

I can hear the shower running, so I take my time braiding my hair in the mirror, giving myself two French braids. I then hide some treats for Henry, since I have a feeling we won't be home until late. I am on my hands and knees, peering through his glass, looking for any sign of movement when I hear Pax come in.

He clears his throat, and I sit up on my knees, turning to him. He tosses his dirty clothes in his hamper, clutching a towel around his hips. His torso is still shimmering, wet, and his muscles glisten in the late afternoon sun. His wet hair is tousled, and his face is clean shaven. He smirks at me, standing halfway between his closet and the bedroom.

I still don't know what *sexy* means, but I think I am beginning to understand it better. I feel my face heat up as he continues to stare at me, and something in my stomach is doing these flips and flops. He looks like he wants to pounce on me.

He finally moves, grabbing some clothes off hangers.

"I like your outfit."

"Th-thank you, for getting it for me," I say. He hums and nods, tossing his clothes to the bed. He pauses to smirk down at me again before he shakes his head.

"No leaving my side tonight, not even for the bathroom, got it?"

I gulp, nervous.

"Why?"

He snorts, sitting on the bed, his towel precariously wrapped in place, as he pulls on some socks.

"Because, you're showing off a lot of skin."

I suddenly feel self-conscious.

"I...I'm sorry?" I attempt, confused. He chuckles.

"I don't mind the view, but I don't take kindly to anyone else staring at what's mine," he says, his voice lowering to a growl at the end. Again, those feelings erupt within me. I like it, how it makes me feel when he says such things. I feel special and protected. I don't want anyone else besides him staring at me, either.

He smirks, standing and turning around. He doesn't warn me, and I don't have the chance to avert my eyes fast enough. He drops the towel, exposing his sculpted, muscled butt to me. I can't seem to look away as my mouth snaps shut and runs dry. His legs are long, muscled, proving yet again his superior strength. He slides a pair of tight but long shorts up, cutting off my staring.

When he turns back around, he is still smirking.

"Why are you staring, Livy?"

I cross my arms, throwing him a glare. I can feel how hot my face is, betraying me. He makes his way over, bending and wrapping his arms around my waist, but I wriggle to escape him. His hands clamp down harder, and he's chuckling.

"Have I embarrassed you?"

"No," I huff, still squirming as he pulls me to the bed and squeezes me. I am perched on his lap, my back to him. I used to hate this, but I am getting more used to it. He nuzzles his face into my neck, and I can't help but laugh, feeling so ticklish.

He finally pulls away, letting me catch my breath.

"I like your hair like this. It's unique," he says, gently tugging on one of my braids. I lean back into his chest, resting my head on his shoulder so I can see him.

"Thank you," I quip. "My mom taught me how."

His arms tighten around me a little more. He always gets this sad look on his face when I talk about her.

"How are you feeling about staying with my parents?"

I feel a stone sink into my stomach. I give a small shrug.

"They are kind people, Livy. They will take care of you, and I shouldn't be gone too long."

I feel a burst of anger.

"Are you going to kidnap more humans?"

"Watch it," he grunts, his hand trapping my cheeks quickly. He is being stern, not mean, but I am mad all the same. His eyes blaze as they stare down at me, fiery, and there is always that faint shimmer when they catch the light just right.

"I took you to save your life, and I don't regret it."

I feel awash with guilt for being so brash, but now I am too embarrassed to say anything. He keeps his fingers on my cheeks, his hold getting slightly tighter as he stares at me. His look changes to something I recognize but can't quite place. I feel my heartbeat thump through me, nervous. His fresh scent surrounds us both, and the feel of his warm, smooth skin on mine sends tingles through my nerves wherever we touch. He leans in, slow.

I suck in a breath, my eyes fluttering closed. I know something is about to happen, but I do not know what. I feel his lips on mine, gentle, plush, warm. When Brutus did it, he was rough, forcing my mouth open to accept what I did not want.

Pax moves slow, tender, and his fingers leave my cheeks to instead cup my face as he smooths his rough thumb over the bones beneath my eye. My stomach is a rioting mess, and deep, deep down within me, I feel something burning, but I like it. He pulls away, the kiss only lasting a few seconds, but it would forever be ingrained in my memory.

My eyes shoot open, wide, searching his face. He is brooding, his brows pulled together, his face serious.

"That is so you remember who you belong to tonight," he says, his voice a deep, possessive growl. More of that burning pools into my lower stomach, somehow centering between my legs. I nod my obedience automatically.

He drops one hand, smoothing it over my bare thigh before he grips it. And then, he leans in again. I feel less prepared this time as his lips crash to mine. He is more hungry as he moves, and I do my best to mimic him. I want to kiss him back, for some crazy reason, because the way he is making me feel is unlike anything I have ever felt before. I do not feel like a slave. I feel like a woman—a woman that is desirable to a man who is so devastatingly attractive and powerful and strong.

He pulls away, leaving my lips tingling from the force in which he kissed me, and I am panting, shivering in his grasp.

"And that, Liv, is the other reason I took you."

We arrive at Jeven's early. There aren't any others here yet, but

Deidre greets me with a smile. My mind is still elsewhere, though. All I can think about is Pax's lips on mine, on how fire courses through me every time his skin brushes against mine now. I feel him pull me into his side, pulling me out of my thoughts. I realize Deidre has asked me something.

"Umm...what, sorry?" I say. She snorts.

"Do you want to come see my room?"

I glance up at Pax for permission. He quirks his brow but hands me my chain.

"I'll come get you when others show up," he says, his eyes dark and glinting. I clamp my mouth shut and nod. Deidre pulls me away, and for a moment I feel as though I can actually breathe. Their apartment is a lot like ours, decorated in dark red hues instead, though, and they are on the ground floor, so I noticed a patio space covered in twinkling lights when we came in.

"You have your own room?" I say, puzzled. She pushes open the door, rolling her eyes.

"Not to sleep in. Jev had an extra room as his office, but he never used it, so he let me do what I wanted with it," she says as she flicks on the light.

"Oh," I gasp, greeted by soft, pastel purple walls, the floor covered in a sheet that is littered with paint splatters. It smells of art supplies, charcoal, and something sweet. There are easels and a few stools and a desk that is covered in pages from a sketchbook. I wander in, taking a closer look.

"Wow, that was nice of him to let you have this," I say, turning to her. She is frowning at a painting with her arms crossed. She is a beautiful woman, tall and lanky but strong. Her black hair is a short bob, just reaching her chin, but she has it pulled back today by a red headband, showcasing her striking cheekbones littered with copper freckles. Her eyes are the same coppery tint, shrouded by dark brows. She even has the most luscious red lips.

I shrink in her presence. Not only is she gorgeous, but she is smart in navigating this world *and* she is talented.

"So," she says, using her thumb to swipe at one of her paintings. "How are things with lover boy?"

She has always been blunt and curious about me and Pax, and I never minded before, but now I am nervous. I don't want to share with her the things that have happened, but I also feel like I need someone who can...help me navigate more?

"Umm...good," I begin. She snorts, finally glancing at me.

"Just good?" she says, quirking her brow. I feel myself blush. I do not want to talk about me, especially since Pax may walk in at any moment.

"Mmmhmm..." I say. "So, you made it seem like Jeven was... mean to you?" I ask, changing the topic. She snorts again.

"I was crabby that day I met you, and I was jealous that you got someone like Pax, looks wise. I already had to suffer through the brothel, and then when he bought me I thought my life was over. He's been...kind, when he wants to be, but we fight a lot."

I am stunned. She is jealous of me? I shake my head, confused.

"But...you said he chains you up...and..."

A coy smile plays on her face as her eyes dance.

"You really know nothing, huh? He has his kinks."

"Umm...what?"

She drops her arms and saunters over to the desk, searching through piles of sketches until she presents a few to me. I do not understand what I am seeing. Hands, for sure, with chains around the wrists, but the hands are actually gripping the chains. And then there's another sketch, two hands intertwined, but one is obviously pushing the other into some soft material.

Her art is beautiful, but it makes those emotions and feelings swirl within me. The ones I had when Pax kissed me. She lowers her voice.

"Sex can be fun. He likes to be dominant, and I let him."

My mouth runs dry. What if...what if Pax wants to chain *me* up? I couldn't...just the thought freaks me out. My chest begins to heave, and she bumps her elbow into me.

"Calm down, Miss Prude. Pax has more of a daddy vibe than anything," she says, and it is then I can hear the jealousy in her voice. I am so confused, and kind of grossed out? I can't tell.

"What...what do you mean?"

"I mean he takes care of you, he's so protective of you. He treats you like royalty. Don't take it for granted," she says, giving me a serious look. I nod. I know Pax treats me well now, after I have seen how others are treated.

I jump as a knock sounds on the doorframe, whirling as though I have been caught doing something bad. Pax stands there, small smile on his face.

"These are amazing, Deidre. Jev told me you're quite the artist."

"Thank you. Liv seems to enjoy them," she says, giving me a sideways wink before sauntering out. I am left alone with Pax, feeling more flustered than before. He walks in, standing next to me as he narrows his eyes at the sketches. His brows are pulled together as he lifts one for closer inspection. I fiddle with my hands, but a smirk eventually etches its way onto his face. He peeks down at me.

"You like these, huh?"

I feel myself flush, my whole body igniting as I remember his lips on mine, remember his words to me. I am his, and he took me because he wanted me. I give a small nod.

"Do you get what is happening in them?"

I bite my lip.

"I think so," I say. I still can't picture it, but these sketches help build some of the image I have already been piecing together. He sets the paper down gently, reaching for me. He pulls me into his side before finding the end of my chain and securing myself to him once more.

"Does it make you curious?" he asks as he does this. I don't want to admit that it does, but I know I should be truthful to him of all people.

"Kinda."

He chuckles, bringing his eyes to me before he sighs. He moves, trapping me between his body and the desk, resting his hands on either side of my quickly heating frame. His eyes swish between mine.

"What are you doing to me, Livy?" he breathes, a small smile on his lips. I am confused. I haven't done anything to him. Sometimes I am a brat, but I've been on my best behavior lately.

"I...I..." I stutter, confused. He reaches up, brushing his thumb over my cheek.

"That wasn't a question you needed to answer."

I swallow, nodding. I can hear more voices out in the living room and kitchen area.

"Remember the rules," he says, his face clouding over. I feel my stomach writhe. I am nervous, being around new people.

"Hey," he says, using his fingers to lift my chin to raise my eyes to his. He gives a gentle smile.

"I'm here, and we will have fun, alright?"

I feel reassured, but Deidre's words are still swirling in my mind. He is protective. He cares for me a lot. Does he have this thing she calls a kink?

"Do you have...a...kink?"

His face falls, going pale before bright red. Shit. What have I done? He coughs, clearing his throat.

"Deidre?"

"Yup."

We are both embarrassed, unable to meet the other's eye.

"No, I don't. Umm...yeah..." he says, scratching the back of his neck. I bury my face in my hands, mortified. He pulls me into a hug, chuckling.

"You're so damn cute with your innocence."

I growl into his chest. He rubs my back.

"Let's go get a spot at the poker table. I can teach you how to bluff a little better."

I take a deep breath, allowing him to pull me out into the party.

∾

Pax

I grab a beer, leading Liv out to the table on the patio. Theo is here, along with Kel and Kip. Kip is married, his wife a vivacious blond. They own a slave as well, but it is a male, and he is near Liv's age. He is sitting quietly on the couch, reading as we pass by. I feel a surge of protectiveness as Liv stares at him.

Dax is already at the table, shuffling cards as we approach. He is joking with Kel and Jeven. I seat myself in the middle of the table, pulling Liv onto my lap. The sun is setting, but it is still warm outside, muggy, and there is a fire pit off to the side.

Liv squirms, getting comfortable. I keep one arm over her hips, holding her to me. I notice she isn't looking anyone in the eye. I have told her not to stare before, but now I believe it is out of nerves. I lean around her, grabbing my beer and bringing it to my lips.

"So, Pax, what changes can we expect to our schedules when you take over?" Dax teases, dark eyes glinting, reflecting the firelight. I clear my throat, chuckling. Tark announced his retirement today to our platoon, and everyone seemed genuinely happy for me.

"I'm thinking of four-day work weeks and extra vacation."
Jeven raises his beer.

"I will gladly cheers to that!" he says. Everyone raises their glasses in agreement. There is idle chatter I take part in for a few minutes, mostly about work, until Jev demands Dax to deal us all in. Deidre brings over bowls of potato chips before she seats herself on Jeven's lap.

"Hungry?" I whisper to Liv. Her little fingers rest on my arm that holds her and she shakes her head. I know she is just being shy, so I let it slide.

Kip distributes chips and we decide on a buy-in price, the game shifting from poker to blackjack per Jev's demands. I can tell Liv is confused. She turns her shoulders to peek at me. I shift, pulling her closer to me.

"We are playing against the dealer. We want twenty-one," I say, sliding in the minimum amount of money before pointing to the cards. I explain the value of each and how to add them. She stays quiet, but I can tell she is simply absorbing and learning. I take another sip of my hoppy beer, feeling happier than I have been in a long time.

I hadn't intended to kiss her today, but I felt like if I didn't, I would do something more, something that would scare her. I can only keep myself from her for so long. I want her, and I feel I have made that abundantly clear. I am glad she is curious, less scared of the unknown, and that she is growing more comfortable with me.

If I can continue to show her that I will never hurt her, perhaps she will be relaxed enough to want more. I feel giddy at the very thought. She is so beautiful to me, human or not. I don't care anymore about the differences between our species. Her heart is what matters, and she has a kind, pure one—one that I want to protect.

"Yes," she hisses as we are dealt. I am shocked, checking her addition once more, but we have been dealt twenty-one. I chuckle, pressing my cheek to the side of her head.

"Looks like someone is good at math."

"Looks like I am just lucky," she whispers back, raking in our chips. I chuckle at her tenacity. She becomes more relaxed as the night wears on, some of my crew even making idle chatter with her, but she mostly talks to Deidre next to us.

Before long, it is clear we are winning. Jeven is coming in at a close second, and every time he is dealt a good hand, Deidre smiles and cheers. He nuzzles her neck, kissing her often. I can see, from my view, that his hands are wandering all over her thighs and ass. Her cheeks are ruddy as she sips a cocktail. I am surprised Jev lets her drink. I smirk, squeezing Liv.

"Thirsty?" I ask.

She shrugs, too enveloped in the game, even leaning her elbows on the table. Her position makes her round ass grind harder against me, and it takes all my willpower to calm down, but my jeans begin to feel a little too tight.

"Here," I say, holding out my fresh beer to her. She turns, glancing at me in confusion. I prod her with it. Gingerly, she grasps it, frowning as she brings it to her lips. She takes a swig, her face contorting in disgust as she forces herself to swallow. I shake with laughter.

"Eww...that's...bitter," she says. Deidre leans over with her drink, handing it to Liv.

"Can she?" she asks to me. I nod, smiling.

Liv takes a sip, much more careful this time. It looks like vodka and cherry soda. She hands it back, carefully considering.

"That is *waaaay* better," she says. I brush my fingers up her thigh.

"Stay here, I'll go make you one. But you have to eat something," I say. She flushes, nodding as I stand. I unhook her, passing the chain to her. When I return, she is eating buffalo wings with Deidre and smiling. I enjoy watching her, seeing her make friends, seeing her safe but also free, in some capacity.

She beams up at me when I get back, standing. I pull her back onto my lap.

"Keep eating and you can have two drinks, alright?"

She bobs her head, reaching for more food. The game is soon abandoned, but we all stay chatting with one another about different topics. Liv is mostly talking to Deidre in hushed tones, but they giggle often, and I keep catching snippets of their conversation. It is all innocent, lighthearted.

Liv shivers as a breeze rises. She hasn't brought a jacket. I lean in, wrapping both of my arms around her.

"Cold?" I ask. She leans back, nodding. I chuckle.

"I'll be right back, do you need anything?"

"Mmm, my other drink?" she quips, turning to smile pleadingly at me. I snort, shaking my head.

"I've created a monster," I say. But as she stares up at me with those big round eyes, I can't deny her. I fetch a jacket from my vehicle and make her another drink. She beams as I come back out, standing up. Setting her drink aside, I open my coat for her. She gives me a sheepish smile as she lets me envelope her in it.

We sit back down. I can feel she is becoming tired, especially as she curls into me, resting her head on my shoulder. Conversations have shifted to more serious topics of politics, so I tune in, listening carefully. Liv yawns against me, and I trace patterns on her bare thighs, rocking her gently to the slow beat of the music that is coming from a hidden speaker.

Kip's wife pipes up, holding her wine glass by the stem.

"I've read through these new policies so carefully. Anyone who votes for Opponent Two has no soul," she says, quite vehement. I am glad to hear she thinks this way, and I want to encourage this discussion. Theo speaks up, setting aside his beer.

"You can't make such a statement over politics," he says, dismissing her easily. Kip's arm is around her, and he frowns at Theo, but she has no problem defending herself.

"Yes, you can, especially when they have no restrictions on children. Imagine the kinds of things they will be subject to with such loose regulations!"

Deidre's eyes fall to her lap, and I notice Jeven holds her tighter. Liv is wavering in and out of sleep. Her and alcohol must not mix too well, but I don't mind holding her close, keeping her warm. Theo shakes his head, crossing his arms. Most Erathians still think women should be demure and quiet and not involved in politics. I do not think that way, but it is becoming clear Theo does.

"So say you have a daughter someday. You want to live in a world where she can be sold to a brothel or some freak with fetishes when she is ten?"

"Not the same. Humans and Erathians are on completely different levels."

She shakes her head in disgust.

"Are they, though?" I say, giving him a dark look. He frowns, still holding tight to his beliefs. Everyone is hushed.

"Yes, clearly they are, or our kind wouldn't have been able to take over so easily."

"So they do not have the same capacity to feel emotion? Pain?"

He sighs, annoyed.

"Why does that even matter?"

I feel instantly heated. I can feel Jev's eyes on me, even Deidre's. Kip's wife is smiling as she sips her wine. My arms tighten around Liv, and she sighs. She is fast asleep. I don't want her hearing this, anyway.

I shake my head, feeling my muscles tense in anger.

"What one of us does to a human reflects on our character. If you are content with harming a sentient being for no reason —if you are fine turning a blind eye to children being subject to torture, sexual or otherwise, then you clearly have morals that need adjusting."

"And what of her? She is obviously old enough to understand the way this world works, to know her place."

I grit my teeth in fury. I am about to speak, but a dark, angry voice rises above it all.

"Erathian men paid to use me. Sorry, *use* is too nice a term. They raped me, sometimes up to six men a day. I was sold to a brothel when I was nine. You think that's ok?" Deidre hisses. I am shocked as I glance at her. Jev's eyes are tight; it pains him to hear this, that much is clear in how he holds her, how he looks at her. My stomach churns. I want to vomit. If Liv had endured that before me...nothing would stop me from hunting down every single one of them.

Theo is glaring at her as though she has spoken out of turn, as though she is the scum of the earth. He is about to speak, but Jeven raises his hand.

"Whatever you have to say to that will never excuse what she has been through. Maybe it is time for you to leave."

Theo grits his teeth, glaring at Deidre, then at my sleeping, innocent little Liv. I sit straighter, using my body as a shield around her. I regret ever taking the time to train him. Theo polishes off his beer and exits.

Kip's wife's eyes shine with tears.

"How can anyone be that cruel?" she whispers, shaking her head. I tuck Liv under my chin, and she shifts, sighing against my neck. Jeven runs his palm up and down Deidre's back.

"He obviously has his own issues, hun," Kip says quietly. She shakes her head, still quite angry.

"We adopted Charlie before we got married. No one wanted him because he wouldn't talk, and no doctor ever

cared to find out why. We finally found someone who specializes in humans. He has something they call Autism," she says
to me and Jev. I am curious, having never heard of this
before.

"What does it mean?" Jev asks.

"He thinks much differently than anyone. He doesn't speak
much, but damn...he goes through books like he goes through
food. He is so smart," Kip says with a grin. I feel myself relaxing,
smiling. It is clear they view Charlie as a sort of child—as their
child. It warms me.

"What about you, Paxton? What is this story?" she says,
motioning to Liv and I. She is giving me a kind smile. I sigh
before I chuckle, reaching up to brush a few strands of loose
hair from her face, but her braids are still intact.

"We raided an empty building. She tried to rescue her
friend, sacrificed herself, really. She knocked me on my ass," I
say, grinning down at her. Everyone at the table chuckles. My
memories grow dark. I hadn't wanted anything to do with her
at first, because I was scared of how attracted to her I was right
away, because of the memories her very presence dredged up. It
made me feel low, disgusting. I see now that that was just a
byproduct of my society's expectations.

"It was touch and go for a while. It's been...pretty damn
hard, getting her to see that I...I won't hurt her. I think she
believes me now," I say, unable to meet anyone's eyes. I hear
Deidre chuckle.

"She does, don't worry."

I smile over at her.

"I just...I never expected humans to be so complex, but I am
thankful, all the same. I don't think I can imagine coming home
to an empty house now. She gets so excited to show me things
when I get off work," I say with a smile. Jev laughs.

"So does Dee, every day it's something new."

"It is not," she growls, pouting. Kip and his wife are smiling warmly at us, and even Kel and Dax are listening closely. I feel my smile fade again.

"All I want to do is keep her safe. It's been difficult, because people are hell-bent on hurting her. I had someone offer me any amount of money I wanted to breed her," I say with disgust. Kip's wife gasps. I nod.

"I may own her, but...it sort of feels like she controls my every move, now. I work so I can provide for her. It's made me much less selfish of a man," I say with a laugh. Jeven joins in.

"Kinda hard to be selfish when you have someone pointing that out to you all the time."

Deidre rolls her eyes.

We all laugh. Livy sighs again in her sleep, her eyelids fluttering, her lips twitching. Kip's wife smiles again.

"She's so little and beautiful. I can see why you're enamored."

I normally would bristle at such a word, but now I know it is true. I grin down at Liv before I press a lingering kiss to her forehead.

Enamored is too weak a word for how I feel about her.

Love is more accurate.

17

Pax

"Don't forget to pack warm clothes, Livy," I remind her as I pack my own suitcase. She huffs, still not quite happy about this little upcoming trip. It has been a few weeks since Jev's party, and things have gone rather smoothly between us. We haven't kissed since that day, but it has become more natural for more innocent kisses on the cheeks or on her forehead. She even seems to get upset when I don't greet her that way.

We leave tomorrow for Halifax, where my parents live. We will be able to spend a few days there together before my swearing-in ceremony, and then I will head out on my first mission as ranger 001.

I took today off to spend some time with her and pack. She is carefully putting all of Henry's things in his own bag. I already warned my parents she came with an extra companion, but my mother was all too excited to host us all. Her suitcase, however, remains empty.

I sigh, tossing my uniform aside before I bend down and

scoop her up. She protests, wriggling, clearly mad at me. I bring her out to the couch. I have been cooking a roast all day, and from the kitchen wafts a delectable scent.

"I don't want to cuddle," she grumbles, still fighting me. I chuckle, laying down with her on top of me before I roll, pinning her beneath me, careful not to put my full weight on her. She gasps and attempts to get away from me without much success.

"I'm just going to nap, I think," I tease. I feel her pinch me, but the pain is minimal. I bury my face in the crook of her neck, and she screeches out a laugh. She hates it, but she cannot control her giggles every time I do it.

"P-Pax," she pants, struggling. I press my lips to her jaw, slow, gentle, changing the tenor of this moment. She stills, and I can hear her breath hitch, can hear her heartbeat change.

"What if *I* want to cuddle?" I say against her. She growls. I reach up, winding my fingers through her hair as I stare down at her. She is confused, trying to figure out my angle. I doubt she will ever realize how badly I want her.

"I'm going to miss you," I say. Her face is composed, but her eyes well with tears, and her lip begins to tremble. She pulls her eyes from mine, unable to move her head in my grip. I sigh, the sight of her crying killing me.

"Shh, shh, Livy," I soothe. She heaves a breath, sniffling. I swipe her tears with my thumb.

"You...are you going to l-leave me there?" she says before she hiccups.

"Never, Olivia. I will come back as soon as I am done. You think I'm excited to be away from you? To not get to read more of our book, or play with Henry?"

She gives a shrug, petulant. I smirk, leaning down and pressing a kiss to her nose. I watch as a deep blush blooms across her cheeks.

"I'll miss you, too," she grumbles. I chuckle.

"Forgive me yet?" I say. She nods, and I lean up to press a kiss to her forehead.

"Go finish packing. We need to eat and get to bed early, okay?"

She obeys. I take the roast out of the oven, placing the enameled Dutch oven on a hot pad. My mouth is watering.

"Careful, Liv, this is hot," I call. She just nods, darting from the washing machine to our room. I run through my list in my mind again, getting my toiletry bag and going to the bathroom to pack all my necessities. I take a piss, but when I go to flush the toilet, the handle doesn't catch. Annoyed, I take the tank lid off to see if the chain broke. My eyes hone in on something wrapped in plastic. I reach in with a grimace, pulling it out. Through the clear cellophane, I can see what it is.

A knife.

I stand there, thousands of emotions swirling in my chest. When did she hide this? Was it recent, since my guard has been down? I doubt it as I grit my teeth. She was just crying over the thought of me leaving. She must have hid this a while ago and forgot about it. She wanted a way to protect herself in case I turned on her, and I can't blame her for that.

I check the chain but let the knife slip back into the water. I can't deal with this before we leave, and I can't punish her for protecting herself. She didn't know me back then. I feel myself smile sadly before I put the tank lid back on and flush.

I wash my hands, and then my blood runs cold as a devastating scream echoes from the kitchen. I storm out, finding Liv standing near the Dutch oven, holding her bright red hands up as she sobs.

I rush to her, gripping her wrists, turning her palms up. Every inch of the insides of her hands are already beginning to blister. She must have grabbed the pot to move it without thinking. She is shaking, crying, but I pull her to the sink and crank on the cold water, forcing her hands under the flow.

"Shh, shh, baby, it's going to be ok," I say, trapping her between my arms and the counter as she tries to pull away from the pain.

"Breathe, Liv, breathe," I say. She is shivering, breathing so fast. I know she needs a doctor right away.

"Stay here, keep your hands under the water, ok?"

She gives a shaky nod, still crying. I rush and get my shoes, wallet, keys and phone, before I pull an ice pack out of the first aid kit and pop it.

"Keep this between your hands," I instruct, pulling her into my arms and rushing her out the door.

She is sniffling, her eyes swollen, her hands trembling and flaming red. I hold her in my lap in the treatment room, waiting for the doctor. I gently rock her back and forth, trying to calm her.

"Ow, ow," she whimpers as the ice pack shifts.

"I'm sorry, Livy, they will take care of it, ok?"

She turns her head, pressing her face to my neck as she cries. I believe she is more afraid of being at the doctor than she is in pain. A knock on the door has her stiffening and whimpering.

A dark haired woman pops her head in with a bright smile. I am on edge, considering how Liv was treated last time at the doctor. The woman comes in, a sympathetic smile on her face.

"I hear someone has some nasty burns," she says, washing her hands before pulling on some gloves. She addresses Liv directly, who is too frightened to move.

"She grabbed a Dutch oven right after I pulled it out of the oven," I say. The doctor sits on her stool and scoots close, her face contorted in sympathy.

"Oh, sweet pea. That has to hurt. Do you mind if I take a look?" she asks Livy.

She sniffs, and I can feel her peeking up at me.

"Go ahead," I say gently to Liv, helping to take the ice pack away. The doctor grabs her wrists carefully, inspecting the burns. She sighs, clucking her tongue.

"Sorry, I forget the formalities. My name is Dr. Whitter. What's your name?"

Liv sniffles.

"Um...Livy..." she says.

"What a beautiful name!" Dr. Whitter beams. I feel Liv relax in my arms slightly.

"Well, Livy, you have suffered from second degree burns. Common in cooking accidents, but treatable," she says, giving her a warm smile. I am still defensive, wondering how this doctor will choose to treat her. Before I can voice my concerns, Dr. Whitter speaks up.

"Thankfully, Erathians developed something called heals-all. It can treat anything from burns to broken bones, and it will take the pain away immediately."

"You use that on humans?" I ask, confused. Erathians heal faster than humans naturally, but things such as broken bones can still take a few weeks. Her dark eyes jump to mine, and her smile falters.

"If you wish to go the traditional route—"

"No, no. I'm just...pleased. You're the first doctor who has... been so kind to Liv."

Her face warms again.

"I'll go grab my supplies and go over instructions with you, then."

She comes back a few moments later with a clear plastic tub filled with translucent blue goop. I smirk. I've endured heals-all many times in my life.

"Alright, Livy, what this does is coat and sterilize your

injuries before it forms a stiff impenetrable cast. You won't be able to move your hands or fingers until you are healed," she says, prying off the lid.

"You'll know when it is done because it will turn a nice violet color."

Liv is transfixed with the tub of goo. The doctor reaches for her wrist, and Liv allows her hand to be dipped in. She sighs, the pain clearly leaving her. The doctor reaches for her other wrist, putting that hand in as well.

"Should take about five minutes to set. Now, as far as healing time, we are looking at five to seven days, due to the severity of the burns and because she will not heal as fast as an Erathian. She will need to keep her hands absolutely dry. If this gets wet, it will eat away at the protective shell. When the casts turn violet, you can soak her hands in warm water and they will dissolve."

I nod, remembering from all the times I broke my bones or burned myself as a rambunctious youth. Liv finally takes her hands out, and the goo has hardened into a protective cast.

"Feel better?" the doctor asks with a grin. Liv nods, staring at her blue hands in fascination.

"Thank you, Dr. Whitter," I say, truly meaning it.

"Ahh, it's nothing, Mr. Harper. You've got a sweet girl under your care."

It is the first time Liv has been referred to as a person and not a slave. I feel myself smile. She gives us a few more instructions, and even gives Livy a bunch of candy. By the time we arrive home, we begin to realize just how troublesome this week is going to be.

"Umm...Pax?" Liv says, standing in the hall.

"Hmm?" I say, clearing the mess from earlier. My eyes jump to her. She is bending her knees, standing by the bathroom door. She pleadingly holds up her hands, and my face falls.

Fuck.

"You have to go to the bathroom, huh?"

She blushes a furious red, attempting to swipe the hair from her eyes, but without use of her fingers, it doesn't help much. She is completely immobilized by this injury, and now we are in a real pickle.

I come around the island, stowing my thoughts of attraction away and focusing instead on her helplessness. I have always been good at focusing solely on the mission at hand. This is no different, right?

"Ok, let me help you," I say.

"What—no!" she gasps, backing away from the door. I frown at her.

"Liv...you're going to need my help. I won't look at anything."

"It's...that's embarrassing..." she whispers.

"I've done worse things, trust me. And I have seen worse things."

She shakes her head, obstinate. I cross my arms.

"How are you going to bathe, wash your hair, do anything without getting your hands wet?"

She is becoming flustered and frustrated.

"Can we just take these off?"

I quirk my brow at her as she holds up her hardened blue hands.

"You really want that pain to come back? Plus, we can't soak them off until they turn violet. If we do it now, we'd have to scrub them off, meaning those blisters will become a lot more painful."

She growls, bouncing her knees. She knows she is running out of options.

"Look, I can help you until tomorrow, and then my mother would be more than happy to take care of certain needs."

She is considering, but she shakes her head.

"I...I don't know her," she whispers. I hide my smile.

"She is kind, Livy, and she's a surgeon. This wouldn't be weird for her at all."

She looks at her feet, turning beet red.

"I just...I want to try on my own, but then if I need help I want *you*..." she mutters. I feel warmed that she is giving me so much trust. I decide to allow her the chance to try.

"Ok, just call me if you need me."

She doesn't meet my eye as she skirts past me and into the bathroom. I shake my head with a chuckle to resume my packing as well as hers now. Near dinner time, I have us sit on the couch to eat. She was successful at going to the bathroom on her own, though it took her a while and I noticed she wasted almost half a roll of toilet paper.

I seat her on my lap, both of us facing the TV as I bring the fork up to her lips. She is annoyed; she is very independent, so maybe this will be good for her. Maybe this will teach her to lean on me a little more.

She takes her bite, and then I take my bite, and we switch off until our plates are cleared. I clean up, stowing things away for our trip. I have her go over her suitcase, ensuring I have packed the right things. She blushes and nods, eyeing her lacy underwear. I may have packed more sexy things on purpose, but I couldn't help myself.

"Alright, what do you need me to help you with for your nightly routine?" I ask. She has her pajamas draped over her arm, and she is frowning. I can tell her hair is annoying her as it keeps falling in her face and she keeps blowing it away.

"Brushing teeth? Bath? Shower?" I press, raising my brows to show my concern. She stares at the ground, becoming mortified. I can't help my chuckle, and she glares at me.

"Livy, it's ok, what are you so worried about?"

She shrugs, still not meeting my eye.

"I just...don't want you to...umm...you know..."

"I don't know unless you tell me, silly."

"Ugh. *See me naked*," she rushes out. How do I politely tell her that I would fucking love to see her naked without sacrificing this conversation?

"I will only look at your head, I swear."

I wait as she chews her lip, growing more frustrated by the second. Still staring at the ground, she hunches her shoulders and speaks.

"Can you help me wash my hair and stuff, please?" she mutters. I smile.

"Of course, Liv."

We make it to the bathroom and decide a bath may be the best option. I find some plastic bags and tape them to her hands to avoid any accidents. She sits on the toilet as I run the bath, and I can feel how nervous she is. I hold up a hand towel.

"You can put this over yourself if you want," I say. She is blushing, biting her lip, even shaking. I feel bad, feel awful that she is so nervous, but I understand why. I want to make her feel better, more relaxed.

"There's no one else here, just you and me, and you trust me, right?"

She is peeking at me from under her lashes as I sit on my knees by the tub. She nods.

"What about this makes you nervous?" I say, motioning to the bath. She squirms, shrugging. I frown.

"Do you think I would hurt you, Liv?" I ask, keeping my voice gentle. She doesn't meet my eye, but she shakes her head quickly.

"I will only do what you tell me to do, ok?"

"Okay," she says, her voice small. I stand up, and she follows. I don't know whether to take her shirt or shorts off first. She holds her hands out helplessly, her round eyes so wide and glossy as she stares up at me. I reach for the hem of her shirt, pulling it up and over her head before tossing it aside. She hugs herself in her simple white bra, but the sight wreaks havoc on my desires. This is going to be harder than I thought.

I reach for the buttons on her shorts, my knuckles brushing against the smooth, warm skin of her stomach on accident. She tenses, stepping back a pace. Her chest is heaving, her eyes avoiding mine. I remember the two times I found her with her pants unbuttoned—both while she was being attacked. It is easy to see where her mind is, and it makes my heart clench.

I work fast, pulling them down. She steps out, shivering in her bra and thong. I make good on my word, looking only at her face, but I cannot control what I see out of my peripherals. I take a moment, letting her adjust, letting her calm.

"See, not so bad, huh?"

She gives a soft laugh and shakes her head. I step closer, reaching around her as though to hug her as my nimble fingers find the hook of her bra. I twist, unclasping it. She doesn't let it fall right away, and she refuses to look at me. I reach for her chin, forcing her eyes to mine.

"It's just me here, remember?"

She nods. Keeping her eyes on me, I reach down to the band of her lacy underwear, gently pulling them off. She stands before me completely naked. I've yearned for this so many times, but now that I have it in such a strange situation, it just isn't the same. She is helpless, and I need to be her protector more than anything, even if that means shoving away my desires until she is ready.

I put my arm around her shoulders, walking her to the bath and helping her in. She sinks down, keeping her knees up as well as her hands. She eventually turns to me and gives me a sheepish smile.

"How are you feeling?" I ask.

"Better," she mumbles. I chuckle.

"I'm glad."

I let her soak for a while before I ask what needs to be done.

As she is pointing to her shampoo and other bottles, she slips, sliding down. I reach in, catching her as she flails, effectively soaking my shirt and pants. She is giggling by the time I right her.

"Not funny," I say, though I cannot hide my smile from her. Attempting to get her hair wet is a whole other process. I try holding her with one hand, but she keeps sliding every time she leans back, and more water ends up outside of the tub than in it. Soaked and frustrated, I reach for the plug on the tub, draining the water.

She gives me a quizzical look as I stand, peeling off my shirt. I smirk down at her. She isn't going to like this.

"You're getting a shower buddy for the next few days, sweetheart."

Olivia

I gulp as I stand under the cascade of water, and though it is warm I am shivering. I have seen Pax naked, but only briefly, and it was by accident. Now, he stands just beyond the curtain, waiting for me to tell him I am ready.

Am I? Will I ever be?

It's not that I think he will somehow turn vicious and attack me. It's more...that I feel ashamed of my nudity. I was raised to be modest, and even while on the run I made sure to never expose myself. I stare at my hands, annoyed that I did something so careless and stupid. I suppose I have to pay the price for not listening to him, now.

"You ready, Liv?" his deep voice calls. I clear my throat, using my arms to hide my breasts as I face the wall.

"Umm...yeah, yeah I am," I say. I hear him chuckle. I'm glad he thinks this is *so* funny. Asshole. The curtain is pulled aside, and I am dwarfed by his shadow. My chest heaves, and I jump as I feel his hands on my shoulders, turning me so we are both facing the same way. He brings me backwards until my head is under the flow of water, soaking my hair.

"I never realized how damn long your hair was until now," he says, his voice gruff. I feel myself smile, relax.

"Tell me what to do, Livy," he says, and I can hear him smiling. I turn my head, nodding to the shampoo.

"That first."

It's kind of nice, bossing him around for once and having him be so eager to listen. Maybe this isn't so bad. It really is just the two of us. No one has to know what we do in our own home, right? He squeezes some shampoo into his palm, the scent of roses mingling with the steam in the shower. He holds out his hand.

"That enough?"

I laugh, for his whole palm is full.

"More than enough," I say. He sets the bottle back, and his wide palm is soon cradling my head. He gathers up my hair, using both his hands now. I sigh. The way he uses his fingers, so gentle but with just the right amount of pressure, is making me relax. It is like a massage on my head. I hear him laugh.

"Someone feels spoiled, huh?"

"Maybe," I smile. He rinses my hair, and I point to the conditioner. He lathers some up, making sure my hair is coated. His fingers find my hips, gently pushing me forward out from under the stream.

"My turn," he says. I oppress the urge to look. I want to see his body again, all of him. I am curious, less afraid now. I chance a peek over my shoulder, keeping my eyes directed up. His face is pinched, eyes closed as he lets the water cascade over his head. I take my chance, my stomach in knots, as I let my eyes dart down.

I cannot help my blush, or the way my eyes widen. His *thing* is long, thick, intimidating, and behind that hangs something else. I have nothing to compare this particular part of the male anatomy to. I don't see how that would fit inside me. Deidre said it gets bigger—hard. Right now, it looks kind of hard, but not all the way? I am confused.

And then, I hear him clear his throat. Mortified, my eyes travel up his scarred, sculpted torso. I've never realized how expansive and impressive his muscles are before now. I want to...to reach out and touch his hard stomach, or his chiseled chest. I have laid my cheek on him so many times, but I have hardly ever touched him. He said I was his, and that he was mine, so I can...right?

"Careful, Livy. You keep staring like that, and I'll have to do something about it," he says, his voice low and husky. I gulp at the dark look in his eyes. Does he mean punish me? I shake my head, but he smirks, reaching for my hips again, pulling me back beneath the flow of water. He rinses the conditioner out, but then I feel his body, slick, hot, pressing against me from behind. My breath catches in my throat. I like it, how powerful he feels against me, and I like this foreign feeling growing in the pit of my stomach and between my legs.

It aches, but it doesn't hurt, per se. It feels like...like I am yearning for something, but I do not know what yet.

"Where's the soap for your body?" he asks, his lips at my ear. I tremble, letting my eyes slip closed as his fingers clamp around my waist.

"O-over there," I say, pointing to the shelf as best I can. He grabs it, squirting some into his hand. I am confused, wondering why he hasn't grabbed a washcloth, but then he rubs his hands together in front of me, creating bubbles.

And then, his hands find my body. I tense, ticklish as he starts on my sides, but before long my mind is a sweltering mess. He is careful not to touch any areas that are too private, but the way his hands feel on me, so strong yet gentle, is making my knees want to buckle. I never want him to stop touching me. I want more.

The ache between my legs grows more pronounced, and it is as he chuckles that I realize I have leaned back into him, that a small moan has escaped my lips.

"Do you like me touching you, Liv?" he asks, lips at my ear. My knees are shaking, but I nod.

"Say it," he growls.

"Yes-yes," I stutter, panting. His lips press against my slick neck, his tongue darting out to lap at the spot just below my ear. My heart races, wild and uncontrolled, as the pressure between my legs begins to throb. It hurts, now, more and more prominent. I want...I don't know what I want.

His hands continue to cleanse me, going up and up, until he is just under my breasts. Gentle, he pries my arms away, giving him access to me. I whimper, nervous.

"It's just me and you, baby," he says in my ear. My stomach writhes in pleasure at his word. I never thought having someone call you *baby* could make you feel this way. I am startled as he palms my breasts, cupping them, one in each hand. My eyes dart down, watching as he dwarfs me, his skin tanned compared to mine. The tendons and veins in his hands prove how strong he is.

"Fuck, you're so beautiful, Olivia," he says in a groan. He tilts his hips forward, and I feel *him*. He is hard, long, hot. My thighs tremble in anticipation. I know he knows how to take care of this ache between my legs. He knows everything. And he cares about me. Maybe...maybe it isn't so bad that he is making me feel so good.

One of his hands leaves my breast, traveling down my stomach, pausing above another area, an area that seems to want him to touch me.

"Do you like this?" he asks, holding me tight to him. I decide not to think about anything, to just let my body take over. I nod. He is kissing me again as he growls, and the hand still on my breast begins to roll my nipple between his fingers. The motion sends electric waves of pleasure down between my legs, and I gasp before I bite my lip.

"I'm going to touch you, Liv, I'm going to make you feel good, ok?" he says, panting behind me. I whimper but nod. He presses a kiss to my temple.

"Good girl."

His other fingers continue down, and I tense, afraid, remembering the pain and humiliation of being tied to that tree. Pax continues to whisper in my ear, keeping me planted in this moment with him. His long fingers move down between my legs, hovering over my opening.

"Fuck," he groans. "You're so wet, baby."

Well *duh*, we are showering.

I feel relieved when he doesn't stay in that spot, the part of me Brutus violated. Instead, I feel his fingers tracing slow circles over something a little way above that. I buck my hips, whimpering, for it is so sensitive, but his rhythm is gentle, languid, and I begin to adjust.

He is kissing my neck again, pinching my nipple, making ravenous sounds, grunts, growls, and his hardness is ever present behind me. I am lost in the clouds, blissful, until I feel a tightening in my core, and I panic.

"Pax—Pax!" I gasp. He slows down but doesn't relent.

"It's okay, it's okay, do you feel it?"

I am panting, shaking. I don't know what he means, but at the same time, I do know. It is somehow instinctual. I nod. I feel like I am on a precipice, about to jump off. His fingers pick up their pace again, and my legs are quivering.

"Ahh...ahh," I moan. And then, my whole body tenses. I cannot breathe, or make sense of anything as I tighten. He pushes me over the edge with his fingers and his kissing, and I cry out, spasming, but he is holding me up. I feel awash in pure bliss—as high as I have ever been before or could ever hope to be again. I feel weak as I pant, leaning into him. Deep inside of me something is clenching and releasing over and over, before it slows and stops.

"Fuck, that was so hot," he growls.

"What...what did you...do to me?" I breathe. He squeezes me, kissing my cheek, my neck, the side of my head before he chuckles. I feel special, warm, safe—protected and cherished, here in his arms right now as my heart still hammers away.

"I made you orgasm for the first time, baby."

18

Pax

Liv is dressed in one of my shirts, sitting cross legged on the ground in front of me as I towel her damp hair. She hasn't spoken much since the shower, but her cheeks have remained a deep shade of pink ever since we emerged. I reach around her, fingers curling around her hair brush.

I begin at the bottom, untangling her fragrant, long locks. She sits still, and I can tell she is in deep thought.

"What are you thinking?" I ask, keeping my tone light. She lets her heavy, casted hands fall to her lap as I smooth her hair down. She turns suddenly between my knees, biting her lip as she stares up at me.

"You...liked that?" she whispers, eyes searching mine. I snort, letting the brush fall to the couch cushion.

"I've wanted to do those things to you for a while now, Livy."

Her eyes bulge, and she blinks quickly.

"Wh-why?"

I shrug, feigning nonchalance as I smirk, picking her brush

back up and motioning for her to turn around. She obeys as I resume the detangling.

"Because, every time I imagined you moaning, I knew nothing would top the real thing," I whisper in her ear. I feel her shiver, can see her nipples harden against my white shirt. I chuckle, pulling all her hair back and peeking at my phone for the instructions on how to braid.

"I like making you feel good," I continue as I twist her hair into submission.

"I like making you happy...and..." I say, tying off her hair at the end. She turns around again, her face clear and bright and expectant. I reach down, cupping her cheek, smoothing my thumb across it.

"I do not want to do those things to anyone else, Olivia. I hope that's alright with you," I say. Her brows furrow as she bites her lip, but she soon blushes and gives me a small smile.

"Come here," I say, gripping her hips and pulling her up onto my lap. She straddles me, unsure of where to put her hands. She pouts, frustrated. I chuckle, leaning in to peck a kiss on her nose. I grip her wrists, putting her casts behind my shoulders, our chests touching. I am wearing nothing but shorts. In the dusky light offered by the fireplace, Liv's skin seems to glow.

"Is it...bad, what we did?" she whispers. I can tell by the look on her face this is a deep concern for her. I am confused, though. Is this cultural? Erathians are sexually active starting rather young by human standards I would think, and it is neither taboo nor discouraged.

"Not at all, Liv. Did you want it, like it?"

She nods quickly, eyes wide. I feel reassured that I haven't scared her. What, then, has her so concerned?

"Umm...I just...no one has ever seen me...naked..." she whispers, looking away. I feel a gentle smile on my face.

"I feel honored, to be the first."

She blushes deeply.

"I was...just told it was bad, unless you're married," she says, "to let someone touch you like that."

I nod in understanding. A custom, then, albeit strange.

"It is not that way in my culture."

She is processing this news slowly, thinking hard about it.

"My mom said...that...a man should cherish a woman's heart before her body."

I smile, though I try to contain it. If only she knew that was the case. But how do I tell her I love her, when she has no real concept of what love entails? I cup her cheeks, searching her eyes.

"I more than cherish your heart, Livy. It is...the most precious thing in the world to me. I hope you can see that, or at least understand it."

"But...but I am your slave..."

I sigh, frowning.

"I don't view you as such. When was the last time you did extra chores?" I say, quirking my brow. She snickers, because she knows she's been escaping all that. My hands fall to her hips. All I want to do is kiss her until the sun rises. I want to bury myself in her, but I know that cannot come just yet. She is still too new to this.

But I want to test my limits, especially since I am leaving so soon. I want her to yearn for me while I am gone, for I will surely be aching for her every day we spend apart.

I scoot forward, bending up to press my lips to hers in a brief kiss. When I pull away, she is blinking quickly, her cheeks warming. I take it as a good sign, pressing my lips to hers again. I move slow, gentle. She surprises me by mimicking my movements. I smile against her, allowing my tongue to glide across her bottom lip. I feel her gasp, and I reach up, holding the back of her head as I slip my tongue in, swirling it against hers.

She makes the most intimate sounds, mewling against me,

and her hips begin to rock upward. I don't know yet if it has been a mistake to not wear compression shorts as my length begins to harden. She is only wearing a thin pair of cotton underwear, and as she straddles me, there is no way she doesn't feel me.

Her gasp as her hot center comes into contact with my throbbing cock is confirmation enough, and I pull away with a chuckle. Her wild eyes are blinking at me, her cheeks and neck crimson.

"I won't hurt you," I say in encouragement as her eyes dart down to my lap.

"I want to...see..."

My chest burns, and I feel ready to explode this instant.

"I'll make you a deal. You can see, but only after I've pleasured you again."

She bites her lip, pretending to think on it, but I can see the fire in her eyes, the excitement. After a moment, she nods. I grip her ass, standing us up before I set her back on the couch with me eye level with her knees.

"Pax," she breathes, nervous. I reach up, curling my fingers around the band of her underwear as I slowly begin to slip them off. As I do, I press a kiss to the inside of her knee. She sighs, letting her head fall back. I rid her of her panties, gripping her hips and giving a slight yank, pulling her closer to the edge.

"I never want you embarrassed around me, Liv, do you understand?"

She peeks down, biting her lip. I keep my eyes on hers as I press a kiss to the inside of her thigh.

"Mmm," she moans, her eyes fluttering closed.

"Is that a yes?" I chuckle against her.

"Yes, *sir*," she teases. My chest ignites with possessive fire.

"Good girl," I tease back, sliding my hands up under her shirt, cupping her breasts, rolling her perky nipples as she gasps. I trail a few more kisses up, closer and closer to where I know she needs me. She shivers as I fan my hot breath over her sensitive spots. She is so eager already, her body so responsive to me.

I dart my tongue out, trailing it as slow as I can from her core to the very top. She writhes and moans, raising her hips to meet my tongue. I cannot hold back. I flick my tongue over her bud fast, then slow, before I dip it as far into her as I can. I repeat this process, lost in my own world of ecstasy. I reach down, pulling my cock free.

I wish she could touch me, but I don't even care at this point. I need a release. I've been aching for far too long. I stroke myself as I devour her. I know she is close again just by how shallow her breathing goes. She tenses, but no noise comes out, and I feel her muscles contract and spasm. I moan into her as she cries out, panting.

I am going to come, and soon.

"Liv," I rasp. Her heady eyes fall to mine, her chest heaving. I reach up, tugging her shirt off, kneeling between her legs. Her eyes widen at my hardened length as I grip it.

"Are you alright with this?" I ask. She is entranced, not even looking at me. I groan, stroking, slow at first as my other hand palms her pert little breast. I feel my own release looming, and staring at her sprawled beneath me after just feeling her come on my tongue has me tensing.

"Can I...come on you...?" I pant. I hope she says yes or I'll be cleaning the couch.

"Yes," she breathes. I groan, the sound guttural. I stroke faster, and then I feel pure bliss. I spurt my seed onto her stomach. There is an embarrassing amount, but her wide eyes seem to just absorb it all.

I am panting, nervous, as I come down from the high. Have I scared her?

"Liv? Liv, are you alright?"

Her eyes dart to mine, shocked.

"That...goes inside of me? And does...that?" she asks. I chuckle, nodding. Her eyes turn surprised.

"I'll clean you up, I'm sorry—"

"When are we going to do that, Pax?"

Although I just had the most mind-blowing climax of my life (notably without even having sex), my cock surges again at her blunt question. I feel a wicked smile of pleasure curl onto my lips. My God, how did I get so fucking lucky?

The drive from Sardone to Halifax is north and takes a little over four hours to complete. Liv has been glued to the window the entire time so far, more excited about the scenery than nervous about staying with my parents. As soon as we left the city and entered the countryside, she seemed to fully relax.

She huffs, reaching a casted hand to her back for the thousandth time as she shimmies against the seat. I chuckle, one hand on the steering wheel. She's been quite stubborn this morning.

"Liv, where do you itch?" I ask, exasperated. She grumbles something incoherent, trying to scratch her back against the seat, her face pinched in annoyance. I redid her braid this morning, but it was much more difficult a feat with dry hair, and it is now springing loose around her face.

I reach over, itching between her shoulder blades with a smirk. She crosses her arms, annoyed. I was able to dress her in shorts and a tank top, but she was still apprehensive being nude around me. I suppose it is simply how she is as a human —modest, demure. I do not mind. I find it cute how easily she becomes flustered.

"Is that attitude I see?" Her frown deepens, and she has the audacity to roll her eyes at me. I grit my teeth, my palms tingling. I haven't had to punish her in a while, and though our relationship has changed somewhat, the fact that I demand respect has not. I know she is being surly on purpose because she is mad at me for leaving.

"Last warning, Livy," I say, cocking my brow at her. She simmers, moving to the other side to better look out the window again. She is becoming antsy the longer this drags on. I know we are close as we enter Halifax, but my parents' home is further out in the country. I smile as we draw near my child-hood home.

As we roll to a stop, Liv is stuck staring, her mouth agape.

"This...is this like a castle?" she breathes, turning to stare wide-eyed at me. I chuckle, shaking my head.

"No, it's a home, Liv."

"That is not just a home!" she argues, shaking her head. I feel slightly embarrassed as I scratch the back of my neck. Yeah, their home is sprawling, and the grounds are well kept and luscious, but my mother is a surgeon and my father is retired military—both high paying jobs in Erathian culture.

"Come here, before the chaos ensues," I say, pulling her to me and seating her on my lap. She seems to pay closer attention when I hold her this way. She is biting her lip, her cheeks flushed. I raise my hand, brushing her hair behind her ear.

"My parents are kind people, so I will ask you to not take advantage of their kindness and do anything you know is wrong."

"Like...stealing?"

I nod.

"Or running away. I know you're mad at me, but don't make them pay for something that is between you and I, alright?"

She drops her eyes but nods.

"You will mostly be around my mother, but my father is your ultimate authority figure. He will be told the rules I have for you, and he will ensure you follow them."

Her eyes widen.

"He will...punish me?" she whispers, aghast. I smile, gentle.

"No, but he will tell me if you have broken rules, and I will take care of that when I get back."

She seems relieved. I glance past her to all the greenery, to the tall, grey-stone manor with its high windows. My grip on her tightens.

"They also have slaves. I am not sure how many. I...I understand, if you are excited to be around more humans, but I need to warn you," I say, searching her eyes. She is excited, that fire growing in her gaze.

"Stay away from any and all males that are not my father. Do you understand, Olivia?"

I know my voice is low, authoritative. I can tell by the way she tenses that it scares her. True to her nature, she glares.

"Why?"

"Because I said so, that is why."

I am glaring back at her, feeling possessive, but only because I want her to be safe. I would never forgive myself if someone hurt her, and I know my father would feel horrible as well. As soon as I see her bottom lip begin to tremble, I know I've upset her. I sigh, pulling her into a hug, holding her head against my chest as she sniffles.

"I just don't want anything bad to happen to you. It would... kill me, if someone hurt you," I say against her hair.

"Then don't go," she mumbles. I sigh, squeezing her tighter. I wish I didn't have to. I press a kiss to her cheek.

"Can you forgive me?"

She shakes her head, but I can see her small smile. I grin, sneaking my hands up under her loose tank top, feeling for myself her flushed skin. She gasps against me, stilling.

"Maybe tonight when we shower you'll forgive me," I say against her jaw before I lower my lips to her neck. I feel my jeans tighten, my hands roaming from her hips to her back as I kiss her more eagerly and begin to slowly grind my hips against hers. She lets out a breathy moan, only making me want to fuck her even more. I open my eyes, ceasing all motions immediately as a figure clad in white and light blue walks toward us down the drive, a wide-brimmed straw hat on her head.

"Shit," I hiss, recognizing my mother. Liv is panting, bright red. I sit her straight, fixing her hair and clothes, but nothing will ever escape my mother's keen eyes. She is close enough now to see us, and she starts waving.

"I'll grab Henry if you can carry some bags," I say. She nods, eyes glossed from a moment before, still flushed. I grin at her, leaning up to press a kiss to her lips.

"To be continued."

∾

Olivia

I am flustered still as Pax helps me from the vehicle, and I stand there awkwardly as he begins to unload. A woman approaches, a bright, beaming smile on her face. She has a small nose and mouth, is slightly wrinkled, and has the most beautiful blue eyes and thick brown hair. I don't see many Erathians with blue eyes.

"Well, hello there!" she says, slowing her approach, hands splayed on her thighs. I smile, but I am so nervous it is hard to breathe. Not only do I not know this woman, but she is Pax's mother. That automatically makes her way more important, right?

I stagger back a step, bumping into his sturdy body. He reaches up with one hand, cupping my shoulder and giving me a gentle rub.

"Hey, mom," he says. I can hear the smile in his voice.

"Oh, Paxton! You grow more muscles each time I see you!"

she says, coming a little closer. I wince, shrinking into him, and she notices, holding up her hands, her face worried.

"Oh, dear, I'm so sorry, my name is Iris, what is yours?"

She waits as I fumble, trying to hide my annoying hands. Pax gently rubs my arm.

"L-Livy," I finally manage. She grins, her eyes flashing to Pax.

"She's gorgeous, sweetheart. I am honored to meet you, Livy."

I feel myself give a small smile.

"It was a long ride. She's kind of tired, and as you can see, we had a little mishap yesterday."

"Mmm, heals-all. I remember putting you in that a time or two," she says to Pax. He chuckles. She waves us forward.

"Come on, come freshen up and I can have someone bring your things in."

Pax moves, dropping his hand and gripping my wrist above my cast. I pull against him, worried about Henry. His mother crunches along the gravel to the massive front doors.

"I'll grab him, you just follow, alright?"

I nod.

We make our way inside, and I am stunned by the sheer size of such a cavernous space. It is stunning, with dark wood accents and paintings and hundreds of windows that let in so much natural light.

"Pax told me of a little companion, dear. What is his name?" Iris says to me as we walk into the foyer.

"Umm, Henry," I say, keeping my voice quiet.

"How lovely!" she says. "I have you in your room, Paxton, and Miss Livy can stay with Mabel, my littlest one."

"Thank you, mom, but Liv will be staying with me until I leave."

I glance at Pax, and his eyes are dark, his arm muscles bulging as he holds Henry's cage. I feel warm, happy that he isn't making me sleep apart from him. I am already dreading sleeping alone when he leaves.

"Oh, sure, dear, go on up and I'll have Mr. Fox and his son bring your things up."

Pax nods, jerking his head to the stairs, and I follow without hesitation. The door is already ajar, so he nudges it open with his knee and steps back to allow me inside. The room is huge, decorated in fine, rich yellows and flowers, with a four poster bed dominating the middle of the space. The windows here are floor to ceiling, and to the left is another open door, leading to a bathroom. There is even a TV and a couch with a coffee table.

Pax nestles Henry in a spot away from any sunlight and sighs, hands on his hips.

"Welcome to my childhood home," he says, glancing at me with a small smile. My eyes feel like they will permanently be this wide.

"This is...amazing..." I breathe, wandering forward. I don't hear his stealthy approach, but he soon has me by the waist, picking me up as I screech out a laugh before he tosses me to the bed. I am sprawled on my back with my legs dangling over the edge. He leans over me, his hips between mine as he grips my waist. In his eyes is that hungry look—the one that makes my stomach flip, the one that makes heat pool between my legs.

Whatever he did to me last night, he can do to me forever. I never knew being naughty could feel so good, but to have Pax being the one making me feel that way just makes it even better. He hums his amusement as he smooths some hair from my forehead.

"I say we just shower right now, what do you think?" he teases. I feel him, then, through his jeans and through my shorts. Hard, eager, thick. I gulp. He told me we wouldn't actually have sex until he thought I was more ready. As nervous as I am, I can't help but be excited as well. He said he only wants to do these things with me, and I believe him.

He leans down, placing a kiss on my chest, and I sigh at the euphoric feeling this gives me. His lips trail up to my neck, then to my jaw, and then latch onto my own. I find myself moaning into him, before I gasp as he grinds himself against me, his hips moving so fluidly. I break our kiss, looking down, watching the way he moves, and a thrill chases through my veins, leaving me breathless. If that is what he looks like *with* his clothes on...

"Fuck, Liv. You're not going to make this easy on me, are you?" he growls, gripping my hips as he pulls away.

"Wha—"

He flips me over more quickly than I can blink, until I am on my stomach, but he is soon pressing himself against my backside, leaning over me, his lips at my ear as my heart races.

"You like this, don't you?" he whispers, grinding his hips into me. I whimper, but can't help nodding. He has me so worked up, so ready for a release. He chuckles, the sound dark.

"My innocent little Livy, all to myself," he growls. A thud sounds in our ears. He is off me in a flash, and my eyes fly open to the door. A man is standing there, holding our bags, and next to him is a younger man, near my age. That one is smirking, his eyes staring deep into mine. I feel so guilty—so dirty, knowing someone saw us. Pax said not to be embarrassed when it was just us, but now these men have walked in on a very private moment. I am mortified.

"Thank you, just leave them there," Pax says, his voice deep, commanding yet still kind. The older man nods, keeping his eyes low out of clear respect. The younger one, however, sets my suitcase down, and his eyes never leave mine. They are the most startling shade of blue I have ever seen, and coupled with his black hair, they jump out even more.

I have seen a look in someone's eyes like that before, but I can't place it right now. Either way, there is something...chilling, about him, about the small smile that lingers on his lips. Pax clears his throat, his hand sneaking up the back of my thigh at the same time before it slides to my hip, his fingers curling in hard enough to startle me. The young man's eyes bounce up, a sneer wavering on his face. Just as quickly, his eyes drop to his shoes.

The older one bows a little as he backs out, but they both turn and leave, shutting the door behind them. Pax doesn't move, and my heart is still thumping hard against my ribs. Slowly, his hold on me loosens.

"Stay away from that boy," he growls. I want to argue with him out of spite, but something is nagging at me, something my mom used to call a 'gut-instinct.' She told me to always listen to that, and I have. It is what kept me alive for so long out in the Ruins and the wild.

He flips me over once more, and I stare up into his dark, stoic face. I know he isn't frowning at me because I did anything. I know he didn't like the way that boy stared at me. My stomach writhes pleasurably. I kind of enjoy how protective Pax is. Sometimes it is annoying, but I know it's just because he cares about me.

"Ok," I say, biting my lip. His eyes swish between mine, but he reaches down and helps pull me up into a sitting position.

"I think a shower will have to wait. Let's go see my parents."

19

Pax

I lead Liv down to the kitchens where I know my mother will be. I am resisting the urge to pummel that kid who stared at Livy, but I will make sure I bring it to my father's attention when I see him. That boy will not go near her.

We pause outside the kitchen, hearing a few lighthearted voices inside. I turn to Liv, straightening her shirt, tucking her hair behind her ears. She stares up at me with thousands of emotions in her emerald green eyes. All I want to do is make her mine, more than I already have. Now that we have a taste of how we make one another feel, I know it will become one of the main aspects to our relationship. I hope she sees how much that means to me, as a man and as a person.

She gives me a soft, nervous smile.

"My parents raised me, and they are kind, Liv," I assure her. She nods, shuffling closer. She never says what she wants, but I somehow know when she is seeking my comfort. I open my arm, folding her into my side. We make our way into the kitchen together. There is a long table, and the scent of cinnamon and coffee. My mother stands at the wide, deep sink, trimming lavender, while a child around ten or so sits at the table, dutifully arranging the flowers into vases.

I feel Liv tense. The little girl is cute, dressed crisply (no doubt my mother's doing), and her blonde hair is swept back into a neat ponytail. She glances up, her blue eyes soft as the sky, her face open and innocent, and when her eyes fall to Liv, she beams in excitement.

"Mama, is this the new girl?" she whispers to my mother. She turns, jumping as she sees us.

"Oh, yes, dear, this is Livy, and my son Paxton."

It isn't lost on me that the girl calls my mother *mama*. I wonder at the origin—of how my mother came to own her, but I will save those questions for later.

"Hello, Miss Livy and Mr. Paxton," she quips, kind, intelligent. I chafe Liv's side, encouraging her to speak, but she is too overwhelmed.

"Hello, Miss...?" I ask.

"Mabel," she says, swinging her little feet. My mother dries her hands, coming around as I pull Liv to the table and usher her into a seat.

"How nice to meet you, Miss Mabel," I say, standing behind Liv's chair.

"I trust Mr. Fox got your things up to your room?" my mother asks, peering over Mabel's work. I feel my stomach turn sour, but I nod.

"Liv, dear, would you like a roll and some coffee or tea?" my mother asks, hand on her hip. Liv turns her red face to me, seeking permission. I smile down at her.

"Go ahead. I need to find my father and discuss some things," I say, bending down as I place my hand on her shoulder. I press a kiss to her heated cheek, before straightening and leveling my mother with a look that tells her not to ask questions.

She tuts, eyes wide with a knowing smile on her lips as she moves to get Liv a plate and a mug. I begin to back out.

"Be good, Livy. I will be back soon."

Her wide eyes are nervous, but I give her another reassuring nod. She can make friends with Mabel and my mother. It would be good for her to have a feminine presence in her life. I can't expect her to watch sports and war movies with me every day.

My feet tread the familiar halls, bringing me to my father's study, where I know he is likely reading or working on something. He enjoys the history of this world prior to the Erathian conquest, and he has worked tirelessly over the years to compile an amazing amount of knowledge.

The door is ajar, but I knock anyway. He is seated at his desk, pen poised over some paper, but his eyes jump up as I push the door open. He gives me a smirk, pushing his chair out and standing as I enter. We are almost the same height, with me just an inch or so taller, and though we used to be just as built, he has lost some of his muscle since retiring from the service. Other than that and the wrinkles around his eyes, we could be the same person.

"Pax," he says, clasping my hand in greeting.

"Father," I say, sitting across from him and leaning back. His office is warm, cozy, the scent of old books thick in the air.

"How was the trip up?"

"Long," I say, folding my hands as I relax. He chuckles, picking his pen back up.

"It seems your mother has already made a new friend," he says. I snort.

"Is she that excited?" I ask. His eyes find mine, glimmering, coy.

"She's excited that you seem to be quite smitten with the girl."

I grit my teeth. Of course my mother would run off and tell

my father what she thought of Liv and I. There are no secrets with that woman.

"Smitten," I grumble, crossing my arms. He quirks a brow.

"To each his own, son. Humans and Erathians are mingling more and more these days. Perhaps some from our species are learning we aren't all that much superior."

I snort.

"I would like to hope so, but then there are...others," I say, thinking back to the man who offered to pay me to breed Liv. I clench my fist in anger.

"There will always be others, son," he says, dropping his pen and folding his apparent letter.

"So, I suppose you wish to impose your rules for her onto me, as I am the one she will fear."

He folds his hands on his desk, leveling me with a serious look. I sigh, scratching at my jaw. I do not want her to fear my father, but to respect his authority.

"As long as she doesn't steal any knives—and trust me, she's made a habit of it—and as long as she doesn't try to run away, then there isn't much else I am concerned with. She will be respectful, and kind, or I will deal with it when I return."

He nods, leaning back as well.

"I am sure she will be just fine. There's plenty to keep her busy with this time of year."

"Good," I say, but then my thoughts turn dark.

"That Mr. Fox and his son—"

He waves a hand with a nonchalant frown.

"I will keep her away from men. I understand your concerns there."

"Thank you," I say, feeling relief. He is still giving me that knowing look, and I shoot him a glare.

"What?" I say, gruff. He chuckles.

"Just wondering when you'll admit you're in love."

I choke, clutching my chest as I spasm with a cough of

shock. My eyes are watering by the time I glance back at my father, but he is just giving me a simpering smile.

"I'm...I am n—"

He holds up his hand.

"Don't lie about those you love. That's low, Paxton."

I grit my teeth, glaring at him, wondering how to navigate this.

"Just be careful. She is a wild, free spirited being, and you will always stand in the way of what she truly wants."

"And what would that be?" I growl. His lips twitch into a frown.

"Her freedom."

We exit his office, meandering through the halls as we catch up and he congratulates me on my promotion. We are just nearing the kitchen when we hear it. The crash of glass, the harried voice of my mother, and then more crashes and metallic clangs.

I rush forward, storming into the kitchen to see Liv backed into a corner, a knife held precariously between her casted hands. Mabel is on the floor, holding her split lip as she cries in a pile of water and vase shards. My mother stands between them, hands outstretched, panicked. My jaw clenches in rage. I don't even care what Liv has done—I am utterly pissed that she has caused this.

"*Olivia Donne*," I say with a sternness reserved for commanding my men, crunching over the glass as I take her arm in my hand and give it a shake. The knife clatters to the ground, and her wide, frightened eyes lands on my face.

"What the hell is going on?" I growl down at her. She whimpers before she winces, shielding her face from me as she cowers.

"Pax, it is fine, it was just a squabble—"

I loosen my hold on her, feeling as though my body has flooded with guilt and dread. She was afraid of me—*is* afraid of me. I release her, wiping at my jaw. I turn, glancing at the mess, wanting to help clean it up.

"Mom—"

"It's fine," she says, more stern this time. I grit my teeth, nodding. I turn back to Liv. She is hugging herself in the corner, shivering like a wounded animal. What have I done?

"Let's go," I say, my voice more gentle. When she doesn't move, I reach for her, but she whimpers again and flinches away. She really thought I was going to hit her. All these months of work, and I ruined it in the span of two seconds.

"Liv, come with me upstairs, please," I say, keeping my voice low, gentle. I back away, allowing her space to move. Chest heaving, she dashes past me and my father. I sigh, moving to follow, but as soon as I make it to the foyer, I see she has not gone for the stairs, but for the front doors. She leaps over the threshold, giving me no choice but to follow.

I run after her, shocked at how fast she is, especially with bare feet. Her trajectory isn't sneaky by any means; she sprints across the front lawn, making for the trees on the other side. I am close, but she still makes it into the forest before I reach out and grab her.

I yank her to me with a thud, skidding us to a stop as I pull her feet off the ground. She is struggling, sobbing, hitting me with her casts and kicking me with her heels. She hasn't acted this way since we were in the Ruins and the surrounding wilderness.

"Liv, Liv, calm down," I chant. She lets out a screech of anger, pushing against me. I clamp down harder.

"For fuck's sake, Olivia, I'm not going to hurt you!" I yell. She finally stops struggling, but she collapses in my arms, sobbing. I have tracked her cycle, as Jev instructed, but she shouldn't be that close to her next period yet, so I can most likely rule that out for her wild emotions. Whatever she is going through is from her past, from things that happened to her when I took her.

I pull her over to a log, sitting down with her in my lap. She is shuddering with each sob, and she surprises me as she straddles me, wrapping her arms and her legs around me as tight as she can. Her tears wet my neck. I hold her back, rocking us side to side, running my hands over her.

"It's okay, Livy, I'm here," I soothe. She is eventually hiccuping. I don't want her to fear me, and I know I have a huge apology to prepare, but for the moment, I only want to hold her tight. She doesn't stop trembling when her cries quiet to nothing.

"What happened?" I ask, keeping my voice low as I continue to rock.

"Pl-please don't leave me," she whimpers. My heart shatters.

"I'll be back before you know it, baby," I whisper, pressing my lips to the top of her head. She sniffles, gearing up to cry again.

"Shh, shh, calm, Livy. If you can just relax, you'll have so much fun here. And you can even go to my ceremony with me and see Jev and Kip and his wife, how does that sound?" I attempt. She gives a petulant shrug.

"Am I going to be punished?" she mutters against me. I sigh. I don't necessarily want to, but it depends on what happened.

"Tell me what went down, and we can discuss it, ok?"

"I don't like Mabel. She's a brat."

I chuckle at the irony, because Liv has perfected being a brat to me.

"Oh yeah? How so?"

Liv sniffs and pulls away, her red rimmed eyes landing on mine. All I want to do is kiss her pain away.

"Your mom gave her a bowl of peanuts. She asked if I wanted some, and I was polite and said no because I am allergic. And then your mom turned her back, and that little shit started throwing peanuts at me. I gave her fair warning," Liv explains, crossing her arms. I can't help but chuckle, reaching up to smooth her hair away from her blotchy face.

"Is that how you would have handled it in the wild?" I ask with a quirk of my brow. A little smile forms on her lips.

"Yeah. If I had my hands, she would have a black eye."

I bark out a laugh at her scrappiness. My hands fall to her hips as my emotions sober. She seems to simmer down as well.

"You're not off the hook for holding her at knife point, Liv. That cannot fly. You know better. She is a child and you're a young lady, alright?"

She huffs but nods.

"I'll have a talk with Mabel as well."

She sits up, her face surprised.

"You-you will?"

I nod. Even though Liv overreacted, she is right; Mabel was being a little shit, and I don't mind scaring her a little so she is on her best behavior for my parents. Liv relaxes, dropping her eyes.

"Liv, you know I would never hurt you, right?" I say. She nods but doesn't meet my eye. I sigh, giving her hips a squeeze.

"Why were you so scared of me, then?" I say, gentle. Her watery eyes reach my face. She wipes at her cheeks with her arm.

"You...you get this look on your face sometimes, and it's...it's super scary, and I never want you to look at me like that..." she mutters. I hadn't realized that was something I did. I feel guilty now for scaring the woman I care so much about.

"I'm sorry. I will work on that, alright?"

She peeks at me but nods.

"You're always safe with me, remember?" I press. I inch my fingers up under her tank top, her skin flushed from her run.

"Yes," she whispers before biting her lip. I smirk.

"Five paddles for holding a child at knifepoint?"

She rolls her eyes. I pinch her side, and she glares, but I am grinning at her.

"No. Just one, thank you."

"Liv, you're lucky it's not more. You also ran away from me."

She slumps in defeat.

"Fiiiine," she drawls. I chuckle, smoothing my hands to her back and pressing down so she falls forward, our noses touching. She blinks at me, flushing a new shade of pink, her eyes confused but also filled with desire.

I press my lips to hers in a deep kiss, skimming my hands over every inch of her bare skin that is available. She rocks her hips forward naturally, something I have noticed she does when aroused. She is seeking me, just as I am seeking her. I doubt I'll be able to keep myself from her for much longer, but I want to try and keep things slow for her sake.

I pull away to catch my breath, looking at her luscious, swollen lips.

"Still mad at me?" I tease. She smirks, mischievous.

"Always."

We make it through dinner, though it is quiet and strained. My father can hardly hide his chuckles, and Liv keeps glancing at him in confusion, her brows pulling together as she tries to figure him out. I know we look a lot alike, but we can be very different in how we handle things. She doesn't want to eat much, embarrassed that I have to hold her fork out to her.

Mabel sits near my mother, her split lip healed, but her eyes are down on her plate the whole time. It is not my wish to frighten a child, but she needs to know her place. Dinner over, we head upstairs. I usher Liv into our room, but pause at the door as my mother and Mabel walk by.

"A moment, please?" I say to them both, closing the door to our room. My mother clasps her hands, glancing down at a demure Mabel. I cross my arms, waiting for her eyes to find mine. When they do, I begin.

"You may be under my mother's care, but Olivia is under mine. If you do anything like that to her again, I assure you there will be consequences, and my mother will not have a say in them. Do you understand?" I say. The child's lip wobbles, her eyes welling with tears, but she nods. I turn my gaze to my mother.

"Olivia is severely allergic to peanuts. I will leave you with an epipen, but she has more. She...will need help administering them, in an emergency."

"Of course," my mother says, but her eyes are tight. She isn't one for conflict.

"Thank you. I will see you both at breakfast."

They continue on down the hall. When I enter our room, Liv is fumbling with the band of her shorts, trying to get them down. I turn and lock the door before going to her, pushing her hands out of the way. I unbutton them, sliding them down her silky thighs. She stands before me in a simple pair of lavender hued cotton underwear.

I reach for her wrist, taking her to the couch. A fire is blazing, giving off the only light in the space. I know she was simply trying to change, but we still have a matter to settle. I sit on the couch, spreading my knees. I can see her jaw clench, but she lays over my legs, resigned to receive her punishment.

I smooth my palm over her ass, knowing now what it looks like with not a stitch of clothing on it. I take a deep breath, feeling aroused already. Liv tenses, and I know she can feel my hardness against her stomach. I need to get this over with, get her in the shower. All I want is to hear her moan again.

I lift my hand, giving her a sharp but tame spank. She jumps, but only a little. The way her ass jiggles is driving me insane. I smack the other cheek. I am becoming more aroused with each passing second, having her at my mercy in such a way. I smooth my palm over her, pulling the cotton out of my way before my hand connects with her flesh again.

This time, a small noise escapes her lips. Not a whimper... a...*moan*? Fuck, my cock is throbbing. I smack her other cheek, harder this time, and her moan is unmistakable. I grit my teeth, her final one the hardest yet. She whimpers, shivering across my legs. I stand her up, making sure she is alright.

Her face is flushed, her eyes glossy, her mouth agape. She looks...frightened, but not of me. Her casted hands move, covering her private area as she twists her legs together. She is hiding something from me. I reach for her wrists, wrestling them away. There, on her underwear, is the stark evidence of her arousal. My body stills, flooding with desire and other emotions.

Me being dominant, spanking her, turned her on. I would be lying if I said it didn't turn me on, too. My mouth runs dry with desire as my eyes find her face. She is blushing profusely, looking so ashamed.

"What's wrong, Liv?" I ask, gentle. She turns her hips, trying to hide herself from my view.

"I...I..."

I pull my bottom lip between my teeth.

"I...don't know...don't understand—"

I pull her forward, cupping her ass, my face level with where I know she is aching for me.

"Did that turn you on?" I say, voice husky. She is confused.

"What...turn me...what do you mean?"

I chuckle at her innocence.

"I mean...did that make you want me to do naughty things to you?"

Her blush is quick to bloom.

"You can be honest with me, remember?"

She considers this, and eventually she nods.

"Yes," she breathes. My hold on her tightens. My mind is swirling in ecstasy. She is so sexy right now, standing there in her little tank top and underwear, her hair a wild mess, soaked and eager for me. Holding back is going to be impossible. Keeping my eyes locked on hers, I reach for the band of her panties, slowly tugging them down. She shivers, her breath catching in her throat.

I press a kiss to the top of each thigh, and then a kiss to each hip bone. I sneak one arm between her legs, cupping her butt and pulling her to me.

"Put your foot on my leg," I demand. She obeys, quivering in anticipation, opening herself up to me like a rare, beautiful flower. I waste no time, darting my tongue out, tasting her, pressing against her bud. She moans, pulling away, but I tighten my hold, keeping her planted as I slowly lap at her.

I build her up to her release, teasing her, bringing her close before backing off. It's easy to do this a few times, until her legs are shaking and she is crying out. I love how vocal she is. It makes me want to do it even more. When I think she is ready, I ask her for the truth.

"Liv," I breathe. She is panting.

"Yes, Pax?"

She sounds confused, annoyed that I have stopped. I find her eyes, using my fingers to keep her turned on. She gasps, loving it.

"Are you alright with going a little further tonight?" I ask. Her eyes are tight, apprehensive.

"What...umm...how?"

"Would you like to feel my fingers inside you?"

She chews her lip, moving to back away a pace, but I hold her to me.

"Shh, baby, you can say no, and I'll still get you off, it's always your choice."

"But...it's...going to hurt..." she says. I smile, shaking my head.

"No, it won't, I promise."

She frowns, but I can feel her relaxing.

"We can...try..."

"Ok," I say, pressing a kiss to her thigh again. I flick my tongue over her bud, gathering her wetness with my finger. She is soft, ready. Gentle, slow, I push my finger in. Fuck, she is so tight. No wonder Jev warned me about this. I begin to worry I will never be able to fit in her.

I pump my finger slowly back and forth, and I smile against her as she begins to rock her hips, seeking more.

"Do you like that, Liv?"

"Mmm, yes," she moans above me.

"Do you want more?"

She gasps as I pick up my pace, but nods. Slow, I add another finger, stretching her to what her limits are for now. It is going to take some time to build up to my cock, but I don't mind. My fingers continue to pump, and she is so wet they glide easily.

She is panting, moaning, so close to her release as I lap at her and thrust, meeting her hips as she rocks to me. My hand that grips her ass leaves for a moment, and I smack her. She cries out, loving it. I am lost as I pleasure her, slapping her again.

"Ahh!" she cries. I feel her walls clamping down on me, hard, but I keep going, pushing her over the edge as she spasms, crying out. I slowly withdraw as the remnants of her orgasm fade away. She stands there, quivering, and I gather her up into my arms, laying on the couch, surrounding her with my body as I kiss her neck and her forehead.

"How was that?" I tease.

"I don't even know," she mumbles, still lost in her daze. I

chuckle. She rolls her shoulder, peeking up at me with a dreamy smile on her bright face.

"Can you make yourself feel good again?" she asks. I smile, feeling warmed that she cares about my needs as well.

"When you've rested a bit, I will shower with you, and then I can do that."

She nods, blushing. It is quiet for a moment, the peace and contentment rather enjoyable. I let my eyes slide closed, nuzzling her.

"Pax?"

"Hmm?"

"Do you...do you love me?"

20

Olivia

I wait, watching as Pax's eyes turn brooding, his lips frowning. There are lines around his mouth and eyes when he looks at me this way. I don't know why I am nervous, but I am. I am not all too sure what love is; I only know what I saw my parent's exhibit, and those memories are blotchy, at best.

I remember my father bringing home bright daffodils in the springtime because they were my mom's favorite. I remember she used to make his coffee each morning before work just the way he liked it. I remember him kissing her on the head or the cheek, or saying her cooking was going to make him fat but he was fine with it.

I suppose that is my definition of love, however loose it is. I know how a parent should love their child, I know how one should love their family, but I am not all sure how a man should love a woman.

Pax kisses me on the head. He holds me close when we fall asleep. He brings me things like cupcakes or ice cream because he knows I love it. He bought me Henry so I would have something to take care of and cherish. And he cares about me and my pleasure—he seems to want to make me feel good while he forgets about himself.

He is protective of me. Even if he comes across as brash and bullheaded, I know he just cares about my safety, because if I was hurt, it would hurt him. Even his rules and punishments make sense to me now; it is all to make me better. Educated, able to take care of myself, respectful.

All of that added up has to amount to something, right?

His eyes warm, shifting from nervous and guarded to open, and a small smile flitters at his lips. My chest feels full. I already know what he is going to say.

"Yes, Livy. I love you."

I awake to the sound of birds chirping, something I hadn't realized I had missed since being in the city. We have been at his parents' house for a few days. Everything has gone smoother. Mabel has stayed away from me, and I simply stick close to Pax or in our room. Each day brings us closer to the time we will have to spend apart, and neither of us want that.

Tonight is his swearing in ceremony. I am proud of him, but we've yet to talk about what exactly his job is. I feel it is time I should know, especially since he has told me he loves me. Before I could say it back that night, he had pressed his fingers to my lips and told me I didn't have to unless I was ready. I feel ready, but maybe he knows more about this than I do. In fact, I *know* he does. I can wait a little longer to share how I feel about him, but I know where my heart is, and it is with him.

I yawn and stretch as the door to our room opens. Pax enters, panting, sweating, not wearing a shirt. He has made it a habit to go running twice a day to prepare for his next mission.

I sit up, eyeing his glistening torso with desire. He grins, hands on his hips.

"Shower time?"

I blush, but I nod. I don't want to seem too eager, but all I want to do is feel that high, that pleasure. Every morning and every night, he takes his time and makes me feel things I never thought I would feel.

I push the blankets away, moving to stand, blushing even more hotly when I remember I fell asleep naked. Both of us, actually. He said that is how his kind bond with one another; a lot of physical touch, more than humans require. He said bare skin to bare skin was the best way to become secure with one another. I understand what he meant. All I want is to be wrapped up by him, tangled together with nothing between us.

There is a wide grin on his face as I stand, and his eyes are directed down. I shift, covering myself, but then I realize what he is looking at. My hands. My casts have turned violet!

"Yes!" I beam, rushing past him to the bathroom. He chuckles, following after as I bounce by the sink. He plugs it, turning it on and letting it fill.

"Someone is excited," he teases.

"I just can't wait to itch my own back. Your nails are too stubby," I grumble, shifting from foot to foot as I stare at my hands, willing the casts to fall off by themselves. He comes behind me, grabbing my wrists. My eyes bounce up, meeting his in the mirror. He doesn't push my hands into the water yet, even with how antsy I am. He simply stares, his gaze dragging slowly from my face down to my breasts. I feel the swell of his sweaty chest as he breathes behind me.

"You still going to shower with me?"

I frown, about to roll my eyes and say yes, but he beats me to it.

"New rule: you must shower with me once a day. Punishment for not doing so will result in ten paddles. Fair?"

My mouth runs dry, and I feel my nipples harden to stiff little peaks. Between my legs, I begin to throb again. His face is stoic and serious. I gulp, giving a small nod. He smirks. I shiver as he pushes my hands into the warm water. He leaves them in, trailing his wet fingers up my arms before he cups my breasts. My eyes flutter closed as I moan. He presses himself tight against my backside, and I can feel his eagerness. It doesn't frighten me anymore, but excites me instead.

He pinches and pulls my nipples, gentle yet firm, and I feel him lean in, his breath fanning across my neck.

"I'm going to miss you being so helpless," he says, his voice husky. I tremble but nod in acknowledgment. His foot nudges mine, spreading my legs. My breathing goes rapid. I know what is coming. His fingers spread me, gathering my wetness before he circles that little nub that is so sensitive. I gasp, my hips lurching, but he remains steady.

"Look at me, at you," he demands. My eyes blink open. I am flushed, blotchy, my chest heaving, my breasts still peaked. He turns my hips to the side slightly, to the floor length mirror on our left. My mouth hangs open, watching his fingers work slowly, building me up. My eyes find his. He is watching me only, a determined look in his eyes.

The look on his face, the sight of his perfect body—of him —pleasuring me, sends me over the edge. I tense, preparing, trying to hold on to that band of ecstasy before it snaps. His other hands snakes up, holding my throat, gentle but firm, pulling me back against him.

"Keep your eyes open," he growls. And I do. I crash around him, crying out, shaking, withering. His lips are at my neck, kissing me hard. I stand there, panting, trying to collect my scattered thoughts, but then I hear him chuckle. I follow his line of sight to the sink. My hands are finally free.

∾

Pax

"Where are we going?" Liv whispers, though there is no need to whisper. I can simply tell she is nervous every time we leave our room together. She wants to make a good impression on my parents, it seems. I interlock our fingers, taking her out the back door and to the stable.

"Don't you trust me, Livy?" I tease, quirking my brow. She peeks up at me, eyes dancing. Every time she looks at me now, she blushes instantly. I cannot wait until we cross that final physical hurdle, but there are a few things we must discuss first, and with my time dwindling, I know today is the day.

I let go of her as I open the barn doors, but grasp her again and lead her forward. She is hesitant; the stamping of hooves and the chuffing of horses may be new to her. I pause in front of a stall, taking my riding gloves out of my back pocket and tugging them on. She stands on her tiptoes, trying to see over the door, but my onyx stallion, Demon, pokes his head out at the same time and gives a loud whinny.

She jumps back with a yelp while I chuckle, reaching up to give his neck a pat.

"Been a while, boy," I say quietly, his great, wide eyes watching me. He gives me a sniff, flicking his tail in anticipation. I know no one here has ridden him as hard as I used to, and I know he is chomping at the bit to let loose.

"Stay there, I'll bring him out," I instruct to Liv. She backs away until her shoulders hit the other stalls, her eyes wide and fearful. I go in, putting on his bridle, securing his saddle. His flanks quiver, and I worry he will be too wild for Liv right away. I need to wear him out a bit first.

"Have you ever been around horses?" I ask as I cinch down his saddle.

"N-no," comes her shaky voice. I chuckle.

"Rule one: never walk behind them. They cannot see

behind them, but they can feel you. If they feel threatened, they will kick, and it hurts like a bitch," I say, gripping the reins. I peer over the top of his door, catching her eyes as she twists her hands together.

"Rule two: you listen and do everything I say without question. Understand?"

She nods. Finally, a rule she can't ignore.

"Last, and this isn't really a rule, but they can sense your fear, and they will take advantage of a novice rider. Especially Demon here," I say. She nods, her eyes tight.

"I'm going to take him out to the arena before we ride, alright? Head out the doors and to your left to the fenced in area."

"O-ok," she says, obeying. I chuckle as Demon snorts again. I can feel his tension building. She has put him on edge. I do not understand how, but animals have an amazing way of sensing things. He either likes her or hates her, but I won't know until she properly meets him.

I bring him out, pulling open the gate and closing it behind me. Liv is standing at the rail, still nervous and jittery. I give her a reassuring smile as I mount. Demon is eager immediately, rearing, but I force him into a trot around the circle before I allow him to gallop. I can feel he wants to run, and he has done well with me after not being ridden in a while. I pull him to a stop near Liv.

"Can you open the gate for me?" I ask. She nods, dutiful as she does so.

"I'll be right back," I call, spurring Demon forward. He takes off before Liv can respond. He is wild, free, his hooves thundering the ground and churning up clumps of dirt and grass as we go. I lean forward, the wind streaking past and making my eyes water. I let him run until he slows to a trot once more, patting his neck as I laugh.

I used to take Demon into Halifax so I could drink. He

always knew the way home, and I slept in the barn with him a few times so my father didn't catch me. I cherish those memories, the freedom a life in the country can bring you. Liv seems more relaxed here as well. She loves our daily walks to the pond, insisting we feed the ducks and look for turtles. She's even shown me how to build a better fire, what tracks to look for if you want a squirrel, what plants make you itch.

She is brilliant in her survival instincts, and I hate to admit she has taught me a thing or two. It is as I am sauntering back that my mind begins to race with possibilities. Being ranger 001 means I can live anywhere, can station my platoon anywhere. What if...what if I moved us out here to Halifax? We'd be close to my parents, the town is small and kind, and the slaves around here are treated very well.

I could give Livy a better life out here, one with more freedoms, one where I don't have to constantly worry whether or not someone will steal her or hurt her. I will have to talk to my father about this later, get his opinion. I know it will make them happy.

As I round the last of the trees, the arena comes back into sight, and my blood instantly boils. I nudge Demon into a trot, eyes locked on Liv. She is twisting her hands, clearly nervous, as that damnable Fox boy talks to her, leaning casually against the fence. They both turn at the rumbling of Demon's hooves, and I pull him up just as I reach them, my eyes searing down at the young man. He nods to me with a cocky smile before he slinks away back to his chores.

I glare down at Liv, but she is shaking, not meeting my eye.

"What did I tell you—"

"He came up to me," she snaps, heated eyes finding mine. I sigh, realizing my misstep. I dismount, walking toward her, but she backs away until she hits the fence.

"I'm sorry," I grunt. She crosses her arms, not looking at me. "Olivia—"

"It's fine," she mutters. I growl. I don't want to ruin our last day together.

"Come meet Demon," I say, gentle. Her eyes shoot to my stallion, and she gulps. I reach for her wrist, tugging her forward. He snorts as she gets closer, and she tries to pull away.

"It's ok, Liv. He won't hurt you," I encourage as I splay her dainty hand across his neck. I show her how to pet him, and he surprises me by turning and nudging at her shoulder and neck. She squeaks with laughter while I am left dumbfounded. Demon, the horse everyone is afraid of, the one who only lets *me* ride him, likes her. I should have known.

"Christ," I mutter. She ignores me, petting him on her own now.

"He's beautiful," she says, mesmerized by his shiny, ebony coat. I pat his neck, smiling as I watch her interact with something for the first time. She is so open, curious, excited. I love this side of her. Hell, I even love it when she's a brat to me. I told her I loved her, and I do, but I hope she realizes just how much. I don't think I could imagine living my life without her now.

"Want to ride with me?" I ask. Her eyes bounce up to mine, still nervous, but she nods.

"Alright, put your foot in the stirrup and hold the saddle—good," I say as she listens. I help hoist her up, and she sits astride him stiffly, panicking.

"You need to relax, or he will throw you, alright?"

Trembling, she nods. I sigh, pulling myself up behind her, caging her in as I grab the reins.

"Ready?" I ask, one hand splayed across her stomach to keep her in place.

"Are we...gonna run like you did?" she breathes. I chuckle.

"No, just a nice little ride until you're used to it."

She relaxes into me as Demon wanders easy down the path. We are quiet for a while as he snorts and flicks his tail, and she is soon calm, leaning back into me, the sunshine kissing her face and hair. I know now is as good a time as any to discuss what is on my mind, for she cannot escape me here, no matter how awkward.

I clear my throat.

"So, there's something we must discuss...about the physical aspect to our relationship," I begin, feeling flushed under the beating sun. Liv stiffens.

"Umm...o-ok...can we not...do those things anymore?"

I can hear the devastation in her voice. She thinks I am spurning her.

"No! No, Livy," I breathe, squeezing her. "I want to eventually do...more, much more, but you need to be made aware that you can get pregnant, if we do that."

"Oh," she says before she falls silent. I clear my throat again.

"Umm...it's your choice, of course. I...I am not quite ready for kids—"

"I don't want a baby right now," she says, stricken. Thank God.

"Good, ok, we're on the same page. So...umm...we can look over some options for birth control. I would take it upon myself to wear what humans call *condoms*, but they do not work on Erathian men..."

She's quiet, absorbing this.

"If...if you don't want to take anything to prevent pregnancy, we don't have to actually have sex to enjoy each other—"

"No I...I want that," she whispers. My grip on her tightens.

"So, you want me to find something for you?"

She nods. I wish I could see her face.

"If this is something you don't want to do, I promise you I am okay with whatever you choose. I will still love you the same no matter what. I mean it," I say, leaning around her. I can see her cheek lift with a smile.

"I...I think I need to be on something...because I just... umm...want you, all the time..."

I press my face into the crook of her neck, and she giggles, shying away.

"I love you," I say against her skin. I never thought I could love something as much as I love her, but I do.

"I...I love you, too, Pax."

We lay in the late afternoon sunshine, Liv resting her cheek on my chest as I run my fingers through her hair. I feel full, overflowing with joy and contentment. She loves me. And I believe her. I smile against her, pressing my lips to her head as she sighs, stretching out. Demon snorts behind us as he grazes.

She raises her chin, setting it on my sternum as she stares at me. With the rays of sun glimmering in her intense green eyes, I would swear she is some ancient wood nymph, here to whisk me willingly away. A small smile is wavering on her plush pink lips.

"What is it, Livy?"

Her smile grows.

"You're handsome."

I chuckle, leaning up to peck her nose.

"And you're beautiful."

She blushes on cue, but her smile fades and she sighs, rolling back onto the grass. I sit up on my elbow, staring down at her in concern. Did the whole birth control thing scare her?

"I like it out here. I feel...better," she says, staring up at the tops of the trees and the sky. I feel a tug of guilt at my heart.

"I can tell that you like it here."

She turns her eyes to me, a devious smile on her face.

"We should just run away together. I can teach you how to survive."

I chuckle, reaching over to clasp her hip, as if she really will disappear from me at some point. I cannot let her begin to think such thoughts. The wild—though beautiful—has its many dangers. As guilty as it makes me feel knowing I have taken her freedom, I know even more so that I have spared her from a worse fate, and that alone is the only thing that allows me to own her in such a way.

"I don't doubt you'd be the one commanding me, my little human," I say. She giggles as I grip her sides and tickle. We tussle and roll as she squirms to get away, but I eventually land on top, pinning her down. She glares at me, though I can see the mischief in her eyes. I brush her hair from her face before I cradle her fragile skull in my hand. My heart is racing—harder than it did when I told her I loved her. The truth I share will change many things for her, for us.

"Liv, there's something I need to share with you...about the wild."

Her brows furrow in confusion. My hand that is holding her face begins to tremble. I grit my teeth, clenching my fist. Even after all this time, the memories—when allowed to rush forth —are still as potent as the days they occurred. I know better than to feel weak, but weak is all I feel. I understand her fear, her trauma, because I have *been* her—helpless, frightened, wondering what I would have to endure before I was given the ultimate mercy of death.

The words swirl in my mind, but they stick in my throat. Her confusion deepens, now mingled with concern. My watch dings, and I glance at it, pulled back from the brink of an infinite fall.

"Shit," I mutter when I catch the time. I pull her up, brushing us free of debris.

"Pax—"

"I didn't realize how late it was. We need to go get ready, or we'll be late."

"Oh," she says, flushed, nodding. I help her back into the saddle before I follow behind. She is still tense, nervous. I squeeze her tight, kissing her cheek.

"I have a surprise for you," I say.

"What—"

"Hold on!"

I spur Demon into a gallop, and she shrieks as we streak through the trees and back to home.

"Liv, dear, let us see," my mother calls, standing in my bedroom with me. I stand at the mirror, fixing my tie, smoothing down my new suit. I had Deidre pick out a dress for Liv for this ceremony. I wanted her to feel beautiful, despite her role in my society. My mother had been kind as she helped Liv do her hair and show her what was expected of a lady at such an event.

But now Liv is refusing to come out.

I sigh, tousling my hair until it sits just right. My mother is dressed in a light blue dress, one that matches her eyes. My father always said her eyes were what lured him into marriage with her. I think I understand what he meant, especially when I look into Liv's eyes.

"I'll get her," I say. My mother tuts, calling my father's name as she leaves. He's not one for being on time to anything.

I knock on the door, but there is no answer. I decide to take my chances as I open it. Liv is standing in front of the floor length mirror, her hair pinned up, wearing a sleek black dress that flutters out and ends just above her knees. My breath catches in my throat. She is simply stunning, even though I think the neckline plunges a little too deep, and even though the straps are a little too thin. I do not want to share her beauty with everyone.

I want to be selfish, keep her locked away so only my eyes

can feast on her beauty. Her gaze finds mine in the mirror, and she lets her hands fall to her sides, clutching at the fabric. She even wears a pair of tiny flats with little bows on the toes. I swipe at my mouth, feeling as though I am drooling.

"Fuck, Liv," I say, taking a few steps closer.

"I...I've never worn anything so nice before," she whispers, blushing. I crack a smile, trailing my fingers over her bare shoulder.

"You should more often. I'll buy you a thousand of these," I say, my voice husky as my desire mounts.

She gives me a wavering, apprehensive smile.

"Stay close to me or my parents tonight. Every man's eyes will be on you, baby," I say, lowering my gaze as well as my hand. I let my fingers slip beneath her dress in the back—pissed off that it is so short, but simultaneously eager, for access to her is much easier. Her breathing hitches, but so does mine when I feel she isn't wearing any panties. My other hand grips her waist, yanking her trembling body to me. She moans, her eyelids flickering.

"You're so naughty for me," I whisper before I press a kiss to her collarbone. She knew what she was doing, choosing not to wear underwear. She shivers at my light touch.

"Paxton Harper! You'll be late to your own funeral!" my mother yells from the foyer. I grit my teeth in annoyance. I don't need a fucking ceremony for a promotion. I continue my pursuit, my fingers hovering over her heated core. I cannot wait to feel how wet she is for me.

Feet stomping on the stairs has us both jumping apart, and Liv dashes for the toilet, shutting herself in. I cough, straightening my tie again as my mother appears.

"Pax—"

"She just had to use the bathroom, calm down," I growl. She sighs, frowning, but there is a knowing smile in her eyes.

She comes closer, gripping my lapels to straighten them out, her words hushed.

"So, shall I be expecting grandchildren soon, or is the moaning I hear day and night a ghost you brought with you?"

Olivia

I am still yearning, aching for the promise of pleasure as we drive to this swearing in ceremony. So lost in naughty daydreams of all the things Pax has done to me, I don't realize we've pulled to a stop, the door open. I snap my jaw tight, scooting cautiously out of Pax's vehicle, making sure my dress stays in place. As soon as I am standing in front of him, I obediently hold out my wrist.

He smirks, his eyes ignited with lust, and my insides melt all over again. He's gentle as he clasps the thin chain around my wrist, securing it to himself, and the trail of fire his fingers leaves along my bare skin makes me tremble. I wish we could just stay home, and I feel myself glowing up at him.

He shakes his head, bites his lip and chuckles as he pulls his eyes away from mine.

"Liv, stop looking at me like that. You're about to make this the sweetest torture I've ever endured."

I press my lips together to hide my smile. Who knew that I, little Livy, could wield so much power over a man like Pax? I really enjoy it, but what I am beginning to oddly enjoy more is being chained up—to *him*. As though he is my anchor, the only one allowed to come near me. I like being his. He puffs out a sigh as his parents emerge from their car, crunching along the gravel drive toward us. It is warm, a humid summer's eve, but the slight breeze ruffles my dress around my thighs, and it almost feels like fluttering fingers stroking me.

I inwardly groan, shifting from foot to foot as I press my thighs together. This ache is only getting worse. Pax pulls me close, bending to whisper something in my ear.

"Be good tonight, please? And...you'll probably see a lot of...interesting things. Remember not to stare."

He pulls away, fixing me with a frown. I want to roll my eyes, but I just settle for a muted nod. Iris approaches, fixing a stray lock of my hair.

"So beautiful, dear! What a figure!"

I blush and duck my head, and Pax thankfully pulls me closer, his presence calming.

"T-thank you," I mutter. She smiles kindly, turning to Penn as he puts his arm around her. They are in love—you can see it in their subtle actions, how they always reach for one another, how they smile, how their eyes light up. I wonder if that is what Pax looks like when he sees me. I feel butterflies in my stomach, and I peek up at him. He's already grinning down at me, his dimple visible.

"Suppose I'm the lucky one, huh?"

"Duh," I mutter quietly so his parents can't hear as we walk forward. I am struck, in complete awe as the edifice of a *real* castle looms into view. It knocks the breath from my lungs, with the deep grey stones, the towers, the lit windows and wide staircase welcoming guests. It is overwhelming as we step inside, and I am more focused on all the artwork and decor than I am on the people that greet Pax.

They ignore me for the most part, as most slaves here are being ignored, I notice, but I don't mind. I am not one for small talk, or big crowds. The entire time Pax chats to a small cluster of older men with his father, his arm is around me, his palm splayed on my waist, his fingers tracing absentminded circles on my hip bone. I lean into him, trying not to stare, but it is such a new environment it is impossible not to.

Some slaves are chained in the corner, some are with their

masters, but all are dressed impeccably and look well-fed. At least there is that. I know it can always be worse.

"Hey there you two!" A feminine voice quips. I recognize Kip and his wife Lana, and they have their human, Charlie. His face is down, hands gripping a tablet fiercely. I try and smile at him, but Pax has told me he's very shy.

"Hey," Pax greets, shaking hands with Kip. Lana smiles kindly at me and rubs her palm over Charlie's back. It warms me, how kind she is to him, and he doesn't seem to mind.

"Liv, you look stunning!" she says. I blush, ducking more into Pax's side. I am not used to such praises from people other than Pax.

"Thank you," I mumble, glancing up at Pax for reassurance. He smiles down at me, that fondness clear as day in his chocolate hued eyes.

"God, you two again," an irritated voice drawls. Pax stiffens, his grip on me tightening, but we all recognize Jev's voice. He saunters up, looking more dapper than I expected in his suit and bow tie. I wonder if Deidre helped him as she helped Pax. Jev lets out a low whistle, eyeing me up and down and then grinning at Pax.

"Think you owe Dee a big old thank you."

"Think you do, too, asshole," Pax grumbles. Everyone in the group chuckles, but with the way Pax is holding me, I can tell he's becoming more and more possessive. Gentle, I pat his side for reassurance, but he's still tense. Before we have to suffer through more small talk, people begin to usher into the banquet hall. We find our respective tables, thankfully sharing with his parents, Jev, and Kip and his small family.

I notice most slaves are left out in the foyer, but out of the hundreds of people, there are still quite a few, and most are plastered to their masters' sides. Pax pulls out my chair and has me sit before he takes his seat next to mine, close enough that his knee knocks into mine and sends a thrill through me.

A speaker takes the podium in front, and though I am interested at first, it soon becomes boring as can be. The Erathian is dull and monotone, and even Charlie seems to be restless. Glad I'm not alone.

Pax sighs, sinking down further and stretching out, and beneath the table I feel his heavy hand cup my knee. I jump a little, peeking at him. He's still staring straight ahead, but there is the faintest hint of a devious smile on his face. I feel my stomach drop. He gets that look when he wants to—

Slow, his hot, rough hand sneaks up to my thigh beneath the hem of my dress. My eyes are stuck wide, watering, and my cheeks flame to life. His hand, though, doesn't stop. The lights dim, and two large screens hum to life, some video playing. I fidget in my seat, for the darkness is only making him more bold. I feel him lean in, and I tense as his long fingers trace circles on my upper thigh.

"Spread your legs for me, baby."

Oh, God.

I gulp, wild eyes looking around at everyone, but they are all focused on the screens, and there's a master and slave a few tables away that are blatantly kissing.

"Liv," he growls when I don't obey. Trembling in my building anticipation, I listen, bringing my knees apart.

"Wider."

My fingers grip the edges of my chair, but I do as he demands, heat flaming into my gut. I can already feel how wet I am, and I flush with utter embarrassment. The pads of his fingers continue to trace circles on my inner thighs, and I feel the rush of air, but it does nothing to cool me. I should have worn underwear. Why didn't I wear underwear?

"Gotta make it a quick one, Liv. Try not to scream."

His words, though teasing, send my heart into a frenzy, and if any of these aliens can hear it, they thankfully act as if they don't. I grip the edges of my chair even tighter. My lip feels like it will be bruised from how hard I am biting it.

Slow, he inches two fingers into me, and though his angle is awkward, he still makes it feel amazing. I bite my lip harder, widening my legs, secretly begging for more as I tilt my hips up to give him better access. He curls his fingers inside me, hitting a spot that makes me see stars, and he begins to slowly thrust them in and out, his thumb jutting up to circle the nub that sends sparks through my veins.

I whimper, unable to keep all noises in my throat, because I am already so close. I was aching back at his parents' home, and now he's soothing me, promising a release. My eyes flit around the room again as he thrusts his fingers a little harder, and I clench a gasp between my lips.

The slave that had been making out with her master is gone —until I see him leaned back in his chair, his fingers knotted in her hair. She's on her knees, below the table, and though I cannot see much from this angle, my mind bridges the gap. She's taking *him* in her mouth, bobbing her head at a furious pace. Everyone around them seems to know, but they also seem to not care.

I'm not sure why, but the sight makes my insides clench and flutter, makes my cheeks flame even more. Pax leans back into my ear, burying his nose in my hair, and before I can figure out what he may be trying to say, his tongue darts out and grazes the shell. I shiver, biting my tongue to keep from crying out. I can tell he's enjoying this, too, just by his breathing.

"Let go, baby, I want to feel you get tight around my fingers."

His huskily whispered words are my undoing. My knuckles grip the chair so tight they crack, and my whole body goes rigid as deep, deep within me, something clenches *hard*. I feel as though I am on the crest of a tidal wave. I pinch my eyes shut, holding my breath, trying to chase that high, to hold out and prolong it. But with one more hard pump of his long fingers through my slickness, and with his thumb furiously circling that sensitive bud, I come unglued.

I tense, sucking in a breath as my body rebels and prepares to rat us out to the entire castle filled with his peers. Quick, he claps his free hand to my mouth, and before I can stop myself, I bite down on the meaty flesh of the underside of his thumb to prevent the high, keening cry from leaving my lips.

I am left floating, panting, completely delirious and spent from that high, that euphoria. He removes his hand from my lips with a grimace and a chuckle, reaching for a napkin and slyly dragging it under the table. I turn my head, blinking lazily and dreamily over at him as the video continues to play. No one else at the table is the wiser—save for Jev, who quirks a brow at Pax before knocking back the rest of his drink. Heat floods my cheeks.

Pax's chuckle is low, and he withdraws his fingers from me. After a moment, I feel the rough, starched fabric between my thighs, cleaning me. He leans in once more, and I feel warm all over, buzzing with the most amazing feeling ever flowing through my veins. I feel...complete, euphoric.

"How was that?"

"Mmm," I answer languidly, my body the consistency of jelly. He chuckles again.

"Fuck, that was so hot, Liv."

I turn my eyes to his, seeing the way they reflect in the darkness, seeing how glossed they are with that now-familiar hungry look. He wants more. My thighs inch closed. I want more, too. He quirks his brow at me, and I blush on cue. Clearing his throat, he scoots his chair back, motioning me to follow.

"Excuse us," he says quietly to the table. "Liv needs the restroom."

Ugh. He's being so obvious. Jeven snorts, and Lana turns

her attention to us, shooting me a wink. I hug myself as I stand, feeling as though everyone at the table knows.

"Hurry back," Jeven says. "You miss your cue, I take your job."

"Shouldn't take too long," Pax jests back, and I am walking away before he can embarrass me further. We make it barely to the hallway before we are laughing and he sweeps me up into his arms, whisking me away with the promise of more pleasure.

21

Olivia

I cannot help the moans that escape my lips. The morning has dawned, cool and rainy, barely even blue, but Pax woke me up, saying he still wanted some time together before he left. I couldn't argue with him on that. His strong hands grip my hips, his fingers leaving permanent marks in my flesh. I grind my hips against his tongue, seeking the release he's been teasing me with for a while now.

I grip the headboard, my legs quivering, tensing. I am so close, and he stops again, pulling his face free, panting. I have never sat in such a position before, straddling his face, but he was adamant I try, and now I am hooked.

"Pax," I whine. His grip tightens, his eyes dark.

"No attitude."

I glare at him, but it is wiped off my face as he slaps my butt, hard. I can't control my high moan, can't control how this makes me feel. Why does him spanking me turn me on? I'll have to ask him. He will know the answer, and I am not ashamed with him anymore. I glance behind me, watching with wide eyes as he slowly strokes himself. He promised me I could touch him this morning, could make him feel good, but only after me. I do not understand his reasoning, but maybe it is part of his culture?

"Like what you see?" he teases. I tense on top of him, wondering what it will be like when we actually do it. He says it may hurt at first, but only for a little bit, and he promised to take it slow. I don't get what that means. Sex can have speeds?

I watch as his big hand grips his length, slowly rubbing up and down. Something leaks out at the very top, and I remember watching him the first time he came on me, how it spurted like a hose and then calmed. His stroking picks up its pace.

"Fuck Liv, stop staring or I'm going to explode," he growls, and his tongue laps at my opening again. I gasp, lurching forward and gripping the headboard once more. I hope he lets me go soon, because I am starting to burn and ache. He says this is a trick to make my orgasms feel more powerful, and I hate to admit they do. *Patience will be rewarded*, he says. Sometimes, I just want it, and I want it *now*.

He is building me up again, and I cannot help but rock my hips to meet his tongue. He likes it when I do this, I've noticed. Finally, I feel close, and he doesn't let up, even when I become so sensitive I feel like I'm going to scream.

He grips me hard as I try to pull away, but one hand tosses a pillow up to me. I bury my face in it, biting it as he slams me down on his face, relentless. I tense, unable to breathe, my vision going white, and then I scream, thankful he knew I would need a pillow. By the time I come down, I am shaking, sweat plastering my hair to my forehead.

He lays me down, curling around me, and I can feel him chuckling. I don't care. I can hardly think straight.

"I can't wait until we have our own house and I can make

you scream just like that every night," he says, trailing kisses along my shoulder. I smile, my breathing calming.

"Mmm," is all I can manage in response. I gather myself, rolling, intent on making him feel good. But I have no idea what to do. He lays on his back, his hands behind his head, letting my eyes feast on his perfect body. I would love him no matter what, but he is my Pax, my protector, and I cannot picture him looking any other way.

I sit up on my knees, biting my lip. He isn't as hard as before, but his thing still bobs against his toned stomach.

"What is your thing called?" I ask, finding his eyes. His grin widens, but he wipes at his face, laughing.

"What is *your* thing called?"

I blush immediately. I know what it is called, but it sounds so...vulgar. *Thing* is better.

"Pax," I grumble. He reaches over, gripping my hips and sliding me so I am straddling him, except this time there are no clothes between our parts, and I can feel him grow harder beneath me. My hands splay on his chest as I gulp.

"The more scientific name, at least for human males, is penis, and Erathians simply adopted that."

"Oh," I say, nodding. He smirks, still holding my hips.

"But, a lot of guys just call it a dick, or a cock."

I bite my lip. Both of those sound better than the first word, but I still like *thing*. Slow, without warning, he moves his hips, and his...cock...slides between me easily, for I am still so wet. I bite my lip even harder, for it feels amazing—*erotic*, another word he taught me.

"Why do I...get wet...when you turn me on...?" I ask as he continues to languidly stroke himself between my legs.

"So I can fuck you without hurting you," he grunts, eyes focused down at our hips, his cheeks blotchy, his eyes tight.

"It means you love me, you trust me...you want me..." he

says, rocking his hips faster. I begin to rock with him, rewarded when the tip of his thing pushes against my sensitive bud.

"When I get hard like this, that is the equivalent," he says, still watching as he saws between my legs. I feel aroused, I feel like I want him again even if he just made me come.

"Will you touch yourself when I am gone, Liv?" he asks, breathless. I hadn't thought about that; I'd only thought about how badly I would miss him in every aspect, not just the physical.

"I...I..." I stutter, nervous. One hand leaves my hip, grasping my wrist, sliding it to where I am throbbing again.

"Touch yourself. Do what feels good...think of me..."

"What...what is this called?" I say, obeying him as I circle the little bud, as he continues to thrust beneath me, his cock meeting my fingers when he slides all the way up.

"Clit," he grunts, his pace quickening. "Faster, Liv, make yourself come on me."

His demand, the way he dominates these situations, has me feeling free to fall apart, knowing he will be in control while I tip over the edge. I work my fingers against my *clit* as he thrusts against me quicker, spurring me into another orgasm before I even know what has happened.

I am still clenching when he sits forward, forcing me onto my back. He grabs my hand, wrapping it as far around his thick cock as it can go. My fingers don't even come close to meeting. With his hand around mine, he strokes, fast, his forehead creased in concentration. I understand what he wants, and he lets go, allowing me to pleasure him. I keep the same pace, watching as the tip of him swells.

"Yes, keeping going, baby," he pants. I do, entranced. He tenses, his mouth falling open as he growls, and I feel his hot liquid spurt onto my stomach and everywhere, really. I keep stroking until he pulls away, fascinated at such a sight, at what I made him do. This was the first time I have been able to touch him, and I only want to do it again, right now.

"Liv?" he breathes. My eyes jump to his. He is concerned, his eyes tight. I give him a wide smile, reassuring him that he hasn't scared me. He returns my smile, skimming his fingers up my sides. I know we are running low on time, but I want more. Biting my lip, I bat my eyelashes at him the best I can.

"Can we do that again please?"

Olivia

"Livy, dear, bring your laundry down when you're finished with your studies!"

I groan into my hand, staring at the workbook in front of me.

"Yes, Miss—"

"Iris!" she corrects, her dissonant voice echoing from the foyer. I sigh. It feels weird to call her by her first name, so I try not to call her anything. I am sitting in a makeshift classroom with Mabel. Pax has been gone a week, and every day—per his stupid rules—I am to complete four hours of schoolwork before I help with chores. Each day without him, I fall a little further down the hole of depression.

It has been raining ever since he left, but I enjoy it, from the scent to the gloomy feel. I don't want to venture outside without him, anyways. Mabel sighs, flipping through the chapter book she is reading. I glare at her. All of her work has the number seven on the side, meaning she is three levels ahead of me.

It makes me hate her even more. She is the perfect child. Does everything the Harper's ask, and they dote on her as one would dote on a biological daughter. She's steered clear of me since the peanut incident, which is good for her. If she didn't, I'd have to show her what a wild human really was capable of.

She peeks over at me with her big blue eyes, and my glare deepens. Her cheeks flush red, and she averts her gaze, shifting in her seat. I can hear Iris approaching again. She is around the house like a worker bee; moving and cleaning and cooking non-stop. I feel a small smile on my face as I trace my sight words. My mother had been the same way.

I finish the day's lessons with a lecture on history. This teacher gives a timeline of Sargas and puts it next to one of Earth. I like that he doesn't try to hide the history of humans, and I am fascinated. I even catch Mabel trying to peek over to my tablet, her little feet swinging, clad in frilly socks and shiny black shoes. She is always dressed so nice.

I meander down into the kitchen, hoping to nick a few sweets to hide in my room. The Harper's haven't been that strict on food, but we only eat three times a day, and I have to sit at the table with them. I am used to living alone with Pax, going to the cooler or pantry when I am hungry. It gives me anxiety, not having control over my food once more. That is one thing I do not miss about the wild.

I am just hiding an apple in my sweatshirt pocket when Iris comes into the kitchen. Frightened, I drop the fruit, and it rolls to her feet, betraying me. Her brows furrow as she sets down her basket of laundry to pick it up. I back away. Pax specifically told me not to steal, so I know I am in for it now.

"Are you hungry, dear?" she asks, doing a decent job at faking concern. I flush, shaking my head. She sighs, giving me a look like I am some poor, starved animal that she wants to care for.

"You can always come grab anything you want, just keep it tidy for the next person," she says with a smile, handing me the apple. I wonder what her angle is as I take it. She is still staring at me with that little grin, like she knows more than she is letting on.

"Oh, I forgot, there is a matter we must discuss."

I tense, but I nod. Has she heard from Pax?

"My son asked me to help you with some feminine issues."

I am confused until I remember the birth control conversation we had. He told his *mother*? I feel myself go bright red. I want to kill him. She laughs, moving to put the kettle on the stove.

"I say we have a spot of tea and discuss some things, woman to woman. I'm sure he has told you I am a doctor—nothing fazes me, dear," she says, grabbing mugs and a tin of loose leaf labelled Earl Grey. My mouth waters. I haven't had a London fog since I was very young. I wonder if she knows how to make one.

"Cream?"

"Yes, please, and...do you have lavender, and vanilla?"

She gives me a curious look but resumes her search.

"I believe so—ahh, I knew Penn had an extra stash. He takes vanilla syrup in his espresso."

She lays it out on the tiled island counter, nodding to it.

"May as well make me whatever concoction this is as well. I love to try new things," she says. I move forward tentatively, giving her a small smile.

"It's called a London fog," I say, pouring out the tea and other ingredients. She is hovering by my shoulder, watching me closely.

"No doubt named after that beautiful city on the Thames," she says, catching my eye. I give her a quizzical look, but I can't help my smile.

"Yes...my mother lived there for a while."

She lets out a heavy sigh as she shuffles around a cupboard and finds some biscuits.

"Shame our kind were so brazen and ruined something so beautiful."

I almost miss the teacup as I pour the cream, stunned. I try not to let it show, but my mind is racing.

"Normally, I'd make my own biscuits, but these do well in a pinch," she says with a wink, bringing the plate over. I carefully carry our tea, sitting down opposite her.

"You...you've been to London, then?"

"Oh yes, many times. I hear there is a group of human architects that have been granted permission to rebuild parts of the city. Funny, how one destroys something and then regrets it."

She brings the tea to her lips, a blissful smile on her face as she tries it. I follow suit, awash with memories as soon as the fruity, creamy flavors hit my tongue. It pulls me up short, how much such a small thing can impact your memory, can flood your body with such terrible yet comforting emotions. I clear my throat, my mind jumping to what she has said.

"Wait...we are in Halifax?"

"Yes, dear," she says, reaching for a biscuit. I frown.

"What was this city once called? And what was Sardone once called?"

"Oh," she says in thought. "I know Halifax was once Dufftown, famous for its castles and whisky distilleries. Scotland, I believe this country was called. Shame they changed the name to something so...*boring*," she says, whispering the end as she leans in, like a gossiping school girl. I can't hide my little laugh, my chest feeling light.

"Scotland," I say. I can picture the map in my head. I do not know where in Scotland that leaves me, but hearing it called its proper name makes me feel warm—makes me feel like a human.

"I'll have to ask Penn what Sardone was once called. It's a tricky name, if I am thinking of the correct word. He is fascinated with the history of Earth, of humans. He is on a preservation council, here in town. You can always pick his brain."

I smile. Rain batters the windows, the sound comforting as my fingers grip my warm tea. I would love to talk to Pax's father about history, but he makes me nervous. He is just as stoic and austere as Pax, so I understand now where his son gets his demeanor.

"We are in what is known geographically as the Highlands. Oh, the culture—the richness of the people. It is stunning. I feel blessed to live in such a beautiful place."

"So...so you like humans, then?" I say, my stomach churning. That coy smile is back on her face, and so is the mischief in her eyes.

"More than my own people, at times," she whispers, leaning in. I flush, but I smile, relaxing in her presence.

"I run a free clinic for humans in Halifax on Saturdays. Most that live around here are well looked after by their respective families."

I raise my brows, looking down into my tea.

"It's not like this in the city."

I can hear her sigh.

"No, I doubt it. The mindset there is much younger."

I nod, feeling the sadness deep in my chest.

"I do hope my son treats you as well as you deserve."

Her words shock me, and I glance at her. She sips her tea, eyeing me over the brim. I nod, wondering what else I can say.

"I...hated him for a while," I begin. She chuckles.

"I should hope so, damn brute. He left Halifax because he thought our ways were too conservative, our restrictions too loose. I sure hope you've made him eat those words, dear."

I snort, nodding.

"I think I have."

"Good. A man should lead the household, protect the family and provide. They should be the head," she says, giving me a curious look. I bristle. I don't like what she is saying, until she speaks again.

"But the woman, dear, is the neck that turns that head."

I return her coy smile. I think I like Iris quite a lot.

I lay in bed, grimacing at the pain that ripples through my lower abdomen. Not only is it the first day of my cycle, but today was the day I received my birth control. Apparently, they like to add insult to injury. Iris was kind, and so was the other doctor who helped me. I have learned more in these last few days about sex than I have in my entire life, but at least I will be better prepared for when Pax gets home.

Iris made sure the contraceptive was an implant, one that lasts a long time but one that does not give out any hormones. She said natural is always the best, so we need to mimic that in every way we can. At the moment, I don't believe her, because my stomach is in knots and all I want to do is cry.

She told me giving birth was a thousand times worse, though. I stopped resisting after her detailed explanation of *that*. I roll onto my back with a groan. She is letting me take the next few days off to recover, but laying in bed only makes me miss Pax more.

There is a timid knock on my door, but I don't have the energy to move.

"Yes?" I grumble. I hear the door open, and little footsteps shuffling in.

"Mama said I should bring you some tea," Mabel says, her voice quiet, anxious. I open my eyes to see her standing by my bedside, nervous, holding a tray of tea. I grit my teeth. I want to hate her, but she is a child, and a human. If we were in the wild, I would be protecting her, even if I didn't like her.

"Thank you," I mumble. She sets it on the coffee table,

lingering by the door as she turns to leave, her eyes on Henry's cage.

"Why is there only one teacup?" I say. She turns, flushed and eyes bright. I quirk my brow at her. Soon, we are sitting in bed, eating all sorts of cakes and sandwiches she stole from the kitchen.

"I can't believe you're from the wild," she says, popping a grape into her mouth. I roll my eyes, hugging a pillow to my stomach.

"You're not?"

She shakes her head, her blond ponytail swishing.

"No, I was born into another family, but my parents died when I was a baby, and then I was adopted."

I find this curious, reaching for another sandwich. I feel like I can eat the whole plate today. How strange, to be born into this society. We chatter about trivial things for a bit longer before she turns red, avoiding my gaze.

"I'm...sorry, for throwing peanuts at you," she mutters. I roll my eyes, frowning.

"I'm sorry for pulling a knife on you and splitting your lip."

She gives me a sheepish smile, but it soon fades.

"Your master...Mr. Pax...he's awfully scary when he's mad."

I frown, wondering what Pax said to her that day. I understand where she is coming from, though; he can be scary when he wants to be.

"Yeah, he can be an asshole," I say. She giggles, hiding her mouth.

"He really seems to like you, though."

I sigh, letting my head thump on the headboard.

"Well, I really like him. A lot. I...I miss him," I say. She giggles again.

"You have a cruuusshhh," she teases. I bump her shoulder with mine.

"Shut up. You probably think he's cute, too."

She shrugs.

"He is, but so is Johnny."

I tense. Johnny Fox. The boy Pax was adamant I stay away from. He came up that day at the arena to introduce himself. He didn't seem to like Pax, but I assumed it's because he's an Erathian.

"Johnny is trouble," I say. Mabel grins.

"Yeah, but he has friends from the other farm, and they hang out late at night in the stable. I really want to get invited sometime."

"You're too young, Mabel. Stay away from boys," I growl, crossing my arms. She sighs, flopping back.

"I'm twelve. Well, almost."

"And I'm eighteen, and I managed to stay away until I was caught. Trust me, you shouldn't get mixed up in that."

I feel worry gnawing at me about her. Johnny seems harmless enough, but I know that Pax can see things that I cannot, and so I trust his judgement. In the same way, I can see Mabel getting taken advantage of; not necessarily in a sexual way, but I'm sure teenage boys could coax her into doing any number of bad things, like drinking or drugs.

"They are all getting together tomorrow night. They race horses and drink," she says, her wide eyes on mine. I frown.

"Whose horses?"

"Mostly the other farm's, but..." she bites her lip. I glare at her.

"You'd better tell me, Mabel, or I'll tell Pax when he gets home," I threaten. She straightens up immediately.

"I heard Johnny say he was going to try and race Demon tomorrow night," she whispers. My stomach clenches in dread. That's *Pax's* horse. That insolent, spoiled, rowdy boy is going to get himself hurt, and he's going to do it while stealing Pax's property.

"Oh, please don't tell Johnny! Or Pax! They will be so mean to me!"

I turn to her with narrowed eyes. I don't want to make her life more difficult, but I need to stop them.

"I'll take care of it," I say with conviction. Her blue eyes widen to saucers.

"H-how?" she asks. I smirk.

"Don't worry about it. I'm from the wild, remember?"

I wait until dusk the next night. It is well after dinner, and I know Iris is reading to Mabel, but only because Mabel helped me concoct this plan. Mr. Harper should be in his study, and so I have to take my chance and go. I am wearing black from head to toe as I creep out the back door and dash to the stables. There is still enough light from the sunset so that I can see my way, but I need to get there before they show up.

I wrench open the doors, met with the snorting of horses. Mabel told me Demon likes apples. I have three in my pocket, the lumpy bulge getting in my way. I close the door, walking quickly to Demon's stall. I pause before it, closing my eyes, trying to rid my body of fear so he doesn't sense it. When I open them, his big black eyes are staring down at me, and his ears are cocked forward. I fix him with a glare.

"Ok, let's be rational, now, bud. You be nice to me, and I'll make sure no one touches you. Deal?"

He lets out a whooshing snort. I take it as a good sign, sliding open his stall wide enough for me to fit through as I sneak in. He shifts, his massive body swaying as he flicks his tail. I slide the stall door closed. In the corner is a pile of hay, and thankfully his area has been cleared of manure. I reach up, patting his neck.

"Please, *please* do not shit while I'm in here tonight," I

whisper to him. He lowers his head, sniffing at me, right where I am hiding the apples. He raises his top lip, nibbling at my sweatshirt and leaving a trail of slobber. I pull away, smacking his nose. He rears his head, but I fix him with a glare.

"If you can't be polite, you don't get a thing," I hiss. He watches me, flicking his tail, but makes no other move to find his treats. I am beginning to become comfortable around him. He is intelligent, keen, sleek and beautiful. I reach into my pocket, holding out an apple for him. He snatches it greedily, frothing at the mouth as he chews.

"Ugh," I say, swiping my hand on my leggings. I move to the corner where his hay is and settle down. It is comfortable, springy, even if it pokes through my clothes. He lowers his head, sniffing at me again.

"Be good, and I'll keep you safe," I say, wondering how long I will have to wait. I cross my arms, sinking into a stupor as the hours tick by, the lights dim and calming, the space warm, Demon's presence reassuring. Before I know it, I've fallen asleep.

22

Pax

The rain has been relentless, and hiking through dense wilderness while sopping wet has been more a feat than not. But, this is my job—keep my platoon safe while taking out targets. Tark identified these threats well before I transitioned into his position of power, and for that I am thankful. It is eerie, how close they have ventured into what is considered Erathian territory.

After the takeover of my kind, we supposedly came to some sort of tense agreement; their numbers were so small, we were sure they wouldn't pose much of a threat. But we had been sorely mistaken. I clear my throat, studying my map for the millionth time today, memorizing the terrain, swiping through the drone footage so I know every tree, every rock, every fern.

I will not lose my men to these demonic beings. Humans had an infatuation with spiritual entities well before the first Erathian landed on Earth's soil. Perhaps there was truth to their legends, but either way, they replicated them without fault, without mercy.

I pinch my eyes closed, taking in a shaky breath. Moments before I knocked Liv out in that abandoned building, I'd killed one. It would have torn her soft, delicate flesh to shreds, assuming it had no self control, starved as the rogue had been. If it had been in a pack...her heart would have given out from pain before they would have been merciful enough to kill her.

When I open my eyes, Jev is frowning at me. He knows what we face. He's never experienced what I have. I pray he never will. But he is understanding of my rampant fear in the face of these monsters.

Humans created them to combat Erathians when the wars started. They called them Hybrids, when in reality, they are Chimeras; beings that hold more than one set of DNA. They are skilled. They are ruthless. And they find joy in pain, whether that be their own, or another's.

Liv thinks I only go on raids to kill or enslave humans, but Erathians don't really care about her kind unless we come across them. Our job now is to protect ourselves against such a monstrous force, against the Chimeras, the Hybrids. I can still feel them, peeling my flesh away, and I can still hear his screams in the quiet of the night as they pulled his body apart, limb for limb.

My little brother.

The reason for my scars.

~

Olivia

I awake to the sound of hushed voices, to the noise of Demon snorting, agitated. Shit. I can't believe I fell asleep when I was supposed to be watching him. I stand, brushing the hay from my clothes before peeking over the top of his stall. Three boys near my age are sneaking into the stable with flashlights, one of them being Johnny Fox. I set my jaw, glaring. Mabel wasn't lying, then.

They are jesting each other, and I can smell the stench of booze from here. My stomach flips in nervous anticipation, but I will stand my ground. They are humans. I know how to handle myself around my own kind, and if they don't leave, I will make them regret it.

"Ok hold on, hold on," Johnny laughs, and I hear the clank of glass.

"He's not as wild as you say if he's letting two people ride him."

"You mean one freak and his whore pet."

"Yeah, I tried to ask her if she likes the guy, but he came back and almost killed me before she could answer."

I know they are talking of me and Pax now, and I bristle, protective. Demon paws at the ground and throws his head, swaying his massive body and nearly crushing me against the wood wall. The door starts to slide, and I slip in front of the horse, fixing Johnny's shocked blue eyes with a vehement glare.

"Liv—"

"What do you think you're doing?" I hiss. He blinks, taken aback, but his friends are laughing, jostling one another. They both have sandy hair and light brown eyes—brothers, it would seem. They must be the boys from the other farm.

Johnny sobers, frowning down at me. He is tall, but not nearly as tall as Pax, and he is skinny as a pole.

"Look, this is none of your business, so move along," he says. The boys behind give a cocky smile. I cross my arms.

"It is my business if you're stealing things that aren't yours."

He rolls his eyes.

"Seriously? You care about that freak?"

I grit my teeth.

"I'm trying to save your asses. If he finds out—"

"She does care about him. Look at her blush," one of the

brothers says, disgust tainting his voice. I feel this situation beginning to slip through my fingers like sand. Johnny takes a step back before he sneers down at me.

"You do, don't you? I saw you that day, on the bed. I felt bad for you, but you *like* it when he uses you, don't you?"

"Stay out of my business," I hiss. He shakes his head, shocked but clearly disgusted.

"You're a fucking traitor, a *whore*. Just like that little cunt Mabel," the taller of the brothers pipes up.

"You're a human, Liv, and Erathians don't give a fuck about humans. They use us. Has he brainwashed you that badly?"

I blink, stunned, wounded. My chest aches. I yearn for Pax right now, for him to hold me.

"I bet he tells you he does all this to protect you, that life could be so much worse, and then he shoves his cock in you and you actually like it," Johnny spits. I blink again, my world shifting. Pax hasn't lied to me. He would never say those things to me unless he meant them. But...how do these boys know the things he's told me? Is Pax just saying those things so he can get what he wants from me without me putting up a fight?

I feel like I want to throw up.

"See? He does, and you fell for it, dumb bitch. Get the fuck out of here," one of the boys says.

I shove aside my hurt regarding Pax, focusing instead on my anger toward their demeaning words.

"Shut the fuck up and get lost," I growl.

"Or what?" the taller brother says, leaning forward, a bottle of whisky tight in his grasp. I am fumbling. I wasn't expecting so much resistance from humans, and now my threats feel rather idle. I didn't even think to bring a knife with me. Demon snorts behind me, my only companion in this moment, but he can't understand me if I ask him for help. I am screwed.

I take a step back, my shoulders bumping into Demon's velvety nose.

"Get out of the way, or you're going to get hurt," Johnny threatens. I feel tears of anger well in my eyes. I shake my head. He sighs, exasperated, a softness entering his gaze.

But before anyone else can react, the taller brother passes off his bottle to his shorter brother and lunges for me. I gasp, readying to scream, but he grabs my shoulders and yanks me out, slamming me into the stall door hard enough that I lose my breath.

"Adam, dude, calm down—"

"No, I'm fucking tired of these little whores running around, getting all hot and bothered over fucking aliens!"

"Dude—" Johnny tries. Adam whirls, slamming his fist into Johnny's jaw, and he stumbles back as Adam turns to me, his eyes glossed with drink. Johnny lunges again, but the other brother catches him, and they scuffle across the straw strewn floor as Demon whinnies, locked away once more. I am panting as I try to dash away, but he catches me by my hair, yanking so hard tears spring into my eyes. He forces me onto my knees as tears leak down my cheeks.

He unbuckles his belt with one hand, slipping it through his loops.

"Adam, fuck off!" Johnny yells. My eyes fall to him. He is pinned on the ground, bloodied as the brother on him reels back and hits him again. Johnny goes limp, leaving me utterly alone.

"Hold her," Adam demands. His brother chuckles, gripping my hair as I slap at them both, but Adam soon hands my wrists bound with his belt.

"Such a foul mouthed bitch. Want to show me what else that mouth is good for?"

I whimper as the fingers that grip my hair pulls strands from the roots. Behind me, Demon is pacing, loud, agitated and angry. I feel the cool kiss of a bottle on my lips, but I press them tight together, trying to avoid the force as best I can.

A slap echoes, and my cheek stings horribly. I kick out at Adam's legs, but he easily dodges it, both of them laughing.

"Trust me, you'll want to be drunk for what we're about to do to you. Traitor whores deserve to be punished."

I am frozen. Punished. The Facility. No, no, no. I am back there, I can't be back there, I will die, Pax promised me he would never leave me there again, but he lied, he's always lied to me. Panicking, I scream, but as I open my mouth, fiery liquid douses me, and a hand clamps over my mouth, forcing me to swallow the burning liquid. I gasp when he lets up, but he pours more down my throat as I choke and sputter.

The sound of his zipper has me tied back to that tree, awaiting Brutus and his vile touch. I want to curl under a rock and hide forever. I pinch my lips closed, feeling his fingers trying to pry my mouth open. I gnash, biting at him, but he slaps me again.

"I swear to God, if you bite me, I will slaughter that fucking horse you're so fond of, and I'll rip your little friend Mabel from her bed and give her the same treatment," Adam growls. I whimper, shaking so hard my teeth chatter. I can't let them hurt Demon or Mabel. I can do what they want if they leave everyone else alone.

His fingers pry my mouth open again, and I resist, but it is futile. I breathe harshly through my nose, confused yet somehow knowing what to expect. Demon is roaring behind me, so hard the entire stable is shaking as he throws his body against the walls. I feel Adam's stiff length at my lips, so much smaller than Pax.

"Be a good girl and suck," he growls. I've never done this before. I don't know how, but he is waiting as Demon continues to thrash. Adam growls in anger, grabbing the back of my head and slamming his length down my throat. I gag, heaving as I feel vomit rise. I hear a metallic clang, and as he is pulling out of my mouth, I bite down, hard. He screams, yanking away from me. They both let me go as I roll to the side, Demon having ripped the hinges to his stall door completely off. My eyes widen, and through my tears I watch as the door falls on Adam, pinning him to the ground. Demon rears, kicking his front legs out, before he lets every ounce of his weight come crashing down onto the door.

Adam can't even scream. The crunch of his bones is a sound that will play in my mind forever. I blink, retching up the contents of my stomach as Demon rears again, chasing off the petrified brother, the heavy thuds of his hooves like thunder in my ears. I slump to the side as darkness consumes me.

I blink my eyes open as my head pounds, throbbing through my skull with voracious power. It takes my mind some time to adjust to what I am seeing. Everything is sideways, but it looks like I am in a study. There is warm light from a blazing fire, and books littering every inch of space. The cushions beneath me are plush, leathery, and there is a thick blanket draped over my sore body.

My mouth tastes of blood, whisky, and horrid memories. My wrists burn, the feeling all too familiar from my time being dragged through the wild by Pax. *Pax.*

His name sends a jolt through my heart—a jolt of longing that turns to sorrow. He's lied to me. He only wants me as a compliant slave. He cannot possibly love someone like me—a weak, pathetic human. I sniffle against the tears, and a deep voice greets me.

"Ahh, welcome back to the world of the living."

I sit up quickly, the blanket falling from my shoulders. It is still nighttime. My eyes fall to a wide oak desk, and behind it sits Pax's father, his eyes trained on a thick book. I feel sick, remembering what happened in that stable.

"What—"

His dark eyes flash to mine in warning, and I clamp my mouth shut as tears waver.

"I think it best you keep quiet and let me do the talking."

Petrified of his retribution, I simply nod. I do not want to endure whatever punishments he has planned for me, but I know they will rival Pax's.

"You are a lucky girl. Lucky that Demon broke down his stall door and saved your life."

He folds his book, clasping his hands together. I feel utter guilt, praying they found the horse.

"I will not mince words with you, because I do not believe in doing so with anyone. I know what those boys did to you. The evidence was quite clear. Adam is dead, and his brother Joel has been taken into custody by the guards. Johnny being under our care, I will ask you once whether or not he should be spared from being sent off as well."

I clamp my mouth, my eyes flying to his. He's letting me choose?

"He...he tried to help me..." I rasp, my throat aching. He nods once.

"I do not know what they told you to justify their actions, but it is common out here in the country for humans to turn against one another—to humiliate and torture those who are sympathetic toward Erathians."

I feel my heart thud faster. Am I not going to be punished?

"My son Paxton has chosen to care for you in every way he is capable. He's never once brought a woman home for us to meet, even as a teenager. He is a serious man, and he weighs his decisions very precisely before he makes them, because he knows what the consequences of this world can be."

I chew my lip, shivering despite the fire. Mr. Harper's eyes are boring into mine, but I cannot seem to look away. He is stoic, and I feel like his words alone are a form of punishment.

He reminds me of my father, what little memories remain of him.

"It is clear as day to me that he is in love with you, Miss Donne. Whatever else you heard tonight is scurrilous lies."

His words should make me feel better, but I only feel sick. Sick for doubting Pax loves me, sick for questioning our relationship, sick that I didn't fight harder to get away from those boys. My shoulders heave as I shake, trying not to sob in front of his father.

"I-I'm sorry..." I cry. It is quiet as my emotions flood me. He waits until I calm down, but even then he doesn't speak.

"He won't want me now...I...I didn't stop them...he-he..." I can't form the words. I feel defiled, used. Pax won't want me after another man has forced himself on me in such a way. I hear the creak of the floorboards, and my head snaps up. He is standing at the mantle above the fire, fingers gracing a photo. He grasps it, bringing it to me. I peek at him as my fingers curl around the cool, ornate edge of the frame. He sits in an armchair beside the couch.

There are three men in the photo. Pax, beaming, wearing his uniform. His father, also smiling wide, but then a third. He is young, still taller than his father, but just a smidgen shorter than Pax. He has the same dark brown hair, but his eyes are their mother's. I never knew Pax had a brother.

"Ollie," his father says, voice filled with longing. I glance up. He is smiling sadly at the photo.

"He...he never..."

He sighs.

"That doesn't surprise me. He never speaks of his little brother. Rare, for Erathians to have more than one child, but we were blessed with two, and only three years apart."

I smile, tracing Pax's cheek, my heart aching. I long for him, but my mind is a mess. How can he want me when all I do is cause trouble? When I am nothing more than a toy for his kind and for humans as well?

"What happened to him?" I ask. He looks young, strong and fit.

"Have you ever wondered how Pax got his scars?"

My eyes flash to his as I tense, my heart thudding to a stop before picking up again. I give a small nod, my hands trembling. He nods, wiping at his jaw the same way Pax does.

"I will tell you, because I know he will never be able to fully explain the horrors he's survived."

I am on edge, but I wait, holding my breath.

"I only know because I was forced to listen to the debriefing. It took over a hundred hours of intense psychotherapy for Pax to even begin to tell us what happened."

I am shaking, cold, nervous. He reaches over to his desk, grabbing a thick folder. He opens it, the pages within covered in print. His eyes flash to mine once more.

"These are Pax's words. Whenever I begin to doubt my strength, I read them."

I grit my chattering teeth, hugging the blanket tighter about me. His eyes pull back down to the pages, and he begins.

"I am Paxton Harper, ranger 002. My brother, Ollie Harper, was ranger 003. We were sent on a mission to clear a section of the Ruins of the Chimeras, or Hybrids. It was night, dark, raining. We fell into an ambush, and my brother and I were split up from our unit. We were captured by a pack of them. I do not remember the initial count, but once we were taken to their camp, there were fifteen."

His eyes find mine, sensing my confusion.

"Hybrids, or Chimeras, were a human experiment. They developed weapons to defeat our kind, but when those beings turned on their creators, there was nothing they could do to stop them."

I feel icy dread in my veins. I am about to speak, when he

holds up his hand. I clamp my mouth shut as his eyes return to the page.

"I was chained to a tree, Ollie across from me. They questioned us for coordinates, but we refused to comply. Our suicide tablets were destroyed upon entering camp, so we had no escape. They began by torturing me. They enjoy the taste of flesh. Human, Erathian, their own kind—it did not matter to them. They carved me in front of my brother, and ate bits of my flesh. That was the first night."

I feel bile rise in my throat, but he keeps reading.

"I do not remember which day it was, but they found out Ollie and I were brothers because he tried to protect me. They began to torture him the same. Burned his feet, carved him up. They found a group of humans. They took the men. We couldn't see what they did to them, but they did not die without much pain. They kept the women with us. They made it a game, letting one loose, giving her a head start before they would hunt her. They kept them alive even when they caught them. They would assault them in front of us each night. On the last day they kept them alive, they forced the stronger one to hunt the weaker one. She didn't make it far. We watched as she killed her friend with a blunt club."

Silent tears are streaming down my face, but his father's words only come faster, the pages flipping and fluttering as the fire crackles and a storm outside begins to brew.

"They knew we would not give up information, and so they simply used us as sadistic entertainment. They attempted to force us to fight one another. We refused. They found more humans, women again. They told Ollie he would be freed if he fucked one of them. He wouldn't. So they did it for him, right in front of us. Every day, they ate from our flesh because we heal so fast. They were becoming agitated the longer we were captive. On the last day of Ollie's life, they castrated him before cutting him from below his waist all the way to his chest. They then pulled him to the middle of their camp and ripped him apart, limb by limb. He called my name. Over and over. He screamed for me, and I could do nothing. I knew he was dying when he begged for our mother. The next day, our unit found us."

I am leaning forward, my elbows on my knees as my head swirls, as vomit rises. The world is tilting. Heaving to and fro. The man I have fallen in love with has endured a hell I will never understand. A hell he was trying to protect me from since the very beginning, and all I did was hate him and try to run away.

Mr. Harper shuffles the papers back in order and closes the folder, tossing it to his desk with a soft thud. I swallow hard. I am still reeling in shock, but then something else creeps over me, some sense of premonition. Pax kept saying he wasn't leaving on this raid to kill or enslave humans. He left because—

"Do you understand now, Miss Donne? The lengths my son has gone to and will continue to go through to protect you, to protect us?"

My eyes flash to his. Pax is out there, right now, facing these monsters, and I have no way of knowing if he is alright. And he…he saved me, from his own kind, but also from those monsters. He kept me close, tying me up nearest the tent before he made me sleep curled up next to him. He knew the price of my freedom, and he saved me.

Saved me from myself.

PART III

THE END OF INFINITY

"When you consider things like the stars, our affairs don't seem to matter very much, do they?"
—Virginia Woolf

23

Pax

It is late—just after one in the morning. I enter the familiar confines of my childhood home, letting my monstrous frame pack slide to the floor as I breathe a heavy sigh of relief. The rain stopped as soon as our mission was completed. Ten less Hybrids now stalk this land. I can rest a little easier tonight. Only a little.

My father was able to get a message through to me regarding an incident with Liv. I didn't need many details to know it was bad—and fortunately for the boy who assaulted her, he's dead. He escaped his fate rather easily, for if he had faced me, it would have been a thousand times worse.

I try not to think about such things. I don't want to ruin what should be a happy reunion. Nothing else matters right now; I only want to hold the woman I love. Our mission lasted longer than expected—three weeks. I have missed her every second of every day. The ache in my chest begins to loosen as I mount the steps.

The latest message from my parents told me Liv was

sleeping in Mabel's room because she was so lonely. She will not have to be lonely anymore. I am here, and I don't intend to leave anytime soon. I pause outside the door, gently pushing it open. I can make out Liv on the right side of the room, curled in a ball on a twin bed. Moonlight kisses her pale face, making her glow like a goddess. My heart lurches.

She is wearing my shirt.

I draw near and crouch next to her, keeping my voice as hushed as possible. I know better than to touch her while she is sleeping. I call her name, but she barely stirs.

"Liv, I'm home," I urge. Her eyelids flutter.

"It's me, baby, wake up," I say. I can feel the grin stretching my face. I have never been so happy to see anyone in my life before. What did I ever do without her?

Slow, she blinks her eyes open, her gaze taking me in with utter confusion.

"Hey, Livy," I say. She gulps, blinking fast as her eyes flood with tears.

"Pax?" she cries, lip trembling.

"Come here—"

Before I can stop her, she throws the blanket back and flies into my embrace, wrapping her legs around my torso and her arms around my neck, clinging to me like a desperate barnacle. I teeter, almost toppling, but I catch us. She buries her face in my neck and sobs, *hard*.

My heart throbs painfully. I stand up, gripping her butt as I carry her out and back to our room. She is inconsolable as I drop to the couch, squeezing her tight, running my hands up and down her back. Whatever happened to her while I was gone was worse than I thought, and now I am livid. Her pain echoes in my soul, and I wish I could take it away for her.

"I'm back, Livy, and you're safe," I soothe. She cinches her arms tighter around me, her strength surprising. I try to pull her away, needing her to calm down before she passes out. I hold her cheeks, slick with tears, and her sorrowful eyes find mine through the darkness.

"Liv, breathe, ok? I'm here, you should be happy—"

"I'm...so...s-sorry for...for everything," she cries and hiccups. I feel my brows furrow. Did she do something else while I was gone?

"For what, Liv?"

"For...for hating you...for trying to-to get away—"

She is shivering, her chest heaving as she gasps for a breath between her words. My eyes swish between hers quickly, my brows knotted in the center. I clasp her cheeks as she continues to ramble off every bad thing she has ever done since I took her. I can't take it anymore, the way she is degrading herself—the way she seems to be hating herself.

"Olivia Donne, listen to me right now," I demand. She whimpers, her lips trembling as she ceases her harried words.

"Do not apologize to me for those things. *Ever.* You did what any normal person would do. You tried to maintain your freedom at all costs. I never shared with you the real reasons, and that is my fault...I will try, someday—"

"He told me," she whispers, her voice strained, pulling me up short.

My heart thuds hard in my chest. I feel awash with ice. More tears flood her cheeks.

"W-who told you?"

"Your dad," she says, her voice cracking. She wipes at her nose.

"I...that boy...he...he shoved his thing all the way down my throat, and I was so scared you'd never want me again after that, but then your dad told me how much you loved me, what you protected me from, and I..." she falters. I am reeling. Seeing red. Hearing what that fucker did to her. But I am also adrift in those woods, watching my baby brother die, knowing there was nothing I could do to save him.

I should be pissed at my father for telling her. I should hate him, for it is my story to tell. I should choose when to tell it.

But I know, in my heart, I never would have been able to tell Liv everything. Some memories are too painful, and I know how easy it is to drown. And right now, she is drowning. I need to be her strength. I grip her face harder between my hands, and her eyes snap to mine, wide and nervous.

"Nothing, Olivia, *nothing* that you have been through or will go through will ever make me love you less. You are my world, you are the reason I get up every morning and put on that uniform. My life was empty before you, lonely. I was miserable, but you changed me in the best of ways, can't you let yourself see that?"

She stares, a deep longing in her eyes.

"I just want to move forward with you...and I want you to think about forgiving me for what I've done..." she whispers. I give her a gentle smile.

"You never need to ask my forgiveness, Livy. It is unconditionally yours, as is my entire heart."

"Forever?" she says, earnest.

I nod, leaning up, my lips hovering over hers.

"Forever," I say, kissing away her tears.

Silence hangs thick in the air of my vehicle as we get on the highway heading south toward Sardone. Liv is curled up next to me, holding my arm in both of hers as she rests her cheek on my bicep. My hand curls around her thigh, giving her a gentle squeeze. She's not let me go for more than a few minutes since I returned. I have no complaints, even if it feels as though our relationship has somehow changed.

It feels deeper, more real. Lust is fleeting, but choosing to love someone despite their flaws and shortcomings is where it really counts. As much as I enjoy Liv's body, I can see now that we are compatible in more ways than just the physical. Not to mention the fact my mother cried when they parted. Liv promised we'd visit more often.

I smile, leaning down and kissing the top of her head as I take the next exit, heading west. Liv doesn't notice, not familiar with this area or how the roads work. I can tell she senses something is amiss as we drive further into the country before rolling through a quaint town. She stiffens, sitting up straighter.

"Where are we going?" she asks, nervous. I rub her thigh in reassurance.

"I have some old family friends out this way. You don't mind if we stop, do you?"

I feel her confused eyes on me, but I continue to watch the road.

"No, I don't mind," she says, though her voice is quiet and strained. I feel my smile grow. We pull off the main road, down a gravel one for a ways. The area is lush, surrounded in dense wilderness that is interrupted by wide fields of green dotted with rocky outcroppings. I slow the vehicle to a stop in front of a modern home, the edifice stone, with angular windows in wide shapes. A tall blond woman awaits us outside, grin on her face and tablet in hand.

I get out, waiting for Liv. She hesitates.

"Pax—"

"Come on. Humor me."

Her brows furrow, but she obeys. Hand in hand, we greet the woman.

"Hello! I am Bex, if you'd just follow me down the path here I can let you inside."

"Thank you, for meeting us on such short notice," I say. She turns, beaming at both of us as she opens the dark, heavy front doors. We are greeted by a wide open space, already furnished, everything crisp and modern yet somehow still cozy. Liv's grip on me tightens.

"I'll let you two wander around. Let me know if you have any questions," she says. I nod to her in thanks, eyeing the fireplace, then the spacious kitchen with brand new appliances. On the back stone patio is a gas fireplace and a hot tub. I pull a hesitant Liv after me through the office, then the guest room, and then the master bedroom and the ensuite bathroom. Her eyes remain wide, her mouth slightly agape. I can feel her staring at me, can feel she wants to ask me what the hell we're doing.

We get done, and Bex holds out her arms.

"Well?" she smiles. I pat Liv's arm, glancing at her in all her utter confusion.

"We need a moment to discuss, if you don't mind," I say.

"Of course! I'll be right outside."

She clacks off in her heels, and Liv pulls her hand from mine.

"Ok, what is going on?"

"Do you like this house?" I ask in rebuttal, quirking my brow. She flushes, clearly annoyed with me.

"Pax—"

"Do you like it?" I say, more firm.

She throws up her hands.

"It's gorgeous—huge. Why are you asking me this?"

"So you could see yourself living here?"

Her face goes pale, her eyes bulging.

"Wh-what?"

"Is that a yes?" I say, reaching for her with a smirk. She shakes her head, connecting the dots slowly.

"Yes," she finally breathes. She is blinking rapidly as I pull her close.

"Pax, wh-what did you do?" she stutters. I flash her a grin.

"Welcome home, baby."

Olivia

"Don't forget to box up Henry's stuff, Liv!" Pax calls from somewhere in the living room. I roll my eyes and grumble. This moving idea sounded great—until it came time to actually do the work to move. Pax keeps telling me I'm whiney. It's not that I'm not ecstatic, shocked that he bought a house for us. It's just...there are things about here that I am going to miss a lot.

Even though some of the memories of this city are impossible for me to think about, I know I'll miss Deidre, Kip's wife Lana, the familiar grocery store, that place Pax took me out to dinner. Smiling to myself, I tuck Henry's food and rolling ball into the box that's on the bed. It will be better out there, in the country, closer to his family. I've grown to feel as though they've accepted me, and I already hate being away from them, too.

"Can you grab my keys from the nightstand, please?" Pax calls. Puffing out my cheeks, I skirt around the barren bed, swiping his keys as my hip knocks into the side table.

"Ouch," I hiss, glancing down. It's normally locked, the code one only his fingerprints can give access to. I have wondered if he kept anything in there—not that I am looking to get into trouble anytime soon, but curiosity always gets the best of me. Chancing a peek, nothing but matte-brushed steel meets my eyes—guns, knives. I gulp. I understand his job now, understand his need to feel he can protect himself as well as me. But something white catches my eye, the corner of a slip of paper. It looks so out of place next to things built for destruction.

My heart stutters a few times as my shaky hand reaches in, fingers pinching the thin sheet. Tears well in my eyes immediately. With all this moving and the highs and lows of excitement mingled with sadness, my emotions are kind of rampant.

The piece of paper brings back so many memories. Memories of a really low point in my life not that long ago. We'd fought that night, and he'd sent me to bed on the floor. The next morning, I'd woken up with all the blankets on me. I knew then he cared, I just didn't realize how deeply.

On the slip is my name, my writing still as terrible as I remember it being. He saved it. He barely knew me, and I'd been so mean to him that night, but he'd still saved it. Heaving a shuddering breath, a smile finally crosses my face. I have Pax. No matter where we end up, I have him. He is my home.

And how lucky am I to have him?

"You're sure you want to do this, Liv?" Pax asks for the millionth time, his heavy hand resting on my thigh as he drives us through the city to Deidre's and Jeven's.

"Yup," I quip with a smile, a fluttering in my chest. He sighs, the sound exasperated. He's tried to talk me out of it all day. I think he's worried about me but doesn't want to let on that he is. I peek over at him, hiding my smile. He's so perfect in the falling light; sharp jaw, straight nose, arms flexing as he shifts and returns his hand to my thigh. Even just looking at him gives me butterflies now.

"You can call me any time and I'll come get you, alright? And be polite to Jev...and no getting into trouble...and—"

"Paaaxxx," I groan. He's so good at ruining the mood with his damn rules. His lips twitch down into a frown.

"I'm sorry, Liv...it's just hard for me, after everything..." he trails off, his iridescent eyes finding mine for a moment before returning to the road. I feel my cheeks warm. Those memories of the farm...I push them away. Nothing is going to happen tonight at Jeven's. Since we are moving, Deidre asked me over for a slumber party. I've never had one, clearly, and she says her older sisters used to have them, but she was uprooted before she was able to. So we both concocted this plan and presented it to our guys.

Jev didn't care at all, of course, promising snacks and pizza. Pax, on the other hand...I glance at him again. His grip on me tightens.

"I'll be good. I won't even go outside."

He smirks.

"You have a knack for finding trouble no matter where you are, Liv."

"Ok, fair," I mumble.

"Speaking of which," he says, pulling into the parking lot of Jeven's. He parks, and his eyes find mine. "You need a better hiding place for knives, baby."

I feel my face slacken, blanche in utter horror. I feel the panic rising. Is he going to punish me? Tonight? Tomorrow? Oh god, all the good stuff is going down the drain because of that stupid move—

He chuckles.

"Livy, calm down," he says, pulling me into his side, squeezing me and pressing his lips to my head. I let out a whimper, a soft plea of an apology against his shirt and warm, muscled body.

"I'm not mad, and you're not in trouble. I can...see why you did it, now," he says, his voice growing a little dark at the end. Although relief floods me, guilt soon surges to replace it. I hadn't known any better at the time, though. He chafes me as my mind races, and I peek up at him, biting my lip. I hid things, but so did he.

"Why did you save the paper with my name? The one I wrote?" I say. It's his turn to be shocked, for his face to pale a few shades. His eyes skirt out the windshield, and he brings his fist up, coughing once to clear his throat. When he speaks, his voice is deeper.

"Uhh...I..." he waits a beat, but then he rushes out his

explanation. "I thought it was cute...I've had a soft spot for you since we met, Liv, but that night, in the tent...when I held you close...I don't know. It was like I could feel my world shifting to accommodate you, and everything you did was intriguing to me, but that was just plain endearing. I saved it because...I think I knew even back then that I was going to be yours."

I blink up at him in shock, but he's staring out the window again, frowning, his face so serious like it always is. Warmth spreads through me, centering in my chest and unfurling out like a blossoming flower, igniting every inch of me down to my toes.

I shift, carefully climbing into his lap and snuggling down into his embrace as he plants another kiss to the side of my head. His arms are sturdy and strong, wrapped around me. I realize it's my favorite spot in the entire universe.

"Let's get in there so Jev doesn't crack any jokes," he says, sounding irritated already. I pop my head up, and he has to crane his neck back to meet my eyes, but he smiles, and my heart melts all over again.

"Who cares. You're all mine."

He lets out a bark of a laugh, bouncing us both with the beautiful sound.

Leaning in, his lips hovering over mine, he smirks.

"And you're all mine."

"So," Deidre says, laying on her stomach as she flips through a gossip magazine. I remember my mom reading them occasionally, but she always said I was too young to look. Now, though, I wonder at the differences in the subject matter. I am leafing through one as well, and though I can read better than before, it is still too confusing and distracting with the bright colors and obnoxious text. It seems Erathians have a love for certain human things, like Leonardo da Vinci's work, and they replicate it onto clothing. I frown, glancing up at Deidre. She pops a piece of popcorn into her mouth.

"Hmm?" I muse, pretending to find the next article more interesting than the last.

"You two left here so peachy last time. God, he was all over you."

I feel myself blush.

"And?" I murmur.

"Annnd," she teases, bumping her shoulder with mine. We are sprawled in the living room, glasses of 'mocktails' in front of us, the box of pizza discarded as we munch on snacks. Jev has promised to stay in his room and give us space, but we can both hear him yelling at his video games.

"And, we haven't talked since then. How are things? He's not too pushy with you, right?"

I bite my cheek to hide my smile as I give a nonchalant shrug. She grins and gasps, so bubbly and excited for the gossip. Pushing herself up, she crosses her arms over her ample breasts. With her long legs, thin neck, and subtle curves, she could be one of the models in the magazine.

"Oh my God, tell me *everything*," she gushes.

"Uggghhh," I groan, rolling onto my back and shielding my face from embarrassment. She smacks me. How do I share such intimate things with her? It feels so...awkward, yet still somehow normal. Like it is something I should be able to do. I peek at her with one eye and glare at her grinning face.

"We've...kissed..."

She gasps, clapping her hands to her mouth with a little giddy squeal.

"Ok, and? How was it? And *please*, I know you've done more. You have this glow about you, and it took him forever to leave!"

I sit up as well, circling my arms about my legs. Sighing, I can't keep the grin or blush from my face. It's still so new, and it feels good that someone is excited for my own excitement.

"He kissed me the day of the party...but it wasn't until the night before we were supposed to leave for Halifax that he... uhh...did more things with me..."

Deidre makes me go into an embarrassing amount of detail, and by the end of my shower story, my face feels like it is on fire.

She seems smug as she crosses her arms.

"Jev told me you two were pretty handsy at the swearing in ceremony. Can't say I blame you. A guy that sexy in a suit? Fuck me," she says, fanning herself. I hide my face and giggle, feeling a weight lifted off my shoulders now that I've shared with someone who I can trust, someone who is more experienced.

"So...how big is it?"

"Deidre!" I hiss, shocked and peering down the hall to make sure Jev's door is still closed. She leans back nonchalantly, picking up her glass and giving the ice a shake. There is a coy, satisfied smirk on her lips, and I feel my chagrin morph into a sly smile as well.

"I mean...his is the only I've seen, so..."

"Show me, dork! Use your hands!"

"Like...this?" I say, gesturing out a measurement.

"Holy fuck, girl," she says, her eyes widening. "And how about that girth?"

"Dee!"

"You've come this far," she says with a sip and a shrug. "May as well spill all your secrets now!"

I laugh, and then attempt to show her with my fingers, making an oblong 'o' shape. All I know is that when I gripped his cock, my fingers couldn't meet. I peek at her, abashed, and she's shaking her head.

"Lord have mercy when you two actually fuck."

I scrunch my nose, nervous.

"Is it going to be that bad?"

She frowns, eyeing me, and then shakes her head.

"I mean, you seem smitten with the big guy, and he obviously adores you, so I think he will keep it tame the first time. But yeah, you'll be sore with a piece that big," she says with a laugh. Butterflies erupt in my gut. I wonder when it will happen. It feels like it will soon, but I don't know.

"Any advice?" I ask hopefully. She snorts.

"Let him do all the work. And then when you're more used to it, if you ever want *anything*, just initiate some sexy time, and he will give you all your desires," she teases. I laugh, but it turns serious.

"But...like during..."

Again, she sighs, her coppery eyes searching past my shoulder as she ponders.

"Honestly, Liv, just enjoy it. You only get one first time, and to have it be with someone special...don't take it for granted, alright?"

I can see that she's saddened, likely thinking about her past, and my heart sinks for her. How did I get to be so lucky when so many other women didn't get that chance? Why are most Erathians so horrible to us humans, especially the women? And will it ever change?

There's a sharp knock on the door, and we both tense, not expecting it. Deidre sits up straighter, brows pulling together. The knock sounds again, and she stands and pads down to their room while my heart races. No one else was supposed to come over, I thought, and without Pax I don't want anyone else near us. I begin to panic, feeling uneasy.

Jeven comes out in front of Deidre, and his face is stoic, pinched. It makes my panic worse. He's normally the joking one, not the serious one. Deidre hangs back as he peers through the peephole, and then his shoulders drop and he chuckles, opening the door.

"Seriously, dude, she's fucking fine, look," he says, opening the door wider and motioning to me in a pile of blankets and snacks. I feel like Henry right now. Pax stands at the door, a disheveled, serious look on his face, but his eyes brighten when he sees me.

"You weren't answering," Pax growls to Jev.

"Yeah, dumbass, I was gaming. Calm your tits."

I stand and make my way over, for as annoyed as I want to be that Pax is here ruining my slumber party, the other side of me sees how worried he is and how sweet he's being. I stand to the side of Jev, crossing my arms. He chuckles to me and backs off.

"You two sort this out. Dee, how about a quickie—"

"I'm on my period!" she pipes up from the hall, sauntering to the kitchen. I shake my head, and then it's just us. Before I can say anything, Pax reaches for me, fingers finding the back of my neck as he pulls me close. My cheek collides with the hard muscles of his upper stomach, and as soon as his cedar wood scent coats my throat, my eyes close and my itty bitty anger disappears.

"Sorry, Liv, I just got worried when he didn't answer, and I..." he stops, cutting himself off. I grin against him, wrapping my arms around his torso and burrowing my face deeper into his warmth.

"I missed you, too."

He breathes a heavy sigh of relief.

"I'll, uhh...let you two get back to this sleeping party. You're not sleeping though?"

"It's a *slumber* party," I remind him. Apparently, Erathians don't do this human rite of passage when they're teens. "It means we eat and gossip and watch movies and then sleep."

"Oh," he murmurs, absentmindedly stroking my hair with the hand that is on the back of my neck. It sends shivers through me and feels so good. As much as I will miss being next to him tonight, I want my one last hurrah with my only human friend that is my age, one that can give me advice, one that is beginning to feel like a big sister to me.

I pull away, my fingers gripping the belt on his jeans. Giving him an encouraging smile, I pat his back. He chuckles, shaking his head.

"I'll never not worry about you, Liv. Best get used to it."

I frown, quirking my head at him.

"Yeah well as long as you know I worry about you, too," I mumble. He reaches up, stroking my cheek with the backs of his knuckles.

"I know you do, my fierce little human."

I grin, because his endearment makes butterflies soar through me.

He leans down, pressing a kiss to my head, and then, because no one is looking, he steals a lingering, hot kiss from my lips.

When he pulls away, I'm left blinking and stunned, and heat is pooling in my gut.

"I'll be here tomorrow at ten."

I nod, mesmerized by his chiseled face and the feel of his hard muscled body beneath my fingertips.

He jerks his chin toward the living room.

"Go have fun, Livy. I'll be here in five minutes if you need me."

I grin again.

"I know, Pax."

24

Pax

I t takes us two weeks to move, but the process is smooth, and I have never seen Liv more vibrant and happy. The patter of her bare feet on the marble tiled floors as she dashes around to put things away brings a smile to my face. I even allowed her to browse through a home decor catalogue so she could pick out what linens she wanted for our room.

She stands before our new mattress and headboard, tapping her chin. It is huge—bigger than any bed I have ever slept in before. The down comforter is fluffy, the duvet a crisp white. I understand her taste; she likes clean, modern, but with dashes of greenery in the form of plants. I am exhausted from putting everything together, and I am silently praying she doesn't instruct me to move something else.

"Well, Princess?" I grit out. She flashes me a glare.

"I hear the hot tub calling our name," I say, coming up behind her, encircling her in my arms as I press a kiss to her temple. She relaxes, holding my arms. We've been rather tame these few weeks, but mostly because we have been so busy with this massive shift in our lives. I don't mind. I already know she is more than ready.

I sneakily check my watch. I have two hours until my order is ready at the local florist. I have filet mignon marinating in the fridge. I took forever deciding on a fine wine to compliment dinner, and even longer deciding on a champagne for dessert. There is a box hiding in the closet, black with a silky bow, and what's inside will make my knees give out as soon as she puts it on—only for me to rip it off. I have about a thousand candles hiding in the garage, and a new fluffy robe for her to wear tomorrow morning when I make her breakfast in bed.

I want her first time to be blissful, memorable—absolutely perfect.

I hope she likes what I have planned. I hope she sees my effort as a gesture of my love for her, just as buying this house was. I want what she wants; to start a new life together, more equals than not, more a team than a dictatorship.

We've taken many steps forward lately, but I know this one tonight will be our first into our forever.

Olivia

"Liv, you've got some mail!" Pax calls from the kitchen. I peck Henry on his little head, letting him down back into his cage. I stand, smoothing down my shirt before I tap the bedroom light off and make my way out. It is cool today, and the marble floors send a shiver up my spine. Pax has been gone for hours, saying he had to run errands, but when I see him in the kitchen sorting mail with a frown, he has no bags.

He glances up as I seat myself on a barstool, tossing me a thick envelope. I have never before received mail, but as I read the name carefully, a smile graces my lips. Pax drums his fingers, small smile wavering on his scruffy face.

"I'm going to start on dinner," he says. I nod absentmindedly, ripping open the letter from his father. It takes me longer than I care to admit to read it, and there are a few words I am stumped on. Pax sees me struggling and comes around behind me, a bundle of asparagus in his hands and a dish towel thrown over his broad shoulder. I point to the word I am most confused by. He chuckles.

"This is one of those examples where English makes no fucking sense," he snorts. I don't even attempt to sound it out for him.

"*Edinburgh*," he says, and it really doesn't look anything like it sounds.

"Thank you," I say, turning to give him a sheepish smile. His eyes are warm. I wish we could skip dinner and just curl up in bed, or go hot tub. It's been raining all day, and summer feels close to over.

He leans in, pecking my lips before he returns to cooking. I tuck Penn's letter away. He did some research, per my request, and found out Sardone used to be called Edinburgh. My fingers play at my lips as I chant the name over and over in my mind. A small link to my humanity has been restored.

"Did he find out about your home, Livy?" Pax asks from the stove. Whatever he is cooking smells amazing, and my stomach growls. He glances at me when I don't answer.

"Oxfordshire?" he prods. I frown, shaking my head.

"Not yet," I mumble. He mirrors my disappointment.

"Don't worry, this is all he lives for. He can find out anything," he says, reassuring. I lean on the cool countertop, clasping my hands as I watch him work. This meal seems more difficult than what he usually makes. I feel bad for not helping, but he's been more insistent that we share chores so I feel like less of a slave and more his equal. I'm still getting used to all these changes, feeling more out of place than I did before.

"Why don't you go study, and I'll come get you when this is ready?"

Lost in my thoughts, I nod, making my way to the office. He has his side all set up with fancy screens. He works from home now, which I love; I get to see him way more often, and after being apart, all I want to do is be near him.

My desk is much simpler, and it faces a floor to ceiling window with a view that leads into a wide open field. It reminds me of that moor we crossed before we entered the kingdom. I smile, reminiscing on how much has changed since then. I don't get much done as I daydream, and I can hear Pax clunking around our bedroom, but he soon calls me to dinner.

"Pax, can we go on a walk tomorrow?" I ask before I stop short. He is grinning, the lights dimmed, our dinner table lit with two long candles with a single rose blossom in a thin vase right in the middle. He holds the back of my chair, nodding to it. My chest swirls with emotions—light, happy, but also nervous. This is meaningful—this isn't just dinner.

He encourages me forward, and I sit before he gently nudges my chair into place. There is a glass of red wine placed in front of me, and he dashes to the kitchen before coming back with our plates. My eyes find his as he sits across from me.

"Pax—"

He holds up his hand.

"I wanted to take you on a date. You know, dinner, movie, ice cream. But...I felt like tonight needed to be more about *you*."

"What do you mean?" I whisper, throat tightening in my angst. He takes a deep breath, his muscles stretching his shirt tight until he exhales.

"I mean to say I love you, more than you can fathom, and I wanted to spoil you. This is the start of a new tradition," he says, reaching for his wine glass. Tentatively, I follow suit, and we gently clank our glasses together.

"Tradition?" I ask. His smirk deepens.

"Once a week, we go on a date. It can be out on the town, it can be a quiet night at home, it can be whatever we want. I want to show you what it's like to be loved by me."

His eyes are earnest, but I can see he is nervous, too. I feel a deep blush coat my cheeks. I've never been on a date before—never dreamed I would ever get the chance to, really. I should have expected something so romantic from Pax. He's always been kind to me, understanding, gentle when I need it. And now that our relationship has grown deeper, I shouldn't be surprised he's doting on me so much.

I feel small, my shoulders hunching. I can never do for him the things he is able to do for me. I don't have money of my own. I can't leave the house without him by my side. I can't go buy him something as simple as his favorite coffee. I feel the weight of slavery once more, but I lock it away to think on later. I will not let it ruin this night he has planned for me.

We eat and chat, laughing often. The food is amazing, as I would expect from him, and so is the wine. He even brings out a chocolate torte for dessert, and hands me a flute of champagne. By the end, my mind is buzzing and I am stuffed. I move to clear our plates and get ready for bed, but his hand clamps on my wrist. I glance at him, confused. His eyes are dark, and in them wavers the now-familiar look of desire. I gulp, my knees weakening, knowing without him saying a thing that I will be at his mercy tonight.

And then it hits me.

Is tonight *the* night? Am I ready for that? By the look in his eye, it's been put off long enough. I am flooded once more with nerves, but the pit of my stomach tingles in forbidden excitement.

"In the guest bathroom is a box. Open it, follow the instructions."

His tone is demanding, deeply woven through with lust. I clamp my mouth shut and nod without question. I seal myself in the bathroom, the black box jumping out at me from the counter. Shaking hands pull the ribbon until it flutters to the ground in silky tendrils. I lift the lid off, and then my confusion sets in.

Something black and lacy and stringy lays there, but next to it is a note. It is Pax's trademark blocky lettering.

Put this on and wait for me in our room

I gulp again, pulling the small stretch of fabric out. I catch my eyes in the mirror, nervous, jittery. I take a deep breath, flattening my hands on my stomach. I shouldn't have eaten so much.

"I can do this," I chant with conviction. Even my voice sounds shaky. I strip down, taking my time to figure out this contraption, but I soon have it sitting right...I think. It is the thinnest thong I have ever worn, and the bra is see-through lace, pushing my small breasts up until they almost spill out of the cups. I brush through my hair with my fingers, then rinse my mouth. I have taken so long, I know he's probably worried about me.

I open the door, peeking out, but he is nowhere in sight. I dash to our bedroom, ready to dive under the covers, but I gasp at the sight before me. Candles. Hundreds of them. On the floor, on the nightstands. And rose petals are strewn over the duvet. My heart is thudding hard in my chest. This is it. This is the final step we take as a couple to become as close as intimately possible.

I am frozen in the middle of our room in the soft candlelight, but I can feel him behind me as he draws nearer. I drop my hands to my sides, wanting to cover my skin but knowing there's no reason. He's my Pax. He loves me. He will take care of me.

My eyes flutter closed as his fingers lightly trail up my sides, leaving goosebumps in their wake. I feel the heat of his body as he leans in, lips at my ear.

"You look stunning, and I haven't even seen all of you yet," he whispers, voice husky. I tremble in anticipation. His lips find my neck. I am thankful his hands are on me as my knees shake. He pulls away and turns me around quickly, my chest heaving as his shimmering eyes stare down at me like a starved wolf. He is wearing only his jeans, but I know that won't last long. His eyes feast on me before he holds my gaze.

"If you aren't ready for this, Livy, you can tell me," he says. I shake my head, biting my lip, and he looks crestfallen for a moment.

"I'm more than ready," I whisper. His face breaks into a grin, and he bends, cupping my butt and lifting me off the ground. I yelp, wrapping my legs around his waist, pulling myself close so that our chests touch. He is so warm, so strong.

He lays me down on the bed, crawling in on top of me. The bands of muscles in his arms are taut, his veins throbbing. He presses our hips together, and I feel his eagerness through his jeans. I let out a blissful moan, the ache between my legs growing rapidly.

"I'm going to take my time with you tonight, baby," he says, kissing my jaw. I moan as he rolls his hips into me, a promise of what's to come.

I reach up, wrapping my arms around his neck and pulling him down. I want him close to me, as close as possible. He chuckles, pecking my cheek, but he extracts himself.

"I am right here, and it's just you and I, right?"

I stare up into his eyes, feel his body on mine, feel our soft, plush bed beneath me. I am here with him and no one else. I am home, safe, with the man I love, the man who cherishes me and protects me. I nod, giving him a smile.

His eyes fall to my breasts, one hand sliding up my side to cup it, possessively. A guttural growl sounds at the back of his throat, and I release a breathy moan as he pinches my nipple through the lace. He presses kisses between my breasts, before he pulls down the thin cup, baring my stiff peak to his swirling tongue. My back arches, and my hands find his hair, encouraging him.

I am a mess, writhing beneath him, bucking my hips up, searching for a release as I try to press against his hard cock through his jeans, but he pulls away before I can build myself up. He chuckles against my stomach.

"Someone is excited for more," he teases. I roll my eyes, freezing, but it is too late; he's caught me. His face changes in an instant.

"On your knees and elbows," he demands. He releases me, allowing me to shakily move into this position he wants me in for my punishment. My head rests on a pillow, my butt in the air, exposed to him.

"Six paddles?"

"Y-yes," I stammer. I cannot see him, but I jump as I feel his hands caress my cheek. He pulls away, and I tense. The first spank is tame. I relax, readying myself for the next one. This one is harder. I bite my lip, quaking in desire. I feel wetness pool in my new thong. His next spank makes me moan before I can stop myself.

By the fourth, my toes curl, and I cry out as the throbbing between my legs reaches new heights. At the fifth, I am clenching the comforter in both hands, the insides of my thighs coated in my slickness. And by the sixth, I feel close to the edge, my release already built up and he hasn't even touched me where I ache most yet.

He waits before touching me, but when he does, his fingers

slide up between my thighs, feeling for himself what his punishment has done to me.

"Fuck, Liv. I want to take this slow and you make it damn near impossible," he growls, toying with me through the lace. I whimper into the sheets; the feel of my wetness, coupled with his probing fingers and the roughness of the lace, I feel like I am about to come.

In a flash, he rips the thong off me, nudging my knees further apart. Gentle, I feel his fingers enter me, his other hand splayed on my lower back.

"Pax," I pant desperately, "I'm...gonna...I'm gonna—"

"Come on my fingers, baby," he says, thrusting into me while his thumb rubs against my clit. I tense, seeing stars, before I fall apart, withering as I cry out, clenching and releasing over and over. I slump to the side, rolling to peek at him. He is chuckling at me.

"You're so sexy when you come," he says. I blush, pulling the comforter over my breasts as I shiver, giving him a bashful smile. He is staring at me as though I am the most rare and precious diamond in the world.

"Do you need a break, or do you want more?"

The way he is sitting on his knees clad in only his jeans and washed in the soft glow of the candles makes me want him. *All* of him. Without one shred of doubt left in my mind, I know I want him, and I want him tonight. Right *now*.

"I want you," I whisper. His eyes darken, his muscles tense, but slow, he unbuttons his jeans, unzipping them before he slides them down. His thick cock springs free. I gulp, still not convinced that will fit in me. When he is free of clothing, he climbs over me, slow.

"Take this off," he says, gentle. I sit up, pulling the ornate bra off and tossing it to the ground.

"You're sure about this, Livy?" he asks, cupping my cheek, his eyes so sincere, so concerned. I smile, nodding.

"Yes," I breathe, absolutely sure. He smirks, pressing his lips to mine as he lays me back, covering me, shielding me with his body. He nestles himself between my legs, and I freeze. He chuckles.

"I'll tell you when, baby, ok?"

I nod, breathless. We continue to kiss, his tongue swirling around mine as he winds his fingers into my hair. He kisses my entire body, from my head to between my legs. I gasp as he laps at me, teasing my entrance and my clit with his expert tongue. Soon, I am on the edge again, and he pulls away as I start to tense. His face has changed into one of determination, and he grasps his length, stroking as a bead of liquid seeps out the top.

"When I come, don't pull away from me, alright?"

I nod, confused.

He gives me a reassuring smile.

"We'll be joined for a little bit. It's something where our species differ," he explains. I've never slept with anyone, and so I know there will be no comparison on my end. He continues to stroke himself, but his other hand toys with me, slipping his fingers easily through my wetness.

"If it hurts too much, tell me to stop, Liv. Promise?" he asks, his eyes boring into mine. I feel a flutter of trepidation, but as his fingers thrust in and out of me, that fright flees.

"I'm ready, Pax," I say. He bites his cheek, his eyes glossed in lust. He withdraws his fingers, leaning over me so our chests are close, just how I was hoping he would be. I want him to hold me, want to feel that security his embrace brings.

I feel the tip of him, sliding up and down my wetness, and he groans. Slow, I feel him stretch me. It burns, and I do feel like I am being ripped in two. I whimper, clawing at him as he pants.

"Holy fuck you're tight, baby," he breathes. I begin to feel full, so full, so stretched, and it hits me that this is happening. We are having sex.

"Are you ok?" he asks. I clutch him and nod.

"Words," he grunts.

"Yes, yes," I say. He's somehow still inching into me, but the burn is fading, and then I feel it. His hips meet mine, and deep inside me I feel *him*, nudging against what feels like a sensitive wall. We take a few shuddering breaths together, and he wraps his arms tight around me.

"You're doing so good, Liv," he praises, pressing kisses to my forehead and temple.

"What...what are you hitting in me?" I ask, wriggling my hips. His hand flies down, stemming my motion as he chuckles.

"Cervix, I think," he says, breathless. His dark eyes find mine. "Does it hurt?"

I frown, considering. No, it doesn't, not anymore. I shake my head. He pulls his hips away, leaving me feeling empty, but then he slides slowly back in until he hits that wall with a gentle nudge. My eyes roll back in my skull as I moan.

"I...I like that," I say, digging my nails into his shoulder blades. He cusses again, repeating the motion. He slides in and out of me at a gentle pace, and each time he is pulling away, I feel his absence, and I want him back.

Soon, his pace is faster, though he is still gentle. He pulls himself almost all the way out, and I whimper, but he slides back in. I cry out into his shoulder, feeling that euphoria building. This time, though, it feels deeper, and I know it's going to be stronger than any I have experienced before.

I let my eyes dart down, watching as his hips thrust against mine, the sound of our skin slapping echoing in the room, his cock glistening before disappearing into me again and again and again. He reaches down, circling his thumb over my clit, and I immediately tense.

"More...more..." I gasp out.

"Scream for me," he growls. I know I don't have to hide it this time. This is our room, our home, and this will be what we do every night for all eternity. I grit my teeth against the impending noise, but my body betrays me. I feel myself floating, feel myself clamp down on him, and then I do scream as he pounds through the most intense orgasm I have ever had.

"Stay...still..." he grunts, gripping my hips as I wither around him, still moaning. He thrusts into me harder than before, and then he sucks in a breath, releasing it in a growl. He is deep within me, buried, his cock spasming against my wall. I feel him spill his seed, and it almost makes me climax again.

He collapses on top of me, and I shift my hips, forgetting what he told me.

"Ahh," I hiss, feeling him tug painfully against my insides.

"Shit, Livy, are you ok? Don't move, I'm sorry," he chants, cupping my face, our hips glued together.

"I f-forgot, I'm sorry," I whisper, giving him a reassuring smile. He sighs, pressing our foreheads together, staring deep into my eyes. I am left drained, but I feel full at the same time— loved. He loves me, and I love him.

"How was it?" he asks, smoothing his thumbs over my cheeks. I give a contented sigh, grinning up at him.

"I want you forever, Pax."

A wide beam splits his cheeks.

"You have all of me forever, Olivia."

25

Pax

Gentle as can be, I wrap my arms tight around Liv and roll so I'm on my back and she is laying on top of me. It's only been a few minutes, and I don't even want to try pulling apart yet—she feels too fucking good still, and I also don't want to hurt her by accident. Sleeping with her was better than anything I have ever experienced in my life. Though Jev was right in how small and tight she is, I still feel as though her body complements mine in a way I never knew one could.

I catch her peeking at me, see the rise of blush in her cheeks, and I chuckle, pressing my lips to her hairline.

"Are you embarrassed?" I ask gently. She tucks her head under my chin, hiding herself from me. I skim my fingertips up and down her back, and she shivers. She shakes her head, but I know the innocent part of her is, and that is fine with me. It is quiet, but I feel like she wants to ask me more. I enjoy her honesty with me—it means she trusts me.

"Why do you get stuck in me? Is that what humans do?" she asks. I run my fingers through her hair, soft, soothing.

"No. It's to ensure our kind procreates effectively. I...swell, and it locks me into place. The more we do this, the less time we will be stuck together," I explain. She raises her head, resting her chin on my sternum. A longing smile wavers on her swollen lips.

"I kinda...like it..." she whispers. My mouth runs dry. If she keeps that up, I'll never be out of her. I clear my throat, brushing the hair from her face with my fingertips.

"Well I kinda like it, too," I say, pressing a peck to her nose. She blushes again and buries her face while I chuckle.

"How...how was it, for you?" I ask, nervous for her response. I know she climaxed—I could feel every centimeter of her muscles clenching around me when she did—but I still want to ensure I haven't hurt her or frightened her. She has her dark blotches in her past, and I would hope she would be honest with me if anything was too much.

"It was...like nothing I've ever felt before," she whispers against my chest, drawing circles on my skin. I nod, knowing what she means. This was different than any other time for me. Physically, our bodies are about as opposite as you can get, but emotionally...there was just more. It wasn't just two people having their primal needs being met. It was two people expressing their love and trust. The way my chest feels so full right now has a smile stuck on my face.

"How did it feel?" I ask. I can feel her cheek warm against my skin at my question.

"Amazing," she whispers, wrapping her legs around my hips to get closer to me.

"I'm glad," I say, cupping her butt. She giggles.

"How was it for you?"

Her voice is small, tentative. She is nervous for my answer. I snort.

"Liv, if you weren't so new to this, we'd be fucking for the rest of the night and probably all day tomorrow."

"So...good?" she teases. I chuckle.

"Amazing."

"You've...umm...done this a lot?"

I still beneath her, worry creeping into my mind. I haven't slept around a lot by Erathian standards, but to her it will probably seem so. I don't want her to think less of me, or think that her innocence meant little to me, but I also want to be honest.

"No, not a lot. But I have slept with Erathian women before."

"Oh," she says. I frown. I can tell she's deep in thought.

"What are you thinking?" I prod. She curls in on herself as best she can. I am thankful we are stuck together—she can't get away from my questions so easily.

"Just...umm...that they are so beautiful—"

I grip her hips, hard, and her head snaps up to look at me, worry etched between her brows.

"Never question your beauty again, Olivia. You are the most gorgeous woman I've ever seen, but that isn't even the most important aspect to you."

She gnaws her lip before she speaks.

"What is, then?"

"Your heart. Your kindness. Your fire. One day we will both be wrinkly and grey haired, but who you are will always shine through, right?"

She nods against me, a little smile on her lips. I sneak my hands to her butt again before I edge to the side of the bed.

"What—"

"Hold on to me," I say. It is difficult to stand and not cause her any pain, but I manage. I walk us to the bathroom, cranking on the taps to the tub. We haven't shared a bath together yet, so now feels as good a time as any, especially when we disconnect. I want to take absolute care of her for these next few days, to show her that I love her. She rests her head on my shoulder as we wait for the bath to fill up.

"When we do this in the future, it's a good idea to use the bathroom after," I say gently to her. I catch her confused eyes in the mirror.

"Why?"

"I was told it helps flush out any bacteria that may have been introduced during sex."

She flushes hotly but nods. She isn't fortunate enough to have Deidre or even my mother that close by, so topics that I would typically avoid will be ones I need to help her with. I don't mind, though. I see it as another extension of my love for her.

When the bath is half full, I step in, carefully settling down with her straddling me still. She sighs in contentment, her body slack around mine. She's exhausted. I wrap her in my arms as the warm water laps at us. I figured she would be tired after all that—from the actual act to the high emotions.

"You wanted to go on a walk tomorrow?" I say. She yawns as she nods against me. I chuckle.

"Well...maybe we can sleep in?" she asks, sounding hopeful. I kiss her again with a laugh.

"As long as you want, sweetheart."

I shift my hips slightly. There is still a pull, but it is loosening. I sit up straighter, and she leans back, giving me a quizzical look.

"I think we'll be able to come apart soon," I say with a frown. She's so tight this is lasting longer than usual. She smiles and then gives a little moan as I shift again.

"Are you ok?" I breathe, stilling. She bites her lip and laughs, nodding.

"I can still feel you. It feels so...good..."

I grit my teeth. She *would* say something to make me hard once more. She's playing with fire. At this rate we will be stuck together until one of us falls asleep.

She notices the look on my face and covers her laugh.

"Are you laughing at my misery?" I say, hiding my smile. She presses her lips thin and shakes her head.

"I think you are," I say in a growl.

"No!" she squeaks, too innocent.

"If you keep saying such naughty things, I'll just have to fuck you again and start this whole process over," I say with a quirk of my brow. But, true to her insatiable nature, she flushes a beautiful deep pink, biting her lip. I grow hot and flustered, my hands tightening their hold on her hips. Slow, she rocks forward, sending jolts of pleasure down into my cock, making it harden again.

She grips my shoulders, her eyes closed tight as she begins to grind against me, finding her own pleasure without much help from me. I groan, my head falling back. The sway of her hips becomes more fervent, and though I have given over control to her, I need to take it back. I thrust my hips up, being forceful but still gentle, meeting her as she is coming down. She cries out, bouncing faster, harder. The water in the tub slaps the sides and spills over onto the floor.

I clasp the back of her neck tight in my hand, my tongue finding her nipple as I ravage her. She is mine. And I am hers. I know she is close as she begins to tighten around me.

"Not yet, baby," I say, panting. She whines, falling onto my chest, breathing hard. I feel close again as well. I grit my teeth, knotting my wet hands into her hair and yanking back, exposing her neck to my lips. I feel a moan bubble up from deep within her, the vibrations against my mouth sending me into a frenzy.

"Now," I growl. She tenses, holding her breath, and then squeezes my length like a vice before she cries out. I shudder and coat her insides with my seed for the second time today. She is shivering, still moaning as I twitch inside her.

We stay silent for some time as I stroke her skin and press kisses to her sticky forehead. I am locked inside her again, but I am hoping it will loosen quicker this time. Her breathing becomes deeper as the water around us cools. I smile as I hold her sleeping form tight to me. She knows I will take care of her tonight.

She knows I will do so for eternity.

Pax

I stare at my tablet screen, reading and re-reading the latest news that has been granted to me first before the public gets a chance to see. I rub my fingers together, lost in deep thought. It is just past dawn, and after getting a few hours of sleep, I couldn't shake the restless feeling I had in my chest.

Perhaps it was intuition, as humans call it. A feeling of foreboding. Maybe humans are much more astute than my race believes. I certainly think so, now. I lean forward, my eyes skimming the print again.

The election is next month, meaning both opponents are throwing out every last ditch attempt to sway the minds of the people. Opponent Two, however, has just released his most intense and thorough documents yet. I grit my teeth, but my blood is beginning to boil

It is stated under section forty-three, part five, that Erathians, as a race, are dwindling. There has been talk of this for years already, but the statistics have finally been issued to the public. And it is dire. Both sides acknowledge that, but Opponent Two has formulated a solution.

Any female human of mature, child-bearing age, is to be plucked from factories, stores, Facilities—anywhere where they are not of 'essential use.' Meaning they will be placed with families and used to procreate as a way to save our race.

Opponent Two is using fear—fear of the end of our kind,

fear of humans once more taking control of their world, fear of
failure as a species—to get what they want. And I know more
than most just how potent the use of fear is to control anyone.
With one month left before voting commences, this ship has
drastically changed course for the worse.

I rub at my exhausted eyes, my mind jumping to Liv. She is
safe here with me, but I have to begin wondering if they will
implement rules on my ownership of her. More specifically, a
timeframe in which I have to impregnate her before they take
her from me. It seems far fetched, but I know to never underes-
timate the powers that be. There is something more sinister
going on here, and I intend to unearth it.

I lean back, tapping my tablet off as I stare out the window-
wall into the dawn. The sun rises a bloody red over the field—
our property. Liv wanted to go on a walk today. I will not let this
news dampen what has transpired between us. I feel myself
smile as I remember last night, remember what she felt like,
remember how she was eager to go again.

Blood rushes to my cock. I try to keep my thoughts from
getting too racy; I need to give her body a break. She may be
more than willing, but I don't want to hurt her. She fell asleep
in the tub last night in my arms, and even when I was able to
pull out, she barely stirred, grumbling nonsense at me as I
cleaned her up and took her to bed.

I snort to myself. I have never met anyone so motivated by
food or sleep—and now intimacy. I should count myself lucky
she is such a simple, wholesome woman. I reach for my phone,
clicking through a few restaurants I have saved. The town we
live in is called Wallace. It is small, much smaller than Halifax,
and so our resources are few. One grocery store that doubles as
a hardware store, a few quaint restaurants and coffee shops, a
boutique or two, a bakery, and Liv's favorite—an ice cream
parlor.

She noticed it when we drove to get groceries the other day

and nearly jumped from my moving vehicle when she saw it. I check the forecast. It will rain all morning and afternoon, so a day trip into town may be out of the question.

I can hear her heartbeats before I hear her footsteps. I turn my chair as she approaches, rubbing her eyes, wearing my shirt. I open my arms, and she quickens her pace before she climbs into my lap and curls up, snuggling into me.

I feel she has fallen asleep, but her calm, tired voice quietly speaks.

"What did you do to me?"

I chuckle, pressing my lips to her head and keeping them there while I formulate a response.

"I made you feel good?" I attempt.

"Mmm, you did," she says dreamily.

"You're not in pain, right?" I ask, nervous. She wriggles her hips.

"No. I just feel...floppy," she says. I laugh.

"Floppy, huh?"

"Mmm hmm. Like my legs are jelly."

"I'll take that as a compliment," I say, leaning us back. She yawns, wrapping her arms as far around my torso as she can manage. I shift her so she is facing me.

"Go back to sleep," I encourage.

"I want you with me," she mumbles. A thrill runs through my veins. I can never deny her anything. Jev would say I'm whipped—and I would have to agree at this point. She has me wrapped around her finger and she doesn't even have to try.

"I think I can manage that," I say, standing. She holds me tight as I bring her back to bed. I lay her down as I pull off my shirt, climbing in after her. She sighs, melting into my embrace. She used to hate me holding her from behind, but now she accepts it without hesitation. I press a kiss into her neck before my lips nuzzle it. She giggles against me, curling into a ball.

"Pax?" she asks.

"Hmm?" I say.

"Have you...have you ever been in love before?"

I still, but for once her question will be a breeze to answer.

"No."

"Oh..."

"Does that surprise you?" I ask, confused. She shrugs.

"I just...everywhere we go women stare at you," she grumbles. I laugh, giving her a squeeze.

"And all the men stare at you."

"No, they don't," she says, defensive and perking up.

"Trust me, Liv, they do. I'm a guy, I think I would know."

She huffs. Is she jealous? Another thrill runs through me. It's adorable, her jealousy, but it just makes me want her even more. To show her that I am completely hers, to show her she is mine. I am still half-hard, being around her while she wears nothing but my shirt. I press myself to her ass, and I can hear the hitch in her breathing as her heart rate picks up speed.

I lean in, my lips at her ear.

"Do I need to show you how much I love you, baby?" I tease, nipping at her ear. She shivers in response as my cock hardens to its full length. There will be no break for her at this point; we both want each other too badly. She pulls away quickly, though, and I let her go in confusion, feeling stung.

But in her eyes is mischief as she bites her lip. She wants to play, then.

"Aww, fuck," she says, wide smile on her face as she jumps up and dashes from the bed. I chuckle, shaking my head, preparing to give chase. For some reason, she loves this game, and I have to admit that I do as well. The predatory ranger side of me enjoys a challenge.

I run after her, chasing her around the house as her bare feet patter on the marble and as she shrieks her laughter. Of course, I let her win, until my desire overtakes me. I have her cornered in the office when I grab her.

She is breathless, giggling, as I cage her against the window wall and the sunrise. My eyes flit behind her. There is no one that way for miles. It is just us and the wild, separated by a few panes of glass.

I grip her hips, hoisting her up. She wraps her legs around me, resting her arms on my shoulders.

"You win again," she says with a frown. I chuckle, sliding a hand up her shirt as I press her against the glass. She shivers, her skin erupting in goosebumps. I roll her nipple between my fingers, and she lets out a soft moan.

"I think you should know by now I always win, sweetheart," I say. She whimpers as my mouth hungrily kisses her throat. We are desperate, clawing at one another, our lips locked in a fervent dance as I rid her of her shirt. She is bared to me, pressed naked against the window for the wild to witness.

I yank my shorts down, centering myself against her hot, dripping core. I groan as I tease her, as she moans and raises her hips to meet mine, seeking pleasure as well.

"I'm not going to go as easy on you today, Livy. I can't hold back," I growl in warning.

"I want you, right *now*," she cries out, raising her hips again. I obey her demand, thrusting into her. She drops her face to my shoulder, biting me, her nails clawing at me as I let her adjust.

"Are you ok?" I pant. She whimpers but nods. I pull out slowly before I slide back in at the same pace. I keep my thrusts deep, my pace slow. I feel like I am going to explode any second, even if she depleted me last night.

I pick up my pace, the sound of slapping skin and her ass hitting the window music to my ears. I can feel her walls tighten, and I reach down, circling her bud with my thumb.

"Ahh...Pax," she moans, tucking her face into my neck as she wraps her arms around me. I hiss as she clamps down, but I grit my teeth and ride it out, until she is pulling away from me, sensitive, exhausted.

"I'm not done with you yet," I grunt. She is trembling, but she knows what she is in for. I gave her a taste at my parents' home.

"You can scream as loud as you want here," I say. She is breathing hard, and I know she feels her next climax building, because she is moaning louder than before. As she tenses this time, her mouth falls open. I pause my thrusts, my fingers strumming on her clit as she clamps down again. And then, I thrust into her harder than I ever have before.

She rewards me by screaming, leaving her nail marks on my back and shoulders. I groan as I spill my seed into her, both of us sweating and panting. When we've calmed, I walk us to my desk chair, carefully sitting with her in my lap.

"I love you," she breathes against me. I smile, holding her tight. Before I can tell her how much I love her in return, she's fallen once more into sleep.

~

Olivia

I cross my arms, standing before Pax as he leans back into the couch with a heavy sigh, a devilish smirk on his face. We spent our day napping. Well, I did, at least. I think he snuck off to work and bring me lunch, but I am exhausted from everything we've done lately, and so it all feels like a blur. A wonderful blur, but still.

"Is that attitude I see?" he says, quirking his brow. My arms fall, and my mouth runs dry. A tingle of anticipation buds between my legs, but I am sore now. As much as I want him, I feel like I need a break, to adjust more.

"You said I could pick dinner, so I chose pizza," I grumble. His eyes dance as they watch me. I know we already had pizza this week, but still. I think I deserve it after living in the wild and Ruins for most of my life.

"Liv, I was joking when I said no," he says, glancing at his watch. When his eyes find my face again, he smirks. The doorbell rings on cue, and I beam down at him, bouncing in excitement as he stands to go get it. He returns carrying two flat boxes, nodding to the table.

"Sit down, I'll get it for you."

I obey, my mouth watering. Soon, he slides a plate in front of me with three slices of pepperoni, along with a can of soda. We usually don't indulge like this, but Pax has been more relaxed on our rules lately. I enjoy it. I feel more free now.

"Did you pick a movie?" I ask, taking my plate to the sink. He sits back with a groan, rubbing his stomach. Somehow, he ate a whole pizza all to himself. We agreed today was a movie and dinner at home kind of day, and that tomorrow when the weather was better we could go on a walk.

He stands, bringing his plate over to the sink as well before he traps me against the counter in a bear hug, kissing my temple. I smile. He gives me butterflies all the time, even when he just hugs me or plays with my hair.

"I did pick a movie. I hope you like it," he says. I frown. There is mischief in his voice.

By the middle of the movie, I am curled into a ball on the couch, wrapped in a blanket, hiding my face in my knees. Pax is laughing—hard. I don't understand him. This movie is the scariest thing I have ever seen, but he thinks it's *funny*. I make the mistake of peeking to see why the music has turned so intense, when a clown pops out, his teeth jagged like razors.

I yelp, hiding my face once more as Pax chuckles. He drops his arm around me, pulling me close to his side, but I am mad at him for choosing something so frightening. I grumble that he's being an ass, but he doesn't hear me. He simply strokes my side gently before he runs his fingers through my hair. I hate to admit I love the way he feels next to me—warm, his muscles hard yet somehow soft and accommodating to my body.

It feels safe, protected. I know, after what Penn told me, that Pax can keep me safe from anything. I chance a peek once more, but this time at him. He is grinning, that dimple visible. He's been growing out his facial hair, and it makes him look more rugged—wild. The men out in the Ruins all had beards. His dark brown hair is a perfectly arranged mess atop his head, and he just got a trim the other day, so the sides of his hair are short and spiky. I like the way it feels when I touch it.

He chafes my hip absentmindedly. His chest muscles contract and expand with the simple movement, pulling his shirt taut for a moment. He is so handsome to me—so *sexy*, as Deidre would say. I feel myself blush as I remember what it has been like to have sex with him. He was so patient, gentle. I felt... like I was safe, to fall apart, to feel good. It was kind of embarrassing to fall asleep in the tub last night, but I woke up clean and warm snuggled up next to him.

He's my protector, my love, my Pax. Even the fact that he took me against my will is diminishing into nothingness in my mind. I am free with him. I have food, and love, and a warm bed and Henry, and a new house. I still wish that I could give him something in return. I wish I had something that was entirely my own to bring to the table. I know he would say it's unnecessary, but I don't want to feel like a bump on a log while he risks his life to keep me happy.

I would be just as happy in a tent on the run with him.

His eyes flash down to mine, catching me staring, reflecting the light off the TV. When I was in the wild and saw that at night, I knew a predator was near, and I hunkered down and prayed it would leave. Now, I see it almost every night, and it makes my heart skip a beat for much different reasons.

He cracks a smirk.

"Scared, sweetheart?"

"No," I shoot back, defensive. He chuckles, pulling me closer and leaning in, his lips at my ear.

"I think you are."

"It's a stupid clown," I mumble. He snorts.

"This is a human movie. A classic, or so I have been told. Should I tell you the plot twist?"

I frown, pulling away. I am tempted, because I hate surprises, really. Especially in movies or books. I like to know the end first. He refuses to tell me how *The Lord of the Rings* will end.

"Ok fine," I say.

"It ends with me and you, in the hot tub, naked," he says, lowering his voice. It is husky, deep, and his breath tickles my ear. I shiver in desire. Soreness aside, I just want to be as close as possible to him again. I don't think I will ever get tired of it. He makes me feel so loved, and even though he is dominant, I don't mind. I like that he knows what to do and can tell me what to do.

"Right now?" I ask, breathy voice shaking. He chuckles, flicking off the TV. I glance behind us, out the wide windows and into the black void that is night. My chest clenches in fear. What if a damn clown pops out? What if something more sinister is out there right now?

Pax moves, pulling me onto his lap as he traps my cheeks, forcing my eyes to his. His gaze is serious, protective.

"Nothing will ever happen to you, Livy. I am here. I would die a thousand times over if it meant keeping you safe from the monsters of this world."

26

Olivia

My stomach grumbles, my wide eyes adjusting to all the colors behind the rounded glass. The scent of sugary waffles tickles my nose, making my mouth water. I am chewing my lip, unable to decide what flavor of ice cream I want. The chain around my wrist tinkles softly as I go back to the end and begin my process of elimination over. No one else is in here, save for the teenage girl behind the counter and Pax.

I feel his fingers brush my lower back, and he leans in, keeping his voice low.

"You know, you can pick two flavors, and we can always make this a weekly trip," he says, his voice light, happy. It has been a little over a week since we first started...well...sleeping together, and each day since then has only gotten better and better. Every day is something new, from surprises, to elegant dinners, to time spent simply together in any capacity.

I turn, standing straight as I blush, giving him a timid smile. He returns it, and in his eyes is a new look, one that has been there ever since we started being intimate. I think it is love, or adoration. He looks at me as though I am the most precious thing in the world to him. And his actions mimic that. I don't even mind wearing the thin chain around my wrist when we go out anymore, because I know in his mind I am no longer a slave, but a person, and a person he loves.

"I choose chocolate, then. And strawberry," I add, unable to decide. He chuckles, rubbing his palm up and down my back as he nudges me to the register. He orders for me, and the young Erathian girl's eyes are wide, her cheeks pink. I glower, crossing my arms. Pax doesn't notice, nor does he give her any extra attention, for which I am glad. I'd probably hold a knife to her, too, if she made a move right in front of me.

She scoops our ice cream into waffle cone bowls, and Pax hands me mine before we exit to sit out in the sunshine. I love how small and quaint this town is, and everyone smiles, even at me. I feel more normal. Summer is drawing to a close, and the day is warmer, but Pax has said there will be a thunderstorm later.

I take my time as I eat my ice cream and people watch. A group of guys around Pax's age pull up in a truck and get out, loud and boisterous, jostling one another as they head our way down the sidewalk. I study them; five in all, muscular, tall, but nothing else remarkable about them. They are definitely Erathians, though.

As they draw nearer, the blond at the front of the group locks eyes with me, and his smile fades before turning into a look of disgust. I frown, averting my eyes, but I can still feel them watching me. Pax gently pats my knee, gaining my attention as they pass by and disappear into the liquor store.

"You alright?"

I force a smile and nod, but my stomach is churning. Pax is concerned, his eyes fixed on me.

"I think I just ate too fast," I lie. He chuckles, shaking his head.

"You and sweets."

I smile back. I remind myself I am safe with him, and that no one would attack me here of all places. Maybe I am seeing things, making things up in my mind. Maybe that man wasn't glaring at me.

We finish our ice cream, and Pax takes our empty bowls and used spoons inside to throw away. I stand, brushing off my shorts. He often leaves me with my chain in my own hands now. I have no intentions of running anymore. Not now that I love him, that I see all the sacrifices he has made for me.

I stand dutifully by the door, waiting for him to return so we can walk to the pet shop to get Henry some more food and bedding. The chime of the bell on the door from the liquor store rings in my ears, and the group of men emerge, brown bags in hand. The blond one has his eyes on me still, and he looks just as disgusted as before. So, I wasn't seeing things, then.

I shrink in on myself, avoiding their stares. I expect some Erathians to be hateful towards me, for whatever reason, but I have been surrounded by such nice people lately that their attitudes are throwing me off. I hear their approach, and my eyes snap up to the tall blond. He sneers down at me.

"Sure have a nice owner, buying a piece of shit like you ice cream," he hisses. I grit my teeth against the sting this causes in my chest. Pax is not my owner. I am not a slave. But in their society, I am, whether we see our relationship that way or not. The reality is crushing.

I don't respond. I'm not looking to get into trouble, or to drag Pax into anything. I just want to leave and have a good day like we planned.

"You deaf?" another asks. The group laughs. I grit my teeth harder.

"I hope he doesn't have feelings for you," the blond one says, leaning in and making his voice quieter. I am confused, and my eyes flash to his dark ones. A smirk plays on his lips, his eyes alight with malicious fire.

"How sweet, he does. Careful, 'round here, we don't take too kindly to human-fuckers. Make sure you warn your boy," he says, stepping back. I shiver, but I deepen my glare. The door to the ice cream shop opens, and Pax emerges with a pint of ice cream to go. He immediately stands in front of me, squaring his broad shoulders, his muscles tense and flexing.

"Is there a reason you're harassing her?" he grits out. The group chuckles.

"Not harassing her at all, sir."

I can hear the disrespect in his voice as he addresses Pax.

"I should hope not. Wouldn't end well for any of you," Pax says, his voice low, cool, promising violence. I reach up, my heart skipping, my fingers grasping the back of his shirt out of stark fear. I try and keep the memories from the front of my mind, try not to think of the stable, or Brutus, or the Facility. I am here, with Pax, and he won't let anything happen to me, ever.

"I bet it wouldn't," the blond says, holding Pax's gaze as his eyes dance. After a lingering moment, he winks, and the chuckling group jumps back into the truck. Once they've driven away, Pax turns to me, frowning.

"You alright, Livy?"

I nod.

"Come here," he says, wrapping an arm around me. I lean into his warm, steady side, all my fears fleeing at his touch.

"Thank you," I mumble. He waves his hand as we start down the street.

"Some people like to try and get a rise out of others. They'd be in for a shock, though."

I laugh.

"I know they would."

He holds up his bag with the pint of ice cream, and I glance up at his smiling face.

"I saw you staring at cookie dough, so I got us some to share for later," he says. I grin, and he chuckles, leaning down to kiss my forehead.

"After dinner?" I ask, already hopeful. He snorts, shaking his head.

"I'm thinking after our first round. Give us some energy for the next go," he teases. I blush furiously, slapping a hand to my face while he laughs. I am warm, happy, content. This is how I wish my life had always been, but waiting for someone like Pax was worth every obstacle.

$\sim$

Pax

We enter the pet store, and containing Liv is a lost cause. She pulls away to go look at the fish while I browse for Henry's brand of food. It seems we are alone here, and I am thankful. After the run in with those assholes, my mood is sour. I don't need any more reminders that my society sees Liv as nothing more than an animal, a means to an end. If there are still such attitudes out here in the country, then I cringe to think of who will win the election.

I bring his bedding and bag of food to the counter, and an elderly lady shuffles out from a back room, her white hair a halo about her head. She is a human, that much is evident by her glasses and her gnarled hands. These are afflictions Liv will face some day, while I simply grow old with little resistance. I push those thoughts aside and focus on all the years we will have together before then.

The little old lady smiles up at me, her eyes tight, but then

Liv approaches, slyly sliding freeze dried strawberries onto the counter. I turn, quirking my brow down at her. She simply gives me a cheesy grin. She loves to spoil Henry. And I love to spoil her.

"Well, someone must have a hamster," the old lady says, pushing her thick rimmed glasses up her nose. Liv beams and nods, seeming relaxed to be in the presence of her own kind. The woman smiles as she rings up our things.

"Do you have a name for him, dear?"

"Henry," Liv says, cheerful. She leans into me, her little hands both reaching to grip one of mine. It warms my heart, how often she seeks out my comfort, my touch.

"An astute name for such a shrewd creature," the woman says, eyes dancing as they stay stuck on Liv. I feel myself smile. It is not uncommon for humans to work in places owned by Erathians, and she seems well taken care of. My eyes fall to her arthritic hands as she bags the treats. On her left ring finger is a band of gold. Her owner must have let her marry, then. I find the notion romantic and kind.

"I thought so, too, but Pax made fun of me," Liv says. I am shocked as I stare down at her. She is fake glaring at me. The old woman chuckles.

"That's what us women are for, dear, to show these men a sense of good taste."

I chuckle, squeezing Liv's hand.

"Liv certainly keeps me on my toes with her taste," I say, smirking down at her. Liv's eyes widen, her cheeks turning bright pink as she catches my double meaning.

"You two are awfully adorable. New to town or just passing through?" she asks as I hand her my cash. Though Erathians can use their phones or other instruments to pay, they have found cash and coins a commodity—an antiquity that is trendy and therefore fun. I often find myself accumulating such currency with a need to get rid of it.

"New to town, just moved onto some property," I say.

"We have a hot tub!" Livy quips. I chuckle, extracting my hand so I can wrap her up and rub her hip.

The woman chuckles.

"That sounds lovely on a cold day. These old bones need a warm soak every now and then," she says.

"Your master must be super nice, letting you work here," Livy says. I tense, wondering if this woman will be offended, but she laughs louder before leaning in.

"I should hope so. Dumb brute is stuck with me for life," she says before she winks. I can feel Liv's confusion, but my heart is suddenly warmed. She is married to an Erathian, which is why she's been allowed the freedom to run her own business.

"I'm thinking Livy here will have to be bound to me for life as well, huh?" I say, peeking down at her. She bites her lip as her blush grows more prominent, but she nods, all the same.

"Oh, young love. I miss seeing it."

"Wait," Liv says, catching on, her eyes widening. "You're married to—"

"An Erathian? Oh yes, dear, for close to fifty years, now."

Liv's eyes bulge, bouncing between me and the old woman. She chuckles again.

"My name is Gladys, dear. My husband's name is Vox. We have three wonderful children, too."

"Woah," Livy breathes, still stunned. I am surprised as well, but I realize she most likely married before the takeover.

"And how long have you two been together?" she says, a twinkle of mischief in her eye. Liv peeks at me again, her wide green eyes full of love. I can't wait to get her home, stripped bare. I need her as I need air to breathe.

"Not long, but we're happy," I say.

"I can see that. Shame our society is going down the shitter."

I chuckle at her wordage, and I feel Liv lean more into my side.

"Yes, very disappointing. It's why we moved here from Sardone."

"Ahh, good choice, though there's still some...bigots," she says with disdain.

"Mmm, I think we may have just met them," I say. Gladys folds her hands, leveling me with a serious look.

"You look after this little peach here. And if you have any problems, you go to the Station. My oldest son is Guard Chief," she says, mouth pressed in a hard line. I feel a sly smile on my face.

"And if you have any problems, you can always come to me. My name is Paxton Harper, ranger 001."

Her eyes widen, her back straightens.

"Bless my soul. You've got yourself quite a hunk here, darlin'," she says to Liv. I snort, leaning down to press a kiss to her hair. Gladys watches us with kind, faded blue eyes.

"We should have Miss Gladys come meet Henry sometime," Liv says. I rub her hip again, smiling at her kindness.

"Sounds like a great idea, sweetheart," I say.

"Thank you, Miss Gladys," Liv says, "I wish I could have a pet store, too."

Gladys leans on the counter, chuckling.

"I'm not one to brag, dear, but I am quite old. If you ever want to earn some extra money, you can always come help me out."

Livy stiffens in excitement, glancing up at me. I can see she wants to take Gladys up on this offer, and though Liv has everything she could ever need, I can see why she would want something of her own—something I do not pay for. She is an independent woman, and she has every right to earn her own money. Part of me would be nervous, leaving her alone for a few hours, but aside from those men earlier, we've had no problems in this town.

"Can I, Pax? Please?"

I frown down at her as I consider.

"How about we discuss it tonight."

She looks crestfallen at my words, but nods.

"Only because I worry about your safety," I say, trying to reign her in. I don't want her feeling low because she is human. She simmers down and nods.

"You've got a good one," Gladys says to Livy with a wink. No, I think. *I* have a good one.

Olivia

I stand in front of the long mirror in our bedroom, frowning as I stare at my body. Pax bought me a swimsuit—sight unseen—and I can't help but feel self-conscious. I know that he has seen me—all of me, but it still feels weird to be wearing basically a bra and thong into a hot tub.

I slide my hands over my waist and hips. I am pale, for one thing, but since I have been with him I've put on a lot of weight. My ribs don't stick out anymore, and neither do my hip bones, but it also makes me feel like I've gained too much weight. I remember my mother always fussing over her thighs and belly, and even though my father would say sweet things to her, she would still find something about herself to be displeased about.

I bite my lip, turning to the side, blushing as I eye my bare butt cheeks. He *would* buy me something that shows off as much skin as possible. I turn back, cupping my breasts and lifting them. They look so much rounder and perkier when I hold them up. I let them go, groaning as they sag in the bright red swimsuit.

There's a knock on the door, but I'm not ready to go out just yet. I suck in my stomach, chastising myself for eating so much damn ice cream and always requesting pizza. I sigh, throwing my hair up into a bun, and when I stand straight, Pax is right behind me in his black and grey swim trunks. I jump, pressing my hand to my fluttering heart.

He chuckles, striding over to me and wrapping me up from behind, resting his chin on my shoulder as he eyes me through the mirror.

"Fuck," he hisses, pecking a kiss to my cheek. I blush, avoiding his gaze. His fingers trap my chin, and when our eyes meet once more in the mirror, his gaze has turned dark.

"What's wrong? Do you like it?"

"I...I love it, thank you," I mutter. His grip tightens.

"Tell me the truth."

I sigh. His skin against mine is a few shades darker, sun kissed, beautiful. Where his body is hard and defined with muscles, mine has turned soft, plush. I don't think myself fat, but...it's difficult to be in his perfect presence when I feel less than.

"I just feel...I don't know," I mumble, covering my stomach with my hands. His eyes darken even more.

"If you're feeling ashamed of your body for whatever reason —stop it right now," he growls. I blush, avoiding his penetrating gaze.

"Olivia—"

"I'm sorry," I mumble. He sighs, sounding frustrated, and it is quiet for a moment, tense.

"New rule," he says, voice coated in authority. My veins jump, and that familiar sensation tingles through my body before centering between my legs. I begin to tremble as his warm body holds me, his rough fingers blazing against my skin.

"You don't have to talk to me about these things, but you will discuss it with someone. And if you continue to get down on yourself, then I'll have to remind you whose opinion is the only one that matters outside of your own."

I gulp, my knees trembling. His eyes are angry, but not at me. He is just being stern. He cares what I think of myself. Maybe I was being a little too extreme.

"O-ok," I say. He frowns, but he presses another kiss to my cheek, his hand moving from gripping my chin to lightly cupping my throat.

"I love you, Livy. I love everything about you. Don't get down on yourself for how you think you look," he says, still stern, still holding me. I lean back into him as I agree.

"Because," he teases, one hand sliding down my back to squeeze my butt. My mouth runs dry as I watch his hands explore me, the one on my throat tightening the smallest degree in his possessiveness.

"Every time I see you—even if you've just woken up, I still want to fuck you."

I bite my lip against my mounting arousal. He sweeps me up as I yelp in surprise, walking us out to the back patio. The hot tub is ready, string lights guiding our way. There's even two glasses of champagne in the cupholders. I'm beginning to relax, to just chill out and enjoy this date he has planned for me.

He helps me in, and the swirling, frothing water makes my skin prickle, makes my joints melt into bliss. It is chilly outside, but that makes this even better. I sip on my champagne, my back to the house. He knows I don't like sitting in his spot; his back is to the field and the woods beyond. Ever since his father told me about the hybrids, I can't look at the woods the same.

He turns, reaching for something behind him, and produces a tray of chocolate covered strawberries. Screw being 'skinny'. Food is way too important. My mouth waters instantly as he laughs and holds the tray out to me. I dry one hand, going to greedily reach for one, when he pulls the tray away.

"Ah ah, come here," he says, eyes glinting in mischief. I

pout, setting aside my drink before I wade to him. He smirks, opening his arms, and I settle onto one of his legs.

"Good girl," he teases, holding up a strawberry for me by the stem. I glare at him, but I know this is all part of him feeling like he is caring for me in every aspect, even if it means him being romantic and feeding me chocolate. I don't care. It's chocolate. I'd lick it off him if he wanted me to.

He holds the fruit to my mouth, and I obediently open and bite down, the flavors exploding blissfully across my tongue as I groan. He laughs again, nuzzling me with his nose. I turn and smile at him as I chew.

"Fanks, Pax," I tease. He shakes his head, his free hand tracing patterns on my thigh, slowly inching closer and closer to the band of my swimsuit. I finish off a few more strawberries before I melt into him, both of us facing the house. Muted light spills from the wide windows, painting us in a soft golden glow. I still can't believe he moved out here—bought a *house*—for my benefit.

Before I can bring up the topic of working at the pet store, his lips are at my neck, kissing me slow but hungrily. I shudder, leaning back into him more, feeling his cock harden between my cheeks. His tongue darts out, swirling against my skin, and I whimper, needing him, wanting him. He knows this. He always knows what I need and what I want, and he always ensures I am satisfied.

I whimper again as he loosens the ties on my top, and it flutters down into the roiling water, leaving my chest bare. He reaches up with one hand, cupping my breast as he kisses down to my shoulder and back up to below my ear. His other hand skims up my thigh before he spreads my legs.

I suck in a breath, but his lips are hot at my ear.

"I'll take care of you, baby," he purrs. His fingers slide under my swimsuit bottoms, finding me already dripping wet. I whimper again, pushing my hips up.

"Shh, shh, be good," he says. I grit my teeth as he rolls my nipple between his deft fingers, and then I moan as he slips his middle finger into me at the same time. I am gasping as he slowly thrusts in and out of me. I need more, but he seems to want to take his time with me tonight.

He thankfully adds another finger, but it's not enough. I need him. I can feel him, hot and hard and eager. His thumb finds my clit, and it nearly drives me over the edge as I cry out. He growls a command, and though I don't understand it, my body reacts. I stand between his legs, and he rids me of my bottoms.

"On your knees, lay over the edge," he pants, quickly untying his trunks. I gulp, obeying, but not before I watch his cock spring free and thud against his abs. I am quivering with excitement as I feel him behind me. We usually have sex facing one another, so this is new—this is exciting.

He leans his body across my back, his wet hand trailing up my spine before he grips my hair, giving a firm yet gentle yank. I moan. I only like it when he is dominate in these situations, but even if we aren't being intimate, if he commands me to do something, it usually turns into sex not long after.

"I don't think this is going to last long, Livy. Can I be hard on you?" he asks. A ripple of anticipation runs through me, and I nod.

"Yes," I breathe, feeling small with him surrounding me in such a way. Despite the chill air, I am sweltering as the water writhes around us and fogs our vision. He fists his cock, stroking me with it until he eases in. I feel so full, and when he's all the way sheathed by me, I let out a loud moan. His grip tightens in my hair, and his lips are at my ear once more.

"Remember how much I love you," he says, his words a warning and a comfort. I brace myself. He presses a kiss to my shoulder before he pulls almost all the way out and thrusts back into me, *hard*. I don't even have time to think straight as he pounds into me at a furious pace, going so deep, stretching me so wide to accommodate him. He is kissing my back, my neck, fondling my breasts, pulling my hair so my neck is exposed. I am lost in ecstasy as my first climax hits.

It is so mind blowing I can't even make a noise, but Pax acknowledges it, grunting in satisfaction. Water splashes over the side of the hot tub and smacks against the patio concrete, but he isn't done. He pulls me up quickly so I am standing with him still inside me. I feel like he is going to saw me in half with his deep, fast thrusts.

I am soon back on my knees as he grips my hips. He angles me a certain way as I let out a string of moans. He's hitting me deeper, pumping against my wall. I tense as another orgasm builds, and though I try to hold out, it rips through me, and I cry out to the night.

I feel him hit my wall as hard as he ever has before, and though it sends a jolt of pain through me, as soon as he spills his seed into me, the pain disappears. He is in me—all of him, as much of him as there could ever be.

He is panting, laying across my back, pressing kisses to my slick skin. He is swollen, stuck deep within me. I love it, how I can still feel him, so hard, so present inside me even after we're done. He picks me up, turning us around so I sit in his lap facing the same way.

I lean back into him, smiling. He chuckles, pressing a kiss to my lips before he smoothes water over my chest. Though I am sore and exhausted, his fingers slide down my stomach, circling my sensitive bud. I lurch at his fiery touch, but I am stuck, whimpering and at his mercy.

"Come for me again, baby. I want to feel you get tight on me," he says, his voice low, husky. I am tense as his fingers circle me.

"Relax," he soothes. "You're going to be ok, relax," he says. And I listen. It begins to feel good, and I feel so full of him that the sensations have me moaning again. It doesn't take long. This is so new, so erotic, that he builds me up, teasing me a few times, before he lets me come. He hisses when I cry out.

"Yes, baby, good girl," he says, squeezing me tight to him.

"Fuck, that felt so good," he growls as I pant, ready to pass out. All is quiet for some time as I rest in his arms. He kisses me often, rocking me back and forth. I smile up at the stars. *Pax came from there*, I think to myself.

And how lucky am I to have crossed paths with him?

27

---

1 Month Later

Pax

I thrust slowly into Liv, gripping her hips so she can't slide away. Who knew the island counter would come in handy for such an activity? It is just past dawn; I was up, preparing for my work day when she came out in just my shirt and wrapped her arms around me. She's been clingy lately, but I do not mind. Ever since she began working at the pet shop a few hours each day, we've not seen each other as much.

She moans, wrapping her legs around me, keeping me planted close to her as she wraps her arms around my neck as well. I hold her tight, slowing my thrusts, keeping them deep and hard. I know exactly what she likes now, and I make sure to always keep her satisfied.

I love it when she melts into me, when she sighs against my neck as though this is pure bliss for her. She is still tired—she loves sleeping in, but she won't miss a chance to get me worked up until I give in and fuck her. Her fingers dig into my back as I slam into her and hold my cock against her wall. She shivers, moaning, tightening. It won't be long, now.

In a swift move, I pull off her shirt and toss it to the ground, gently pushing her away. She catches on, leaning back, her palms splayed on the marble behind her, giving me an uninterrupted view of her body, of me sliding in and out of her. I pause my thrusts, gritting my teeth as I breathe through my nose. She gives me a coy smile that soon turns curious.

Without me saying anything, her small hand reaches down, gently wrapping around my slick cock. It's my turn to shiver, for the sight and the sensation nearly drives me over the edge. I pull out, slow, before I thrust hard back into her. She cries out, her hand gripping me even tighter. There isn't one centimeter of me that isn't somehow engulfed by her, and it is amazing.

I quicken my pace, for as much as I want to stay buried in her all day, I cannot. With the election just three days away, I have a ton of work to do and potential raids to plan. I grunt as our sticky skin slaps, and her moans increase, her face lost in her world of ecstasy. Fuck, she is so beautiful, and how lucky am I that she is mine? Never in my life could I have hoped to fall in love in such an intense way before, yet here I am, head over heels and worshipping the ground she walks on.

My cock slams into her, once, twice, and she clamps down on me. I push myself as deep into her as I can go as she cries out, and I fill her completely with me. We pant, gathering our breath, before she gives me a small laugh. I grin at her, pulling her close, kissing her deeply.

"Looks like you'll be helping me make some coffee," I tease. She gives me a warm smile, staring dreamily into my eyes.

"Good, because I need some now."

"Oh? You mean you're not going to go back to bed?" I say, smoothing my hands all over her silky body. She presses her lips thin and shakes her head.

"Nope."

I frown, confused. She hates being up with me this early and typically goes back to bed. What is she planning? But before I can ask, she blushes. I quirk my brow at her.

"What trouble are you going to get into?"

"Nothing!" she squeaks, too innocent. My frown deepens.

"I think you should tell me, because we don't keep secrets," I remind her. It was her new rule; to not keep anything from one another, no matter how embarrassing. It goes hand in hand with honesty, but I understand her need for this rule. It is back-firing for her now, though.

"Ok, ok," she says, biting her lip, "I just wanted to...take a shower...and touch myself..."

My eyes fly wide open. She admitted to me that while I was gone she had been too nervous to do such a thing, and she also said she preferred it when I was the one giving her pleasure, to which I had to agree. But hearing her say she wants to take time to do this herself—well, I won't become unstuck anytime soon.

She is blushing, avoiding my gaze. I reach up, tenderly cupping her cheek before brushing her hair from her face. She peeks at me, looking ashamed. I know this isn't because I don't satisfy her. I wonder, then, why she wants to try now.

"What has you wanting to try that, baby?"

She gives a shrug, leaning in and hiding under my chin. I gently rub her back and shoulders. I press kisses to her hair, smiling.

"As long as you tell me a detailed description..." I tease. She gives a small laugh.

"In all seriousness, Liv, it's your body. You do whatever you want to make yourself feel good. It's healthy."

"Really?" she asks, pulling away, brows furrowing. I cup her cheek again and nod.

"Of course. It helps you...destress. Unwind. And if you don't feel comfortable sharing with me, that is perfectly fine, I promise," I assure her. She bites her lip again, cocking her head to the side.

"I...don't mind sharing with you. I *want* to share that kind of stuff with you," she says, looking determined and serious. I chuckle, pressing a kiss to her forehead. It warms me, how open she is with me about everything. And then I begin to wonder...

"Are you curious about...more than just that?" I ask. Her brows furrow again, and I realize she has no clue what I am talking about. I smirk, smoothing my palms over her hips.

"Like...what?"

"How about I show you some things, and you can order anything you want that looks...fun. Stuff for you, stuff for us..." I say, searching her still confused gaze.

"What kind of stuff?"

I snort, blushing. Never before have I gone into a sex shop. Any relationships I had before Liv weren't this...intense.

"Well...stuff to make sex...more interesting? Better?"

"Better?" she whispers, her brows shooting up. I give a half shrug.

"I wouldn't know. I'd be new to all that, too, but it could be something we explore together?" I suggest. Her cheeks warm as she smiles, giving an eager nod. God, how did I get so lucky to be with a woman who loves sex as much as a man?

"I like that idea," she says. My smirk deepens.

It is lunchtime, and Liv has showered and gotten ready for the day. She is now sitting at her desk, browsing through an online sex shop. I come up behind her, and she holds the tablet up to me, turning her confused gaze to meet mine. I chuckle.

"I don't think we need that."

"What is it?" she asks.

"Lube. It's to make me slide into you easier, but we've got that down."

She blushes a nice deep red, scrolling to the next thing she had saved. A lingerie set—a corset in an emerald green. My mouth runs dry.

"Yup. Add that in your size," I say. She gives a little devious smile and obeys, then hands me the tablet.

"That's all?"

"I...didn't know what everything else was..." she admits, sheepish. I chuckle, retrieving my chair and pulling it over next to hers as I begin to scroll through the photos.

"Stop me if you want to know what something is," I say, peeking at her. She is leaning over, gaze intense. Her little finger sticks out, pointing to something. I click on it, feeling my cock harden.

"What does that do?" she whispers. I cough, clearing my throat.

"Umm...goes in you and vibrates."

"So...so you put it in me?"

"Or you use it by yourself," I say, glancing at her. I can see she is even more intrigued. Without waiting for her to fumble for an answer, I add it to the cart. She smiles, blushing even more.

"Thanks," comes her small voice. I chuckle, shaking my head as we continue to peruse. We are entering the more interesting section, and eventually her small hand reaches up, pointing to another photo.

"Why would you need that?"

It is a length of silky black rope. I frown, for I feel tying her up may not be the best idea.

"It's for tying you up."

"Oh...hmm..." she says. I can tell she isn't as into that idea, and I don't mind. She points again, only this time it is to a small paddle. I smirk.

"Someone likes getting spanked."

She glares at me playfully.

"It's your fault," she mumbles. I reach over, wrapping her in a side hug as I chuckle.

"Did you always like that...?" I ask, truly curious. She is sheepish as she bites her lip and reddens, but she gives a small nod.

"I was...kind of confused why...but...even the very first time I got into trouble...I don't know. I just *liked* it."

I am surprised at this admission. Perhaps there was more trust between us initially than I thought, perhaps there was more attraction as well. I add the paddle to the cart, and she buries her face in my arm as she giggles.

I lean over, pressing a kiss to her head. I wish, for the rest of our lives, that this will be how we remain; open, honest, loving, safe with one another to explore. My society may be shit, but if I can continue to give her freedom in every way possible, I know we will be alright. I know our love and our bond will grow as deep as roots. No matter the future, we will always have each other.

Olivia

It is dusk, the days growing shorter as we approach fall. I shrug on my jacket and pull on my new hat, waiting for Pax to come get me. Every week, I work four shifts at the pet shop with Gladys, mostly helping her close. Pax always brings me to and from work. The first week, though, I caught him working across the street at the coffee shop so he could make sure I was safe all day. It warmed me, his protectiveness, but I still needed more freedom.

We settled on a compromise; he would drop me off and pick

me up, and he even bought me a phone that could call him, his parents, or Jev if need be. This massive leap forward was something I had never expected to happen, but Pax had promised me he would try, and so far he had not let me down.

I grin as his deep green vehicle pulls into a parking spot just down the road from the pet shop, and Gladys chuckles, keys jangling as she comes to lock up.

"I'd be excited, too, if that was waiting for me every day."

I blush, turning to smile over at her. She winks at me, shooing me out so she can close the glass door and set the alarm. Pax is already out and walking toward me, wide grin on his face, that perfect dimple visible even under his scruff. His hands are shoved into the pockets of his jeans, his grey hoodie tight across his broad shoulders and chest. I shiver in excitement, my whole body tingling in anticipation.

The other day, we had to pull over on the way home so we could indulge in one another. Keeping away from each other is difficult, but I could care less. All I want for the rest of my life is him. Him and Henry, our little family.

"Hey, baby," he says, wrapping an arm around my shoulders and pulling me to him. Even though I still wear the chain around my wrist, it is more for show now. Even Gladys has one similar to mine, but no one ever bothers her, and now no one bothers me, either.

"Hi," I breathe, leaning back to look up at him. He bends down, kissing my head, sending butterflies rioting into my stomach. Gladys gives the glass door a tug, ensuring it is locked, before she comes over to say hello to Pax.

"Miss Gladys," he says with a nod. She gives a coy grin, bundling up in her scarf.

"Mr. Harper, you grow more handsome each day."

He chuckles, chafing my side.

"And you grow more youthful."

She bats her eyes and fans herself before winking at me.

"My, my, you're a lucky lady," she says, whispering loud enough for Pax to hear. I laugh, curling more into his side, breathing in his intoxicating, masculine scent.

"I know I am," I say, truly meaning it. I haven't been this happy since my mother died, and I haven't felt this secure or safe since before I was uprooted. Even with all the troubles I faced getting to know Pax, I wouldn't take anything back. I love him far too much.

Gladys sighs, checking her thin, gold watch. An heirloom from her mother, she told me.

"Best be getting home to watch this election," she says, sounding annoyed. Pax's grip on me tightens. I know he has been even more busy preparing for whatever outcome, but I also know he hasn't been telling me everything. He says I don't need to worry about anything yet. I still do, though. I have a feeling this can shape the outcome of the remainder of our lives, and I am nervous.

"I plan to not even turn on the TV tonight and just wake up to a shit show tomorrow," he says, teasing, but there is a tightness to his voice. We say our goodbyes and Pax leads me to the car, helping me in. I sit right in the middle, chilled but also just wanting to be near him. I enjoy having a chance to miss him each day.

He smiles down at me as he starts the vehicle, sliding his hand between my thighs, his skin so warm that it sends chills throughout my body. He chuckles, letting go of me so he can shift and back out. I grin as I watch him.

"You know, I stole a car once when I was in the Settlement," I say as he turns onto the road that takes us home. He chuckles, raising his brows.

"Oh?" he says. I nod.

"Yup. I was mad because I wanted to see my dad, so I got in and got it started, but stalled it on a hill."

"And how did that work out for you?"

I grimace as I remember the repercussions of that awful day.

"I rammed into a tree and didn't get dinner that night, and my mom yelled at me *so* bad," I say. He laughs hard, grinning from ear to ear.

"So, you were always a little shit then, huh?"

"Hey," I whine, glaring at him. He glances at me, his warm eyes dancing in the sunset.

"I'm impressed you knew how to operate a manual. Old technology, but Erathians eat that shit up."

I am curious, watching as he shifts into another gear. It is sexy, watching him do something as simple as driving. I am biting my lip as I stare at his strong hand, his tendons flexing as he holds the top of the shifter.

His chuckle pulls me from my daydream.

"Here," he says, lifting his hand. I am confused.

"Better hurry before we stall," he says with a wink. Panicking, my hand flies to the gear shift, but I have no idea what to do. His laughter fills the car, and his big hand drops over mine, curling around my fingers. He shifts, keeping his hand on mine, and we settle into a comfortable silence.

We drive, and I am mesmerized as I watch him gently command me. It's making me ache for him—something as silly as this has turned me on. His intelligence, his cool, controlled demeanor, everything about him, about this moment, feels subtly charged with sexual promises. I am buzzing with excitement by the time we pull into the garage.

He hops out, helping me down and into the kitchen. I hang up my jacket before dashing to the bedroom, but his arms catch me, pulling me to him in a crushing embrace. He buries his face in my neck and inhales before kissing me tenderly. I sigh into him, relaxing.

"I have a surprise for you," he says. I twist in his arms, curious. He straightens but still holds me, his eyes dancing.

"What is it?" I frown. He surprises me all the time now, and even though I hate surprises, I love the way he spoils me. Now that I am making my own money, I can't wait to return the gesture.

"Dinner first, then put on the warmest clothes you have," he says with a smirk. My confusion deepens.

"What—"

"My lips are sealed, Liv. You'll like it, I promise."

I am nervous, even though I shouldn't be.

"Can't you at least give me a hint?" I say, making my eyes big as I beg. He sighs, cupping my cheeks as he frowns.

"It has to do with astronomy."

"Really?" I breathe, excited. He smiles, pecking my lips.

"Yes, now go before I make you help me with dinner," he says with a chuckle. I stand up on my tip toes, pressing my lips to his. He melts into me, encircling his arms around me as he lifts me off my feet and squeezes. Before I know it, our tongues are dancing as he slowly thrusts into me, our clothes strewn throughout the house, the trail leading to our bedroom.

I am nestled between Pax's thighs as we sit on a thick quilt in our field. His body encompasses mine, warm, strong, reassuring. My legs are still shaky from our earlier lovemaking session, and though I am sore and tired, the ache is a new constant reminder of the shift in our relationship. I find that I crave it, this feeling he gives me even after the act. Like he is still inside me, throbbing, yearning to give me more.

I gulp, torn from my thoughts as an owl hoots nearby. The darkness used to be my shelter; now, I know what horrors lie in wait. I pray I never have to face a Hybrid, but knowing I have Pax is the best comfort of all.

I am bundled up against the chilly night air, stumped and

wondering why we are sitting out here with a thermos of hot cocoa. I lean back into his embrace as he circles his arms around me and tucks his face into my neck. I shiver at the touch of his frigid nose but smile. His affections rival mine; he always wants to be touching me in some way, but I don't mind.

"Ready for your surprise?" he says, his voice husky. I nod eagerly, setting aside my cup of steaming chocolate. He reaches behind us and hands me a long bag made of sturdy material. Puzzled, I glance at him, but he just nods to it.

"Go on," he encourages. I pry the velcro open, the sound cutting through the quiet of the night. I pull out a long, metal, circular object with a bubbled lens at one end. I recognize it, but I am still confused. I feel his chuckle rumble through his chest, and he reaches around, pulling on the thin end until it elongates.

"It's a telescope. A small one, but still super powerful. Look through this end," he says, holding up the tiny end to my face. I am smiling as I obey, giddy with excitement. I press my eye to the scope, pointing it to the sky with his help. It is surprisingly heavy.

Right away, millions of stars come into view—some that I couldn't have seen with the naked eye. I gasp at the sight, and it takes my mind a moment to comprehend what I am seeing. Throughout my lessons, I mostly stuck with astronomy because it simply fascinated me. I never really mentioned that to Pax, so he must have just noticed. I feel warmed at the thought.

But now that I know more about space, what I am seeing is quickly put into perspective. Every star is a sun, the center of different solar systems, and some probably contain life. In the same breath, some of the light I am seeing is still emanating through space from stars that have died thousands of years ago. I gently lower the telescope as my heart sinks.

I blink up at the night sky, feeling my tears, feeling the

weight of it all, but mostly, I feel the insignificance of the mundane. Why does all this matter? What is the point in life, the point in slavery, the point in one race dominating another? Why do we find solace in books, why do we grieve and mourn for things that were or things that never will be? There is an entire universe out there doing all it can to expand, and then there's me. I am nothing, not even a blip on a radar.

Pax remains quiet, but his hold on me tightens. He must sense I am emotional, lost in the speculation of philosophers.

"You can still see Sarg, our sun. It will shine still for tens of thousands of years more, because it takes so long for light to reach Earth," he says, his voice low. I swallow the lump in my throat. I know that he feels connected to his planet in a way I will never understand.

"Can you show me?" I ask. He reaches around me, grabbing the telescope and connecting it to a tripod. He types in coordinates he reads from his phone, and then leans back once more, allowing me the first look. My hands are trembling as I gently cup the eye hole and gaze through it once more. My heart stutters as everything comes into perfect, crisp view. It looks so... normal. So much like my solar system. A simple sun and nothing more. But I know the truth—know that the star exploded and then shrank to nothingness, leaving everything behind in a frozen wasteland.

"This is..." I say, fumbling for the right words. He presses his cheek to the side of my head.

"Amazing?" he finishes. I nod, but the word falls woefully short.

"I just feel so...small...don't you?" I ask. I wait for his response, knowing he is thinking this through carefully.

"I...do. Yes, in some ways. But then I think how...how crazy it is, that I ended up here, that I took a job as a ranger because my father was in the military, and that I went on a raid, and that

I found *you*," he says, his voice growing more earnest as he squeezes me tighter.

"How? Out of all the decisions we both made, how did it lead us to one another?" he asks, sounding stumped. I feel chilled at his words, but also warmed. He's right, though; how, and why? I smile to the stars, burrowing down into his warmth.

"Fate," I say. He chuckles.

"You humans love to use that explanation."

"It's true," I argue, defensive. He is quiet for some time.

"I love you, Olivia," he finally whispers. The tone of his voice has my insides melting, my heart racing. This isn't how he would normally say it; there is more. This time, his words have weight. I am worried, confused. Is something bad coming? Should *I* be worried?

"I love you, too, Pax," I say as my heart races. He chuckles as he squeezes me, pressing a kiss to my cold cheek.

"Calm down, baby girl. I can hear your heart."

I frown at the night sky.

"What's wrong?"

He sighs.

"I'm just worried about tomorrow, about the way our lives may change."

I chew my cheek in thought. He's been worrying more about this a lot lately. But it still feels like he is keeping stuff from me. I don't want to push him, especially not on something like this, something that involves his career.

"Well, guess what," I say, turning to stare him in the eye. His gaze is reflective, and it reminds me of the light from his home star.

"What?" he teases, tucking my hair behind my ear. Using all my strength, I push him until he falls onto his back, a confused smile on his perfect face. I grin, crawling up and over him until I straddle his waist. I grip his wrists, pinning them above his head, but his arms are so long that I am stretched as far as I can go, our chests and noses touching. He quirks his brow at me, but his eyes are playful.

"You're mine, so I say you can't go anywhere or worry about things you can't control. Got it?"

His eyes flash, serious and brooding for a moment, before he relaxes and nods, giving me a gentle smile. He is warm beneath me, his wide torso stretching my legs taut, his grey hoodie soft against me.

"Good," I tease. He grins.

"Anything for you, Livy."

28

Pax

I awake to the crushing weight of an entirely new world. I sit in my office, numb, frozen in fear of the unknown once more. As much as I tried to mentally prepare for this outcome, I don't think anything could really have worked. My phone buzzes again, and without looking I silence it.

Every single person in my unit has called me, and now my parents are as well. It is only six in the morning. They must be as stressed as I am, seeking answers to questions that I know have none. The only thing we can do now is push back against those who seek to dominate an entire race until extinction—against those who seek to exploit them in ways never before allowed.

My phone buzzes again in my hand, but somehow I know who it is without looking. I answer on the second ring.

"Paxton," my father's tense voice says.

"I know, dad—"

"No, you don't. I need you to listen to me very carefully."

The tone of his voice has me sitting straighter, my muscles coiled, ready to spring into action.

"What," I grit out.

"I need you to come meet with me, today. This cannot wait."

I feel my brows furrow. The sun has only just started rising, and though Opponent Two has won the election, nothing will be implemented for at least a week.

"I have a shit ton of work to do now if I'm to keep my men from shipping out in two days—"

"Paxton Penn Harper, listen to me."

My spine tingles. Another feeling of premonition begins to take root in my core.

"I'll leave when Liv gets up," I say.

"Good, good, bring her," he says, his voice sounding panicked and far away.

"What the hell is wrong?" I hiss.

"*Sargas*," he says, and the line disconnects.

We are driving to my parents' house, and though Liv is excited, I can also feel she is nervous. She knows something is wrong. She is astute, empathetic—she can always tell when I have something on my mind, but she never presses me for answers. I used to think it was because she was afraid of me, but now I know that it's just how she is. She is generous, able to give me space to think and process, and I hope I have done the same for her.

The word my father said was the nail in the coffin—Sargas. In the military, each unit has their own extraction word. Once spoken or written, everyone in the platoon should know danger is near—close enough that it can hear you. Hence why our words change often and are not to be shared with anyone.

Sargas was the word given to our platoon when my brother

and I were captured. Only my father and Tark would know it. Which means we are in danger, and whoever poses the threat is able to listen to us. I doubt our home is bugged—that technology costs too much for just anyone to use. But with my standing in the military, it wouldn't be a far stretch to say my phone calls are being tapped.

We pull up, but no one rushes out to greet us this time. With a deep breath, I help Liv out and into the familiar home, leading her to the kitchen. My mother and Mabel sit at the table, talking in hushed tones. Mabel is crying, holding my mother's hands, and the sight of my mother also crying pulls me up short.

Liv holds my arm, shivering. I am about to say something when I hear footsteps behind us. I turn, glancing at my father, and he jerks his head toward his office. I try to extract myself from Livy, but she is refusing to let go. He comes up, placing his hand on her shoulder, his words quiet.

"She needs to hear what I have to say."

I am put even more on edge. I set my jaw and nod, and we quietly leave the kitchen. My father's office is comforting, warm —but right now, I am too tense to settle down. I take Liv to the couch, and we sit, my father settling into his favorite armchair. Livy grasps my hand, and I give her a gentle squeeze.

"Care to enlighten us?" I press, frustrated at such a flamboyant display of secrecy. My father presses his lips into a thin line, his eyes boring deep into my own. Whatever he is about to say, it is serious.

"It is over, and so I can finally speak freely about things I have been forced to keep quiet on for the last three years," he begins as ice floods my veins. My eyes are stuck wide on him. Three years. The length of time an Erathian is allowed to serve in office. Secrecy. Opponents are not allowed to discuss their standing with anyone, even family. Last night was the election. Opponent One has lost the race...

"Dad?" I breathe. His eyes fill with potent emotions, and he gives a subtle nod. He holds his hands open wide for a moment before clasping them once more. I shake my head, confused, dumbfounded.

"You—"

"Yes, son. I just lost the most important election of our lifetime."

Liv's fingers tighten almost to a painful degree on my hand, and my stomach sinks before writhing in utter agony. My mind is racing, unable to comprehend what he is saying. I am fumbling for words when he speaks, holding up his hand to stop me from interrupting.

"I tried my best, son, to give humans back their rightful place in society. Change of that magnitude cannot happen as fast as I would have liked, and so here is my apology to the both of you. I did what I could, I fought as hard as I could. I am...immensely sorry, for not being able to continue such a fight."

My world is shifting, tilting. What is he even saying? Why the hell should he apologize? He's been my leader—unbeknownst to me—for the past three years. A damn good one, too. And now it is crumbling around us all. I hear Liv sniffle beside me, but I cannot bring myself to look at her. I cannot bear both her and my father's devastation. And then, I remember my place in all this.

"Sargas—"

"You're being watched, listened to. I've known for some time. You're not in danger yet, but one wrong move against this new leader, and he will not be so forgiving."

His warning has my vision pulsing in red. No one will threaten my family. No one will hurt them. No one will get to Olivia. Not with me still standing.

His eyes flit to Liv.

"I'm sharing this with you as well, Liv, because you deserve to know there is hope for your kind," he says, his face softening as he gazes at her. I grit my teeth, holding her tighter.

"There is a new kingdom, across the ocean, and there, humans are free—equal to Erathians. I've been...sending humans there for quite some time now. We've just broken the news to Mabel that she is to leave at the end of the week, and we would like to help send you as well..." he says softly. I can hear Liv's heart thudding so hard in her little chest that it is shaking me. I am just as stunned as she is. My parents have been living a double life for years—and I knew nothing of it. I was too selfish, wrapped up in my own little world. But as soon as Liv entered the picture, everything blew wide open.

She is my catalyst for change.

"You should carefully consider this offer, because once this leader imposes his Breeding Rights Act—"

"Dad—"

"What?" Liv breathes, astonished. My father's eyes bounce to mine, confused and then livid.

"You haven't told her?" he growls. I glare at him.

"I was planning to once things were more concrete," I grit out.

"Pax, what's going on?" she asks, sounding so small, so scared. I take a deep breath, still eyeing my father as I move my hand to grip her thigh possessively. There's no avoiding it now.

"This new leader intends to enforce the breeding of humans with Erathians as a way to save our race from failing. Our numbers have been drastically declining, and he will use that as fodder to fuel the fear of our kind into complying," I say, unable to look at her. Her body reacts, tensing.

"But...but..."

I finally tear my eyes from my father's, setting my jaw. She is mine. I am hers. We haven't come this far to stop the fight now, when the fight is only just beginning. I will never run from a threat—ever.

I look down at her, holding her gaze as though it is the most precious and fragile thing in the world. In a way, it is.

"Olivia, they would have to tear you from my cold, dead hands. I will *never* let them have you."

But there, in those deep green eyes, is a flicker of true fear.

Olivia

It has been two days since Penn broke the news to us. I am... confused, hurt, angry. Why didn't Pax tell me something so important? I can't blame him for not knowing his father's position in all this, and I cannot be upset over the fact that freedom is now a real possibility for me.

I can, however, blame him for keeping secrets from me, secrets that he knew I deserved to hear. Breeding humans? Forcing me to have a child? Where will it end?

I am sitting on the patio in the frigid morning air, my arms wrapped tight around my legs as I rest my chin on my knees. My eyes wander across the harsh landscape; it is beautiful, unforgiving. I know what it is like to survive through a brutal winter. I know how to track stags or set gill nets for fish. I have survived in the wilderness with a small band of humans before. I know I could do it again.

What would happen if I simply ran? It had been my goal, until I fell for Pax. And now that I have been granted more freedoms—a real chance at escaping, I doubt I could really do it. I have been weighing my options relentlessly for the past two days. Penn said another cargo ship leaves at the end of the week, one I can board with Pax and leave to start a new life.

I have three days left to decide, but Pax already voiced his decision; no. He refuses to leave, and though I am furious with him for that, I can't blame him, either. He has his duties, and he wants to stay and fight and change things.

I puff my cheeks out, glaring across the field and its dying, yellowed grasses. I don't wish to tell him that he alone cannot change things. Not in such a selfish, brutish society. Hell, his father was their leader, and he could only do so much before he was voted out. It all seems impossible, so I am left with the ultimate decision: stay with Pax and pray he can somehow halt all these new Acts, or leave alone and be free, one way or another.

My heart and my head both ache, throbbing constantly. I want my freedom more than anything in this world—to walk down the street and not fear for my life, to buy things on my own, go places on my own.

But then, there's Pax. I don't want to live my life without him. Just imagining it is unbearably painful. I love him too deeply, but I cannot hold onto both desires at once. It is going to tear me apart. I swipe at the cold tears on my cheek, no closer to deciding on what I wish to do.

Pax has been understanding, giving me my space, walking away from conversations when he becomes too frustrated or pushy. He wants me to decide on my own, without him swaying me one way or another. I think that is the most frustrating part of all.

If he would just tell me what he wants me to do, I would do it. But he won't, and I am left wondering what decision he *would* choose for me. He is too smart, too calculating. As my heart aches in longing for him—even though he is just feet away in the confines of our home—I feel as though I know which way I am leaning, but I still can't completely cement myself. Not yet. I need just a little more time.

I hear the sliding glass door open, hear his heavy footfalls. A steaming mug of tea is placed on the table next to me, fragrant, with cream—just the way I like it. More tears race down my cheeks at his gesture. He would do anything for me, including risky political coups. I feel utter guilt as my stomach twists.

He sighs as he sits, but I can't look at him yet. I will crumble as soon as I do. I am not as strong as he thinks I am.

"Come here," he says gently. I hug my legs harder, shaking my head. I can't. I can't be close to him. It makes the pain even worse.

"Please, Livy? Don't shut me out," he says, voice soft and sounding hollow. He is in as much pain as I am. I swallow hard. Before I can comprehend what I am doing, I stand, shuffling over to him. My shoulders tense as I crawl onto his lap and wrap my arms around him, hiding my face in his neck as I choke out a sob.

He squeezes me tight to him, rocking me back and forth as he smooths his palm over my hair. He is warm, reassuring. I can't leave—I can't imagine going through life without him. He is a warrior through and through, and he has already survived the worse forms of torture imaginable. How pathetic am I to be afraid of mere possibilities?

Even if all this new stuff gets passed into law, I will not be taken from Pax. He's explained we'd be allotted a year or so to procreate. Sure, children were nowhere near my radar, but having a child with Pax wouldn't be the end of the world. He would be an amazing father.

But raising a child in this society, however, would not be so amazing.

His lips are pressed to my head, and he holds them there as I calm down. Life, though unfair, has also given me him. I have squandered many things in my life, but I do not want Pax to be one of those things.

"I love you, Olivia. More deeply than you can fathom."

I pull away, staring into his deep brown eyes, lost in his gaze as my mind swirls. He is so handsome. So open and earnest. I would miss his eyes, his smile, that one dimple, his scent, the way he holds me—everything.

"I love you, too, Pax. I..." I begin, finalizing my decision as I sit there on his lap. I watch as his jaw ticks. He is nervous. I wet my lips, my heart hammering away. I am about to speak when he shakes his head.

"You still have time to decide," he says, his voice gruff, thick with emotion. He sounds as though he is about to cry. I have never seen him look so devastated before. And it is then, as I watch his facade crumble, that I know which decision he wishes me to make.

He wants me to leave.

Pax

We lay in a tangled web of limbs, every inch of our bodies pressed tight together against the dawn. We haven't slept together, intimately, since my father broke the news to us. Our minds have been pulled in far too many directions. Our emotions are too high.

I stare down at Liv as she sleeps. She is peaceful, here in my arms. Funny, that despite how shitty this world is turning, that in her sleep she is able to find some solace and freedom. I wish I could do more for her. I feel the crushing weight of responsibility heavy on my chest every day.

I don't want her to leave. At least, the selfish part of me doesn't want her to leave. She is mine. No one would care about her as much as I do. No one would know to get her chocolate before her period. No one else would cradle her as gently as I would. No one would ever love her as deeply as I do.

But I know this is just the tip of the iceberg. These policies, this rampant, fear-filled propaganda, it is only the beginning. And unless I can find a way to stop them from happening, we are stuck for the time being. It would be safer for Liv to go to this human refuge my father speaks so highly of. They even have Erathians protecting their border. With all the lush greenery, this place seems like a haven. The Appalachians, my father called it. The humans took back their history from my species' greedy fingers.

Liv sighs against me. I smile, stroking my finger slowly down her plump cheek. She is so beautiful. So gorgeous it hurts. I will miss her, the way she smiles at me, the way she holds Henry so tenderly, the way she cries out when I make her feel good. I blink away the forming tears. I haven't felt emotions this potent since Ollie died.

After what we endured, and after all the therapy I suffered through, I became a shell. A man with hardly any room for feelings. I tried, truly, but I was numb, stuck going through the motions. I moved to Sardone to get away from the memories we shared. Ollie had been my best friend. We did everything together. He would get us into trouble, and I was always there to get us out of it.

It became easier to just stop remembering him. When I think back on our childhood, it became mine; the memories of him faded, and all those trips into town on Demon were just me. All those nights sneaking out were just me. Even though I always knew in the back of my mind that Ollie was there. He would never leave me.

Just as I know Liv would never leave me.

But it is too dangerous, and so she must. She has a few more days, but the clock is winding down, and so I need to make her go before she can change her mind—before I can change *my* mind.

I push the deep sorrow away, leaning in closer to press my lips to her warm, soft forehead. She tenses, waking up as I pull away. Her eyelashes flutter, her brows furrowing in confusion as her deep green eyes settle on my face. I cup her cheek, smoothing my thumb over her bones, giving her a gentle smile.

She returns it, melting into my embrace, pressing her lips to the hollow of my throat. I groan, my body betraying me instantly. It hadn't been my intent to wake her up just for sex, but it has been too long, and we are both suffering through this without one another. I need her, and she needs me, at least one last time.

I skim my hands up her sides under her loose shirt, and she wraps her arms around my neck as we kiss deeply, passionately. I cup her breasts, and she moans into me. I growl, rolling my hips, pinning her beneath me. She gasps, and we are both clawing at our clothes in our haste, tearing them off.

Before I know it, I am plunging through her wetness to the hilt, her moans loud, music to my ears. I thrust, greedily, encompassed by her as she holds me tight, raking her nails up my back and across my shoulder blades. Our skin slaps in our fervency, a sound I will greatly miss. I lean down, circling my tongue around her pert nipple, and she shudders, tightening on me.

It doesn't take much longer. She tenses, crying out, and I follow soon after, spilling myself inside her. I wonder if it will be the last time. I know, in my heart, that it needs to be. I collapse, rolling her so she is laying on my chest as we are knotted together. We are both panting, but she lets out a soft giggle.

I smile against her hair, kissing her head.

"I like waking up that way," she teases, her voice light, happy. I squeeze her harder as sorrow overcomes me.

"I like it too, Livy."

She must hear the tone of my voice. Her head pops up, and my arms fall away. She stares at me, her brows furrowing, until she is glaring deeply. Her jaw is set, her lip trembling. I sigh, moving to cup her cheek, but she jerks her face away.

"Liv—"

"You can't do this," she whispers, her voice thick with tears. I feel my own throat constrict with emotion.

"You have to. It will be safer—"

"I'm safe with you!" she yells, her face reddening, her tears spilling. I grit my teeth, tearing my eyes from her.

"You always take all my choices from me," she hisses. Ahh, there it is. The familiar agony, greeting me like an old friend. It washes through me at her words, leaving me weak, my heart shattering. This is why I avoided relationships. I simply do not have the strength to handle the hurt anymore.

"Look at me," I demand, leaving no room for argument. She is spiraling, fuming, but she turns her hate-filled eyes to mine. I capture her cheeks, holding her tight as my heart breaks all over again.

"I love you, Olivia. And I will no longer keep you from your freedom, from living a life you deserve, even if that means sacrificing my heart."

Her eyes waver with fresh tears.

"And what about *my* heart?" she whispers. I swipe her tears as they fall.

"I will cherish it until the end of my days. And that is why you must go."

29

Olivia

Today has been awful. After this morning, we both avoided each other. I was just staring into Henry's cage when Pax asked if I would go get ice cream with him. As much as I wanted to say no and throw a fit, I just as badly wanted to spend time with him. I used to hate him for taking me against my will, and now I hated him for forcing me to leave against my will.

Maybe I was not meant to understand his decisions. They didn't make any sense to me. I want to stay despite the threat posed above us all. He needs me, right? And I know I need him.

He holds my hand as we leave the parlor, the ice cream settling in my stomach like a rock. It is chilly tonight, the stars twinkling innocently above us. Why can't we just run away together? Get on a ship and just *go*.

I turn, glancing up at him as we walk down the dark, deserted street. He is still so austere, so handsome it kills me. I feel a fresh wave of tears mingled with the fiery spite I so wish to fling at him. Maybe I should just run away on my own. I'd be better off in a land where I know how to survive. Even with the looming threat of Hybrids, I know I'd rather be here, closer to Pax in some capacity.

He quirks his brow and peeks down at me, his eyes reflecting the light of the moon. It is beautiful—breathtaking, how animalistic and powerful he is. I wish I could curl up against him, feel the softness of his hoodie, breathe in his scent and feel his strong arms around me. His hand on mine gives a squeeze, and a sad smile paints his lips.

I can't bring myself to return it, knowing what he is doing to me—what he is once more forcing me into. He's a fool if he thinks I will make this easy. When we get home, when he falls asleep, I'll leave on my own terms. I will make him hurt as badly as he is hurting me right now.

His car is still a ways away. We parked by the pet store to see if Gladys was there, but she had closed up early. My heart sinks. I will miss her, too. I will miss everyone. I hadn't realized how many friends I had made, from Deidre to Pax's mother to Mabel. I don't want to make new friends. I just want to cling to what I know, what I have been growing to love ever since Pax took me.

He sighs harshly, his hand on mine tightening even more. I wince, peeking up at him. His jaw is set, his eyes glaring forward.

"I can't fucking do this," he hisses. I am confused, about to voice it, when he yanks me to the side and into the mouth of a darkened alley way. I stumble after him as he pulls me along, protesting, frightened. We are in the middle of the alley next to a dumpster. The other end is a dead end, and barely any light from the moon or the lone streetlamp reaches us.

"P-Pax?" I stutter as he whirls me around and pins me against the wall. My heart hammers as I catch sight of his eerily beautiful eyes, his fingers digging into my shoulders as he glares down at me. Why does he look so pissed? Did he somehow read my mind about running away tonight? Does he somehow know what I am planning?

I suck in a breath as his eyes waver with thousands of emotions, but there is something...primal, about him right now. Something ancient and dangerous. I shudder, a trickle of fear slithering down my spine.

Just as suddenly, his hands leave my shoulders, but my back stays glued to the cold brick wall. He cups my butt, lifting me off my feet as though I weigh nothing. I gasp, wrapping my legs around his hips automatically, and then his lips are at my neck, his fingers winding through my hair, pulling hard enough to make me whimper, but it sends a thrill through me. He wants me, I can feel it—and I want him.

I want to take my anger out on him, and he seems to want the same, his hold bruising, his lips crushing mine, leaving a trail of marks down my neck. I moan into him, egging him on. I need more—*we* need more. We need each other.

I am kissing him back when he pauses. I whimper, opening my eyes, searching his face for why he has stopped. He is not looking at me, however. My heart leaps into my throat as I peer down to the entrance of the alleyway. And then, I hear it, the clank of bottles, the somehow familiar voices.

I count their shadows. *One, two, three, four, five.* Tall, broad shouldered men—Erathians. My legs tighten their hold on Pax as their iridescent eyes lock onto us. Slow, and without tearing his gaze from the men, Pax lowers me to the ground. My feet hit the concrete, and a chill shoots through me.

He turns to face the oncoming group, shielding me with his strong body. I am shivering from head to toe. I feel the threat, deep in my bones. Pax reaches behind, opening his palm to me. I grab his hand, squeezing tight in my fear. He gives a gentle squeeze back, and his low, authoritative voice weaves to me through the dark, empty night.

"Stay as far from them as you can," he instructs as their

boisterous voices reach us. I know them, now; the men that went into the liquor store, the ones who warned me they didn't take kindly to those who were sympathetic toward humans. My gut roils.

"Do not speak, and if I tell you to get away, you listen," he says. I can't even formulate a response. I am frozen in fear.

"Well, well, well," the leader says, his feet skimming over pebbles, the bottle in his hand glinting as he wavers, drunk. His friends fan out behind him, chuckling, jostling one another. The leader points his bottle at Pax, a sick smile curling onto his face.

"I think we warned you about this little slut here," he says, nodding to me. Pax stands tall, stoic, unwavering. I swallow my nerves. He's always protected me. But for some reason, tonight feels...*different*. The odds are not in his favor.

"Get lost," Pax seethes. The blond chuckles, shaking his head, and his friends laugh.

"That is your last warning," Pax says, cool, even. I am shaking from head to toe, my mind wavering between the past and now. I pinch my eyes shut against the memories—of the gym, of the Facility, of the tree I was tied to. My heart is rapidly beating against my rib cage as I fight off the demons of my past.

"Listen to her poor little heart, boys. Wonder how fast it will beat when we take turns fucking her in front of you," he growls to Pax.

He snorts, pulling his hand from my grasp. I feel his absence immediately, and though I want to reach out and grab him, I am far too afraid to move, rooted to my spot in my fear.

"You would have to kill me before that happens," he says, that same possessive note to his voice. The group simply laughs once more at the threat. The leader hums his amusement, his eyes dancing.

"I suppose tonight is the night you die, then."

My heart stutters before it grinds to a halt like the truck I stole in the Settlement. They are close—too close. I can smell the booze on their breath, reeking through the alley and clouding my mind. They have us cornered.

I pinch my eyes closed, taking a few breaths to steady myself. I am not in the Facility. I am not tied to that tree. I am not watching my home be ripped apart, my kind slaughtered in the streets. This situation is still not good, but I am not in my past. There is hope. Right?

My eyes spring back open as I hear the forward scuffle of Pax's boots on the asphalt. At the same time, he shoves me backward, hard. I collide with the brick wall, losing my breath as my eyes take in the scene before me.

They all lunge forward as Pax swings at the leader. His momentum catches the blond off guard, and they are soon on the ground as Pax pummels his face. Shouts erupt, and the others rush to join in the fight as I stand there, frozen, chest heaving, petrified.

When I was in the wild, I witnessed wolves hunting their prey and taking it down. They were voracious, cunning, deft—but more importantly, they were animals, and they had no room for mercy. Not only was that a lesson for me to learn about this world, but it served as a stark reminder of my place in it.

Watching these men attack reminds me of that time. Pax throws them off, fighting them one by one, just as deft, just as cunning. He is skilled—has been trained for this, has survived way worse things. But the foes are relentless, and they are fighting dirty.

One of them growls, clutching at his stomach that Pax just kicked. He takes his nearly empty bottle, smashing the bottom against the dumpster. It shatters, glinting pieces of glass littering the ground, sparkling like stars from below. I am lost, mesmerized, until I realize what he intends to do with the remnants of his bottle.

Two men are fighting to control Pax's arms as he roars and thrashes, kicking out at the blond, connecting with his temple. The man thuds to the ground, silent, still. Pax is panting, a sheen of sweat coating his forehead. My heart lurches as the man with the jagged edged bottle approaches him from behind. I see his intent, and I have no other thoughts.

I jump forward, pushing off the wall to give myself more momentum. I spring up, latching onto the man's back. He is confused, whirling around, trying to get me off. He wraps his long fingers around my bicep, tossing me to the ground in front of Pax like a rag doll. For the second time tonight, I lose my breath, but my eyes blink up at Pax.

He is on his knees, three men holding him down. Why isn't he fighting? Why is he surrendering?

And then, I feel it. The coolness of sharp glass pressed to my throat. I swallow hard, my throat expanding and nudging the shard. I whimper, locking my eyes on the man I love—the man who has saved me time and again. His eyes are hard, cold, calculating. He's angry. But at me?

Blood pours from a cut near his temple, and by the way he is holding his arm, I can tell he's in severe pain. I lurch forward, needing to help him, to see if he's alright, but the hand gripping my coat yanks me back to reality.

"Tell your whore to be a good girl and strip down for us," the man holding me seethes. A shiver of fear runs through me, but I keep my eyes on Pax, for he is my strength in this moment. He heaves a breath, his broad chest expanding.

"Go to hell," he spits. The man holding me yanks me up, slamming me against the opposite wall before I have time to think. He tosses the bottle to someone else as Pax rages behind me, as the man tears at my clothes. I am in a stunned state. I cannot move, blink, process. This is happening. The buttons on my red rain jacket pop off and clink across the ground. Even though the air that hits me is frigid, I still can't move.

Pax is back on his feet, wrestling against the men that hold him. He doubles over as one of them knees him in the gut. The man holding me reaches for my jeans, and something within me snaps.

"Fight, Liv!" Pax wheezes. "Fight, dammit! Fight him like you fought me!"

And then, it clicks. I did fight Pax. He may have won, but I still knocked him on his ass that fateful day. I bring my knee up between the man's legs, fast and hard, satisfied when I hear his pained grunt. He stumbles away, clutching at his groin. Pax fights harder than he has yet, throwing the men off him, laying them out until it is just him and my attacker left.

Pax has regained the upper hand for the moment, and I feel it—*hope*. We can work together, can fight our way through this—

The night is shattered by the echo of gun fire. The man who attacked me staggers, holding his arm out. There, in his hands, is the pistol.

Pax falls to his knees, clutching at his stomach as blood seeps through and stains his light grey hoodie a ghastly crimson.

No no no no no.

I blink, pinch my eyes shut, scream. The man drops the gun, fleeing to the mouth of the alley as Pax slumps to the side.

The blood.

The gun shot.

The way his face has gone pale. The way the blood seeps between his fingers and drips to the ground. The way I cannot hear a thing. The way I feel so helpless, so lost, so alone. I see my mother, her caramel hair splayed behind her as she lay in that field dying.

She smiled up at me, so pale, her eyes lacking their usual gloss and spark. But she had grinned, all the same, as I'd pressed my hands to her stomach, as I'd screamed and begged for help that would never come. I'd sat there, watching her die, feeling her pulse weaken beneath my fingertips, feeling her blood cool.

No one tells you how quickly a body turns cold after its inhabitant dies.

I wish someone had warned me, back then.

I swallow against the mounting fear, eyes locked on Pax's form. He blinks slowly up at me, not saying anything. He knows I am a coward. He knows my past still has a tight hold on me and refuses to let go.

The pool of blood beneath him grows too quickly.

I shake my head, backing away. His eyes follow my retreat. I do the only thing I have ever been able to do.

I run.

30

Pax

I stand in the empty entryway of our home. My left arm is in a sling still—shattered, or at least it had been. I heal quickly, but it is still bothersome. The gun shot to my abdomen burns, though. And with it, the memories burn as well.

It is eerily quiet in our home—my home, I guess. I fight back the emotions as best I can, but my heart still throbs, the wound fresh. I was a fool to expect anything more. She saw her chance to run, and she took it. Waking up in the hospital alone confirmed that. None of the nurses or authorities said anything about her.

I don't even want to look for her. I wanted her to be free, but on my own terms, and that was selfish of me. When I pulled her into the alley, I was about to tell her to stay—stay with me despite everything. Together, we could have made it through.

Now, we are apart, and I feel as though a chunk of me is missing as well. With her, traipsing through the wild. I've played the 'what if' game since I awoke, and knew I had to stop at some point. She has full knowledge of what is out there, and she still chose to run. I understand her fright, the way she reacts in tough situations, but I had thought by the look in her eye that she could make it through.

I sink onto the couch, my mind in a daze as rain bashes the window panes. There is no point, now. What am I fighting for, if not her? This job, this house, this life—it all had a purpose when she was part of it, and now she is gone, and I am left alone once more. Adrift, wondering what the fuck the purpose of this pain is.

I lean forward, burying my face in my good hand as a sob chokes me. I hurt. *Everywhere.* She ripped me apart, diced me up, carved out my heart, and ran. And the worst part of all is knowing I deserve it.

I can lie to myself as much as I want, say I saved her from a worse fate, but I am still part of the problem in this sick society, and I can't even blame her for leaving me bleeding out in that alley, cold, alone. I remember the stars, how they twinkled down at me, privy to my private pain. I remember how weak I felt as my blood stained the concrete in an ever-expanding pool.

But mostly, I remember her eyes as she stood at the mouth of the alley. Wide, frightened, pupils dilated as she stared at me for a few lingering heartbeats. Such a lush emerald green. I will never forget such a color, and I know I will never see anything quite like it again. I wipe my tears on my sleeve, a small smirk on my lips.

That damn moor. Her goal, the last tendrils of the wild reaching into the kingdom. The last stretch of her freedom. Fitting, that it would match her so completely. She is green all around; young, innocent, flourishing, but deep, enchanting.

A knock sounds on my door, pulling me from my misery. I stand, wiping hastily at my weakness, squaring my shoulders before I go to answer. Probably another Guard. I've been questioned relentlessly since I awoke. I killed the blond one. I can't seem to find the guilt for what I did. I saved her, and that is all that matters to me.

I unlock the door, pulling it open, greeted with a blast of icy, rainy air. A guard stands before me in uniform, small smile on his face.

"Paxton Harper?" he questions. I sigh, nodding.

"I gave my statement at the hospital—"

He frowns, brows furrowing, and I stop myself. Did I end up killing another assailant without knowing it? It wouldn't reflect poorly on me—self defense is self defense. But going through the damn line of questioning again sounds agonizing. I just want to fall apart by myself. It is all I have ever known.

"Did something happen, officer?"

His frown deepens.

"I am Gladys' son, Jance."

"Oh...I've, uhh, heard a lot about you," I say, my confusion deepening as I rub the back of my neck.

"We found something that belongs to you," he says. I perk up, looking past him for *her*, but he simply holds out his hand. In a clear plastic bag is my phone, crushed and shattered. I frown in return, reaching for it as my heart sinks to my toes.

"Thanks," I say, nodding once to him. He is still studying me, and it is becoming agitating.

"That all?" I bite to him. His dark gaze turns even darker.

"How do you think you survived, Mr. Harper?"

I grit my teeth. What the hell does this have to do with anything?

"I don't know. Lucky, I guess."

He snorts, pissing me off further.

"I'd say you're more than just lucky."

"What the fuck is this? Look, I'm exhausted, I was in the hospital for two days, my arm is broken, and—"

He takes a step closer, squaring up to me, and in his eyes

dances something sinister. I am completely taken aback at this display.

"My mother's store front window was shattered that night. It tripped the alarms, alerting the Guards. Do you know what we found just down the street?"

I feel my mouth run dry as the rain beats down relentlessly behind him, drowning out my pounding heart.

"What?" I breathe, but my words come out as nothing more than a whisper. The door to his Guard car opens, and out ambles Gladys. My eyes, however, are glued to the brown haired beauty that she pulls along up the walk to my front door.

"Your phone was shattered, and she told us hers was left at home. She remembered my mother saying that if the glass broke, it would trip an alarm that rang straight to our station. She threw a rock through the window, Mr. Harper, and rushed back to you. She put enough pressure on your gunshot wound to keep you alive until we arrived."

All his words are misty, floating past me before swirling around in my mind. I cannot look away from her as she draws nearer, bashful, her head down. But when she peeks up, when her eyes meet mine, I can feel my heart cinch itself back together.

They pause at Jance's elbow, and she finally allows her eyes to meet mine. She is afraid, chewing her lip, that beautiful, glorious blush painting her cheeks. I want to crush her to me, kiss her forever, fall to my knees and worship her for the rest of my life.

She saved me.

She had every chance to run to her freedom, and she stayed.

I feel my eyes water as we stare at one another, but then those tears spill over, and with it, she cries out, leaping to me. I cannot even feel the pain in my arm as she squeezes me and sobs. I hold her more tightly than I have ever held her, and she clings to me with equal fervor. Gladys and her son step back, giving us our space to reunite.

"I love you so much, Livy," I croak into her silky hair. She sniffles, pressing her cold nose to my neck.

"I'm never leaving you," she growls against me, her hold tightening. Despite the heaviness of this moment, I chuckle, overjoyed, at peace. No, she will never be forced into a decision again.

"Never," I affirm. And then, it hits me; she really, truly saved my life, in many ways. I was nothing before her; a hollow man, lost, directionless, so lonely. And then she changed all that— changed my life from the inside out simply by being herself.

And oh, how deeply I love her for that.

"I missed you," she whispers, pulling away to stare at me. I smile down at her, brushing her damp tendrils of hair from her blushing cheeks.

"I thought...thought you'd run..."

Her brows furrow, but she isn't mad; she understands my logic, understands why I would have thought that. After another thoughtful moment of consideration, a slow, bright smile creeps onto her angelic face. She gives a sure shake of her head.

"No," she says, voice gentle, far away, and I feel like we are on that moor again, those many months ago. "No, Pax. *You* are my home."

EPILOGUE

Olivia

"Pax," I whine, shivering, my eyes shrouded by a thick piece of black fabric. Wherever he has taken me, it is blustering, frigid, and insanely loud. I can hear him chuckle, though, and I try to stumble over the uneven terrain as best I can. Without my eyesight, it is almost impossible, but his hands are warm and steady, holding me, preventing me from falling. Finally, we pause, and though I collide with his back, I am thankful for the brief bit of warmth it brings me.

His big hands are on my shoulders, heavy, reassuring. Even with the salty scent in the air, I can still smell him—cedar wood, fabric softener, his minty toothpaste. Everything is heightened with the blindfold on, but it is all a comfort, knowing he is here, that he won't let anything bad happen to me.

He almost died for me.

No one, human or Erathian, has ever sacrificed themselves in such a way. No one except my mother. Watching Pax die beneath my fingertips took everything out of me. I couldn't stand the thought of losing the last person on this Earth that I loved. And so I had screamed at him, hit him, wept, kissed him. I did everything I could that night to make sure he would see another day—and now we are here, months deep into a new regime, still safe, still healthy. I know changes are coming, but this is the breath before the plunge.

I know, though, that I have Pax to take that dive with me. We will never part, never again. I doubt I could handle it. I know for a fact he couldn't.

So much has changed, yet so much has remained steady; our love, for one thing, our home, our routine. There will be hurdles, but at least we are a team now. A team that can change the world, a team that can bring freedom to my kind. Things are never as bleak as we believe them to be. And for that, I am so thankful.

"Ready?" he asks over the din. I nod greedily. He tugs the back of the blindfold, and it slithers away with the wind. I blink, my eyes adjusting to the black expanse before me. It is night—late, well past the time we typically go to bed. Stars twinkle and shine above us, so peaceful in comparison to the roughness of the ocean.

"Oh," I gasp, staring out over a vast, roiling sea. I have always seen photos of the ocean, but I have never been to it. Mesmerized, I take a step forward on the uneven rocks. There is nothing, for thousands and thousands of miles. I know, though, that Mabel is there, across the water, in a new land where she is free. Pax and I will get as many humans to safety as we can. Today is simply the first step.

I feel him approach, but I cannot take my eyes from the new scenery. Bright galaxies and celestial bodies, a massive expanse of writhing water, so powerfully crashing against the dark, craggy rocks. It is immense, and I suddenly feel so very small. If this is the ocean on our Earth, then I wonder how Pax feels about the universe. Does he feel as small? Does he think about such things?

But then, the skyline begins to change. I squint at the darkened horizon as a wide band of a shape takes form, like two ends that are about to meet. The colors are unreal, something I have never seen before, such rich, deep green hues that somehow light the entire sky. Aurora Borealis. I learned about this phenomenon in my studies, but I never dreamed I would be able to witness it, and here of all places. There is something ancient, majestic, about this moment. The universe is unforgiving, and it takes without thought, without pause.

In the same breath, it gives. It gave me life, purpose. It gave me Pax. It is vast and endless, just like the love we hold for each other. The colors on the horizon play like gentle fish, meeting in the center and undulating above the ocean, lighting up the sky in the most fantastic and brilliant display I have ever seen. It makes my heart thump hard in my chest, this feeling of being so alive, so at one with the universe.

With a wide smile on my face, I turn, wishing to share this moment with him. He has already been to the beach many times with Ollie, he told me. He's opened up more about his little brother, to the point now that we talk about him often, celebrating what his life meant to Pax.

My smile falters, though, when I see Pax on his knee, staring up at me with a concerned look on his face. Did he trip? Is he hurt?

I am about to bend down, to help him, when he opens his palm. There, perched innocently in his large hand, is a small black box. His eyes fall to it, and he heaves a deep breath, his shoulders rising with the motion. My heart begins to hammer in my chest, hard enough that it shakes me to my core.

When his deep brown eyes find mine again through the darkness, they are awash with emotions—watery, tear filled.

My fingers fly to my mouth, trembling, but not from the cold. This is happening. Something big. Are we—

"Olivia Donne. I have made you mine in every way, but not in the way that truly counts," he says, his voice strong, sure. I am stunned into silence as the waves behind us crash and break upon the cliffs, as the colors of the Northern Lights reflect in his glinting eyes.

He gently pries open the box, and inside is a dainty, thin, silver ring with a brilliant, dazzling diamond right in the middle. My mother wore one as well. I know what it is. My heart leaps. I feel as though I am going to faint and fall off this cliff.

"I want you, forever. I want you as my equal. I promise to cherish you, protect you, fight for you and your kind—until the end of my days."

I feel a smile growing on my face as tears spill forth and coat my cheeks. He takes another deep breath.

"So...will...will you..." he fumbles, shifting from pale to crimson in the span of a few seconds. I am nodding before he can find his words.

"Marry me?" he finally says, breathless. I leap into his arms, and he catches me.

"Yes, yes!" I say against him, pressing my cool lips to his burning skin. He kisses me back, our lips locked, but he pulls away long enough to slide the ring onto my finger. It fits perfectly, just as perfectly as this moment feels. I stare wide-eyed at it, the way it glints like it is a star itself. There is something strange about the diamond, how depthless the plains are. I am enchanted when Pax speaks.

"It is from Sargas. Very rare. These formed from the dying star," he explains, his voice quiet, deep. My eyes flash to his once more, and my heart beats a tangled rhythm. He smiles, leaning in, pressing our foreheads together. I return his smile.

"How did I get so lucky—out of the whole damn universe—

to find you?" he breathes, his lips nearly pressed to mine. My smile grows into a wide grin.

"The same way I got so lucky," I say. He gives me a curious look.

"That out of the whole damn universe—out of a collapsing star, I also found you, Pax."

BONUS CHAPTER

Pax

I stare into the flames, the orange tendrils muted by the surrounding darkness that consumes all. I lean forward, elbows on knees, my posture relaxed but my mind on high alert. I can feel my spine prickle, as though the monsters from my past, present, and future are watching me, their eyes like hands roaming over my skin before they sink their teeth into my flesh.

Being in the Ruins, in the surrounding wilderness, it always brings back those feelings. The memories I can keep locked away for the most part, but the absolute hollowness and the unrelenting anxiety that flows through me is a constant reminder of the tortures I endured, the abhorrent evil I survived.

I feel my fist clench as my brother's dancing eyes leap at me through the flames, sparkling with the same mischief he always wore. I grit my teeth, pushing his memory away as best I can. Out here, it is almost impossible.

A commotion from my comrades snaps my eyes up to Brutus, and I immediately bristle at the sight before me. The littlest human we captured sits between his thighs, her hair twisted into a strange style but springing loose all about her dirty face. He shoves a morsel of pork past her plush pink lips, and I watch with mounting animosity.

I hate her.

I hate everything about her, about all humans. They are weak, pathetic, sniveling creatures. Their purpose in our society barely keeps them alive. I find them all a waste, but particularly females. My knuckles blanche and I feel my teeth grind so hard they may pulverize into dust in my mouth.

I don't care to examine why I hate humans. I know why, but I refuse to face it at the moment. But as those memories flash in my mind's eye like a firework—as the picture plays out as though it were happening right now in front of me—I can't help but to acknowledge the trigger this tiny human is to me. She reminds me of all I saw and endured, reminds me of Ollie, of how even in his most dire need, he would never stoop low enough to harm an innocent being.

I swallow the lump in my throat; I am a coward.

"Good human," comes Brutus' teasing voice, and my eyes refocus on the sight before me as the group tensely chuckles. "How does it taste to eat your own kind?"

The little human's eyes widen, and my jaw pops in a flash of white hot fury. She lurches forward, vomiting the small bit of pork and not much else. She is starved, too thin, and now she's lost even more nutrients. Everyone laughs at her reaction to the cruel joke, a joke that cuts me deeper than anyone will ever know. Before I can stop myself, my voice rings out through the small clearing.

"Knock it off, Brutus."

The human shivers in fright, her eyes finding mine through the night, through the flames. Brutus grips her hair and gives her head a shake, taunting me. His smile is sick and twisted, but I know my gaze does not waver. I will not back down.

"Why, Pax-y?" he mocks.

I feel my glare deepen. He grips the girl's cheeks, hard enough to elicit a whimper of pain, the sound a soft mewl that strikes a chord deep in the shelter of my chest. I know I am to blame for some of the pain she is now experiencing, but she deserved it for knocking me on my ass in that building.

"Aww, cute noises humans make, huh? What other ones can I make you do, human?"

My stomach writhes in rage. I understand what Brutus means, and his torment only sends me further spiraling into my own personal hell. I can still hear the screams of those women, clawing at my ears, painting the surrounding woods forever with their bloody pleas as they were tortured before our very eyes by those sick monsters.

Brutus stands, and my mind jumps back to reality as he forces her onto her knees and presses her face to the junction between his hips. My blood boils over. Everyone lets out another round of chuckles at her misfortune. He lets her go, and I am relieved, until he reels back and backhands her across the face, the crack of skin on skin like a lightning strike through the rainy night. She slumps to her side, unable to catch herself in thanks to her bound legs and wrists. She is so small in our presence, so seemingly fragile.

"What a little whore, like the rest of them."

"Enough, Brutus," I growl, having had enough of his games.

He huffs a derisive snort.

"That's all they are good for. Cleaning and fucking. May as well break her in now—"

"I said enough," I hiss out through clenched teeth as the tidal wave of past trauma threatens to consume me whole.

"You can't command—"

"By law, you must register to own a human. By law, you must have them screened for diseases and have them inoculated."

Everyone waits with bated breath as Brutus stares me down, a sick, challenging smile plastered to his lips. I hate him more than I hate the girl laying gasping on the ground. I do not let my eyes flit to her.

"And yes, Brutus, I can command you."

I know pulling rank, when done often, begins to mean little, and so I very rarely do so. But here and now, I know I need to. To save the human from further molestation. To save myself from hearing the trigger her cries and pleas would be to me. I cannot fall down that slippery slope while out here in the wild. It could get me killed.

Brutus sneers, rearing his boot back before he slams it into her stomach. I look away. My hatred for her festers.

I awake with a pounding in my chest, my eyes springing open to the darkened tent and the noise of clamoring heartbeats. I roll out of instinct, protecting myself first from whatever is attacking us. If I cannot control the situation, we are all doomed.

A small cry alerts me to the foe, and beneath my hand is a thin throat. It takes me a moment to realize I am straddling the little human, pinning her hard enough to cut her air supply off. I loosen my hold, and my mind races. How the fuck did she get in here? I glare down at her, into those wide eyes, and my hatred for her and her kind surges through my veins.

"You're not allowed in here, human," I hiss, unable to stop myself as I raise my hand and reprimand her with a slap that echoes through the quieting tent. It is too quiet. Too still.

I raise my eyes, and my fury changes course in that small span of time.

"What in the fucking hell—"

I stand, the torment of my own torture pulsing in flashes

before my very eyes. Those women, screaming and begging. Those women, forced to hunt one another down or die an even more horrific death. Ollie refusing to bring further harm to them.

And there Brutus stands, buckle undone, zipper down. I glance down at the trembling human. She's so small, so much thinner and starved than the ones I watched die. I cannot imagine her lasting through one hour with a Hybrid. It sets my teeth on edge as my emotions war. I hate her; the memories her face and her presence bring to the forefront of my mind are impossible to ignore as the war wages within my own body, my heart and my soul. Tears run down her cheeks, coating the red handprint that now adorns her bruised skin.

"What did I say about the laws, Brutus?"

"Listen, Pax, she's nothing. She's going to die before we get home, so we may as well enjoy her—"

My temper rises. Ollie would never take advantage of an innocent being in such a way. *I* would never, either. Ollie was the better of us two, though. Always. Brutus' attitude toward this entire situation is one I will not tolerate.

"That is not what I asked," I grit out through clenched teeth. He crosses his arms, setting his jaw. I can hear the human's heartbeats calm a fraction.

"Fine, whatever, I'll *obey*," he says, his tone mocking. "You may as well just take her since you're already so attached."

Fire ignites my chest once more, and I turn to glance down at the girl. Her emerald green eyes flutter with fear, but there is something deeper, something that is akin to a spark of a potent emotion. Perhaps hatred. I cannot decipher. I need to get her out of here before I'm lured further into this mess than I already am. I reach down, yanking her up before I drag her out and choose a tree closer to the tent. I know, deep in my heart, why I am doing this, but I begin to shut the doors of my past, to cut the memories off before they can drown me anymore.

I find some new rope, reaching for her bound wrists. She tugs away, but I am too lost in my thoughts to notice much. I reach for her again, and she turns her back to me, a petulant little child in her actions. Shaking in quiet fury, my hand snaps out, catching her by the throat as I pin her to the tree.

"You will obey us, human," I spit as I tie her once more to her makeshift prison. She shakes her head, and that fire in her eyes grows immensely, expanding like oil over water. I take the gag from her mouth, giving her the opportunity to lash out, secretly wishing to provoke such a response. I am not disappointed.

"You're all freaks," she growls.

"Some tongue for someone in such a position."

"Go back to your own planet, you fucking leech."

Her words make my blood boil. If only she knew what I was capable of, if only she knew how deeply her words cut me. If only she knew the hell I've walked through to earn the right to even be alive.

"Speak to me that way again, and you will regret it, human."

A wad of spit splats between my eyes, and her smug expression sends me over the edge as I wipe it away.

"I will enjoy breaking you."

I stand, towering over her as she squirms like a bug caught in a sticky trap.

"You will never break me, freak."

I snap, fist connecting with her already bruised cheek, boot connecting with her ribs as red pulses around the edges of my vision. She gasps and cries out, her pain clear by way of her curled up body and tears. I hate her. I hate her. I hate her. I try to convince myself of this, but Ollie's ghost is there in my mind.

I cannot hate her.

It is not her fault, what happened to my brother.

"Sleep, human, you will need it come tomorrow."

I turn and leave before guilt forces me to act against the law, before that guilt pushes me to let her go. Without me, she will die, and as I stomp back to the tent, I realize that despite what I thought was hatred for her and her kind, I do not want that at all.

I don't understand why.

∼

The rush of the river is calming. My nerves, however, are fraying like the wick of a candle. I spent the entire day with the human—and it only made everything all the worse. She'd almost died from consuming a peanut protein bar. She'd been fiery, mouthing off, constantly challenging me. Did she have no self-preservation?

I'd kept her tied close to our tent once more, and finding her pinned there with her pants unbuttoned and inconsolable...

I feel my fingers flex as I stretch them and clench them into a fist. I do not hate her. Not anymore. I can feel the tendrils of that fury slinking away, replaced by curiosity instead. She is strange, enchanting in a way I never thought a human could be —so very complex, not unlike my species. She has needs, wants, emotions (however disorienting I find them), and she's struggling to survive.

I cannot blame her for that.

I turn, peeking over my shoulder. I can still hear her bathing, but the allure of seeing what she looks like under her grimy clothes is strong. My jaw clenches, though, when my eyes fall to her.

She's so frail. So tiny. I can count her ribs, the bumps of her spine. Her back is to me, her hair long and shiny in the moon-light. Her torso is littered with bruises of varying colors. A heaviness settles in my heart, knowing I put some of those bruises there. I will have to be better; my father raised me better. Ollie wouldn't have hit her. I only did because...she's infuriating, for one, but also because she still reminds me of my past.

She shifts, moving to stand, and my eyes sweep back to the forest, allowing her the privacy she rightfully deserves. No one will touch her again as Brutus has. I will not bring her further harm. My heart begins to beat a strong, steady rhythm. I know, before I can fully form the thought, that I am going to keep her.

She will not last without me.

I lay awake, the little human safe in my arms. She told me her name. *Olivia.* I do not know what it means, but I find it strangely beautiful. Foreign, alien. I smirk to myself. Odd, that I think her characteristics are the foreign ones.

She is warm in my arms, even her toes, which took some time to heat up. I stare down at her in the soft light filtering in through the canvas. She is calm, her face young and bright, even if marred by bruises. I cannot help my smile, or the odd feeling she gives me as I hold her. I feel...full, complete in a way I haven't felt since Ollie died. I will do this, in his honor. I will keep her, feed her and clothe her and protect her. If Ollie were still here, he'd have already staked his claim. He'd probably even be able to make her smile with one of his corny jokes.

I reach up, brushing my fingers along her cheek. She is so soft and fragile. I feel my thoughts begin to turn dark. I should have done more to save those women. I should have offered myself to protect an innocent life, but I'd been more concerned about getting my brother out of there alive. I wish I could have done more for all of them.

They didn't deserve the way they had to die.

A hard lump forms in my throat as I continue to trace the planes of her little face. These thoughts are not new; I think them every night when the darkness closes in around me. The only difference now is that I am not alone. Her plush lips part, her brow puckering. I cease my motions. I do not want to frighten her, for her to think I am going to attempt to take advantage of her while she's asleep.

She looks more stressed when I stop.

Cautious, the pads of my fingers resume the exploration of her smooth skin, avoiding the areas where she's injured. As soon as my skin meets hers, a soft sigh escapes her lips, and the faintest smile lights her face. I return the grin. She doesn't realize it, how she makes me feel full once more. How she's unknowingly giving me back a part of myself I thought would be gone forever.

I can sense—with her stubborn attitude as well as mine—that this will not be easy by any means. That I will have days where I question why I did this. But then she rolls, flopping onto her back, and her little hand flies out, smacking my chest. I still, waiting until she settles, and when she does, I push my fingers through her silky hair. She gives a small moan of contentment at my touch, and my smile grows again. I like her like this; sweet, innocent. But I also like the challenge she presents me.

Her fingers grip the fabric of my shirt. I continue to stare at her, mesmerized. *Yes*, I think, I am doing the right thing. And bending down to press my lips to her forehead, I whisper my promise to her.

"I'll keep you safe, little human. For Ollie."

THANK YOU

Tear Me Down was a project that began on a whim shortly before Christmas of 2020. It felt like we were all living a real dystopian novel, and I found myself so busy with so many life-altering changes in my career path that I was breaking down in every sense. I stepped down from a solid job that I had held since I was 18, I jumped both feet first into tutoring and then teaching, and I once more fell in love with life and the beauty of it. I questioned every day why I had done this to myself, especially as it came time to grade so. many. papers! But through all the stress and busyness, I found solace in the words I was writing.

This book is so different from all of my others. I pushed myself to be uncomfortable, to write realistically, to examine choices characters would make that made me want to slam my forehead on the keyboard. Through all that intense introspection, Pax and Livy were born from the ashes of what it felt like my life had been prior to breathing life into them. I once was lost, but through their story, I found myself again. If anyone can take anything away from this book, I would hope it would be this: everyone has a story of their own. Some might make you cringe, some might make you cry, others may make you jealous. The beauty of that is that we do not know an individual's story until we sit with them, until we peel away their layers while also being vulnerable enough to share ourselves. Be kind to everyone you meet. They may have walked through a fire you will never understand, or they may currently be walking through those flames wondering how the hell they're going to make it to the other side.

With all that being said, I have some major thank you's to express.

First, to my amazing readers who've followed me for years and supported me through all my experimental works. You all gave me the courage to put myself and my work out into the world, and I will be forever grateful for your support and kind words. I needed that encouragement to keep pushing forward despite my fears.

To my friends and family, you know who you are. Without you, I would not be here. You've encouraged me when I couldn't see an end to all the bad, you've supported me, you've given me my space to create, and you've loved me unconditionally when I needed it the most. Thank you.

To my awesome editor Vickie Vaughn, bless you for putting up with all my technological issues and for STILL being willing to work with me. You've helped me ensure the best possible product to share with the world. I appreciate you and thank you!

To L.J. Anderson of Mayhem Cover Creations—WOW! Thank you a million times over. You made this process so easy. I am so thankful to have found you, and now my baby has its own unique vibe that is impossible to ignore.

Lastly, as this book (my first published) is dedicated to my momma, I would like to expand just a little on how thankful I am for her in particular. She is the epitome of grace under pressure, a woman who held us kids together and gave us the best life possible despite the circumstances. She's shown me kindness, compassion, an open mind, has battled for me when I needed it, and has allowed me to battle for her when she needed it. Mothers—whoever they are to you—are underrated forces of nature, and without mine, I cringe to think of where I would be. You are my best friend, Mimi, and your time to experience life anew is here. I can't wait to be by your side as that happens.

ABOUT THE AUTHOR

Ruby Medjo is a graduate of the English program at Eastern Washington University, where she cultivated and refined her passion for telling stories. Currently residing in the gorgeous Pacific Northwest, she spends her time reading, writing, drinking coffee (or wine), and teaching her English and History classes. She is blessed to be surrounded by amazing friends and family who continue to push her to pursue her dreams no matter how intimidating. She is still waiting on her Hogwarts acceptance letter, but she is willing to fall through the stones at Craigh na Dune instead.

Made in the USA
Las Vegas, NV
13 September 2021

30216216R00256